A DEATH AT DAWN

*Book 1 of the series WHEN THE
FIRES BROKE THROUGH*

By Gabrielle Grey

ISBN: 978-0-578-63477-7 (Paperback)

This book is a work of fiction. Any references to historical events, real people, or real places are used fictitiously. Names, characters, and places are products of the author's imagination.

Cover Art by Nanette Bollenbecker.

www.gabriellegreybooks.com

To my wonderful parents

Without you guys, this book would not exist.

CONTENTS

CONTENT WARNING

This book contains themes of the following that may be distressing to readers: violence, cursing, suicide (attempted), marital abuse, menstruation, alcoholism, gore, classism, racism, sexism, kidnapping, murder, poisoning, prostitution, rape (attempted), vomit, and weapons.

GENESIS

Part One

GLORIANA

The seasons were changing, and the oak leaves shifted into vibrant shades of oranges and yellows. The long hot summer days had turned cold and short. Summer was no longer; the autumn season now ruled the lands.

The highborn lady of the Mountain Realm sat shivering on a rock under a pine tree trying her best to stay warm. Her fur collar scratched her skinny neck, and the thick wool blue dress weighed heavily on her legs.

Lady Gloriana Wayward had lived in Maryere for twenty-six years, seventeen of those years married, and yet, she still couldn't tell when the first cold was about to begin, but her children knew. Her three beautiful children were born of Wayward blood, just as hardy as their father's.

Her younger children, Josef and Jaslyn, played on their ponies in the grassy green fields outside the Dense Pines. Fields that still felt of summer. *This is nice.* Gloriana couldn't remember the last time she spent relaxing with her two youngest children. *I've been so busy since Borin left.*

She sighed, trying to recall her own childhood. *I wish I was young again.* As a child, Gloriana lived in the Summerlands. In the city of Goldspire, the shoreline went on for miles, and the sunshine lasted all day. During the winter, she swam in the calm rivers and relaxed in the humid jungles. She never had to sleep by a burning fire, fearing snow and death. Instead, Gloriana dreamed of warm rain and summertime. Of life and happiness.

How naïve, she thought, repositioning herself.

Gloriana open and closed her cold, aching hands. Her once smooth sun kissed skin was now grey and cracked. The cold instantly ruined her beauty whenever she stepped out of Winter's Keep. *I should've brought wine. That would've kept me warm.*

One of the guards standing behind Gloriana shifted his feet, reminding her that they were there. She clinched her teeth, picturing the two knights. One was too young and could never look anyone in the eyes. The other was narcissistic and heftier than many well fed lords.

She groaned and turned around. "Go, find Maiden Barda, and tell her to hurry with my gloves and to bring a canister of wine. It is terribly cold, and I'm suffering. I will be able to watch my children just fine while you two are away."

"I'm the Lord Protector's knight," the fat one scoffed. "I only take orders from him, and he said to watch you anytime you are away from Maryere."

Gloriana frowned. "Do as I say, *knight*."

"That is Ser William Cantree, to you." The knight corrected, looking down at her. "I can have you punished for speaking to me that way. You are no mountain woman."

She had heard the insult before, but this time the words hurt. "Threaten me again and I will ensure my husband hears about it when he returns." Gloriana spat, and Ser William's eyes widened. "Now, do as I say."

"Y-yes, my lady," the younger knight interrupted, bowing.

The young man looked at Ser William, waiting for a response. Ser William rolled his eyes. "Fine," he said reluctantly, his lips puckered like a child.

Both men turned and walked toward their horses. "You," Gloriana pointed to the young knight, "Come here."

The shy man returned and Gloriana studied the two trees painted on his breastplate. *A man from House Bradberry*, she recognized, and her eyes widened as she focused on the small mountain peak in between the trees. *No, he's a customary knight with no surname.* She then took in the newly painted snowflake at the top of the knight's breastplate. *He's a man tied to the land, and yet he's a lord knight. Borin must be running out of men to choose from.*

The young man cleared his throat. "Yes, my lady?"

"Make it that he is dead," she commanded bluntly, and the boy's face paled. *I'm always angrier when I'm sober, but oh well.* "When he dies, just blame someone else."

"My lady I,"

"Hush," Gloriana put a finger to her lip. "The Mountain Realm needs knights who uphold honor, not supremacy ideals. You know what the land needs, don't you?" She took his hand, using her beauty to her advantage. "Once the deed is done, you will be rewarded handsomely." Then, she kissed his hand and the young knight smiled excitedly. "You wouldn't betray me by telling someone about our conversation, right?" The knight shook his head, and her grin turned wicked. "Good. Now, go on, he's waiting for you."

The young knight walked to the horses and mounted, leaving the Dense Pines along with Ser William. *I never asked the customary knight his name.* Gloriana sighed, not really caring. She got what she wanted, and that was all that mattered. *Although I was a little extreme.*

A shriek from one of the ponies made Gloriana bounce up from the rock she sat on. The horse reared and Josef tumbled from his pony and onto the cold hard ground.

"I thought a Hero like you could beat a poor ogre like me," Jaslyn teased, trotting around her brother.

"Shut up!" Josef yelled his voice cracking. "You cut me with that sword!"

"I cut you with a wooden sword?" Jaslyn laughed, looking at the blunt piece of wood. "Hurry, we must go tell all the weaponsmiths to stop making steel swords, wooden ones can kill just as easily."

Josef looked over to Gloriana, saying nothing; but his copper-colored eyes screamed. Gloriana pressed her lips together as Jaslyn continued to mock Josef. The young boy watched his sister, his mouth agape. He turned back to Gloriana, still sitting on the ground. "Mother!" he yelled. "Make her stop!"

Gloriana *did* want to make Jaslyn stop, but she also wanted her son to be strong. *He will never be if he doesn't learn.* "You let your sister unhorse you? Didn't you say a moon ago that you were the better rider?"

Josef eyes grew wide. "But...she's older than me!"

"By only a year," Jaslyn continued to tease.

"A young lord cannot be unhorsed by a man. A young lord cannot be unhorsed during play. A young lord cannot be unhorsed by his sister, or friend, or a sack of potatoes." Gloriana glanced at her fierce daughter and sighed, "A young lord cannot be unhorsed at all."

Jaslyn jumped from her horse and helped Josef up. "If we practice instead of playing games for children, maybe I wouldn't be able to unhorse you, little brother," she said, mussing his curly hair. "I can teach you."

"I would like that," Josef smiled and mounted his pony. The two rode off again, but this time the two children were not characters, they were teacher and student.

Gloriana watched as Jaslyn smacked Josef with the wooden sword, teaching him lessons. *Children.* Gloriana shivered, thinking about her daughter's tone. *When did Josef and Jaslyn grow up?*

Time passed, and Gloriana did nothing but sadly watch as her children grew up before her.

I haven't been a very good mother, but maybe I can try now.

Behind Gloriana, leaves rustled, alerting her of someone's approach. *Finally, Maiden Barda is here.* She glanced over her shoulder. *Oh,* Gloriana blushed, examining the young woman who walked toward her. *I forgot. Barda retired.*

The new handmaiden was beautiful. She stood tall over Gloriana, and her long blonde hair swayed as she moved. "Forgive my tardiness, my lady," the maiden stuttered out, eyes glittering like sea glass. "I've only just arrived to Maryere and,"

Gloriana raised her hand to quiet the woman, and the maiden handed her a pair of black leather gloves. Gloriana slipped them on, and the fur that filled the inside immediately gave her hands relief from the frigid cold. She closed her eyes and listened to everything around her. The horses neighed, the wooden swords clanged, and Jaslyn scolded Josef on why she unhorsed him again.

"Did you bring the wine?"

The handmaiden shuffled her feet. "Uh, no, my lady. I didn't know I was supposed to."

"Shame."

"The Lord Protector has returned from Kingment and wishes to see you," the maiden informed, her voice small.

Gloriana freezed. *He's back!?* "Why didn't he write to let me know he was returning?"

"I don't know, my lady."

Her lord husband, Borin Wayward, had left moons ago to visit the Northern Kingdom of Valley Pines. He left without warning, declaring that Gloriana would rule as Protector of the Mountain Realm in his stead. Of course, the highborn disagreed with the idea, but when Gloriana pulled herself out of her drunken slumps and ruled properly, some highborn acknowledged her.

As a leader, Gloriana felt fulfilled. She grew in confidence and rekindled her love for herself. During the summer days, Gloriana wore red and purple again, just as she had as a child. Silk tulle hid her face when she prayed in the chapel, and she even pierced her nose. Gloriana loved being so different from everyone else in the Mountain Realm, especially as their ruler. But the summer days faded, and she found herself once more wearing the ugly wool dresses that kept her warm.

"Children," she waved. *What is Borin going to be like now? Did he change at all?* Gloriana hoped he did. She stood from the rock and walked to her stallion. The young maiden helped Gloriana onto the horse as her children approached. "You don't have anything to ride?" Gloriana asked the maiden.

"No, my lady."

"Get on Josef's pony," Gloriana commanded, pointing to her son. "Jojo, ride with your sister." Her children glanced at each other confused. "Your father has returned," she added simply, and her children silently did as they were told.

The road to Maryere was dull.

On ancient Mountain Realm maps, it was titled the Golden Road, but now, people just called it the Road. There was nothing golden about the muddy path, with its thieves. So instead of taking the Road, Gloriana led everyone through the Dense Pines until it reached the lumberyard outside Winter's Keep.

Unfortunately, the sight of Maryere wasn't a beautiful one either. The city was sad and colorless. It was nothing like Goldspire. When they passed the city's gates, Josef and Jaslyn jumped off the pony and raced into Winter's Keep.

"I will put away the horses," the young maiden informed, sliding off Josef's pony.

"What is your name?"

The young maiden gave a small smile. "Asterin, my lady."

Gloriana handed the reins to Asterin, eyeing the girl. "In the stables, find a strong, hardy horse for yourself."

"Thank you, my lady," the young woman replied gratefully. "Oh, and the Lord Protector is in the Grand Library."

Unease filled Gloriana with every step until she reached the Grand Library. *Please, all the gods, let this man be reinvigorated; ready to lead the Mountain Realm. Let him be kinder and filled with optimism.* She wanted Borin to be a strong leader the people loved. *The people don't love him. They only tolerate him.*

She paused. *Do I only tolerate him?*

When it came to her lord husband, Gloriana was the perfect actress. *I must be if I don't want any problems.* "Borin!" she yelled gleefully, entering the library that was opened to all.

Above her, she heard a hearty recognizable laugh. "Gloriana!" Borin greeted, hanging over a rail. He still acted young, but his face seemed tired. "Come upstairs."

"I've missed you," she exhaled, reaching the top of the steps.

Borin pounced and embraced Gloriana warmly, something he had not done in a long time. *Did he miss me, too?* The hug did not last for more than a second before he pulled away and examined her face. "You pierced your nose?"

Gloriana blushed. "Aye, it reminds me of home."

"This is your home," her husband pouted.

"My *true* home. It helps me remember my family who were slain." Her words made Borin's face pale, and he stepped away.

She frowned at her husband's reaction, and her eyes shifted to the other side of the loft where a man stood quietly by the window. He stared out of the large window, looking down at the bland city. *A lord,* Gloriana recognized, examining the thick fur cloak the man wore over his shoulders. He turned and smiled prettily at Gloriana. *I've seen him before. Who is he?*

"Glory, it's Falk!" Borin exclaimed, breaking the silence. He put his hot, sweaty arm over Gloriana's shoulder as she shrunk into herself.

Glory is a mountain name. I'm a Summeran.

"She's more beautiful in person than what you described," Falk said, gazing at her, smiling so hard his cheeks turned rosy.

"I tried to tell you," Borin replied, grabbing his wine cup and filling it.

Gloriana disliked the men's lingering eyes. "It is very nice to meet you, Lord Osmont," she said through her teeth, trying to sound polite.

"My sweet Glory, quit being so civilized. This man is family," Borin declared, his voice echoing through the library.

She tried her best not to roll her eyes. *That man is not family.* House Osmont were the sworn enemies of her people; her *true* people. She bowed honorably toward the man whose last name bared anger in her soul.

The silence became unbearable as Falk's green eyes stayed on her body. "You do not wear the clothing of your people?"

Gloriana's stomach jumped at the question, and her eyes grew wide.

He's toying with me. She knew why. *House Osmont believes they are superior over House Thoren. He believes that I'm a dirty simpleton, just as his father did.* "It is cold here," she responded emotionlessly.

"Your lady wife seems a bit annoyed, Borin," Falk joked, and her husband laughed nervously.

"No, the library is frigid." Gloriana explained. She then excused herself and exited from the loft of the library.

Borin followed behind. "What was that?" He growled, stopping her, and his copper eyes stared down, burning bright with fury.

Gloriana noticed the grey hairs that seemed to sparkle in her husband's dark brown hair. *He's gotten older.* She thought carefully, trying to not think of her own age. "He said I seemed annoyed, so I left. I didn't want to make Lord Osmont uncomfortable."

"He noticed your hatred," Borin replied, trying to reason with her.

"Hatred? His father murdered my family!"

"You will not embarrass House Wayward's good name. Behave yourself while he's here."

She scoffed. *He will never understand.* "I will treat him with respect, but I will never see him as family. Know that."

"Glory," he sighed, still trying to sound kind. "You must let go of the past."

Let go of the past? She hugged herself in comfort, and tried to steady her breathing. *What does he know of letting go?*

Lord Borin Wayward was a man that let the past control him. Every day his goblet filled with wine, erasing the harsh memories. The deaths of his mother, his brother, and his father—his real family, were all memories that Borin wanted to forget, but never let go.

Borin's goblet made Gloriana buzz with anger. *As if I'm any better, drowning myself in wine any moment I get.* She released her arms from her waist and exhaled through her nose. *He will not tell me how to feel.* Her eyes stung as she focused on her husband. "I cannot."

"You can."

"I cannot!"

Her husband's face grew stern, and her grabbed her shoulder. She eyed his hand and cold sweat dotted her forehead. *Is he going to hit me?* Her muscles tensed at the question. Before Gloriana would've relented, ending the conversation before it got anywhere. *I'm not going to let him stop me. Not anymore.*

"How can you condemn someone for their father's actions?" he finally asked, his voice hushed.

Gloriana's body pulsed. Her face and ears grew warm as she thought about Borin's question. *He's right.* She lowered her eyes and stepped away from her husband. *I hate when he's right.*

She turned and descended the stairs, leaving Borin behind. Her fingers gripped the railing, trying her best to contain her anger. *The Seers are watching now.* The feeling gnawed at her as she kept her head down.

Ice crunched beneath her feet as she stepped out of the Grand Library. She rubbed her hands against the rough woolen sleeves of her dress. Compared to the strange warm breeze that flowed through the Dense Pines, Maryere was nothing but a frozen wasteland. Gloriana paused and looked at the cold grey sky.

Her lips trembled and her husband's question replayed in her mind. *Why should I condemn someone for what their father did?*

She thought about her father then.

His dark blue eyes, friendly smile, and the warmth he brought when they hugged, all swirled in her head. She loved her father. *And he's dead now. Father is dead because of Lord Morvan Osmont, so House Osmont is my enemy.* She nodded at her decision and began her trek to Winter's Keep. *House Osmont is my enemy, so Falk is my enemy, too. No matter what Borin says.*

ALICE

Slowly, Alice Wayward opened her eyes and stared at the icy grey nothingness outside the window. *I'm awake.* The rustling of the blanket reminded Alice where she was; in her room, alone. *How long was I asleep?* Her attention landed on the door that locked her away from the world. *Did anyone come to see me?* She sighed and placed her hand under her chin. *Of course not.* Her nose wrinkled, and her eyes filled with tears. *Nobody ever comes to see me.*

She sat up in her bed and studied the book that sat at the nightside table. Reading usually helped pass the time and took Alice's mind away from the reality that she couldn't leave the Bloody Tower. She grabbed a book and opened it. A strand of her hair fell on the pages causing Alice to frown. *Will I go bald before the year ends?* She released the strand and watched it fall back on the book. *Will I even be alive before the year ends?*

Alice dusted off her hair from the page. *Lismure,* she read, *the city that knows all.* As she read, she dreamed about what would be in the city. *Bustling markets, green parks, and enormous buildings.* It all seemed so magnificent and glorious to Alice. *I wish I could see it.*

A violent cough paused Alice's thoughts. Her throat burned, and her head felt as if it was about to explode with each cough. She groaned when the coughs resided, tasting blood in her mouth. *I don't know how much longer will I be able to take this.*

"Is that coughing I hear?" her handmaiden, Lady Myra Nores, called from outside the room. "Has my Alice finally awaken?"

She sat up in anticipation, waiting for the click-clack of Myra's shoes tapping against the thick cold stone.

Myra strode into the bedchamber. "Alice," she bowed, her amber-colored eyes glittering with excitement. "Good gods, it's freezing in here!" she exclaimed, moving to the other side of the room. Myra's long fingers wrapped around the logs that were set beside the fireplace. "No wonder you aren't getting any better. Do you know how long you were asleep?"

Alice looked away. "No."

"Six days." Myra lit a match and threw it into the fireplace.

After a moment, the firewood crackled, and the room grew warm. Alice closed her eyes and inhaled peacefully. The burning wood made her nose twitch, but she welcomed the stench. *At least it is warm.* Myra eyed her silently, causing Alice's skin to prickle. She opened her eyes, and the two girls stared at each other. Myra crossed her arms, and her frown deepened.

"What?" Alice questioned, unable to take the silence.

"How are you feeling?"

She brought her knees close to her chest and squeezed her legs tightly underneath the covers. "I'm fine," she breathed out.

"You're lying."

"So what?" Alice responded, throwing her hands in the air.

"Your lord father is home," Myra informed, changing the subject, the fire crackling over her low voice.

Alice tried to picture her father. "How does he look now?" she asked, remembering his black hair and long hairy face.

"Older," Myra replied bluntly. "Your lady mother is not happy about his return."

"Oh." Alice replied, puzzled. She didn't understand. Her father was back. Alice thought her mother would be happy to see her husband again. "But, why?"

"He brought Lord Falk Osmont with him."

"Okay?" Alice responded, not understanding. "Why would my mother be upset with that?"

"Because of what House Osmont did to House Thoren."

Alice placed a finger on her cheek, trying to remember what House Osmont had done. She gasped. "Massacre," she growled as fury boiled inside her. *How stupid of my father.*

"Your mother confronted Lord Borin, and he told her that no child should be held accountable for their father's mistakes or crimes," Myra scoffed.

Alice agreed with her father's words, *I wouldn't want to be held accountable for the things my father has done.* Her handmaiden's frown deepened at the silence. *It seems that Myra feels differently.* "Any other news?" she asked, trying to change the subject.

"Aye, this news you will not like," the young woman replied, her voice still cold and angry.

"What is it?"

Myra looked away. "It was reported that your father brought a whore from the Northern Kingdom of Valley Pines."

Alice wiped the cold sweat from her brow. *What? Father?* Her hands shook with embarrassment and anger as she processed what Myra had said. "What is her name?"

"It is unknown," Myra answered carefully.

"Well, figure it out," Alice snapped. Her head throbbed from her outburst, and she only wanted to sleep now. She didn't want to think about her stupid father with his stupid whore.

"I will try my best," Myra bowed. "Your lady Aunt Victoria sent gifts."

Alice continued to stare at her blanket, holding back tears. "What of it?"

"Jaslyn received a horse for her birthday," Myra began, her voice pepping up with excitement. "Josef received a sword. He named it Firestone."

Alice chuckled, and her headache intensifying as she pictured her brother with a longsword fit for a man. "He is too young for a sword."

"He will be old enough eventually," Myra reminded her.

"The boy is only ten," she replied, knowing that Myra was right. *Jaslyn and Josef will grow up to be strong while I am stuck here in the Bloody Tower.* "What did my sweet lady aunt give me?"

There was a long pause before Myra pulled out a necklace. "This."

"Oh, how wonderful!" Alice smiled, taking the gift. She rubbed her thumb against the gold chain before putting it on. "It's beautiful. I will need to write a letter to thank her."

Myra turned away. "My mother once told me that ruby necklaces always lead to blood being shed."

"This is a quartz crystal," she countered, but when Myra's face didn't change she could do nothing but exhale. "Fine, I'll remember the warning," she assured, putting on the necklace. "Is there any other news?"

"Aye, there is a feast in a few days, praising the gods for your lord father's safe return. Lady Gloriana has informed me that you are not required to go if you do not want to."

Alice groaned. "Why would anyone want to celebrate a man who has a whore?"

Myra turned away from Alice. "Your mother does not know."

"She must be told at once!" Alice commanded, almost bouncing from her bed.

"Alice, no." Myra replied, grabbing her arm. "Your mother needs to learn on her own. A child must not know about the adulteries of their parents."

She had forgotten.

Most children grew up blind to what the adults did around them, and some ended up dead without ever knowing why. *I'm different.* Alice's illness forced her to stay inside, hiding away from the world. So, her mother gave her Myra, a highborn lady from the Summerlands.

Alice looked at her only friend. "How do you know all these things?" she asked, sounding sadder than she had wanted to.

Myra's eyes grew wide. "Uh...the uh...from the Seers," she replied stumbling over her words.

"And whom do the Seers serve?"

Myra's expression morphed into confusion. "The Citadel."

Alice nodded slowly, "And who does the Citadel serve?"

"Themselves," Myra replied, her voice low.

That is why my lady mother hates the Citadel so much. "Could the Lord Protectors of each region not just destroy the Citadels?"

Myra shook her head. "If the Citadel disappears, the knowledge of the world disappears."

"What about in Lismure?" *The city that knows all.*

"Lismure gets its information from the Citadel, just as everyone else does. Besides, even if the Lord Protectors revolted against the Citadel, it would not stop them. There are more than just the Citadels here in Mystos."

Nempur, Eeccess, and Ihphy's Archipelago. The names of the continents swirled in Alice's mind. She wanted to travel there. Any place would be better than the Bloody Tower and Maryere. *If only I could become well enough to leave.* She sighed heavily then. Her sickness had lasted for moons now and she wasn't sure if she would ever get better. *Maybe I'll die in Maryere, the same place I was born in.*

Her spine shivered at the thought.

"I am going to the feast," she declared, clutching her new necklace. "I want to show everyone that I am not dead, yet. Since no one even worries to see me, but you."

"That is not true," Myra replied.

"Of course, it's true! I am better off dead," she whispered as tears burned her eyes.

Myra stood and walked to the door, slightly opening it before pausing, "I will tell a seamstress to provide you with a warm dress for the feast," she informed with her back turned. "And never say something like that again."

Then the handmaiden left without another word.

HADRIAN

Rhythmic knocking awoke Hadrian Osmont from a dreamless night. *Another day has come!* He sat up energetically and wiped the sleep from his eyes, wondering who could be on the other side of his bedchamber door. "Come in," he yawned.

His mother glided into the room. "Good morning, my perfect son," she greeted in a sing-song voice. "Do you know what day it is?"

He grinned. "Planning day?"

Lady Arla matched his smile, her eyes glittering. "Are you ready?"

Hadrian jumped from his bed and landed in his mother's open arms. Warmth engulfed Hadrian as she hugged him tightly, squishing his face into her pudgy midsection. "What should we plan first?" he asked, pulling his head up to breathe.

Arla squeezed a bit tighter before releasing her son. She relaxed on one hip and put a finger to her chin. "Let's break our fast, and then we can plan." He agreed with the plan, and Lady Arla Osmont held his hand, leading him through the High Castle.

Hadrian's mother was his world.

When she sang, he sang with her. When she read, he read with her. When she baked, he baked with her. They spent most of their time together, and Hadrian adored every minute.

He glanced at their intertwined hands and noticed the ragged edges of his mother's nails, lightly pushing into his skin. *Did she chew at them?* He examined his own nails and sighed. *Why would she do that?*

"Hadrian," someone called.

He lifted his head and met Patty's light brown eyes. "Good morning, Patty," he greeted, still being tugged along behind his mother.

Patty's mouth twisted as she examined the boy. "Why are you still in your bedclothes?"

Hadrian's vision narrowed on his clothing and he gasped. *I didn't even notice!* He returned his attention to Patty and blushed. "I rushed out of my room and forgot to change," he confessed quietly.

The handmaiden gave a small smile. "Are you excited for your birthday?"

"Aye!" Hadrian beamed, his embarrassment melting away. "I'll become a man tomorrow!"

"Servant, go to the kitchens and get Hadrian and I some breakfast," Lady Arla interrupted, tightening her grip on his hand.

Patty's bright smile dropped and she quit walking. "Yes, my lady," she replied solemnly and turned towards the kitchens.

Hadrian looked at his mother's chestnut-colored hair and frowned. "Her name isn't Servant; it's Patty. You know this, Mother."

Lady Arla turned her head and pressed on a smile. "Of course, my precious son. Now, let's hurry. I want to eat and start planning!"

We get to plan my birthday together! He brightened, imagining the laughs they would share throughout the day. *I love my mother, and my mother loves me!*

The pair arrived at the dining hall and his little sister, Maerwynn, cheered Hadrian's name as he entered. "Sit beside me, big brother!" she told him, twirling behind her chair. Her long light brown hair floated as she spun on her toes. "Big brother, sit beside me!"

"Morning," Leonidas grumbled, lifting a hand.

Hadrian's face enlivened at his little brother's greeting. "Morning Leo! How are you today?"

"Fine," he exhaled, "You're still in your bedclothes," he added, lowering his eyes to the meal, ending their conversation.

Hadrian huffed and rolled his eyes. *Maybe I should go and change.*

"Are you planning something for your birthday?" Maerwynn questioned, bringing Hadrian's attention back to her.

He released his hand from his mother's and walked toward his little sister. "Of course!" he answered, patting her soft hair. Maerwynn gave a bright smile showing her missing front teeth. "I think I see a tooth growing in," he informed, pointing at her mouth.

Maerwynn flexed her muscles like the strongmen did at the annual festivals. "I'm growing up! Soon I will be older than you!"

Laughter burst from Hadrian as he took his seat. "That's not how it works, Wynn."

His sister sat beside him and rolled her lavender-colored eyes. "You'll see! I will become older than you and become the Lord Protector myself!"

"Wynn, enough of the nonsense," Lady Arla snapped as Patty placed a platter in front of her. "You're a girl. You can't be the Lord Protector."

"There's actually no law against it," Leonidas corrected, yet everyone ignored him.

Maerwynn frowned and stared at Hadrian. "Can I help you plan for your birthday?"

He glanced at his mother and gave her a wide smile. "Is it okay if Wynn helps?"

Arla's tiny eyes peered at her daughter before landing on her precious son. "If you're okay with it," his mother answered with her arms crossed, and Maerwynn cheered again. "But if Hadrian doesn't like an idea, you can't whine and complain."

"Fine, fine," Maerwynn waved off, spooning some eggs into her mouth. "Hadrian is going to like my ideas, aren't you?"

Hadrian nodded. "Of course, Wynn."

Patty placed a platter in front of Hadrian, and he took in the tantalizing aromas that filled his nose. "Thank you, Patty."

The servant girl bowed and took her place against the wall along with the other servants, waiting for someone to call for her.

Hadrian's attention turned to his father, who seemed to disappear at the end of the table. *Father didn't say good morning*, he realized, watching the man write. *What is he writing?* Hadrian cocked his head to the side curiously, trying to see if he could read it. *It's too small.*

His father, the Lord Protector of the Southern Kingdom of Valley Pines, Peyton Osmont, was an emotionless man, always in thought. *I have so much to learn from my father*, Hadrian thought in awe, as Peyton pushed the paper he had been writing away and leaned over to grab another piece.

Behind Lord Peyton stood Ser Colvic Rames, one of the most famous knights in all of Mystos. *Ser Colvic is always by Father's side.* He peeked behind his shoulder and smiled. *After tomorrow, I will have a knight constantly by my side too! Then I will have a best friend.*

His eyes went to his mother, who took a bite of toasted bread. *Well, I already have a best friend I can depend on.*

"Dear, what's so important you can't stop writing to eat?" Lady Arla questioned, catching everyone's attention.

Lord Peyton stopped and looked at his wife. "I am an important man, and I have important matters to attend to."

"If it is more important than your family, then you can just,"

"Father, what is something I should do for my birthday tomorrow?" Hadrian interrupted, not wanting his parents to bicker.

Peyton repositioned in the chair. "Eat some cake."

"That's it?" Arla scoffed.

Hadrian mused over his father's answer before turning to Patty. "Could you find someone to make a lemon cake for my birthday? I love lemons. Actually, could you bake the cake, Patty? Your sweets are always so good, it would be the perfect present."

Patty's eyes twinkled as she stared at Hadrian, speechless.

Lady Arla turned to the girl. "You are supposed to say 'yes, my lord,' when Hadrian talks to you, Servant."

"Apologies. Yes, my lord. It would be an honor to bake a cake for you."

The room was quiet once more, and Peyton continued writing, ignoring his family.

"I'm done," Leonidas announced, standing. "I'm going to the courtyard to train."

"No one cares," Maerwynn teased, sticking out her tongue.

"I care," Hadrian intervened, and Leo smiled. "Maybe I will join you later. I want to get stronger, so I need to start training, too."

His little brother nodded with enthusiasm. "I'm still training with sticks, but there are techniques I could teach you." He then turned to the famed knight, who continued to stand silently behind Peyton. "Ser Colvic, could you train Hadrian and me later?"

Colvic shifted uncomfortably. "Aye, if time allows it."

"But Hadrian," his mother whined. "I thought we were going to plan."

"Planning shouldn't take all day," he reasoned, and Arla's downturned face made him frown. "Like Ser Colvic said, if time allows it," he added and his mother's face brightened, but now it was Leo who was frowning. His little brother stomped out of the room, and guilt ripped at Hadrian. *How can I make everyone happy?*

A knight rushed into the dining hall and approached Hadrian's mother. "My lady, you are needed."

Lady Arla's face twisted in confusion before her eyes flickered to Peyton, who continued to write, still ignoring everyone. "I am in the middle of my meal. Can it wait?"

"I'm not sure. It is about your, uh, request."

Arla jumped to her feet with her eyes wide, and her chair crashed to the floor. "You found her?"

The knight hesitated. "As I said, you're needed, my lady."

Hadrian stared at his mother, confused. *What is she looking for?*

Arla met Hadrian's questioning eyes and sighed. "Would you be able to do some planning with Maerwynn without me? We can continue what you two have started when I return." Maerwynn bounced in her chair, cheering loudly, and Arla peered at the girl.

Hadrian pouted. He wanted his mother to be there as he planned his birthday. *Just like always.* He studied the concern etched into his mother's face, groaning. "Aye, that's fine."

Lady Arla gave a kind smile and walked out of the dining hall, following the knight.

"What do you think the request is?" Maerwynn asked excitedly. "Your birthday is tomorrow. It has to be something for you!"

Peyton Osmont groaned, grabbing his children's attention as he rose to his feet. "If you need me, I will be in my study." He then walked out of the dining hall with Ser Colvic and a few servants following him, leaving Hadrian, Maerwynn, and Patty alone.

"Why is everyone acting so tense?" Maerwynn questioned, crossing her arms.

"Who was acting tense?"

"Everyone!" Maerwynn shouted as Patty approached. "Patty, wasn't everyone acting tense today?"

Patty placed a finger to her chin. "Lord Peyton and Lady Arla did seem a bit annoyed."

"A bit?" Maerwynn repeated. "They were agitated. Leo and Ser Colvic were too," she turned to Hadrian, her hair slapping against his arm. "You didn't notice?"

Mother seemed fine until the knight arrived, Hadrian noted. *Father seemed annoyed, but he is always irritated. Leo and Ser Colvic were quiet like usual, too.* He looked into his little sister's bright eyes. "No, I didn't notice."

Maerwynn groaned. "You never notice," she pouted. "Come on, the days are still warm. Let's go to the courtyard where Leo is and plan there." She walked to the exit. "Patty, you come too."

Patty skipped to Maerwynn, and the girls left ahead of Hadrian.

Alone, Hadrian looked at each spot his family had sat. *I never notice,* he thought, remembering Maerwynn's sad face. *What am I supposed to notice?* He stood and walked to the door, deep in thought, when he bumped into someone. "Sorry," he apologized, waving his hands. "I didn't see you."

The unknown woman smiled, her bright red eyes smiling, too. "No worries," she told him, her voice hoarse. She looked him up and down as if she was examining a prize. "You're Hadrian, right?"

A shiver ran down his spine. *Who is this woman? I've never seen her before.* He nodded, and the woman's smile grew.

"You've grown into a handsome boy."

Hadrian blushed and looked away. "Thank you."

"Your birthday is tomorrow?"

"Aye," he replied, eyeing her suspiciously.

The woman stepped closer, causing Hadrian to shrink within himself. "I can see you know the House Ashe tradition of going to sleep early the night before your birthday," she replied pointing at Hadrian's attire. "Did Arla teach you that? Did she teach you why? She was never a very patient person."

Hadrian frowned. "You should be referring to my mother as Lady Arla Osmont."

His statement caused the woman to chuckle before she placed a hand on his cheek, causing him to freeze. "It's hard becoming an adult. Be careful out there." The woman then turned and walked away, leaving Hadrian Osmont alone in the hallway.

Be careful out where? And who was that woman anyway? He lightly placed his hand on his cheek where the woman had touched him. "I'll ask Mother," he declared to no one.

Sh! Even the walls have ears; the strange woman's voice echoed in Hadrian's head. *Be good. Be well. Be safe.*

VICTORIA

L ady Victoria Osmont lounged in the glass room and hummed along
with the rain that showered around her. She thought back to when her
life was better, before her Saavant, Enya, told her that she was slipping into
insanity once again, and would soon die. *I'm not insane. I'm not insane. I'm
not insane.* If she admitted she was as everyone else did, then it would be
true. *I must fight for my sanity. I cannot be afraid.*

The fire crackled and swirled in the fire pit behind Victoria, and goose
prickles crawled up her arms. She turned to the dancing orange and red
flames that brought warmth to the cold room. *I cannot be afraid.*

She was a Wayward in truth, and Wayward's feared nothing. Victoria,
however, had come to fear everything. Every year that she grew older, she
found a new thing to fear. Once it was horses. Another time she feared
elderberries, the only cure to the sweating sickness that had ailed her.

Now, Victoria feared the truth.

She took a deep breath and slapped her cheeks, trying to calm down.
She needed to be sane—to *act* sane. She had to for the sake of her children.
She couldn't leave her four wonderful, beautiful babies behind with their
wretched lord father.

She sighed, thinking about her sons, Doran and Rosert, who were
complete opposites. Doran had grown to be a bit strange like her and
thoughtless like Falk, while Rosert was distant and wild. Neither of them
looked alike, except for their big and bright smiles. Her daughters, Emeline
and Catrain, were Victoria's little princesses of springtime. Each so kind
and so sweet, reminding her of the goddesses in the Clouds.

I can't leave my children. I love them far too much.

Her mind wandered to an old black book Saavant Enya gave her a fortnight ago. The old woman had told Victoria to read the passages in secret,
and learn from it, to take her mind off of her failing sanity. Keeping secrets,
however, made the voices in Victoria's head screech in revolt. She covered
her ears and hushed the noise. *No one must know that I have a book about the
Arts.*

A door creaked opened, pulling Victoria back into reality. Ser Edmund
Archard walked into the room with his face blank. The knight bowed before
Victoria and removed his hawk's beak shaped helm to reveal a boyish face
no older than eighteen. *But a man grown,* she thought, thinking of her own

sons.

Ser Edmund pushed his long mop of blond hair away from his eyes. "My lady," he began, grabbing the hilt of his sword. "I expected you in the throne room."

"I wanted to be in here where I'm outside but inside. What did you need?"

"We found the women sleeping with the Lord Protector."

She blinked. "Women? It's supposed to be *woman*. Enya said one woman!"

The knight shook his head. "There was a brothel the Lord Protector paid weekly."

"What did you do with the women?"

"They were murdered, as you requested."

Victoria Osmont wanted to frown, but the words were sweet to her, and she couldn't help but smile. *No, don't smile. People died!* Her green eyes narrowed on the young knight. "I didn't ask you to murder multiple people. Just the one woman Saavant Enya saw with Falk." She sighed, understanding how unfaithful her lord husband was. "What's done is done."

She opened the book that sat on her lap, no longer wanting to talk. *It was more than one woman.* Her hand shook as she flipped through the book with Ser Edmund still standing awkwardly before her. *I must think of something else before I start screaming and shouting.*

Her attention landed on a random page. *When Axone, the goddess of Life, created the terrafield, she produced the Four Beings to enhabit the world. The Four Beings were the Nature, the Beast, the Arc, and the Darkness. The Arcs were the original intelligent species, created thousands of years before humans. The Arcs separated humans into two groups. The Maras, or Arts users. And the Zuts, or non-Arts users. A Divine Queen created Scholars long ago to document human history. One such Scholar wrote,*

Ser Edmund Archard cleared his throat. "What shall we do with the children?"

Her eyes snapped to the knight. "The what?"

"Children," Edmund repeated with a gulp.

"Whose children are they?"

The knight could no longer look at her. "The Lord Protector's."

Victoria boiled with fury. "How many did you find?"

"Two who mirror Lord Falk. They have fiery hair, and eyes the color of moss, just like an Osmont."

She leaned over, trying her best to stay calm. *I'm still in shock learning about the affairs, but...* She gripped at her hair. *He has bastards. Why would he do that to me? Does he not love me?*

Lady Victoria Osmont realized then that she didn't know who her lord husband was. The man she thought she knew wasn't real. *Is anything real?*

"One child is fifteen and the other is twelve," Edmund continued, watching the rain through the glass ceiling, "but there could be more."

"I did not ask for ages!" Victoria screamed, practically standing. *Rosert is fifteen,* she clutched her chest. *Emeline is twelve.* Her teary eyes returned to Ser Edmund. *How long has this been going on?*

Then another question popped into her head. *Do these children know who their father is?* She needed to know if her husband's bastards thought they were better, because their father was also the Lord Protector of the Northern Kingdom. *If they do, I'll see to it that they are dead.*

No one would jeopardize her children's future.

Victoria relaxed in her lounge chair. "I would like to see the children. Bring them here, but don't tell them why."

Ser Edmund stared back in horror. "You're not going to put them to the knife, are you?"

"I refuse to have the children of whores become sinners. They will be godly children." She smiled, comforting the knight.

"Of course, my lady," Ser Edmund bowed. "I will bring them to the Black Castle within the next moon." He then exited, leaving Victoria alone in her thoughts.

"FALK!" Victoria screeched, rocking back and forth as she chewed at her lip until it bled. "He's a scumbag, giving other women his attention, ugh, disgusting! How could,"

She covered her mouth, remembering a young woman who had all of her brother's attention when he visited Kingment. *Brother,* tears filled her eyes, *he told me she was just a servant girl.* She gritted her teeth imagining the woman's smile as she entered Borin's wheelhouse. *How could I be so stupid? Of course he was lying!* She slammed her hands against the old pages of the book.

Does Gloriana know? Her eyes widened, as the abuses her brother described he had done repeated in her head. *That poor woman. After years of taking hits from Borin... now he can't even stay loyal to her? He blamed it all on Mother, too. Mother would never teach him such a thing! Borin must change before something happens.*

She squinted, picturing her sister by marriage. *I must warn Gloriana; but how?* She paused for a moment. *I'll send a letter. But it must be secretive, something that no one could read—not even the Saavants.*

Victoria thought about her childhood then, back when her life was calm and pleasant. She pictured the times she had spent with Gloriana in Maryere as her older brother, Ser Rodrick Wayward, watched over them. *This is Old Summeran,* a young Gloriana explained, writing on a piece of paper. *It's the ancient language of the Summerlands.* She shut the old book that still laid on her lap and stood up from the lounge chair.

No one must know our words, Gloriana's voice echoed. *No one must know.*

She walked to the abandoned study where Lord Protectors were supposed to write their decrees. *Falk never liked this place,* she remembered, stepping inside, causing dust to swirl.

Her body ached as she approached the desk and sat in the velvet-cushioned chair. The softness eased some of her pain, causing Victoria to exhale loudly. She placed the old book Enya gave her on the desk, and grabbed a piece of paper.

Slowly, she dipped a quill in the thick black ink and attempted to write the letter. *Shit!* The language was so difficult, with its stokes and circles, that it made Victoria's hand throb. *I can't write this*, she realized as her tears splashed against the wet ink on the paper, blurring what she had written. *What do I do?*

"Mother," her youngest daughter, Catrain, called poking her head inside the room. Victoria motioned for the girl to enter and a bright smile spread across Catrain's face. The young girl closed the door and skipped deeper into the study. "Why are you here?"

"I was writing," Victoria explained simply, poking her daughter's button nose, causing the girl to giggle. "Why are *you* here?"

The question wiped the grin off Catrain's face and she shrugged. "I was bored. What are you writing?"

"A letter to my friend," Victoria answered, slowly closing her eyes. Consciousness began to slip away, frightening her. *Is this insanity? Or is this much more?* "There is something I wish to tell them," she exhaled. "Something important."

"Mother, your mind, it's not," Catrain started, but stopped as pity etched into her face. "Is the letter for Lord Borin?" She questioned, her golden eyes twinkling like stars in the black skies as her cheeks turned rosy.

Victoria smiled. *The eyes of the golden bear.* It was a feature House Wayward had for hundreds of years, but as time went by, the golden eyes became rare. When Catrain was born and opened her eyes for the first time, Victoria cried from the happiness that filled her. *When I look at her, she brings me home.* She remembered Borin's reaction the first time he saw Catrian. His big hand mussed her hair and he gave a hearty laugh. *My girl has got the same eyes! We made special children!*

Catrain, however, never saw herself as a Wayward, only an Osmont. She was a hawk, not a bear. Borin was a lord, not an uncle.

"No, my child, Lord Borin is my brother, I said friend," she reminded.

"Well, can I help you?"

"The language may be too hard. It is a dead language."

The girl's face scrunched, still trying to read the letter. "A dead language," she repeated, almost disgusted.

"Aye, it's ancient and from the Summerlands."

Catrain smiled. Everyone in Mystos knew that the Summerlands was the most beautiful of the Five Great Lands, with its rolling hills, black sand beaches, and purple waters. "How did you learn a dead language?"

Victoria picked up the quill and continued the letter. "Nevermind that," she told her daughter, causing Catrain to groan. "Look, I'm already done," she added, folding up the letter. "But you can do something else for me."

The young girl's face brightened. "What?"

"Give this letter to Saavant Enya and tell her to send it to Maryere."

Catrain stepped back. "I don't want to."

"Why not?"

"I don't like her."

She's just an old woman. Victoria sighed, not understanding her daughter's apprehension. "Fine, just go straight to the rookery and tell them to send it to House Wayward. It's written on the letter."

Her youngest child took the letter out of Victoria's hands. "Alright, but I want three cookies for dessert instead of one!"

A kind smile returned to Victoria's face and she pinched Catrain's cheeks lovingly. "Of course, anything for my sweet little girl."

JASLYN

The winds howled around Jaslyn Wayward, fiercely screaming that autumn had arrived in the Mountain Realm. Her knees pressed into the dirt as she stooped behind a dying prickle bush, stalking a little grey rabbit with a pink nose and fluffy ears. She thought it was a pleasant runt hopping around and eating the dead leaves from the ground. *If I kill it, Maiden Barda can make her famous hare stew.* Jaslyn's mouth watered at the thought.

Freezing air swirled around Jaslyn again, sending a chill through her spine. She studied the small aminal as it hopped closer, unaware she was near. Jaslyn chewed on a stick and cut a sharp point into another, trying to concentrate.

The air stilled, but the squawking birds seemed only to grow louder. *I can't think like this!* Little furry hares were the most challenging animal for Jaslyn to hunt and the most rewarding. *Better than a deer or a wild boar, like the ones the lords brag about when they return from their hunting trips. Larger animals are easier to hit,* Jaslyn thought, setting up her arrow. *They cannot escape easily like a bunny can.*

Jaslyn pulled back her arrow and exhaled slowly, waiting for the perfect moment.

"My lady, the wind is ungratefully cold! Why did you demand we come out here?!" Asterin yelled dramatically from behind, scaring the rabbit away.

Jaslyn watched the little hare hop behind more prickle bushes before disappearing. Branches rustled behind Jaslyn as she turned to see Asterin fuddling her way through the foliage. The young maiden was not dressed for hunting. She wore a sheer blue dress lined with black wolf's fur, and underneath the first layer, the handmaiden wore a tight, roughspun garb. The grey cloak tied around the handmaiden's shoulders was made of fur from an animal Jaslyn couldn't make out, but she knew from how Asterin dressed that the handmaiden wanted to be a highborn. *Maybe the maiden thinks she is a queen,* Jaslyn quipped, observing the girl. Even Jaslyn's twin handmaidens, Violet and Evergreen, were smart enough to dress for the dirtiness of hunting.

"What would you like me to do, my lady?"

"Just sit," Jaslyn snapped. Her mother's handmaiden sat on a rock larger than she was before turning her glassy eyes back to Jaslyn. "And stay quiet," she added, and Asterin nodded rapidly.

Once again, Jaslyn embarked on her quest for a kill, her mind wandering. *I hunt better with my handmaidens by my side.* The twin girls were always there for Jaslyn during her trips into the Dense Pines, even though they were as prim and proper as Asterin. They sacrificed for Jaslyn, and she was determined to make their efforts worthwhile by having rabbit-fur gloves made. *Once I get my kill.*

Unfortunately, Violet and Evergreen had to help with the feast preparations, leaving Asterin to watch her. Jaslyn didn't know much about Asterin, only that she was the new handmaiden to replace Maiden Barda. She frowned. *No one can replace Maiden Barda.*

Jaslyn Wayward lifted her attention to an ugly bird perched on a bare branch above her head. She lowered her eyes and noticed Asterin sitting underneath, staring at something else. A devious grin appeared on Jaslyn's face as she shot the bird right in the eye. It fell from the tree and flopped on the young maiden's lap, causing her to squeal. "Clean it for Maiden Barda," Jaslyn commanded.

Asterin frowned and pulled the arrow out of the bird's eye. Thick, dark blood streamed from the wound, staining Asterin's dress. The handmaiden sighed, displeased, and reached into her thick burlap sack, pulling out a dagger.

"You don't skin a bird," Jaslyn laughed, and Asterin paused with the blade at the bird's throat. "You have to pluck the feathers," she explained to the maiden, pretending to pluck an invisible bird.

Asterin's face turned bright red. "Yes, of course. Apologies, there weren't many birds where I'm from." She placed the dagger back in the bag and began plucking .

And where are you from? Jaslyn wondered before a chirp caught her attention.

She scanned her surroundings but couldn't find where the sound originated. Jaslyn focused on the handmaiden, who didn't notice the noise. *What is it?* She walked toward the light chirping, her steps hesitant. The sounds grew louder as she trekked deeper into the thickets, reminding Jaslyn of the whimpers of a hurt animal. She ducked behind some bushes and readied her bow for protection. *Animals that are afraid are the ones more ready to attack,* her father's warnings from one of their hunting trips echoed in her head. *You never want to interact with a hurt animal.*

She pressed her lips together. *I'm not one to listen to advice.*

Jaslyn Wayward quickly pushed back the bushes, revealing a tiny lion cub whimpering in the freezing mud. She stared at the animal with astonishment. *I've never seen anything like it before.* Her golden eyes darted around, but she saw no other animals. *It's alone.*

She slipped the bow on her back and crept toward the cub. "Sh, no crying," she hushed, picking the little cub out of the mud and holding it close to her chest. "What do I do?"

Jaslyn knew she couldn't leave the poor baby lion alone in the Dense Pines. *It doesn't belong here.* She repositioned the shivering animal in her arms, her mind racing. *Will my parents allow me to keep it if I take it home? Will they realize I even have it? Maybe Alice will want it? She loves my gifts.* Jaslyn focused on the tiny, scared animal, bringing its face to her neck for warmth as it cried. "It's okay, I will help you."

Jaslyn traced her steps back to where Asterin continued plucking the bird. In her arms, the little lion shook so severely it brought tears to Jaslyn's eyes. *I can't cry,* she thought, sniffling. *A Wayward is always strong.* "Water," she demanded, seeing Asterin through the trees.

Asterin placed the half-plucked bird on the rock, grabbed her bag, and pulled out a water canister. Jaslyn pulled the cub from under her cloak and showed the shivering animal to Asterin. The handmaiden's eyes widened in shock at the sight of the lion cub. "What is that?" she shrieked, her voice filled with disbelief.

"Pour water over it," Jaslyn instructed, ignoring the maiden's ongoing gasps.

Asterin poured water over the cub, and the animal replied with shrieks, howls, and snaps. "My lady, I don't think you should be playing with,"

"It is only a baby," Jaslyn interrupted, not caring about the woman's concern. "It will not hurt me or you. Anyway, my mother did not insist that you travel with me to think," she snapped, scrubbing the lion's fur until it was clean. "There you are," she smiled, examining the lion. The animal's pale yellow fur looked almost white, and its eyes glowed like fire. "You're beautiful." She said, putting the cub back under her cloak. The cub purred happily, making Jaslyn smile. "It may be too much for Alice to take care of him while she is sick, so I'm going to keep it."

"My lady," Asterin began, still staring at the cub. "The Mountain Realm is no place for a lion. It doesn't belong here. Where I am from, they are uncommon, and the Grasslandi adore the white lion."

"I'm going to name you Kai," Jaslyn continued, chuckling a little, ignoring the woman. She studied the tiny animal in her hands, and the cub looked back, its eyes glowing. "There was a famous Hero from the Embrus tribe who lived high in the mountains, named Kai." She petted the lion, "Maybe you can grow into a Hero lion or something."

"My lady," Asterin started again.

Jaslyn shot a violent look at the handmaiden. "Yes?"

The young woman's face paled, and she took a few steps back. "The feast is in a few hours," Asterin replied cautiously, walking to the horses. "We should start heading back."

Jaslyn had forgotten. *Would anyone miss me if I didn't show up?* Her mother had demanded that she attend the feast, so she had no choice. *Why can't I be forgotten like Alice?* "Aye," she sighed, walking to her new horse, Storm. The Valley Stallion had a black coat with a white mane that reminded Jaslyn of bright lightning striking along the night sky. She loved her horse, and she loved her lady aunt for gifting it to her.

Kai yawned heavily before laying comfortably in Jaslyn's lap as Asterin led her out of the Dense Pines and onto the Road back to Maryere. *Why aren't we staying in the forest?* Jaslyn never traveled on the Road when returning home. *The Dense Pines stretches to the lumberyard outside Winter's Keep.* She remembered the first time she met Asterin only a few days ago. *Mother took that way, too. Why did this handmaiden take such a dangerous route?*

They passed through the snow-dusted green lands and into a peasant village Jaslyn didn't know existed. Her face darkened. "Why did we go this way?"

Asterin turned her head, grinning. "What do you mean? Are you afraid of the people?"

"M'lady," the peasants called to Jaslyn as her horse approached. Their gaunt faces and needy eyes seemed to scream at Jasyln as their voices filled the air.

She pictured the annoyance constantly etched on her mother's face. *The Road is filled with thieves and murderers!* Lady Gloriana Wayward had warned, one of the few times she attempted to mother Jaslyn. *You're a Wayward. Nothing scares you, but just ride through the Dense Pines until you get to the lumberyard.*

Asterin slowed to a trot, and more peasants surrounded the pair.

"M'lady," children called out, stretching their arms to her.

The young cub growled underneath the cloak at all the noise, but more peasants ran to Jaslyn in admiration, and the knights patrolling surrounded the pair, causing them to stop. On their breastplate were the painted sigils of different highborn houses they were aligned to, along with a little mountain peak to indicate they were customary knights without a surname. One knight had the lantern for House Dimwich, another had the white winter rose of House Morlen, and three of the men had the black castle of House Blackmour. Nowhere in the group of shining knights did Jaslyn see the golden bear of House Wayward.

Not even a customary knight.

"Move! Lady Jaslyn Wayward needs to return to the capital!" Asterin waved a hand angrily, making demands she shouldn't make.

"There are too many peasants for a safe exit," a knight responded, staring at Jaslyn with old, tired eyes. "We must separate them."

On the knight's breastplate was a grey pigeon holding a longsword in its talons, indicating that he was from House Millister. *No mountain peak,* Jaslyn recognized. *This knight is a highborn.*

"That will take too long," Asterin groaned. "We can't be late. Can't you like strike them down or something?"

Jaslyn's eyes widened, and she opened her mouth to speak, but the highborn knight was faster. "I will do no such thing," he scoffed before his attention shifted from his men to the peasants and then to Jaslyn. "Apologies, my lady, but I cannot slaughter people for no reason."

"Give me your name, knight, so I can explain to the Lord Protector why his youngest daughter was late for his feast." Asterin continued.

"Ser Lyon Millister," he answered with his head held high.

Kai popped his head out of Jaslyn's cloak and yipped at the crowd. Murmuring swirled around Jaslyn as the cub tried to escape from her grasp. "Stop it, Kai," she scolded the restless lion.

"My lady," the knight exhaled, pointing to Jaslyn. "Where did you find that beast?"

"No matter," she dismissed, tightly holding onto Kai. "I commend you, Ser Lyon, and your defiance. Murdering innocents will not happen today," she told the crowd. "Because I, Jaslyn of House Wayward, will not allow it." The crowd roared at her declaration, and she lifted her hand to quiet the peasants. "I apologize this handmaiden even suggested such a thing."

The crowd of peasants applauded before respectfully moving out of the way so Jaslyn could leave the village. She turned to Ser Lyon Millister. "I will remember your kindness." She reared her horse and raced towards Maryere, leaving Asterin behind.

Jaslyn brought her cloak closer to her chest as the snow slapped her face. *An early snow.* She rode Storm harder, trying to ignore the chill in the air. "Whoa, girl," she called out, trotting into the city. Children filled the streets, enjoying the fresh snow. She jumped off of Storm and led it to the stables.

When Jaslyn left the stables, the snow's pace quickened, and she could no longer see the muddy ground. Instead of going to Winter's Keep, she rushed to Maiden Barda's new cottage with Kai in her hands.

"Maiden Barda!" She yelled, opening the door. The heat from the fire brought immediate comfort and melted the snowflakes in Jaslyn's wavy hair. She sniffed, and her mouth drooled. *Mutton stew.* Maiden Barda stood over her cooking pot, stirring the contents that made everything smell wonderful.

"Close the door, child," Maiden Barda instructed, waving her tiny, frail hands. Jaslyn did as she was told and walked deeper into the cottage. "You have a lion, child?" the old maiden asked, still not looking up from the stew.

Jaslyn smiled. "Aye. I named him Kai."

Maiden Barda turned to the pair and leaned in to examine the cub closely. "His fur is white and his eyes are red like blood."

Jaslyn frowned at the description. "Aye, Asterin said the Grasslandi worship white lions."

"The beast will be loyal to you and the ones you love."

Jaslyn stood silently, repeating the old woman's words. *Of course, Kai will be loyal to me. I saved him from freezing out the Dense Pines all alone.* She hugged the lion comfortingly, and he purred in her ear. A smile spread across her lips, and she focused on the boiling brown liquid in the cauldron. "Can I have a taste?"

The old woman shook her head. "I'll make a pot for you another day."

She frowned. "Fine. Who is the stew for?"

Maiden Barda grinned and continued to stir. "It's for some skinny knight taking orders from an irrational black sun."

Jaslyn shook her head, not understanding the old woman's cryptic words. "Okay, well, I need to go ask my parents if I can keep Kai. See you later!"

"I will be leaving Maryere by the week's end," Barda said in a low voice, stirring the soup. She kept her eyes down, never looking at Jaslyn. "Get your meal before then."

Tears filled Jaslyn's eyes. "What do you mean you're leaving? You can't do that!"

The maiden wiped her hands clean with a rag. "I'm no longer needed here and have things to do elsewhere."

"No, no, you can't!" she cried. "I need you here. I'll be so lonely without you!"

"My dear girl, you will be fine. Besides, your new friend will protect you forever, so worry not." Maiden Barda patted Kai on the head, and the white lion cub yipped happily, licking the old woman's hand.

GLORIANA

Braised suckling pig, blackened miniature chickens, roasted carrots, and hard bread filled the room with a mouth watering aroma. Laughter and music rung in Gloriana Wayward's ears as she sipped on the wine brought from Kingment. Her eyes scoped the room before landing on the man who sat across the table, slowly sipping on a glass of rainwater, keeping his eyes solely on her.

"Let's get on with the feast!" Borin's voice boomed over the conversations. Giggles from the highborn echoed, making Gloriana blush. *My husband is an embarrassment.* She gulped more wine and sighed, wanting to disappear.

The clacking of metal approached, warning Gloriana that a knight was coming to bother her. She lifted her eyes to see the shy knight bowing before the Lord Protector. *Oh, the lord knights don't come to me anymore. I'm not the Lord Protector.* The shy knight's eyes flashed to Gloriana before he focused on Borin. "My lord, a knight has been poisoned."

The Lord Protector of the Mountain Realm gave a serious face. "Who?"

"Ser William Cantree."

Gloriana held in a gasp. *Maiden Barda and the knight work quickly.*

Borin hummed at the information. "Wasn't he the one who had enemies? I'm not surprised. Is there a chance I may be poisoned?"

Why does he ask with such little care?

"The investigation is ongoing," the knight replied, frowning. "We don't know how or when he was poisoned. His body was already decaying when a knight found him."

"Continue the feast. Find someone to deal with the matter in the morning," Borin decided, and the young knight nodded and walked away. Borin turned to Falk with a grin. "Can you believe that? My mother always warned me that poison is a woman's weapon. Which bitch did he piss off?"

Gloriana's blue eyes narrowed. *Poison is a woman's weapon.*

"Aye, men shed blood instead to solve our problems," Falk confirmed, still glancing at Gloriana as he spoke with Borin.

Shed blood. Her mind raced to the day her happiness disappeared.

Lord Robart Wayward's phantom hand touched Gloriana's shoulder, just as it did twenty-four years ago. *Gloriana,* he had started. *It pains me to tell you this, but Lord Morvan Osmont has ordered for the murder of your family. The act already took place. Everyone is gone.*

Afterward, Gloriana spent her days in solitude, only speaking to Borin's older brother, Ser Rodrick. At first, the proud knight was reluctant to protect a little Summeran girl, but after only a few weeks, the two had grown close. They went everywhere together, laughing and enjoying life. Rodrick was kind and gentle, too, reading, singing, and even dancing with her.

Why couldn't I have married him?

Instead, Rodrick was sworn to the sword, and that commitment led him off into battle—never to return. Gloriana reached for her wine glass, and gulped the bittersweet liquid that allowed her to forget.

"Mother, Father, hello," a weak voice called from behind.

Gloriana spun around in her chair, and the room spun with her. "Alice, you're here!" she greeted loudly. *I didn't even know Alice was awake.* She studied her daughter for a moment, trying not to frown.

Alice's limp black hair stuck to her sweating neck, and her tired eyes sunk into her face. Her purple woolen dress seemed black in the dim candlelight, making her skin look as pale as the snow that fell outside. *She looks terrible.*

"You got out of bed. That must've been hard," Borin said with care. "If you become feverish you can return to the Bloody Tower."

Alice frowned. "Do you not want me here?"

The Lord Protector of the Mountain Realm matched his eldest daughter's face. "Of course, I want you here. Please, sit and have fun."

Alice smiled, avoiding Gloriana's lingering eyes, and bowed. "Thank you, Father."

Gloriana pushed the chair beside her, and patted on the soft cushion. "My sweet daughter. How long has it been?"

"Six moons," Alice whispered, sitting down.

She made a face and rubbed her thumb against Alice's clammy cheek. *Has it truly been that long?* "How are you feeling?"

"Fine," her daughter sighed, moving her face away.

Gloriana studied Alice as Asterin approached. "I need more," she told the handmaiden, holding up her empty cup.

"May I have a glass, too?"

She reared her head back at the question. *Even Alice is growing up. Have I missed my children's childhood dealing with my traumas? Why have I realized it too late?* Alice gave Gloriana a sweet smile striking pity into her heart. "Aye," she answered, and Alice lightly bounced in the chair. Gloriana turned back to her handmaiden, still unsure. "Get a glass for my daughter, too."

"Of course, my lady," Asterin bowed and made her way to the wine table.

"Are you Lady Alice?" Falk interjected, causing Gloriana to frown.

Alice lowered her eyes. "Yes, my lord."

"You're a delight for the eyes," he complimented with a squint, smiling brightly.

"Thank you," Alice whispered, blushing.

"My name is Falk of House Osmont, Lord Protector of the Kingdom of Valley Pines," the man declared proudly, practically puffing out his chest.

"*Northern* Kingdom." Alice corrected innocently.

For a moment, Falk's face showed no emotion. Gloriana pressed her lips together waiting for a reply. *Would he claim that Alice is being rude?* "Aye, I guess you're right," Falk laughed, and Gloriana sighed with relief.

"The feast has begun!" A servant announced, as platters of food were placed on the grand table.

Beef broth with onions. Gloriana grabbed a piece of hardened bread and dipped it into the hot broth. *Delicious!*

Borin Wayward beamed, piling food onto his platter. "I've missed the feast food from home," he leaned over to Gloriana. "The food in Valley Pines isn't that good. I don't know how Victoria deals." Borin then stuffed his face with pork and chicken, moaning with each bite. He sucked his fingers from the warm meat juices and gulped his wine to wash it all down. *He's acting like a starving animal.*

Asterin returned and placed the wine glasses on the table.

"Thank you," Alice whispered, hesitating, before taking a sip.

Falk leaned forward. "How do you like it? It's been sitting in a Valley Pines winery for over fifty years."

The girl shrugged. "It's alright. A bit tart." And Falk frowned.

Conversations started meshing together as Gloriana stared at nothing. *Maybe I drank too much.*

"Would you like more wine, my lady?" Asterin inquired leaning over.

Gloriana tried to focus on Alice, and the girl's black hair turned blonde, but she could still see those sad blue eyes. "My sweet summer child," she exhaled, leaning into her chair.

A gasp snapped Gloriana out of her drunkenness. Alice's bright blue eyes welled up with tears and she covered her trembling lips with her hands. Gloriana then studied Asterin who stared back, her eyes filled with pride and excitement.

Shit. Gloriana had forgotten, *Alice* was her sweet summer child.

Her eldest daughter jumped from her chair, glaring at Gloriana. The sudden moves caused the chair to crash to the floor, and a sob burst from Alice, causing her body to shake. Lady Myra Nores, Alice's handmaiden, lightly took Alice's hands and escorted the crying girl out of the dining hall.

Gloriana's eyes met her other children as the room quieted.

Jaslyn stood and awkwardly glanced around the room. She walked from the dining hall without a word, and her two twin handmaidens followed behind.

Josef's eyes snapped from one silent guest to another before he smiled politely. He slid out of his chair and walked past Gloriana, his little head held high. "It's late, Mother. I'm going to bed," He kissed her softly on the cheek and walked away as the conversations returned to the room.

My children hate me. She wiped away the tears brimming her eyes before picking up the wine glass, and finishing it in one gulp. "More please." Asterin filled the cup again, and Gloriana quickly finished another cup. *I'm going to vomit.*

Borin's thick fingers brushed against her sleeve. "Glory, give me a kiss," he told her, his words slurring. "Let's make another one of those ungrateful brats."

She sneered at her lord husband as anger brewed from the name she hated so much—*Glory*. She lightly placed a hand on her head, not having the patience for Borin's shenanigans. "Stop calling me that fucking name," she growled through her teeth.

The Lord Protector's copper eyes widened. "I can call you whatever I want! Now, come to me," Borin stuttered, grabbing her arm; his fingers squeezing into her soft skin.

Gloriana stood frantically, but his fingers dug deeper. "Let go!" Her begging silenced the room again, and Gloriana's head spun. *They're watching me.*

Finally, Borin Wayward released his wife. "Leave, you've ruined my appetite."

He didn't hit me. I must get away before he changes his mind. She rushed out of the room and ran through Winter's Keep, pushed open the doors, and watched the autumn snow fall. An iciness in the wind burned her sun kissed face, as she stepped into the elements. She trekked through Maryere's empty streets as the wind howled. *I'll go to the Sun Keep; there I can think about what I should do next.*

The Sun Keep was House Wayward's old holdfast, located on the western side of Maryere. Gloriana had spent her childhood running through the halls of the enormous castle with Victoria and Rodrick. The day Lord Robart Wayward died, however, Borin abandoned the Sun Keep.

Gloriana pulled the rotted wood nailed to the door and pushed her way through, getting away from everyone and everything. She wrapped her arms around herself for comfort as the scent of pinecones filled Gloriana's nose. *How does the ruins still smell the same?*

Crows hovered the destroyed roof, cawing loudly as if to tell her that she was invading. *I've been treated like an invader all my life*, she wanted to tell the crows. *Your squawks mean nothing.*

Gloriana exhaled, noticing her frosty breath. *I should make a fire.* She collected a few pieces of sticks and walked to the fireplace. *Two dry sticks*, she remembered Jaslyn teaching her once a long time ago. *Back when my daughter tried to spend time with me.* The twigs, however, were damp and cold, and she sat on a fallen beam, defeated. *I wish I wasn't such a failure.*

"Do you need any help?"

Gloriana turned to see bright green eyes meeting hers. She stood from the beam and bowed, "Lord Osmont, hello again."

Falk stepped closer and Gloriana kept her eyes on her shoes. "I can start a fire," he offered walking to the fireplace. "It's so cold and dirty in here! I can't believe Borin let this place go to waste."

She backed away. "Is Borin coming?"

The Lord Protector ignored her question and started a fire. Flames crackled and the decaying keep glowed orange. He stirred the fire carefully, and then turned to Gloriana and smiled. "Is that better?"

"Aye, thank you," she replied, still not looking at the man. "Do you need something?"

Falk studied Gloriana's depressed demeanor, cupping her cheek before sighing. "It's been over a week since I arrived and you've been avoiding me, why?"

Finally, her eyes settled on his. "I was taught my place a very long time ago. I avoid everyone."

He released her face and sat on the fallen beam. "I feel like it's more than that. Like you hate me. I understand what my father did is considered wrong, but I promise, I hold no ill will and like I said in the library, you are very beautiful. I wish my father saw,"

"I don't hate you," she interrupted, not wanting to hear his false words.

Falk Osmont gave a single laugh. "There is no need to lie, Gloriana. I want us to be friends." He leaned in. "Actually, I want to be more than friends." Falk then kissed Gloriana before she could respond.

She pushed him away. "Do you have no shame?" she roared. "I'm a married woman, and your wife is Victoria, someone I love very much."

"You have no idea how long I've wanted to do that." Falk purred, ignoring her anger. "No one has to know."

Her head pounded. "No. Never. You can't just say you want to be friendly, and think I will open my legs for you."

"I do want to be friendly."

"And you also want to sleep with me."

Silence filled the air before Falk sighed. "Fine, yes, I've wanted you since the last time I was here, but you were too busy to care about me. You were looking at someone else."

Gloriana's face grew hot at the man's response. *Looking at someone else.* She thought back on the first time Falk Osmont visited Maryere during the Single King's War. *I didn't care the Osmonts were at the Sun Keep because,* she gasped. *Rodrick.*

He leaned in and stole another kiss, leaving her breathless. When he pulled away, her mind spun. *What should I do? What am I doing?* Her eyes went from his pink lips to his red beard to his green eyes. *Remember who he is.* She didn't move as he kissed her again. *Use him to my advantage.* He fingered through her hair and kissed her longer and harder. *If I give him what he wants, then maybe I will never have to see him again.* That was all she really wanted.

She pulled away. "How long are you staying?"

He shrugged. "A moon, maybe two."

I will get rid of Falk and maybe get a little more power in the end. Now, Gloriana was the one leaning in. "Understand, your father murdered my family, so being friends will never work. So, how about this? When you leave Maryere, I never want to see you again."

Falk looked her up and down, feeling the challenge. "Fine, and what do I get?"

I should have a little fun. Her life in Maryere had been nothing but hell for years. She deserved to be touched with lust instead of anger. *It might feel good to be a little wicked for a few hours.* She slid onto his lap, straddling him, and gave him a small kiss. "Me."

Lord Falk Osmont grinned, showing his perfect white teeth; already frantically untying Gloriana's dress. "Deal."

JARIN

T he agonizing moans of the river people echoed in the Lord Protector's mind. The summer moons brought no rain and intense heat, continuing the drought the Riverlands had been dealing with for over a decade. Farm animals were dying, people were starving, and even the largest river roads had dried up. Autumn had arrived in the Riverlands, bringing with it an unpleasant harvest, and now, everyone suffered. *Just as they did when my father ruled*, Jarin Ayers sighed, looking out the window to his kingdom. *Will this drought ever end?*

Jarin pressed his hand against the window, and the radiating heat sizzled his skin. He stepped away, still feeling the warmth in his palms. "There is nothing I can do," he whispered, repeating the same sentence he told himself daily. "The Riverlands is nothing but a wasteland."

For half a year, Jarin Ayers, the Lord Protector of the Riverlands, locked himself away in his bedroom, refusing to do anything. He didn't speak to his family. He didn't rule his kingdom. He did nothing. *What's the point?* His adulterous wife, Lady Dimia Osmont, constantly belittled him, ripping at his confidence. His sons paid him no mind, further tearing down his spirit. Only his advisor, Hamlin, the monk, tried to help, and in return, Jarin had Hamlin rule the Riverlands in his stead.

I'm pathetic.

Outside, a restless breeze swirled, and the smell of dirt in the air reminded Jarin of his childhood. *Maybe,* he thought, opening the window. *I can go back to when things were better.* His fingers wrapped around the window seal as he lifted himself. Below, was a world that continued on without him. *I can see my family again.*

A gust of wind pushed him back, and he gripped the window seal, determined not to fall into his room. *It's over for me.* He inhaled deeply through his nose, and prepared for the end.

Brother, the breeze whispered. *What are you doing? It's not your time.*

His eyes snapped open. *Brea,* he recognized with tears. "I must!" he shouted to nothing. "There is nothing left for me here."

Go to Hamlin, see what is happening, and Obum will bless you.

The winds blew again, still trying to push him back. Jarin sighed. "Why should I go speak to Hamlin?" After a moment of silence, Jarin knew he was going mad. He stepped down, the air now turning frigid. "Fine,

Sister."

He pressed his hand against his forehead before looking at the door. *I guess it wouldn't hurt to see the old man*, Jarin reasoned. He looked out the window again and took in the clear blue sky. *The god of Rain forsakes me.*

Brea's pretty face appeared in his mind. *No. Obum will bless you.*

Jarin Ayers marched to the reading room where he knew his longtime friend would be. When he reached the door, he inhaled sharply. *Is this wise? Should I return to my room before someone sees me?* Instead of walking away, Jarin knocked on the door.

"Come in," Hamlin called, and Jarin slipped into the room. The old man's small brown eyes brightened. "My lord, I haven't seen you in many moons," he exhaled, relaxing in his chair. "Your hair has grown."

Jarin anxiously pushed his fingers through his hair, taking in the monk's appearance. Before, Hamlin's belly poked out from under his robe, and his face was plump and pink. Now, he was skin and bones and pale and sad. *Is this what Brea meant? No,* Jarin frowned. *Hamlin can't die. Who then will rule the Riverlands?*

"Was there something you need?" the old man questioned, clearing his throat.

He repositioned his footing. "How are my sons?"

"Strong, handsome, and loved by the young women in Waterbrook," the monk answered.

Unease nipped at Jarin. "Do you think I should make Terryn the Lord Protector? He is almost seventeen now."

"Don't be ridiculous," Hamlin scoffed. "There have been no responses to betrothal requests I've sent out. Terryn can't become Lord Protector until he's married."

"The Chapel's rules don't apply to House Ayers."

The old man focused his attention on Jarin. "I suppose, but he is still too immature," he exhaled, rolling up a scroll. "The world is about to fall into the hands of Unmos, so House Ayers should stay aligned with the Chapel and follow their rules."

Jarin groaned, not wanting to hear about alliances with the Establishments. "Why do you think the world is about to be in turmoil?"

"I've seen it in my dreams," the monk replied, sounding insane. "Oubliettes being found surrounded by trees. Cities sinking. The world becoming anew. And there have been news of attacks against the settlements here in the Riverlands. Some say it's monsters reaching the surface."

"It's not monsters, it's bandits," Jarin concluded, and Hamlin nodded. "The cold is arriving, so the attacks should stop soon, but we should keep an eye on it."

The old man smiled. "Look at you, acting like the Lord Protector you are."

Jarin's cheeks warmed. "Anything else?"

Hamlin looked away, his face twisted. "I'm dying," he announced with a croak. "I was going to tell you, but," he inhaled sharply. "The priests have given me a year."

The words struck Jarin in the heart. The monk had told him the terrible truth. *Hamlin's dying. He is going to be another ghost that haunts my days.*

Jarin stared at his friend and held back a sob. "Thank you for watching over me since I was a child," he started, his voice quivering. "And apologies for what I have become since my siblings died. Forcing you to rule over the Riverlands gave you unnecessary stress that has ailed you. Starting today, you will no longer be alone. Please, find a pupil to train."

"Of course, my lord," the monk struggled. "I have news about... your lady wife."

He wanted to laugh. *Hamlin didn't even give me a moment to mourn. Just moves along as if nothing happened. Like always.* "Has she found the gods?"

Hamlin shook his head. "She's disgusting as always. Having sex with anyone willing."

The news of his wife's infidelities always hurt, but it never surprised Jarin. *I must become stronger, become a person who punishes Dimia. A person Hamlin would be proud of. But, when will I blossom into that person?* He studied his old, sick friend. *Is there no way I can be better now? I must do something. I must!* For the first time in many moons, Jarin's mind spun with ideas instead of misery. *I want to change. I want to be better. I must become a person Hamlin would be proud of before he passes away.*

He took a deep breath. "How can we help the people of the Riverlands?"

"We can't."

"We must. I hear them suffering outside my window daily. What if we use Maras and create,"

"NO!" the monk snapped. "It's illegal to employ Maras in Mystos. Plus the Chapel will never allow it."

Jarin Ayers sighed. "We must do something." There was a moment of silence. "What if we have a feast? Like Celebration Day! The river people love the child-goddess of Revelry, Krella!"

Hamlin frowned and put away another scroll. "That's not a good idea. There was no harvest."

"Someone must've harvested something, anything," he groaned. "See, this is why we need Maras helping us."

Hamlin gave an emotionless face. "House Ayers' coffers are full."

"Great! Have Ser Bronston Hedge find some knights and give them ten gold pieces for their harvest." Everything made sense in Jarin's mind. *The Riverlands has the gold, just not the resources.* "Then, get a group of squires and have them travel to different kingdoms, buying food and supplies for our people. Have them dress as the small folk and give the squires wagons and oxen to travel with, no highborn stallions. If necessary, provide women and children to act as a family. Reward them heavily for their service to the kingdom. My people will not starve," Jarin declared, pounding his fist into the hard-mahogany armrest.

He knew he had to be prepared for the winter. He couldn't let his kingdom continue to suffer, it had to prosper. *I must be remembered for ruling better than my father. And that starts now.*

Hamlin stared at Jarin with wide eyes. "You're manic. Let's wait a few days and see if this is something you still want to do."

"No, get it done today. We have no time to waste."

Finally, Hamlin relented. "Very well, I will have knights riding out by nightfall."

"Thank you, now I can return to my bed with an eased mind. I will see you again here tomorrow." Jarin told his advisor and left the reading room without another word.

Honor and pride filled him. *I will become a new man.* For years, he had done nothing to save the broken kingdom his father had left. *That changes today. My people will suffer no longer.*

Jarin walked to his room and opened the heavy oak door. In his bedchamber, his wife, Dimia, sat at a vanity, staring at herself. Her long arms moved around her face as she brushed the waves out of her cinnamon colored hair until it shone. Her clear blue eyes glittered like diamonds in the mirror, as the candlelight made shadows dance around her face and bodice. Her looks always reminded Jarin whose blood she had running through her veins. *She will never love House Ayers.*

"I thought I would find you here," Dimia started sweetly. Slowly, she sat the brush on the table, and popped a candy into her mouth. "I wanted to see you."

We haven't spoken in moons. Why does she want to see me now? Did someone inform her that I left my room? What is she plotting? He frowned and stepped toward her, his body warming. "What do you need?"

She looked him up and down with a smirk. "You seem different. What happened?"

Jarin brightened at the question. *Maybe if I tell her my idea I can make her care about the Riverlands.* "I've created a plan to feed our kingdom." He informed and Dimia raised her eyebrows in interest. "Send squires to other kingdoms to get supplies! Isn't that genius! I've been speaking with Hamlin and,"

Dimia's ivory face turned bright red. "I had that same idea ten years ago," she snapped, breaking the candy with her teeth. "Before things got bad."

He stared at her for a moment. *Dimia's right. She had tried to help in the beginning, and I did nothing. I just sat there and let time pass by.* He straightened his stance. "Apologies," he exhaled, and Dimia turned away to look at herself in the mirror. "The Riverlands will be prosperous again. I'm holding a celebration for the kingdom to lift morale. A large feast for the highborn."

"What?" Dimia jumped to her feet, her face filled with fury, and slapped Jarin's face.

He grabbed his cheek and stared at his wife with wide eyes. *She wants to slap me again.* And deep down inside, he wanted to slap her, too; for slapping him, for hating him, for never loving him. He wanted to hurt her, but he couldn't. He wasn't that type of person, and he still loved her too much.

"So, you're telling me, that the people *you* are supposed to be protecting; are dying. And you, you inconsiderate fool, who won't even leave this stupid castle to see the city or the rest of this worthless kingdom, decides to throw a party?" She took a deep breath and threw her arms in the air. "For what? For fucking existing? You really are as stupid as your father would say."

Dimia's words stung Jarin. *That's not me. I'm no fool.* He refused to be defined by his wife's words. "I'm paying the farmers ten gold pieces for whatever food they can provide, so they can buy more seeds for a better harvest next year," he quietly informed, though not as confidently as he had told Hamlin.

Dimia's attention shifted to the candlelight, and she smiled prettily. "Well husband, at least you aren't just stealing the food like a Warrior Raider," she said in a hateful tone. "Will this plan really help the small folk?" He nodded silently and she smiled again. She kissed his cheek where she had slapped him, her breath smelling of sweet caramel and river wine. "You know, I've missed seeing you look so lively. It makes me want you."

Jarin looked into Dimia's light eyes, suppressing the cruel thoughts that swirled in his mind. *To her, I'm no different than a whore.*

Dimia slipped off her dress, and Jarin looked away uncomfortably. *No, I don't want this,* he realized. *I want to be alone.* "Cover up, please."

She pouted playfully. "You do not wish to bed me?"

"No, I have another meeting to attend to," he lied. "I don't want to keep them waiting."

Dimia's face jumped at Jarin's words. She studied him for a moment longer before moving closer. "You sure you don't want me?" she questioned again, stroking his hair.

No. He knew it now. He hated her cruelness. He hated her spite. He hated that she never loved him. He had never harmed her and yet she blamed him for everything. "Dimia, leave."

"Fine!" she yelled, covering up. "Can I at least see you after your meeting?"

Dimia is asking to see me again? His lady wife's desperation seemed almost silly. "No, I will be quite tired."

The woman puffed her cheeks before leaving his bedchamber without another word.

Lord Jarin Ayers stood alone and sighed. "I have no meeting," he told the nothingness in his room. "And she knows that, yet she acts as if she's jealous."

He undressed, laid in his bed, and soon slipped into slumber. A sleep that he so dreadfully needed.

In his dreams, he sat in the fields outside of Waterbrook. Before him were knights, bards, and fat old women with pies. While the flutes and harps played, his older sister, Brea, danced freely, bringing smiles to everyone's faces. *This is where I always wanted to be.*

"There's my sweet sister," Jarin's older brother, Domeric, called, his horse rushing to the small festival. Jarin met them in the middle, and the three Ayers siblings were reunited. "I've missed you both," Domeric exhaled, hugging them.

Brea's purple-colored eyes looked behind her brother judgingly. "Dom, who's that?"

Another horse approached, and a tall, slim woman with silvery hair and grey eyes slipped off and leaned casually against Domeric. "Hi, my name is,"

Before the woman could introduce herself, more horses appeared over the hill—an army. The dancing, singing, and music stopped.

"All hail King Alen Ayers!" A knight yelled to the crowd.

King? Jarin realized then that it wasn't a dream. It was his memories, and his memories were nightmares. Flashes of his childhood came to him in the form of death and fire.

Smoke filled his lungs, and Jarin retched over the rail. *Where am I?* Something touched his shoulder, trying to comfort him. He turned and saw a person who was supposed to be Dimia, but it wasn't her, it couldn't have been. Her skin was pale green, with scales like a lizard, and pieces had peeled, revealing bone. Her wounds seeped pus and bled, and her right arm was gone. Her hair was falling out, and one of her ears was only a hole. *Is she even alive?*

Finally, Lord Jarin Ayers recognized the disease that ate at his lady wife's body. *Deathskin.*

"Please," he cried out. "Don't touch me."

Then he was awake, hyperventilating.

A *tap-tap-tap* slapped against the window, catching Jarin's attention. He jumped from his bed and rushed to the other side of his room. Dark, heavy clouds poured unrelenting rain over the city of Waterbrook. "Obum has blessed me," Jarin exhaled. "Rain has come!"

Jarin opened his window and the chilly air kissed his cheeks. He looked at the courtyard and noticed Dimia twirling and smiling, her hair and clothes drenched in the rain. As she twirled, a man in armor grabbed her by the waist and passionately kissed her. Neither caring that they were in public. *She will not hurt me anymore.* Jarin promised as tears welled up. Hamlin's sad pale face flickered in his head and his frown deepened. *I'm going to become a better lord... a better man. Everyone wait and see.*

HADRIAN

In his dreams, the woman with red eyes towered over him, as if he was the size of an ant. *Be safe.* The woman's voice echoed endlessly, and he walked closer, only to be farther away. Hadrian wanted to know more. *I wish I could've spoken to Mother about the woman.* He imagined the strange woman's long dark hair, rosy cheeks, and warm demeanor. *Wait, she looks familiar. Who is she?*

Hadrian Osmont's bedchamber door burst opened, and servants flooded in. He shot up from his sleep and brought his knees to his chest, watching people quietly empty his room. *What's going on?*

Click-clack. Click-clack. The sound gnawed at him as someone approached. Lord Peyton Osmont marched into Hadrian's room with Ser Colvic following closely. His stoic eyes scanned the bedchamber, before frowning. "Hadrian, let's go."

"Where are we going?"

"*You* are going to Kingment," Peyton clarified, looking away.

What? Father couldn't mean I'm going by myself, right? Hadrian's lip quivered. "I don't understand! It's my birthday!"

"Celebrate it on the road, or something, but you must leave now."

Shock buzzed through Hadrian as he processed his father's words. "Am I being banished?"

Lord Peyton repositioned his footing. "Is there a servant here willing to travel with him?" he asked, ignoring Hadrian's question.

Hadrian trembled, bringing the blanket to his face. *This can't be happening. My father is banishing me, but why? What did I do?*

"Me," Patty volunteered, stepping up. "I'll travel with him."

The Lord Protector clapped his hands. "Wonderful," he replied, his tone anything but jovial. "You'll be in charge of his things. Go with Ser Colvic to the wheelhouses so you can direct the servants there."

Patty bowed and followed Ser Colvic Rames out of Hadrian's chamber, along with the servants and all of Hadrian's things.

Lord Peyton stared for a moment before approaching. "My son," he started, clearing his throat. Peyton awkwardly placed a hand on his son's shoulder. "From now on, you must be brave and strong."

"Why!?" Hadrian cried with snot coming out of his nose. "Why do I have to leave? Why did you banish me?"

"I didn't banish you. Let's just say you are going on a quest."

Hadrian shook his head, refusing to believe his father. "No, I don't want to go on a quest! I don't want to leave! I want to stay here and learn how to be the Lord Protector!"

His father frowned. "Starting today, Leo will now be the heir to the title of Lord Protector."

Hadrian's vision narrowed. "So, you are banishing me," he exhaled, barely audible. He then grabbed his father's hand startling the man. "May I see Wynn and Leo before I leave?"

Lord Peyton closed his eyes. "I don't think that will be possible."

"What about Mother?" Hadrian begged. "I must say goodbye to her!"

"NO!" His father roared. "You will NOT see her! You are going to go to the courtyard, get on a wheelhouse, and leave this place! I will not hear another word against it!"

Hadrian's mouth dropped. *Father isn't letting me see Mother. I can't say goodbye to my family.*

Lord Peyton Osmont embraced his son. "I'm sorry I wasn't a good father. This is all my fault, you did nothing wrong. You are a sweet boy who could lead great nations. I'm so sorry to do this to you, but you must go. It's for your safety."

Peyton hugged him again, but Hadrian felt empty. *I'm being punished when it wasn't my fault. Did my father commit a crime in my name?* He pressed his lips together knowing there was nothing he could do right now. *Father is making me leave, so I will leave.* He pulled away. "Okay, let's go," he told his father stoically.

The Lord Protector of the Southern Kingdom of Valley Pines gave a rare smile and walked to the window. "I know you probably hate me right now but I promise, it will all make sense in the end," he continued, but Hadrian stayed quiet and moved off the bed. Peyton groaned at the reaction before shaking his head. "I wasn't going to tell you this, but it seems I must. I can't let you leave King's Berth without me telling you that,"

"Peyton, she's up and raging. Should a servant give her more willows tea?" Ser Colvic questioned, rushing back into the room.

"No, it's okay, Hadrian's ready." Peyton then turned back to Hadrian. "I'm sorry son, but Arla isn't your mother."

For a moment, Hadrian couldn't hear anything. *What?* His mouth gaped open and he struggled to breathe as he processed the information. And then he screamed.

✳ ✳ ✳

Staring at the endless sea of brown grass left Hadrian Osmont deep in thought as he traveled on the Oaken Road. Sleep had eluded him since his father knocked him out after learning the truth.

Mother.

He pressed his head against the wheelhouse wall, holding back tears. *How could Mother not be my mother? That literally makes no sense.* The wheelhouse jerked every which way, causing his stomach to twist. *Does Wynn and Leo know too? Will they see me differently now?*

Hot tears burned his eyes. *Oh yeah, I'm never going to see them again.*

Finally, the wheelhouse stopped, causing Hadrian to lift his head and listen to the shuffling outside. Sunshine poured into the wheelhouse as the door swung open. "My lord," Ser Colvic Rames greeted. "We are in Seascape."

He jumped out of the wheelhouse and looked around. A ruined tower sat high on a cliff, blocking the intense sunshine from Hadrian's eyes. The thick salty air filled his nose, reminding him of King's Berth. *Nothing makes sense.* He clenched his fists, and turned to Ser Colvic. "Why are we here?"

The famed knight's eyebrows rose. "What do you mean?"

"Father said I was traveling to Kingment. That is north, yet, we are in Seascape, which is east of King's Berth. Why?"

Ser Colvic slightly grinned. "We aren't going to Kingment."

Hadrian tensed. "Then, where are we going?"

"Here, there, I don't know. Maybe nowhere. It really doesn't matter as long as you're safe."

Blackness engulfed Hadrian.

Agonizing days had turned into weeks since leaving King's Berth. Hadrian daydreamed of traveling to where he was born and learning more about his parentage in Kingment. *I can't go there either. Am I never allowed to speak to House Osmont again?* The pain of losing his family hung over him, and bile crept up his throat. *I must be able to see my family again—to see Mother again.*

A heavy hand landed on Hadrian's shoulder, bringing him back to the seaside town. "There's a tavern here. Let's go for lunch."

Hadrian followed Ser Colvic silently into the town. With each step, his boots sunk into the mud, creating terrible squishing sounds. He stuck his tongue out. "Ew, gross!"

"Don't worry, I can clean your boots later!" Patty chirped.

He blushed and slowed his pace so he could walk with the young servant girl. "Thank you. Hopefully, it won't be too much of a hassle."

She waved her hands nervously, tripping over the soft dirt. "No, no, it's never a hassle." She smiled, and Hadrian matched the expression.

Ser Colvic Rames opened the tavern door for Hadrian, and the faint scent of piss slapped him in the face. Hesitation stopped him from entering the boisterous tavern. *Will everyone know who I am?* He exhaled the anxiety that filled him and took a step forward. Deeper in the tavern, stewed beef cooked on the fire that brought a mouth watering aroma. Hadrian's stomach ached as he imagined the carrots and potatoes that filled the stew. He followed Ser Colvic and Patty to an open table, sat, and waited for the food to appear.

A young woman approached. "What do you want?"

Hadrian's eyebrows furrowed. "Huh?"

"You have to order your food and drink in order to get it, silly." Patty giggled.

Hadrian cream-colored skin turned flushed and he returned his attention to the woman. "I'll have a glass of freshly squeezed mango juice."

"Mango... juice?" the girl questioned, cocking her head to the side.

"Ale for the table," Ser Colvic ordered.

"Ale! Ale! Ale!" Patty cheered, and the woman smiled before walking away.

Hadrian took a deep breath. *I'm not in King's Berth anymore.* He grabbed his knees under the table, studying the divots in the wood. *This hurts so much.*

The woman returned and Colvic grabbed the ale before she could sit it on the table. He lifted the mug and chugged it down, barely taking a breath. When he finished he groaned and placed the mug on the table. "I can see that everyday you question reality," he started cryptically. "But your father wasn't lying. Lady Arla isn't your mother."

He gripped the edge of table as he gritted his teeth, trying to stay calm. *I look more like my mother than my father,* he reasoned. "Then who is?"

"That I do not know," Colvic answered, shaking his head. "I wish I did, I would bring the woman before Arla and beg for mercy."

"Why would you beg for mercy?"

The famed knight frowned. "Of course Peyton didn't tell you everything."

Patty sipped her ale, looking solemn. "Lady Arla wants you dead."

A pounding in his chest brought an intense headache. Hadrian lightly touched his forehead and repeated the young woman's words. *Mother wants me dead.* Hadrian couldn't believe it. *My sweet, kind, and caring mother would never,* he paused, remembering the times Lady Arla would smack Leonidas for misbehaving. *She never hit me. She told me that she loved me too much.* He pulled his shirt. *Now, I mean nothing to her.*

"Sounds like someone wants your head on a spike," a woman commented, entering the conversation. She smiled and the large scar that stretched across her face smiled with her. "You're gonna need more protection than a knight and a peasant."

Who is this woman? Hadrian looked the stranger up and down. *She's so dirty and what happened to her face? I've never seen a scar so thick.*

Colvic grunted. "Stay out of the conversation, girl."

The woman sat beside Hadrian, grabbed his untouched ale, and sipped it, staring only at him. "My name ain't girl. It's Raynese, and I'm just telling you the truth. If someone wants this cutie dead, then they might tear down the entire world just to do it."

"Why?" Hadrian questioned to Ser Colvic, his eyes watering. "Why does my mother hate me so much?"

"You're not her child from what I've heard," the woman named Raynese answered instead, still drinking the ale. "The woman sounds like a maniac."

"Who are you?" Hadrian asked angrily, his voice raising. "Are you the person she hired?"

"Hadrian, calm down," Colvic said, and he relaxed. "Whatever your name is, can you please leave? You're causing unnecessary anxiety."

Raynese finished the ale and placed a copper on the table. "Alright, but I warned you. When you're dying, don't blame,"

"Sh," the knight hushed, not looking at Raynese. Three huge men dressed in animal furs stared at Hadrian, and his heart dropped. *They're only looking at me.* Colvic placed a copper on the table, too. "We should leave."

The woman looked over her shoulder, grinning. "Oh yeah, those look like some fighters." She moved to stand. "Well, have fun."

"Wait!" Colvic called and Raynese paused. The famed knight's face twisted as he thought about what to do. "Fine, you're right, we need more protection. Are you a mercenary or something?"

Raynese winked at Hadrian, as if it was all a game. "For this cutie, I can be anything you need."

Patty frowned. "You're behaving too casual."

"Apologies, peasant girl. I didn't know we were in a castle with the," she paused, her hazel-colored eyes darting around the tavern. "Alright, enough fucking around, they're starting to move. Let's go."

Raynese's sudden reaction left Hadrian no time to process. She grabbed his hand and whisked him out of the tavern with Colvic and Patty in tow.

Huge raindrops fell from the grey sky, making it hard to see and everyone paused at the door. *When did that start? It was sunny less than an hour ago.* The pouring rain chilled the air, and Hadrian shivered.

Raynese groaned and tugged at his hand. "Let's go," she commanded.

They rushed to the wheelhouse, soaking wet. Colvic grabbed Raynese by the shoulders. "Do you have a horse?" The young woman shook her head, and Colvic sighed. "Ride in the wheelhouse and protect the boy."

Boy. Hadrian Osmont chewed at his lip and climbed into the wheelhouse, sitting far away from the door. *Colvic thinks of me as some helpless child, but he's always by my father's side! He barely knows me.* Hadrian crossed his arms before thinking back on his childhood. He rarely trained to ride a horse, he never sparred, and for three years, Hadrian refused to learn how to rule the kingdom. *I am a helpless boy.*

"I'll do my best," Raynese saluted and climbed into the wheelhouse. The young woman sat beside Hadrian and moved close, smiling. Rain dripped off her body, and she smelled of dirt, yet she was still stunningly beautiful.

After a moment, she separated herself, the amused look never leaving her face. The wheelhouse bolted off, and the pair bumped into each other.

The two stayed silent as the carriage swayed wildly, rushing away from Seascape.

We are fleeing for our lives.

Raynese looked out the window and whistled. "Damn, those things are still chasing us!"

"What things? Monsters?"

She studied Hadrian for a moment, her face brightening with excitement. "Even worse, it's the Warrior Raiders."

GLORIANA

ears weighed down the strange envelope in Gloriana's hands. They were tears of worry. Tears of sorrow. Tears that brought unease to Gloriana's chest. *What is this? There was nothing on my desk last night. Where did this come from?* She broke open the seal and read the letter slowly, absorbing every word written in the smudged black ink. *This is Old Summeran.* The ancient letters bounced around in her head as she tried to remember how to translate it. *It's Victoria! What does she need? We rarely write in,* she paused.

Wait.

Gloriana read it again, making sure she understood it correctly. *What does Victoria mean Borin has a whore?! And he brought her back to Maryere with him!* Her hands shook imagining some wretched woman basking all over her naked lord husband.

"Who is it from?"

Her body pulsed, remembering that there was someone else in her bedroom, too. She took her eyes off the letter and stared at a red beard and bright green eyes, feeling sick. *What?* Her brother by marriage was in her bed, smiling at her, naked. *What am I doing?*

Gloriana returned her attention to the letter and touched the dried ink carefully. *This doesn't look like Victoria's usual handwriting,* she realized, tilting her head in confusion. *It's like... she's in pain.* Then, things began to click for Gloriana Wayward. "Victoria's sick, and instead of ensuring she recovers, you're here. Why?"

Falk stood from the bed, "Is that what it says?" he asked, reaching for the letter. Gloriana rushed to the fireplace, and threw the paper into the fire, watching it turn blue, then orange, then black. "Look, I don't know what the letter said," he touched her shoulders gently. "But let's just go back to bed. It's much warmer."

I'd rather die. This was a mistake.

Her eyes turned to the bed. Satin sheets were tossed about, and plush pillows were on the floor. Just the sight made Gloriana want to vomit. *What am I doing?* Receiving the letter from Victoria had snapped Gloriana to her senses. *I should've never made that deal with Falk. What was I thinking?* She tried her best to hold back tears, but there were too many. *Now, I have been unfaithful to my husband,* she paused, *just as he was to me.*

Gloriana studied her bedside table where a half filled wine cup sat. *Did my drunkness cause this madness?* She thought back on all the times she sneered at Borin and his constant drinking. *When did I become like him?* She grew angrier with herself. *I will never drink again.*

"Leave," she cried.

Falk's face twisted with displeasure. "You want to talk about Victoria? Fine! Yes that crazy woman is sick *again*," he confessed. "Our Saavant said that this time she will not make it to the end of the year."

"Is that what she told Victoria? Or is that what she told you when she was laying in your bed?"

"That was not needed, Gloriana."

Her head throbbed. "We are all just women to you. Not even that. Just objects for you to play with because you are a stupid little boy!"

"You're right," Falk said with a smile that frightened her. "Women are just objects to amuse little boys like me. You're not the only one I have slept with in Maryere. There are many whores,"

Gloriana slapped Falk as hard as she possibly could, and he tumbled to the floor. He held his face, staring at her silently. "I am no whore," she declared standing over him.

"Yes, you are." He laughed, standing. "You used your cunt as a trade to make sure I never stepped foot in Maryere again. You paid and got what you wanted. No better than a whore that gets a gold coin at the end of,"

Gloriana slapped him again, her body shaking. *Is Falk right? Is that whay I did?* She had betrayed her family—her real family, for her own comfort. *Mother, Father, Clee, Alice, Roland, Symon.* She marched to her desk, opened a drawer, and pulled out a piece of paper.

"What are you doing?" Falk questioned, but Gloriana ignored him. She pulled out a quill and dipped it in the ink. "What are you doing?"

"I'm drafting how I'm going to tell Borin the truth," Gloriana replied, and stared writing.

"No the hell you aren't!" Falk leaned over, grabbed her arms, and spun her around. "Since you haven't realized it yet, you dumb bitch, I'm going to explain this super easy for you." He leaned in close. "I'm using you, so you can't be truthful with Borin."

She blinked back at him, confused. "You don't frighten me. I can tell him whatever I want."

Falk smiled wickedly, letting go of her. "Not if you want your family safe."

He's going to blackmail me?! Rage ripped inside Gloriana. *Of course he is! He's a fucking Osmont. Why did I bother trusting this evil bastard?*

The Lord Protector snapped his fingers inches from her nose. "Hello, didn't you hear me? I have your family in the palm of my hand. All because of you."

Gloriana swung in retaliation, but Falk caught her arm and twisted it. She shrieked, and he released, pushing her away. The two stared at each other, breathless. "Leave Maryere, tonight," she demanded.

He stood straight, relaxing. "Oh, I can't do that, sweet Glory," he informed stepping closer and lightly touching her hips. "I think I want to fuck you a couple more times before I go. Your forcing me to leave Maryere and never return," he looked her up and down. "That's going to be expensive and I haven't gotten my coin's worth."

Gloriana Wayward dug her teeth deep into his skin until she tasted blood. She pulled back, and Falk studied the wound Gloriana left with his mouth wide open.

After a moment, Falk grunted and licked his teeth, "I wonder if that's going to leave a scar."

"I don't care if,"

Lord Falk punched Gloriana in the face so hard she tumbled over and slammed her head, cutting her eyebrow. *I'm going to kill you!* Her heartbeat throbbed in her ears as she rushed to the other side of her bed. She grabbed a knife that sat beside a platter of hard bread. *I'm going to slice his throat open, just like his father's men did to my sister!*

"Put it down," Falk commanded, his eyes wide. "And calm yourself before you make a true mistake."

She gripped the knife tighter. "I hate you."

He scanned the room, the emotions shifting on his face. "You know, I'm kind of glad that my father committed those crimes against your family. It's clear your *kind* are beasts."

Gloriana's vision tunneled. *I knew it. He's vile just like Morvan Osmont.* Hot tears brimmed her eyes and she clenched her teeth. She wanted to stab Falk in those bright green eyes and kill him.

"I heard none of your family put up a fight," Falk laughed, "No wonder it was so easy to install House Ashmire. None of you dumb Summerans fight!"

"You don't know anything," she growled, still crying. "My family was blessed by Korta, the goddess of the Harvest. They were good people, harmless people." Her heart ached remembering their smiling faces. *Mother, Father, Clee, Alice, Roland, Symon.* "They were kind," she croaked.

Falk buzzed his lips. "Oh please! If your family was blessed by Korta, then House Thoren would exist."

Gloriana pointed the knife at herself. "I'm still alive."

"Aye, unfortunately," Falk chuckled. "But hopefully not for long."

She froze. "What do you mean?"

Lord Falk Osmont walked over to his clothes and quickly dressed. "I've been told that a new era is approaching," he informed, slipping on his shoes. "An era where the dark gods reign and the Wicked thrive, where *I* will thrive. It's going to change everything. All I need to do is ruin your life."

Is that the only reason why Falk came to Maryere? To ruin my life. "Lies!" Gloriana screamed. "My life isn't that important."

"Duh," Falk laughed, gripping the doorknob, "but there are more lives who are important to you." And he walked out of her room with a smug smile.

Alone, Gloriana flung the knife across the room and pressed her hands into her forehead. *Lives who are important to me. He means to hurt the family that I have now, just as his father did all those years ago.* She turned to the door and froze. *I must send my children away to stay safe, but where?* She pressed her lips together in thought. *Somewhere Falk won't find them.*

She walked to her small library and cleared the shelves, trying to find a map. *I need to find a place safer than Maryere for my children to hide.* She wiped her face, and stared at her blood covered hands. *He cannot harm my children as he has harmed me.* She returned her attention to the bookshelves. *Who does he mean to harm?*

Asterin knocked, before entering the room. "Good morning, my lady, how," she gasped. Slowly, Gloriana turned around to reveal her beaten face to her handmaiden. Asterin's bright green eyes widened as she brought her hands to her mouth. "Your face!"

"Get me something to cover myself," Gloriana replied, wiping away more blood.

Asterin grabbed a crimson robe and placed it on Gloriana's shoulders. "What happened?"

"Lord Falk threatened me," she confessed. "He told me would hurt someone I love. He can only mean my children."

"Are you sure?" Asterin questioned. "Your relationship with your children is," she paused, looking away. "It's just, are you sure?"

Gloriana studied the table she pressed her hands against. *Asterin is right. I don't have a good relationship with my children.* A tear fell down her cheek. *Falk doesn't know that, but it doesn't matter. He still can't touch them.*

Asterin wetted a rag and methodically cleaned the blood off of Gloriana's skin. Gasps and whimpers poured out of Gloriana with each touch, and when Asterin finished, the throbbing intensified. "Did Falk do this?" the handmaiden questioned, dipping Gloriana's bloody hair in water.

"Aye," she mumbled.

"You must hurt him back."

A small grin curled her lips. "You're right, but I must be smart. My carelessness is what got me here. Please, watch Falk and report to me. I don't know how he's going to do it, but I need to know before it happens, so I can stop it."

"Of course," Asterin replied, wrapping a towel around Gloriana's hair.

"I can handle the rest," she waved off. "Find information. I told Falk that he must leave, so whatever he is planning will come soon."

"Yes, my lady," Asterin bowed, and left the room quickly.

Alone, Gloriana sat in front of her mirror and smiled. Her cuts and bruises looked horrible on her sun kissed skin, but she didn't worry. She was not going to let Falk get into her head. *I'm going to bring that man down if it's the last thing I do.*

ALICE

Decaying orchids, magnolias, daisies, and honeysuckles filled Alice's nose, reminding her that it was autumn. She pressed her fingers into the ice encrusting the fountain that sat in the middle of Myburn Garden. At the top of the fountain sat the goddess of Life, Axone. The goddess's eyes were closed but her arms were outstretched, as if calling for Alice's embrace.

Alice stretched to lightly touch Axone's marble fingertips, and the soft snow that had collected in the statue's hands slid off and fell to the ground. She retracted her hand and sighed, looking at the clouds. *The gods are so far. Do they even help us when we pray to them?* She turned away from the fountain, and the throbbing in her head intensified. *Maybe it's time to go back to the Bloody Tower and lay down.*

She had only been outside for a few minutes, but her body couldn't take the intense cold that surrounded her. She pulled her cloak tighter, bringing her nose to the collar. *I should've brought Myra*, she groaned, stepping forward. The snow crunched beneath her feet as she made her way to the exit, wanting to feel the warmth from the fire kiss her cheeks.

"Kai, no, get back here!"

Pressure pushed on Alice's shoulders, forcing her to the ground. She clawed the slushy snow, trying to wiggle free as something crushed her. *I am too weak*, she realized, tearfully. *I can't get free. I'm going to suffocate and die.*

"Kai, you big dummy, what are you doing?!"

The pressure lifted and Alice exhaled heavily. She rubbed her icy wet hands against her face. *What happened?* She sat up and was met with long fangs. *A lion!* Alice squealed, sliding away from the beast. Her eyes lingered on the thick pale-yellow mane that framed the animal's face. *A white lion?*

"Alice, is that you?" Jaslyn appeared from behind the animal with a bright smile. "It is! Hi Alice! I haven't seen you since the feast."

She shifted to her feet and brushed the snow off her dress. *I don't want to think about that annoying feast where all eyes were on me.* She smiled instead and pointed toward the animal. "A lion?" Myra had told Alice that a wild beast roamed Winter's Keep, but Alice had no idea the beast was Jaslyn's pet.

Jaslyn smiled cheekily and gave Alice a thumbs up. "His name is Kai!"

Jaslyn wrapped her arms around the lion, and it returned the embrace by licking Jaslyn in the face. "But, it's too cold out here. Why aren't you inside?"

"I came to see fresh faces, and yet there is no one here," she replied, looking around the desolate garden.

"That's because it's too cold," Jaslyn countered. "It hasn't stopped snowing for days. Everyone is inside by the fire, staying warm."

"What about you?"

Jaslyn put a finger to her chin before shrugging. "Aye, I stay by Maiden Barda's roaring fire in her cottage."

Maiden Barda. Alice couldn't remember the last time she thought about the old maiden who had cared for her as a child. *I wonder if she still makes her hare stew.* Alice's mouth watered at the idea of eating a bowl of Maiden Barda's meal. "How is Maiden Barda?"

"She's fine, really old, but fine," Jaslyn answered before her golden eyes focused behind Alice, and her face grew dark.

Someone's here, Alice realized, her heart dropping. Slowly, she turned, only to see her lord uncle walking toward them.

Lord Falk Osmont entered the garden with his head held high, as if he owned it. His beautiful, embellished orange cloak swayed behind him as he walked, and goose prickles crawled up Alice's arms as her uncle approached. *What does he want?* Lord Falk grinned, and his eyes flashed torment in its glints of emerald.

"I gotta go," Jaslyn grumbled, and when Alice turned around, her little sister and the lion was gone.

Alice Wayward now found herself alone with a man she didn't like. *It seems no one but Father likes him.* Lord Falk's eyes gazed at Alice. "You look sick," he cooed. "Sit on the bench; are you alright?"

"Quite alright," Alice replied before walking to a stone bench that sat under a tree, and brushed away the pinecones that had fallen. Her head pounded and her ears buzzed with every movement she made. *I must go back inside, not have a conversation with this strange man.* But the strange man was a Lord Protector and Alice could do nothing but oblige.

Falk stood over her, watching closely. *Why is he staring?* She flashed a look at her uncle, and noticed a strange cakey paste covering pieces of his face. *Is Falk wearing makeup?* His face was wind burnt, his lips were bruised, and his eyes were puffy. *He doesn't look normal.*

Her lord uncle seemed to be in pain, yet he kept smiling.

His horrible, mocking smile reminded Alice of the wretched feast again. The dim candlelight shadowed unimportant faces that sat at the dining table. Only their false smiles were visible.

My sweet summer child, her drunken mother's voice rang in her head, causing her body to tremble. Alice hugged herself, trying to keep her composure.

"Do you enjoy pine trees?" Lord Falk asked, pulling her from the wretched memories.

She glanced at the pile of pinecones that she had swept off the bench, "They're are pretty," she answered nervously, not looking at her uncle.

He licked his lips, and sat beside Alice. "There are many that grow in my kingdom."

Alice frowned and inched away. "I suppose it's beautiful in Valley Pines."

"More than beautiful," Falk smiled, stroking her cheek, "but not as beautiful as you." Alice moved from his touch, and Lord Falk frowned. "There are trees of many species in Valley Pines. It can become sweltering hot during the summer moons, but the winter moons bring rain and snow. There are beaches, too, and mountains! There is everything you could think of in Valley Pines. The gods favor House Osmont, Lady Alice."

And they do not favor House Wayward?

"Sounds nice," Alice squinted, trying to keep her face emotionless. She wished Jaslyn was still there to get her out of the conversation. *Jaslyn left, so I have to get out of this myself.* "Maybe I could visit one day. You know, with the Mountain Realm being terrible and all," she added bitterly.

He gave a long sigh as the snow began to fall again. "Aye, it's worse than when I was younger," he complained looking up at the sky. "It's constantly snowing!" Small snowflakes fell on his face, and he groaned, brushing the icy pieces off.

"Yes," Alice responded, her eyes on the clouds above. "I must go in now. The snow is not good for me." She stood from the stone bench and took a step, before being yanked back. Alice stared at Lord Falk's hand that was wrapped tightly around her arm. "I do beg pardon, lord uncle. I really must be going." Falk said nothing and squeezed her arm. "Please, you're hurting me," she said, struggling to escape his grip.

"You shouldn't hate your home, my dear. You're a very beautiful young woman, Lady Alice, your name might start popping up in betrothal conversations," he gave her a wicked smile. "Then, one day you may find yourself missing home more than anything in the world."

Alice pulled with all her strength and freed herself from her uncle's grasp. *How could I ever miss home if I never leave?* She wanted to laugh at her uncle, but instead, she plastered on a cold smile. "My lord father isn't thinking about that right now. Again, I must be going." She bowed, turned on her heels, and trekked down a broken cobblestone walkway.

Back to her hell that was the Bloody Tower.

JASLYN

The snow had fallen nonstop. Little ice pellets whipped around Jaslyn, stabbing her in the face. She lowered her head into her horse's mane, but the icy flakes showed no mercy. Jaslyn gripped the letter Ser Lyon Millister had written her. *I want to speak with you, alone.* The words swirled in her head as she tried to guess what it was Ser Lyon wanted. *Does he want to talk to me about Kai?* She wondered, noticing a dim light in the distance. *Or Asterin?*

Kai yipped from below, catching Jaslyn's attention.

"What are you doing?" Jaslyn giggled. The white lion continued yipping as he pounced into the snow, blending into the surroundings, and disappearing from Jaslyn's view. She stopped her horse, Storm, and jumped off. "Kai, where did you go?"

Muffled yips guided Jaslyn to her young lion buried in the snow. She sighed heavily before bending down and scooping the heavy lion into her arms. "Kai, you're getting too big," she scolded, feeling like a mother. "When we go traveling, you must stay close." Kai lifted his head, showing the bone he had found. "Gross!" She grabbed the bone from her lion's mouth and tossed it aside. "You don't know where," she paused when the bone hit the snow, making a rattling noise. *What was that?* She shook Kai off and walked to where she threw the bone.

In a small hole sat a skull. *A person?* She bent down and dusted off the falling snow. *Did someone die, and they just left the body out here?* She pressed her lips together and pushed dirt over the skull and the random bone Kai had found. *I will give them a proper burial.*

When Jaslyn finished, she turned on her heels, and walked only few steps before something tripped her. *What the heck?* She dusted the surface and noticed another pile of bones. She scanned her surroundings, shivering. *How many people died?* She wondered, carefully stepping away. *Why aren't they buried properly? Does Father know about this?*

She shook her head and sighed. *I must speak with Ser Lyon. Maybe he knows about this.* She rushed to her horse, mounted, and kicked it to run.

From afar, a figure waved. *Ser Lyon.* She kicked the horse to trot faster, and the cold wind burned her skin. The first thing she noticed was the new fencing built around the village, and her eyebrows rose in confusion. "What is this?" Jaslyn asked Ser Lyon when she approached.

"Well, hello to you too, my lady."

Jaslyn blushed and dismounted. "Sorry," she exhaled before brushing off the snow that dusted her hair and shoulders. She stepped up to Ser Lyon and smiled. "Hello! How are you?"

"I am doing well, my lady. Thank you for asking."

She frowned. "Please, call me Jaslyn. I am no lady."

Ser Lyon eyed her for a moment. "Aye, I believe you are right." He turned on his heels and walked into the village.

Jaslyn stood there for a moment with her mouth wide open. *Did he insult me?* Her attention turned to the ground and she lifted her leather boots caked with snow and mud. *Whatever. I'm not dressed like a lady nor do I really want to be one. So, who cares?*

She rushed to Ser Lyon's side. "So, the fence?"

"The lion has grown since we last met," Ser Lyon Millister replied instead. "Can it stay outside of the cottage while we talk?"

Jaslyn clenched her fists and nodded, following Ser Lyon to a small cottage. *Why is he ignoring me?* The knight opened the door, and warmth from the fire melted her face.

Inside the cottage was a small family. "It's the queen! It's the queen!" the children cheered, rushing up to her.

Her heart dropped. *Queen?* There were no queens in the Mountain Realm.

"Children," their mother called. "Stay by the fire. It's too cold to go toward the door." The children ran back to their mother and sat beside her.

It's too cold, sleep by the fire. Jaslyn remembered Maiden Barda's warning. *You don't want to wake up with frostbite.*

Ser Lyon's heavy footsteps approached from behind, making her gulp. "The fence is for protection," he finally answered.

She studied the knight. "From what?"

"Everything."

"Lyon, let her get warmed up first," the mother cooed from the fireplace. "Lady Wayward, my name is Katia. Come sit with me and we can wait for my husband to return."

Jaslyn's cheeks warmed at the mother's kindness. She walked to the fireplace and sat with the family. *They're not much different than me*, she realized, looking around. *But they are peasants, and I am a highborn.*

"My name is Amyn!" the little girl sang, waving to Jaslyn.

She waved back. "Hello, Amyn, I like your name. Mine is Jaslyn."

"Your name is not Jaslyn, you are the queen," the young boy informed, causing her to frown. "I'm Sien, by the way."

The whipping wind from outside swirled, making the fire flicker. Jaslyn turned to the door and an axe met her in the face.

"Honey, shut the door!" Katia scolded.

The man with the axe shut the door behind him. "Sorry, my love." He laid the axe on the table and locked eyes with Jaslyn. "So, you are the highborn girl with the golden eyes."

Jaslyn gulped, unsure of what to say. Her head spun trying understand what was happening. *Maybe it was a mistake to come here alone.*

"Father, that's the queen!" Amyn cheered.

She stood and placed her hands on her hips. "What does Amyn mean I am the queen?"

"Please, sit at the table," Ser Lyon said with a small smile.

Jaslyn studied the knight for a moment before relenting. The wood creaked underneath her feet as she stomped to the table. She flopped in the chair and sighed. "Now, explain."

The husband groaned and took a seat. "The peasants want to rebel."

What? She tried to blink away the burning tears that were forming as she pieced together what was happening. *The peasants want to revolt and they are telling me. Why?* She turned her attention to Sien and Amyn. *They called me queen.* She frowned.

"There's no food and no where to find warmth."

"Does the Lord Protector know?"

Ser Lyon's wrinkles frowned as he took a seat. "He was told about it four years ago, and every year since. The peasants are no concern to the highborn."

"Is that why, outside the village there are,"

"Shallow graves," Ser Lyon finished. "Aye, many have died."

Jaslyn shook her head. "How?"

"No food and no warmth, remember?"

Tears welled in Jaslyn's eyes. "Someone should do something!"

"I thought you might say that," the husband interrupted. "You think you're so different from the other highborn."

Her eyebrows furrowed. "How could you possibly know anything about me or the highborn?" Stillness filled the room, but Jaslyn refused to back down. "Tell me who you are."

"Friar," the man replied with a huff. "Does that make you feel better?"

Jaslyn's face burned. *Why am I here?* She wondered, averting everyone's eyes. "So, the peasants are cold and dying. Is that why they want to revolt?"

"That's not the only reason. Many, apart from a few blacksmiths and tailors, are farmers. Every year, the Lord Protector forces peasant farmers to pay sixty percent of their harvest as taxes for nothing in return." Ser Lyon explained.

Sixty percent, Jaslyn repeated, pressing her hands against her thighs. *Why does Father need that much?*

"That leaves the farmers with barely enough to survive," Friar added. "With such little food, they cannot sell their harvest to buy more seeds for the next year. Nor can they buy goods from the blacksmith, the tailor, or even the cobbler. Everyone suffers."

"Why can't the farmers become something else?"

"Many become the same profession as their parents. That's just how it is," Ser Lyon answered.

Jaslyn placed a finger on her chin. "Why don't the farmers ignore the yearly requirements?"

"The Lord Protector's knights will take the taxed harvest regardless," Friar informed, repositioning in his chair. "Even using violence."

It should not be this way, Jaslyn understood, her lip trembling. *How could Father do something like this?* She wondered if either of her parents thought about the peasants and small folk that lived in the Mountain Realm. *If they won't help, then I will*, she decided, *I don't know how, but I will fix this mess that my parents have ignored for far too long.*

"We want you to be a queen the peasants can follow."

Her knuckles buzzed as she slammed her fists against the table. "That will start a war!" *I'm no queen. I'm nothing but a little girl who feels pity for the weak. Am I willing to betray my family for them?* "I can't."

The freezing wind howled around the cottage, and the fire flickered again. "I need to seal the cracks," Katia declared, running to another room. She rushed right back with a tub of paste and a flat metal piece. "This is the best way," Katia smiled, trying to lighten the mood.

You will never be able to seal the stone. Jaslyn wanted to tell the woman. As Katia pressed the thick paste into the walls, Jaslyn realized that there was nothing else to keep in the heat. *If she doesn't use that paste, they will freeze.*

She turned to Friar. "Why me?"

"You are Jaslyn Wayward. Second daughter of the Lord Protector, Borin Wayward and Gloriana Thoren," Ser Lyon answered instead. "You were born with the ancient eyes of the golden bear, and the white lion rides with you."

"What does Kai have to do with this?"

Friar sighed. "A moon before you visited the village, a Saavant arrived. He made the people gather in the middle of the village and declared that winter was coming, and summer will come even quicker." Friar paused, examining Jaslyn's confused face. "It was a warning for the harvest. The Saavant told us that the way they are living cannot continue. Finally, the Saavant proclaimed that the white lion rides high in the winds, roaring an end to the suffering. Roaring for a new dawn."

They believe I'm part of some prophecy. Sweat dripped down Jaslyn's back at the realization. *What should I do? What would my family do?* She thought about her siblings then. *Josef would try to get his way out of it. While Alice would ask the opinons of those in the room.*

"And you believe it's me?" Jaslyn questioned, and Ser Lyon's hesitation caused her to frown. She didn't want this responsibility. She wanted to run wild in the forest, and fight beasts that mimicked the monsters in Maiden Barda's stories. She wanted to do things on her own terms. She wanted to be free. She squeezed her hands into fists. "I'm no,"

"Lyon, are you sure she can help? She is a highborn. They know nothing of this world," Friar interrupted.

"I've seen her command a mob of peasants. When she puts her mind to it, she can do anything."

She brightened at Ser Lyon's faith. *He believes in me. He believes I can do it, but should I?* She turned to Amyn and Sien who sat shivering by the fire. *They believe that I can be queen.* She wondered what her family would think. *They are the reason the peasants are suffering in the first place.* She paused. *That's right. It's their fault that the peasants want to rebel. They didn't choose me off of some whim. I was their last choice.*

Jaslyn Wayward knew then what she had to do.

She turned to Friar. "I'm willing to do what is necessary for the realm to prosper. Even if that means committing treason against my family." The words choked her, but she swallowed her fear. She had to speak the truth, and the truth was treason. "It seems I'm the best you got."

"You're the ancestor of Rayleen the Righteous and bear the same golden eyes. Queen Rayleen would be proud of your decision. She always did what was best for the kingdom," Katia replied.

She didn't want to think about her family; the past nor the present. She was dishonoring them, killing them, destroying the house's name, all for the sake of the kingdom.

Jaslyn's reality frightened her.

She imagined the war that would come if she declared herself as queen. The blood, the fire, the anger; it all brought terror to her soul. She wanted to run away and see nothing. Instead, all she saw was the proud smile plastered on Ser Lyon's face.

Jaslyn looked outside the cottage window, and far off in the distance, she saw the outline of Maryere. The capital city was so close, and yet, from where Jaslyn stood, the village seemed like a different world. She wished there was something noble and not treasonous that she could do for the village, but there wasn't.

Friar leaned back in his chair. "Fine, as the leader of this peasant village, we back your claim as queen."

Queen, Jaslyn couldn't believe it. They wanted *her* to be queen. *I should make changes now. There is no time to waste.* She brightened. "Let's build up the village."

"What do you suggest?" Katia questioned with a smile.

Jaslyn thought for a moment, scanning the cottage. *Everything is small because no one can afford anything. We need jobs.* "Let's expand and create more shops and housing."

"Stone is hard to come by," Friar grumbled.

She frowned. "Well, there is a lumberyard right outside Maryere. Let's build using that. I will figure out the funds and give the wood to the village."

"What a wonderful idea, my queen," Ser Lyon praised.

Jaslyn nodded. "Building could give more jobs, and needing more shops could bring some specialty merchants like in Maryere."

Katia started writing down the ideas. "Brilliant! We've wanted to do all these things, but there is no money."

"Wait, back up," Friar interrupted. "What do you mean build everything with wood? We need raging fires in our homes daily just not to freeze. We shouldn't construct our buildings with only wood."

"We can make the hearths with stone," Ser Lyon counseled, threading his fingers together. "We can hire people to contain small fires and create more jobs."

"That's a great idea," Jaslyn agreed, glancing at the annoyed man with a sly smile. "I will do what I can to obtain stone as well."

Friar rolled his eyes. "Whatever."

"Honey, please give some faith to our queen," Katia pleaded, her voice soft. "Jaslyn, since you wish to care for the village, I think you should name it."

"This village doesn't have a name?"

Friar groaned. "Peasant villages are not granted the pleasure of having a name."

Everyone's attention snapped back to Jaslyn. She shivered and brought her eyes to the ceiling. *Gods have mercy for what I am about to do.* "The village should be called Queen's Cove."

JARIN

For years, as Lord Jarin Ayers tried to sleep, he imagined faceless figures pleasuring his lady wife, bringing him nothing but madness. He usually cried himself to sleep, but not tonight—tonight, he was pissed. The depression Dimia carelessly caused Jarin was exhausting. *She doesn't care about me.*

From the moment they got married, he had let Dimia's actions control him. *I don't want to be that man anymore*, he thought, folding his arms. He pictured Hamlin, his sons, his knights, his people. *I want to be a Lord Protector they will be proud of.*

Jarin rolled over. *This ends tonight*, he decided. *I'm going to banish Dimia from the Riverlands.* He jumped from the bed, exited his room, and marched down the hallway to Dimia's bedchamber.

At the door, he heard a woman's voice, a man's voice that sounded deeper than the sea, and then he heard hers. Dimia's voice, smooth as glass, echoed in the air as she talked to each of her lovers, unaware that Jarin stood right outside her door. He hung his head low and listened through the door to the conversations.

"Once I slew a man who was fifty feet tall!" the deep voiced man bragged, and Dimia moaned and giggled with pleasure.

"How did you kill him, my love?" Dimia exhaled.

"I took my longsword and dug it deep into his belly like this," the man said, and Dimia moaned louder as more voices giggled. "You feel that? Right in your belly?"

"So, you pleasure me the same way you killed a great big giant?" Dimia asked, and the entire room erupted with laughter.

She's so vile, Jarin tensed with tears in his eyes. *And I loved her. I loved a woman who does not deserve love.*

"It's not fair, I want to have some time with Dimia!" the other woman whined.

"You'll get your turn; you have to wait."

"I've waited for so long that I've already pleasured everyone else," the young woman continued.

Dimia sighed. "Alright let me just,"

A scream rang on the other side of the door, as footsteps raced around.

What happened? Jarin placed his ear closer to the door and listened as someone vomited violently. *It's Dimia! She's sick!* At first, Jarin wanted to slam into the door and play hero. Dimia was his wife, and he had to protect her. That was his job, but he was horrible at the task.

He never protected her, not once.

"What should we do? We can't leave her here, but we can't go and get help. The Lord Protector will realize that we were here with her. We can't risk that."

"We have to find help! She is the Lady of the Riverlands. We must risk everything to keep her alive," the man's voice boomed. "Someone needs to wake up Lord Ayers. He must know she is ill."

"No!" the little voice cried. "There's been a sparkle in Jarin's eyes recently. He will punish us!"

She said my name so casually, Jarin observed. *Who is this woman?* Jarin stepped away, his heart beating wildly. *I must go.* He hurried back to his room, shut the door, and locked it before people started moving around the once silent hallways.

Outside his room, people banged on the doors, screaming for help. Jarin pulled out his sitting chair and placed it in front of the window, sighing miserably.

His doorknob turned, but the lock prevented it from opening. The door jiggled desperately, as if the person behind it begged Jarin to open it, but he didn't.

Jarin turned slowly and looked out the window. Candlelight dimly lit the city, and thick black clouds filled the sky. He sat in his chair and looked out to his kingdom. *Dimia is sick.* He didn't know what to do and he blamed no one but himself. *If I'd stopped her sooner, none of this would've happened.*

He drifted to sleep and stared at the blackness from behind his eyelids as he prayed to the gods for the morning light to come soon.

The next morning, Jarin awoke to the pale sunshine trying to poke through the morning clouds. His tired body ached as he sat up and studied his red, tingling hands. *I'm getting old,* he thought unhappily.

Jarin grunted as he stood, and his joints cracked from stiffness. He shuffled to the window and took in the sight of Waterbrook working busily. *Everyone is doing their job.*

The milkmaids cared for the goats and dairy cows on the hills outside the city. Lines had already accumulated at the shops in the Obsidian District. The market opened, and the once quiet streets filled with people buying, selling, and trading. The Defenders of the Oar marched down the streets of Waterbook, upholding law and order.

He smiled at his city. *The coin I paid the knights, farmers, and artisans is circulating. My plan is working.* He rested against the wall. *Dimia was right.* He realized, wanting to laugh. *Give money to the poor, and everything will fix itself.*

Screams suddenly filled Jarin's head.

He grabbed his hair, stumbling backward. *Brea. No, Dimia.* He regained his footing and leaned over, panting. The wretched sounds echoed in his mind, as he walked to the watering bowl and splashed his face with the icy water, trying his best to forget. *I need to go for a walk.*

Jarin moped over to his clothes, and pulled out a blue tunic and black rough spun breeches. His fingers pulsed as he laced his boots and tied on his black wool cloak. The cloak's hood shadowed his face, and Jarin smiled, pleased that no one would be able to recognize him.

Jarin quietly exited his bedchamber, and began his trek.

He turned left and right through the Water Castle's maze of hallways with his head low. He passed the library, the kitchens, and the dining hall. He passed the young maidens gossiping, and the older ones dusting and groaning as they always did. Children's laughter filled his ears, and he smiled, knowing he was walking through Brea's Skyway, where the walls were the sky, and it now constantly smelled like rain. *One more turn and then the exit to the courtyard.*

People strolled down the grand hall, and the knights silently stood guard. Everyone was safe and happy. Jarin grinned, feeling like a true Lord Protector.

The door to the throne room swung open, allowing light to flood into the hallway. Jarin Ayers smacked his teeth. *I didn't want to be bothered today,* he complained. He was Lord Protector, and the Lord Protector did his job by counseling with his advisors. *Hamlin will want to tell me about Dimia. I can't do that today. Another day, one day, any day, but not today.*

His attention flipped to the door that led to the courtyard. *I'm so close.* Jarin rushed down the hallway, trying his best to reach the door before anyone approached him. *That means passing the open throne room,* he thought, willing to take that chance.

He quickened his pace, and every step ached, but Jarin kept on. As he walked, the door seemed to move farther and farther away.

"My lord," Hamlin called from behind. *Not today.* "Jarin!" He faced the old man and the monk smiled, revealing his gums the color of sour milk. "Someone has arrived to meet with you."

Arrived? To meet with me? He leaned over to Hamlin's good ear and whispered, "Tell me true, who is it?"

Hamlin looked back at Jarin confused, and pointed into the throne room. "You told me to bring them when I could."

Jarin moved away from the monk and entered the room, noticing a young woman knelt before a small statue of the goddess of Animals, Citia. She stood as the men approached and her sunset-colored eyes sparkled at Jarin.

The Lord Protector hobbled to his chair, and felt instant relief sitting on the plush cushion. He studied the two that stood before him. *Hamlin must have seen some potential.* "What is your name?"

"Lysane, my lord,"

"You have no surname?" The girl shook her head, and Jarin frowned. "You're a bastard?"

Her face darkened. "No, my lord. I am an orphan."

"Who raised you?"

"A woman named Lady Vera Withers."

"And you did not take on her surname?"

"No, my lord. I am an orphan."

Jarin didn't understand the young woman's blunt answers. *I guess she's more like Hamlin than I thought.* His eyes narrowed. "Will I be able to put my complete trust in you?"

Lysane smiled. "Lady Vera told me it is never wise to give all your trust to one person. She also told me to never lie, for lying is a grievous sin. And I wish to stay on the gods' good side, for all is not well when the gods are angry."

Hamlin nodded, "She's right. The gods become angry when their children sin against them."

Jarin stared at the two for a moment, "Hamlin, do you trust Lysane?"

"The girl is wise and obedient. She would be an excellent member on your council," Hamlin concluded.

Lysane's eyes lit up with excitement. "Council? My lord, you want me to be a part of your council?"

"Only if you want to," Jarin replied and Lysane squealed with excitement. "Then it is settled. Lysane, you are now a part of the Council of the Riverlands."

Lysane dropped to her knees. "Thank you, my lord."

"Rise, girl. More things need to be said," Hamlin instructed.

Lysane stood and Jarin repositioned in his chair. "For now, you will be the stable master's apprentice," Jarin began and Lysane's smile withered away. "No one must know that you are training with Hamlin to become one of my advisors, but you must stay in the castle. You will go to the Shadow Tower daily to train, but only once the sun goes down. You will learn to speak with the Dykon, priests, Voyagers, Saavants, and merchants. You will go to Hamlin with information before coming to me." His eyes narrowed. "You must never obtain the black eyes. You are not a Seer. You do not work for the Citadel or the other Establishments. You are my advisor." Lysane signaled in acknowledgment at the directions. "Good. The faster you learn, the higher you will move in the ranks and will no longer have to be the stable master's apprentice. You can become anyone you want."

"Anyone?" Lysane inquired excitedly.

"Aye."

She turned to Hamlin, "And you chose to be a monk?"

Hamlin gave a goofy grin. "The Riverlands are hot and it's always much cooler in the chapel for an old man to sit all day and listen to the confessions of sinners." He replied and Lysane giggled. "But, no, I am a godly man, child. The gods chose for me to be a monk before I was chosen to become an adviser."

Lysane nodded, "Would I be able to become the head of the Defenders of the Oar?"

Jarin smiled. *And replace Ser Harrwyn, one of Dimia's lovers? I would love to make that happen.* "I said anyone, didn't I?" he asked, and Lysane gleamed with happiness. "Remember, the faster you learn, the higher up you will move. But first, you must learn."

"Yes, my lord, of course."

Jarin was about to dismiss Lysane and Hamlin, when a sea of knights marched into the throne room.

"You cannot march into a council meeting!" Hamlin boomed, turning and waving his bony finger.

"Quiet old man before I cut you down faster than the gods ever can," Ser Harrwyn Brooks threatened.

"You will not speak about the gods that way!"

"Stand down Hamlin," Jarin commanded.

The knight smirked. "You better listen to your lord."

"Hopefully, Varva will hear my prayers tonight," Hamlin finished, his eyes closed.

Jarin stared at the knights. "What is the meaning of this?" The sea of silver platted metal separated in two, and Dimia's handmaiden appeared before him. *Jossa.* Sadness puffed her cheeks, and the raw skin around her eyes signaled hours of sobbing. "Why did you come in here with knights interrupting my counsel?" Jarin questioned, already knowing the answer.

Not today. He didn't want to hear what the young woman had to say. *Please, not today.*

"Dimia," Jossa started in-between sobs, "Lady Ayers, she hasn't woken up. Things are happening to her that I cannot explain. A Saavant is caring for her now."

Her voice... it's the one that screamed. Betrayal choked him as he looked at the handmaiden. "Where is she?"

"In her bed chamber, my lord," Jossa answered, sniffling.

"Place her in the Black Tower until she awakens, and the Saavant believes she is healthy once again," Jarin commanded and the young woman wailed, dropping to her knees. "Hamlin, give the poor girl some willows tea to calm her nerves." The old monk shuffled to the crying handmaiden, helped her to her feet, and led her from the throne room. "Daya, come here," Jarin called, and a young girl appeared beside him instantly. Daya moved like a shadow, quickly and silently, and her sudden appearance sometimes frightened Jarin.

Daya pushed her short black hair out of her sand-colored eyes. "My lord, you've finally called upon me. What can I do for you?" she questioned, displaying the large gap in her front teeth that made her look even more childish. Her skin matched Jarin's, tan and glowing, and little brown freckles plagued her round flat face. *She looks so innocent.* Jarin glanced at the tattooed eel that coiled around Daya's arm and remembered who she was. *A Dykon. A re'in. A killer.*

Dimia loved Daya, as if the girl was her own child. And even though Daya despised Dimia, the girl played the part quite well. *Daya will find pleasure in supervising Dimia's departure to the Black Tower*, he thought, smiling deviously.

"Knights, escort little Daya to Dimia's bedchamber, and move my wife's things into the Black Towers for her *short* stay. Alright?" Jarin glanced at Daya who met his eyes before beaming. She skipped down the dais, and disappeared into the crowd.

All the knights marched out without word of rejection to Jarin's swift plans.

"Who was that girl?" Lysane asked when they were alone.

"Daya is a Dykon."

"Dykon, like an assassin?" she inquired and Jarin nodded in confirmation. "Is she on your council, too?"

"No, but soon she will come to you with secrets, like a little whisperer. She is one of the few who can be trusted."

Lysane accepted the information, finally understanding what her true task was: to replace the old monk who would teach her the way. "How old is she?"

"Dykons don't tell their age," Jarin replied, "but most start as children. Maybe Daya could teach you how to stay hidden so my wife never learns of you. Many in this castle sell secrets to my wife, and she would be more than happy to get rid of you."

"No need to worry, my lord," Lysane smiled confidently, placing her hands on her hips. "I know how to become invisible. I've ran away twice and my mother never found me, no matter how many she hired."

VICTORIA

An overwhelming scent of piss and salt filled the grand room as seventeen bastards filed in. Victoria sniffed her sleeve, where she hid a stick of lavender incense, and her stomach turned at the sight of all the children. She saw House Osmont in each as they smiled, and her rage grew. The door to the grand room closed, and the crowd talked amongst themselves. The children laughed, gossiped, and acted like children. It made Victoria Osmont's heart ache. *I must get rid of them.*

"My lady," Ser Edmund Archard greeted, kneeling.

She frowned, sniffing her sleeve again. "There are more than what you reported."

"Apologies, my lady."

"Bring me the eldest and you, get me some damn wine," she commanded pointing to a young maiden, who hurried away to get the wine.

Ser Edmund bowed his head, and turned to the children. He tapped the hilt of his sheathed sword on the ground, and the room silenced.

"Will the man, age of twenty-three, step forward?" Ser Edmund commanded.

She sat up as a young man walked to the dais. *When did all this begin? We married when I was only twelve!* The maiden skipped back up the steps and handed Victoria a wineglass. "Thank you," Victoria said, and took a sip.

Her heart dropped staring at the man's body. *He's strong. Much stronger than Doran. What if Falk decides his actual first-born son will be Lord Protector when he dies?* She frowned. *I cannot let that happen. He must disappear.*

"What is your name?" Ser Edmund boomed.

"Ivar, ser," the man replied.

He knows how to respectfully speak to a knight. Victoria cleared her throat. "Ivar; what kind of name is that?"

"My mother speaks the tongue of the old Forestlands. Named me from the language."

"So, she is not dead?"

"No, my lady. She has been gone for three years now, on a trip."

"You did not go with her?"

"No, my lady," Ivar frowned. "My mother said I was too special to put myself in danger. She wouldn't let me train with a weapon, and she wouldn't let me leave Kingment."

"Strong woman," Victoria replied bluntly, "Smart woman." *And I am a weak woman. A dumb woman.*

"Thank you, my lady," the man smiled.

"Are you married?"

"No, my lady. I'm a blacksmith's apprentice."

Victoria nodded slowly, taking another sip of her wine. "Any siblings?"

Ivar turned and pointed to some of the children, "Only four." Little heads popped up from the crowd and smiled.

"Only?" she blurted, spilling some of her wine on the marble floor. "Do you all have the same father?" Ivar nodded, and behind him four other little heads nodded with his. "Who?" She wanted to trap the man. *Tell me who your father is, boy.*

Ivar shifted his feet. "I don't know, my lady. My mother only told us that we all had the same father."

Victoria relaxed in her chair. *He knew the answer I wanted. He's smarter than he looks.* "What a shame," she exhaled, rolling her eyes, "I'm done with you, next child."

Ivar bowed and disappeared into the small sea of children.

A young woman now stood before Victoria, and curtsied awkwardly, her lips trembling. Victoria's eyes went from the girl's chestnut-colored hair to her deep brown eyes. *She looks more like me than Falk.* "What is your name?"

"Raina," she whispered, looking at the floor.

Victoria rolled her eyes. "Speak up girl. And your age?"

"Sixteen," Raina replied hesitantly, but much louder.

"You say, my lady, after you speak," Ser Edmund informed Raina, his voice filled with authority and the girl nodded nervously.

"Who is your mother?" Victoria asked.

"A woman named Rebekah," the girl's eyes darted around the room before adding, "my lady."

"Has she left you, too?"

"Aye, but she will never return. She is dead now." Raina strained to say, and Victoria felt no pity.

"What is your occupation? Are you a whore?"

"No!" the young woman shouted. "My lady, I am the bastard of a merchant. I live in his compound in the Green Hills, and he claims me as his own."

Victoria slowly turned to Ser Edmund Archard, and the knight refused to meet her eyes. She scrunched her face, trying to stop herself from screaming. *I can't prove these bastards to be Falk's if they already have fathers claiming them as their own!* She wanted to throw her wineglass at the girl. Instead, she gripped the neck of the cup as tightly as she could. "Very well," she managed to say through her clenched teeth. "You may leave."

Raina stepped forward, grabbing at her hip as if she had a sword before standing straight. "Thank you, my lady."

"Do any others have fathers?" A few more children rose their hands. "Get out. I have no interest"

When everything settled again she took another sip of wine. "Next!"

Another girl approached and placed her hands on her hips, radiating Osmont attitude. Victoria covered her open mouth with her hand. *Catrain? No this girl is taller than Catrain.* The girl had sparkling moss colored eyes, and matted bright red hair that stopped at her ears. She had a jawbone like Rosert and was as tall as Doran. Cold sweat beaded on Victoria's forehead. *She could pass for one of my children.*

"My name is Cleric, my lady," the girl began, not waiting for Victoria to ask questions. "My mother was a whore, but my father is the Lord Protector of the Northern Kingdom of Valley Pines." The children in the room gasped, at Cleric's declaration. Cleric grinned and walked closer to Victoria, causing Ser Edmund to step in front of her. "I know what a pain that this might be to you. He loved my mother very much."

Victoria was not prepared for one of the bastards to be as bold as Falk. Cleric handed Ser Edmund a stack of letters and the knight placed them on Victoria's lap. Her hands shook as she opened one of the letters. *My love,* it began. *That's Falk's handwriting.* She blinked slowly, feeling the tears burn her eyes. *There is no use in denying it.*

"I'm sorry, my lady." Cleric said sincerely, jumping up the dais and into Victoria's arms, hugging her sweetly.

The crowd gasped, and Ser Edmund pulled Cleric off, throwing her onto the ground. "Quite alright," Victoria exhaled, as Cleric helped herself to her feet. *I want them all dead, but my rage isn't their fault. I must show mercy.* Victoria pulled Ser Edmund closer. "I've decided what to do," she announced. "Please send them to the Evaluation Block."

"That place is hell," Ser Edmund informed with wide eyes.

"So give them to the Yellows! They are the kindest of the Evaluators, are they not?" The knight stayed silent, causing Victoria to sigh. "Look, it's far better than the original option I had. Ivar, his siblings, and Cleric won't be sold. Ivar is too old. If he is a slave, Falk will always be able to find him. Also, out of the kindness in my heart, I'm allowing his siblings go with him. And Cleric," she sighed. "Cleric *is* Falk's daughter. There is no denying that."

Ser Edmund gave Victoria a disapproving look. "Yes, my lady," he said and the knights ushered the sea of bastards out of the grand room, causing the children to cry. *They know they're not going home.*

Ivar, his siblings, and Cleric stared at Victoria. *They must go far, where there will be no trace of them. A place where no one will ever find them, not even the Seers.* "I called you all here, to send you on an important quest," Victoria began, making it up as she spoke. *The White Abyss! No one ever returns from there.* "Please to go to the White Abyss and bring me back the ancient relic, the Crown of Wonder. When you return, I will repay everyone handsomely for it."

"My lady," Ivar started uncomfortably, "I cannot do this mission. I'm almost a master blacksmith, and my sister Gilly is sickly."

"You cannot deny your lady," Cleric reminded him.

"How right you are," Victoria smiled. "These knights will escort you to the stables, where you will each find a strong horse. Then to the Lord Protector's blacksmith, where you will receive your weapons for defense. It is not a safe journey from here to the White Abyss," Victoria warned. "The knights will give you food, water, and clothing for travels and you will leave by nightfall."

"Nightfall?" one of Ivar's younger siblings yelled out angrily.

"Yes, my lady," Cleric replied confidently.

Two knights surrounded the group and marched them out.

"No!" Ivar screamed. "You can't do this! I must inform my mother! You just can't send me away like this! No!" He then dashed toward Victoria, and she could see murderous intent in his eyes. The knights tackled Ivar, blackening the man's eye, and causing the other siblings to cry. "You won't get away with this!"

"Take them away," Victoria commanded. "Cleric, however, can stay." The young girl stopped and turned to Victoria. "Come, girl." And the young bastard ran to her. "You will not be taking this travel to the White Abyss only to not return." she explained. "Does my husband, your father, know what you look like?"

Cleric shook her head. "No, my lady. My mother had told me how he visited when I was a baby, but not anymore, now that I am older."

"Good," Victoria smiled, suppressing the pain inside. "Let's keep this a secret between me and you."

"Of course," Cleric promised. "Whatever you need of me, I will do."

"My daughter, Catrain, is in need of a new handmaiden and friend. That will be your new job."

Cleric made a face, "Do I have to wear a dress?"

Victoria laughed, "No, I will not force you."

"Thank you, my lady!"

She snapped and a servant approached. "Maiden Woolfe will bathe and dress you in new clothing, but no dresses," Victoria explained, turning to the old woman. The maiden made a face but agreed. "And she will teach you how to be a maiden for my daughter."

Cleric nodded and walked out of the throne room with the old woman.

Ser Edmund stepped in front of her, smiling. "That was kind of you, my lady."

"She was honest with me. I need that in this god-awful kingdom. People lie and scheme so often it makes me want to kill myself."

The knight frowned. "You didn't speak to all the children. They could've become servants."

"Oh yes, let's have a hoard of Osmont bastards running around the

Black Castle. That won't cause any issues," she said sarcastically, rolling her eyes. "Don't be ridiculous!"

Edmund sighed. "Those children could've been honest, too."

"It doesn't matter," Victoria replied, grabbing for her wine glass as a headache grew. "I didn't want to look at those little Falk faces for another minute."

ALICE

Crackles and hisses from the roaring fire woke Alice from a deep sleep. She had been asleep since walking through Myburn Garden, and knew her body would ache from the lack of movement. She sat up and yet, the pain melted away. Suddenly, she felt alive. *This isn't how I usually feel when I wake up.* She observed her hands moving in different directions. *I haven't felt this energetic in years!* She hopped out of bed and twirled in her small room, her hands stretched joyfully. *Am I better? Has my illness finally been cured?* She scampered to the window and watched the endless snowfall. *This is great! I'm finally better!*

A strange pulse ripped through her head, causing her to frown. *I should go out while I still can. Just in case.*

Alice slipped on her favorite golden winter dress, embellished with bears stitched in green thread, to represent House Wayward. *But where should I go?* She moved to her mirror and brushed her matted hair until it shone. *My hair seems so thick,* she thought, gritting as she pulled out the knots. After washing her face, she placed a few golden bear clippings in her hair and clasped the necklace her aunt Victoria gave her around her neck.

She stared in the mirror, a smile growing. *Let's see what's going on outside.*

Alice Wayward rushed down the Bloody Tower's stairs and pushed open the door, but it didn't budge. *What's going on?* She continued her struggle to exit, but nothing moved. *Did they lock me in?* Her family often locked her inside the tower when Alice had her bouts of sickness so no one would take advantage of her motionless body. *I'll get out the other way.*

She sat on the fourth step and shifted a loose brick. Once one crumbled, three more fell, just enough for Alice to slip through. *I'm going out no matter what.*

She trekked into Winter's Keep, unpleased by the sight. *Where is everyone?* She wondered, noticing only a few servants.

"Alice?"

She smiled at her handmaiden. "Hi, Myra! I'm finally awake!"

The girl's face brightened and the two embraced. "That's great! And you look wonderful, too."

"Thank you, but where is everyone?"

Myra's dark brown eyes scanned the hallway before leaning in close.

"Apparently, some super important meeting is happening in the throne room, but not everyone was invited."

Her eyebrows raised at the information, and she gave her hand-maiden a devious smile. "Let's go sneak in."

The two girls rushed to the throne room and entered through a side door to see only her father, her mother, Lord Falk Osmont, and his knights. The attention landed on them, and Alice stepped back. *We aren't supposed to be here*, she realized at once.

"Perfect," Falk Osmont grinned.

Tears filled Gloriana's eyes. "Wait, no,"

"Silence!" Borin roared, his face twisted with anger. "Continue."

Falk bowed. "As I was saying, I can forgive insults, but a scheme to murder my children to amend for my father's sins is inexcusable. I mean, what kind of mother does that?"

What's happening? Alice backed into the shadows, and the room's attention left her. *Why does it feel like death is in the room?*

"But," Falk continued, his voice slightly louder. "I don't want a useless war with you, Borin. We are friends and have known each other for many years. So, I would be willing to ignore your wife's misgivings if you betroth your eldest daughter to my son, Doran."

What?

"No!" Gloriana shouted, now on her feet. "No way! Alice is too sick to leave the keep, much less go to another kingdom."

"I thought I said silence," Borin growled.

Gloriana looked down at her husband. "You do not believe this man, right, my love?"

"I don't know what to believe," Borin replied, his eyes on his lap. "To think you would allow your hatred to target innocent children is unimaginable." He paused then and shook his head with a groan. "But my mother always warned you would bring misery onto House Wayward."

"Borin, you cannot be serious,"

"And you've been acting strange as of late," he interrupted. "Constantly near me as if you've done something wrong and want to be there when it comes to light. Well, here you are, now sit down." Slowly, Gloriana took her seat with her mouth wide open, and Borin cleared his throat. "Falk, thank you for bringing this information to me, and I sincerely apologize that my wife dared to put your children in danger."

"I didn't," Gloriana started.

"But I cannot accept a marriage between Doran and Alice. My daughter is far too sickly to marry. Her moonblood has never flowered, and we don't know if she will survive the journey to Kingment. It's too risky."

Falk turned his head to the shadows, and Alice's heart dropped. He moved his finger, directing her toward him. "Alice, come out here. I'd like to take a look at you."

Alice Wayward shuffled into the middle of the room.

The Lord Protector of the Northern Kingdom of Valley Pines looked her up and down before grinning. "She looks fine to me."

"Aye, she may look fine today, but her condition is constantly changing," Borin explained. "She has been asleep for three weeks and isn't healthy."

She gasped internally. *Is that true? Was I genuinely asleep for three weeks? That's one of the longest times I've ever slept!* She didn't understand her body. *If I was that sick, why would I feel better now?*

"Well, if you refuse the betrothal," Falk started, and his knights grabbed their hilts. "Then I will be forced to arrest Gloriana."

Alice's body moved without thought. "No!" she shouted, getting in between everyone. "No!" Alice's bright blue eyes landed on her lord uncle as she waited for his relaxed stance. *I must save my mother. I cannot have her punished for her feelings of bitterness. It's not her fault. She was getting justice in her own way.* Alice grabbed the red crystal attached to her necklace. *I don't want to do this, but leaving would be better. It's not like my family will miss me when I sleep most of the time. I will save my family by sacrificing myself.* "Maybe if I leave, I'll recover," she explained, her voice shaking. "Maybe it's the cold that makes me sick." Her attention bounced between her father and mother. "Maybe this is what the gods wanted."

"My sweetest child born of summer," Gloriana exhaled, moving to her feet. She walked down the dais, her body swaying with grace. "Sacrificing yourself... to help me... is too kind," she added, placing a hand on Alice's shoulder, "but I cannot allow you to do that." Her determined blue eyes landed on Lord Falk Osmont. "Arrest me if you must!"

Falk's face scrunched at the declaration. "I would much prefer to connect our families than to spill blood."

"You are married to Victoria, in case you forgot," Gloriana frowned. "Our families are already connected."

Lord Borin stood suddenly, grabbing the room's attention with his enormous stature. *Father looks like a real Lord Protector*, Alice observed, almost in awe. *But he's about to make the wrong decision.*

Borin Wayward inhaled deeply. "When Alice becomes a woman, we will send her to Kingment to marry Doran."

"Borin," Glorana exhaled, her lips trembling.

"That won't do," Falk responded. "She will be coming with me when I leave at the end of the week." A deafening silence caused Falk's evil grin to grow wider. "Or I'll be taking Gloriana and hanging her for her crimes."

Gloriana Wayward lifted her leg swiftly, pulled a dagger attached to her ankle, and launched at Lord Falk. Before the woman could strike, Omsont knights tackled her to the floor and pinned her down.

"I guess your wife has made the decision," Falk chuckled, "Men."

"No!" Alice cried.

The knights began to handle Gloriana, and Borin's face roughly turned red. "Release my wife, take Alice, and leave immediately!" he roared.

Falk motioned, and his knights dropped Gloriana, causing the woman to smash her face into the stone floor. "Stop acting like this is so unreasonable," he smiled. "Your unwanted daughter is wanted now." He then turned on his heels and marched out of the room.

Alice dropped to her knees and embraced her mother, crying. Cold hands wrapped around Alice's arms, pulling her away. Her attention focused on the lord knights who slid a downtrodden Gloriana out of the throne room. Alice turned to her father. "Wha,"

"I'm putting your mother under house arrest for her crimes," he motioned to the shadows. "Handmaiden, please escort my daughter back to the Bloody Tower and begin packing her things."

Myra Nores helped Alice to her feet, but Alice's eyes stayed only on her father. "Will you punish her further?"

Lord Borin sighed. "You won't be saying goodbye to her. That's her punishment."

I'm being punished, too. Alice pressed her lips together and nodded, not wanting to argue. "I sacrificed myself for our family. Please, Father, promise to keep our family together."

Myra guided Alice to the throne room door, leaving the Lord Protector of the Mountain Realm behind.

"I will do what I can," he answered as they stepped out of the room.

Alice's handmaiden leaned close. "What he can do is nothing," she whispered. "For if he could do anything, he wouldn't have accepted a bribe full of lies."

HADRIAN

The creaking wheels made Hadrian twitch. He inhaled through his nose and exhaled through his mouth, trying his best to stay calm as he stared at the wheelhouse floor. *Stop creaking*, he begged, now clutching his hair. The wheelhouse hit a bump in the road, and the creaking worsened. Hadrian groaned loudly, waking up Raynese.

"What's wrong?" she asked, rubbing her eyes.

"I'm going crazy in here. I want to get out."

Raynese sat up and shook her head. "The Warrior Raiders are after you. It's best to keep the stops to a minimum."

He trembled. *That's right. Mother brought back the Warrior Raiders to kill me.*

Everyone in the Kingdom of Valley Pines knew about the scavenger tribe who wreaked havoc on the people for hundreds of years, pillaging, raping, and murdering. They cared nothing for the usual standards of civilization, still living in their old ways. As the kingdom expanded, the Raiders became too much, forcing Lord Peyton and Lord Falk to eradicate them, pushing the tribes to Unmosis.

None of it made sense to Hadrian. *Would Mother truly bring the Warrior Raiders back? It seems so unlike her.*

"The sadness in your eyes hurts to see," Raynese exhaled, bringing Hadrian's attention to her. "Let's talk about stuff."

"Like what?" he mumbled, picking at his nails.

She placed a finger on her freckled cheeks. "So, I'm guessing you're a highborn?"

He frowned. "Talking about stuff isn't asking questions."

"We've been riding in this dumb thing for weeks, and I barely know you! Whatever, just know you can ask me anything."

He rolled his eyes. "Fine, where are you from?"

"The Grasslands, what about you?"

"The Kingdom of Valley Pines, duh."

She grinned, and the scar across her nose upturned. "What city?"

"You didn't give me a city, and anyways,"

"Oroketi," she interrupted, her face unchanging. "Your turn."

Hadrian looked away. "Arkmore."

"Hm," she replied, sounding serious yet holding back a laugh. "You're a terrible liar. Work on that. I interrupted you with my answer, so you didn't second guess it. You, however, hesitated with your response. Think about the differences."

"Wait, you were lying?"

Raynese shrugged. "Who knows?"

Hadrian studied the woman, annoyed. *Why does she toy with me? Does she not understand that I'm in misery?* He paused. *Is this her way of comforting me?* Hadrian held in a groan. "It doesn't matter. We don't need to know about each other. Just protect me like Ser Colvic instructed you to do."

Raynese frowned. "You don't like me?"

His heart dropped from the young woman's changed demeanor. *What's wrong with me? I've been rude to someone willing to risk their life for me. If she's willing to do that, I can trust her, right?* He sighed. "I do."

"Yay," she cheered, jumping into Hadrian's arms, startling him. She pressed her cheek against his before releasing him. "I was nervous another person hated me."

"Another person?"

Raynese nodded, reclining into the cushions. "This world is wicked, yet unpredictable," she warned, pulling out one of her many daggers. She pressed the blade's tip into her palm as if it relaxed her. "Even the person you love more than anything could end up hating you."

Mother. He balled his hands into a fist and pressed his lips together. *I can't keep wallowing because she wants to kill me. That isn't going to bring my old life back.* The time had come for Hadrian to grow up. *I must be ready, or else I'm going to die.*

He leaned forward, his mood shifting. *The first thing I should do is make Raynese my closest companion. She's strong. I can feel it.* A smile appeared. "Who would hate a beautiful woman like you?"

Raynese's hazel eyes widened. "Well,"

The wheelhouse stopped, and Ser Colvic immediately opened the door. "A horse died. So, we will stay here for the night."

Raynese leaped from the wheelhouse and stretched. "Finally! Sleeping under the stars!"

Hadrian stepped out and took in the blended colors of the evening sky. *It's beautiful.* A few servants rushed around, setting up camp as Raynese twirled, completely carefree. *Is she always like that?* He didn't know whether he loved or hated it. *I sort of want to be like that.*

Patty approached with clean clothing. "Hi Hadrian, I,"

He embraced the servant girl tightly, causing her to gasp. He wanted to hold her longer, but Patty's tense body caused him to pull away. He took in the girl's bright red face and smiled. "I haven't seen you in a while. Apologies."

She lifted the clothing for him to take, looking away. "It's okay. I was just surprised."

"Would you help me dress? Like when we were younger?" he questioned, taking the outfit.

Patty hid her face with her hands. "Hadrian, you're acting different."

"I must become bolder if the Warrior Raiders are after me. I can't continue being the little boy, never leaving the castle. My mother is forcing me from home, so now it's time to see the world."

The servant girl inhaled sharply at his reasoning. "It seems that rude woman has rubbed off on you."

He frowned, stepping back. "Was I being rude to you?"

"No, of course not! It's just,"

Another servant approached. "My lord, your tent is over there."

Hadrian grabbed Patty's hand. "Thanks," he replied, walking in the direction the servant pointed. "Come on." Patty nervously followed behind, and they rushed into the tent. When they entered, he twirled around, taking in the massive tent before pausing. *Wait, Patty is right. I'm acting like Raynese.* He stopped and focused on Patty, still standing near the entrance. He sighed. "If you don't want to be here, it's fine. I'm sorry, but I'm just sad. You bring me a comfort no one else can. I want to be near you forever. You're my best friend."

Patty rushed to him, and the pair embraced. The hug felt so real and so right, and it was everything Hadrian ever wanted. *I didn't realize how much she meant to me until now.* Patty pulled away, and he stared into her bright green eyes. *She's beautiful, just like the evening sky.*

The servant girl laid her head on Hadrian's shoulder and sighed. She took his hand and placed it on the scar on her upper thigh.

He rubbed his fingertips against it, and Patty's breath hitched. *The scar is thick like the one on Raynese's face.* "Who did this?"

Patty smiled at his concern. "The Warrior Raiders. They murdered my family and slashed my legs as I escaped. When that happened, I wanted to give up on life. Everyone near me was gone, and even though I escaped, I became a servant and worked my way into the Lord Protector's castle. I was broken and often thought of ending my life to be with my family again, but then I met you." She lifted her head and smiled. "You are kind, understanding, and a wonderful human. I love you." He gripped her soft skin in reaction, feeling his body grow warm, yet Patty's smile grew. "Please, don't change, Hadrian. Yes, life sucks, but don't give up. Stay you."

Ser Colvic Rames stomped into the tent, and Patty stepped as far away from Hadrian as possible and lowered her head. The famed knight looked at the pair and shook his head, pushing away a smile. "Hadrian, go bathe."

He groaned as Patty rushed out, saying nothing. "Can I in the morning? I'm tired, and it's already so cold."

Colvic rolled his eyes and sighed. "We won't be staying long in the morning, so bathe at first light," the knight turned before pausing. "Although, if you're trying to get close to Patty tonight, I'm sure she would prefer a clean you to lie next to."

Hadrian's brightened. "Okay, I'll wash up now. Where is it?"

"They set up a small tub behind your tent."

He rushed out of the tent, stripping with each step before hopping into the tub. The cold water caused his teeth to chatter, but he pushed forward, cleaning himself as quickly as possible. *Patty could sneak in during the night. I would love to sleep in the same room with her instead of,*

The trees rustled, and Hadrian lowered himself in the water. *What is that?* His eyes darted every which way, unsure of what to do. *Is it the Warrior Raiders?* He stepped out of the tub, now nervous. *I should leave.*

Hadrian returned to his tent, where Raynese laid on his bed, relaxing. "What are you doing?"

She sat up. "We didn't get to finish our conversation earlier."

"Well, I'm naked, so could you please leave?"

Raynese grinned and put her hands over her eyes. "I won't peek."

He groaned and decided to get dressed, ignoring the woman. "Done."

"Yay!"

Hadrian scoffed and sat beside Raynese. "Alright, what were we talking about?"

The smile dissipated off Raynese's face and the large scar on her face frowned with her. "You had asked who would hate a beautiful woman like me."

"Alright, so answer."

Now, the young woman's eyes were watery. "You don't want me here, I get it." She stood, hunched over. "I'll leave."

Hadrian's face matched Raynese's and he grabbed her hand. "No, we can finish our chat. Who hated you?"

The woman beamed and returned to the bed. "Well, long ago, I traveled across the Amethyst Sea to the biggest island in Ihphy's Archipelago. This island, however, wasn't tropical but parched and cursed."

Images of human-like beasts with silvery scales, giants that roared fire, and people whose skin was blacker than the night sky filled his mind. Hadrian then pictured a desert that stretched farther than he could see. *Can something like that exist?*

"I traveled to the kingdom of Lyks, and the people had shades of hair color that I had never seen before. A rich merchant prince invited me to a hair-dying festival. When they saw my tanned skin, the inhabitants thought I was a mermaid-turn person. So, they gave me a shade of blue for the sea they thought I came from."

"Blue!" Hadrian laughed aloud. He couldn't see Raynese's gorgeous brown hair, a blue hue.

Raynese giggled with him, and his face grew warm again. *Even though she's wild, her smiles and laughs are still so pretty.* "Yes, but my hair was much brighter than the Lykans. They were amazed by the color and named me Ihphy reborn." She paused as if she was remembering the praise. "But it was all too much. I couldn't be the goddess they loved. I wasn't that person. I was a traveler. So, I ran away from Lyks and traveled to Mikos, another kingdom on the other side of the mountain that the Lykans prayed to."

Patty entered the tent and stared at the pair, her eyes wide. "Uh," she started, stepping back. "Um."

"Come and listen to Raynese's story!" Hadrian invited, patting on the bed. Patty hesitantly sat beside Hadrian and he found himself sandwiched between two beautiful women. *I need them both by my side. One will be my sword. The other will be my heart.* He turned to Raynese. "Continue."

Raynese frowned, no longer animated. "When I entered the kingdom, the Mikosi turned me into an outcast because of my dyed hair."

"Why did you dye your hair?" Patty asked quietly.

The traveler woman groaned. "Well, you missed that part, servant girl. I went to a hair-dying festival."

Servant girl, Lady Arla Osmont's voice echoed in his head.

"Her name is Patty, and you will call her as such," Hadrian commanded, his voice stern.

Patty smirked while Raynese glared back.

The young woman scoffed and leaned against Hadrian. "Anyways, the people treated me like an outcast. They yelled, cursed, and even threw rotten fruit at me. So, I shaved my hair and started again." She smiled simply, but Hadrian saw darkness in her hazel eyes. "Well, not before I made sure the Mikosi were no more."

"How terrifying!" Patty squealed.

Raynese ignored the girl and kept her eyes on Hadrian, her face moving closer to his. Soon, their noses were almost touching, and Hadrian felt Raynese's warm breath on his lips. "You're an interesting boy," she purred. "I like interesting boys."

Patty stared at the pair, her mouth wide open. "You're being too casual. Please stop touching Hadrian!"

Raynese's cold hands touched his chest, but he didn't move. Everything about the woman felt sinful, yet Hadrian wanted more. Raynese leaned in to kiss Hadrian and he leaned back. "A kiss from me is something you must earn."

The woman grinned at the declaration. "Bet."

Patty's eyes watered. "Wait, Hadrian, you're,"

Scents of smoke and ash filled Hadrian's nose, causing his eyes to widen. "Fire," he interrupted. The two young women looked at him confused, but the crackling of wood pierced Hadrian's ears. "Fire!" he yelled again, and Raynese breathed in the tainted air. She stood up and ran out of the tent without saying a word. "Wait!" Hadrian cried out standing up.

He stumbled out of his tent, with Patty following behind, and watched as the forest twinkled oranges, reds, and greys from the fire and smoke. The thick air burned Hadrian's lungs and he coughed uncontrollably.

"This doesn't look good. I'm going to grab a few items from my tent," Patty informed. "I'll be right back."

"No, you should stay with me."

"I promise. I'll be right back."

Hadrian Osmont nodded reluctantly, watching Patty rush away. *What is going on?*

Raynese crawled out of her tent, dressed in a new outfit with a dagger in hand as Colvic appeared, staring at the blazing fire. "Run!" the famed knight yelled when his eyes caught Hadrian's. Hadrian continued to stand there, motionless and afraid. "Raynese!" Colvic screamed rushing towards them, "Go north to the River Lilia. Cross it and I will meet you at the border."

Raynese grabbed Hadrian's hand, and suddenly, they were running. As they ran, figures formed in the trees before morphing into humans. The figures, however, were bigger than stallions, and wider than big oaks. The beastly humans charged towards the camp, yelling, and screaming like squawking crows. "Oh shit," Raynese cursed, quickening her pace. "The Warrior Raiders found us."

A huge man with a shaggy black beard jumped in front of Raynese and Hadrian, "Which one of ye is the lil' lord?" he asked his accent thick, and his stench thicker.

Raynese responded by poking the dagger in the man's belly and ripped his skin across with all her strength. Hadrian saw the man's eyes go wide, while his face went pale. His entrails spilled from his body before the man hit the ground. *She killed him so easily.*

More Warrior Raiders poured from the forest, attacking the camp, and separating Hadrian from Raynese.

A rough looking woman dressed in furs caught Hadrian's attention as she moved her longsword around gracefully and cut off the carriage driver's head in one strike. The head rolled on the ground, and the woman stuck a knife into his eyes before eating it.

"Duck!" Patty's voiced called from behind.

Hadrian dropped to his knees. *I'm going to die. They are going to kill me, just like Mother wanted.* He turned and a man lifted his sword, causing Hadrian to cover his face. Patty's shrill scream forced Hadrian's eyes to snap open. *Patty!* He watched as the young woman collapsed. She hit the ground, and the Raider laughed.

"No!" Hadrian sobbed, crawling to Patty. He scooped the handmaiden into his arms. *She saved me. She jumped in front and saved me.* "Patty!"

Metal clanged above, and Hadrian looked up. Raynese deflected the Raider's second swing, causing the man to take a few steps back. Raynese lept forward, engaging in battle.

Hadrian returned his attention to Patty, who bled out from a deep slash on her chest and stomach. She touched his hands softly, her skin already cold. "Hadrian," she struggled.

Tears flowed out of Hadrian as he hugged Patty. "I'm so sorry. This is all my fault."

"No," she replied in a soft tone. "I didn't have to come with you. I

chose to. I didn't want to spend a day without my lovely lord by my side."
She blinked slowly and touched Hadrian's cheek. "Hadrian," she whispered.
"I love you, but it's time to see my family." Her hand fell from his face, and
her breathing stopped.

"PATTY!" Hadrian held her tightly as destruction happened all
around. "Patty, please wake up," he begged, pushing her bright red hair
away from her face. His tears splashed on her forehead, but she didn't react.

She's dead.

"Hadrian!" Raynese shouted, rushing back to him. She paused when
she saw Patty dead in his arms. "We have to go."

Hadrian shook his head. "I can't leave Patty."

Raynese bent down and cupped Hadrian's face. "Patty died defending
you. Don't let that be in vain. Mourn for her later. For now, we must leave."
She grabbed his hand and lifted him to his feet. Patty fell from his hands
and laid on the ground. He stared at the slash that had cut through her
torso. *She's dead because of me.* "Let's go," Raynese commanded, and they
started to run.

They entered the darkened forest, as the fighting continued behind
them. The heat of the fire no longer burned Hadrian's skin, yet the pair kept
running.

Colvic said we should go north to the river. "How far is the border?"

Raynese looked back at him with dread. Her tan skin was covered in
ash, and her breath sparkled in the cold air. "Far."

And the birds started screaming.

JASLYN

Big, bright brown eyes sparkled in Jaslyn's mind as she stepped into her new village, Queen's Cove. *Lord Osmont proposed a marriage between Alice and his eldest son, Doran because Lady Gloriana tried to assassinate his children. The Lord Protector secretly accepted, arresting your mother, and Alice will be leaving in a few days,* a voice echoed, and Jaslyn could still see the tears streaming down the young Summeran handmaiden's face. *There are whispers of what you've become, Lady Jaslyn. Please, save us. Save Alice.*

Jaslyn had searched for answers within Winter's Keep for hours, but her mother's bedchamber was locked, and her father was nowhere to be found—so she knew she had to do something.

I had to be queen.

Jaslyn Wayward prayed to the gods for their protection before working with her handmaidens to communicate with Ser Lyon. *I'm sure more than just the peasants are tired of my father's fruitless reign. If Alice's handmaiden learned about me being a queen from the whispers, then people are taking the claim seriously. I must take advantage of that.* Jaslyn gathered information, wrote to any possible allies, and finally, she was having a meeting. *My first meeting as queen.*

"Wow, Jaslyn, this is so nice!" Evergreen exclaimed, her hands by her face and fingers interlaced.

She blushed, her eyes on the fresh snow underneath her boots. "Thanks, but I haven't done much."

"Oh please, I saw you giving a knight your allowance," Violet chuckled, walking ahead. "I've already stopped by and spoken to some peasants. Just your interest does a lot for them."

"What do you mean you've already stopped by?" Jaslyn questioned, pouting.

Violet grinned and turned toward Friar's cottage. "Come on! They are all waiting for you, my queen."

The three girls entered the cottage, and Jaslyn Wayward strode across the room with her head held high. *I must get something done today. I must save Alice.* She squeezed her hands into fists and attempted to calm her breathing, but it was all too much. Her eyes scanned the unrecognizable sea of faces that filled the room. *Knights.* Jaslyn examined their breastplates, her frown deepening. *Knights from almost every house in the Mountain*

Realm, but House Wayward.

"A lot of men," Violet whispered, her green eyes wide.

Evergreen buzzed her lips. "It doesn't matter. They are men with swords. Men who fight. Men we need."

Jaslyn agreed. *I'll take anyone who wishes to help me help the people.*

"My queen," Ser Lyon Millister began, grabbing her attention. "Thank you so much for coming today."

Not like I had a choice, she thought resentfully, kicking a chair's leg and sitting down roughly as her twin handmaidens stood behind her. Jaslyn studied the knights again. *These are the people Ser Lyon believes will help me, but can I trust them? How do I know when I do trust them? When did I start trusting Ser Lyon?* She thought back. *The moment I met him.* Jaslyn frowned at the realization. *Being that trusting can kill me.*

The weight of the situation pressed down on her, causing sweat beads to dot her hairline. "I would like to thank all highborn and customary knights for traveling to Queen's Cove," she started, nodding to the crowd.

"No need for the formalities," a knight said, startling Jaslyn.

She noticed the painting of the bear in a creek on his chest plate and frowned. *House Myster.* The old matriarch that lived in Crimson's Quarters did not support Jaslyn, so she didn't understand why a knight from that house would be at the meeting.

"Tell us your plans," another knight added in a huff.

Jaslyn bounced in the rickety chair. *Plans; what plans? I just want Alice to stay in Maryere.* She glanced at Ser Lyon's concerned face and decided to tell the knights what they wanted to hear. *I want to help the peasants. That is what a queen would do.* "Starting today, I want you to pick a peasant village to sponsor. Let me know, and I will name it and help smuggle goods from the closest city to the village."

"Won't doing that cause a shortage in the city?" a House Mason knight inquired, his eyebrows raised suspiciously.

She blushed. *I don't know.*

"We aren't taking away all the food. Just some so the villagers can eat," a different knight responded with a smile.

Jaslyn Wayward matched the knight's face. "That is correct. What is your name, ser?"

"Neeman, my lady."

"She is not a lady. She is a queen." Ser Lyon corrected.

Jaslyn waved at Ser Lyon's words. "It's fine." She looked at the man's breastplate and raised an eyebrow. *A bow?* "I'm sorry, I don't know the house you are aligned to."

"I'm with the Rangers," Ser Neeman smiled. "Although we are assassins, Lord Protector Aleister Wayward created a division of knights to protect the people from religious zealots."

The Rangers? Assassins? Religious zealots? Jaslyn had never heard of those things before. *Does my father know about this?* Her body tensed as questions raced through her head. She blinked at Ser Neeman, realizing there was a world out there that she didn't know. *The world is more complex than I ever imagined. Must I learn all of this to become queen?* Finally, she relaxed. *If it means ensuring Alice's safety, I'll know everything this horrible world has to show me.*

Jaslyn gave a false smile. "I was unaware that the Rangers supported me."

Ser Neeman's eyes widened, and he looked away. "I, uh, wouldn't say they support you, my lady."

"Jaslyn is a queen, not a lady," Ser Lyon repeated, and Jaslyn paused. *Ser Neeman is here to determine if the Rangers should support me.* She looked at each knight that stood in the room. *Are all of these knights here to do the same? Do I have the support of anyone?*

She frowned. "Well, after this conversation, I hope you will let the Rangers know I am worth the support." Ser Neeman nodded, disappearing into the crowd, and Jaslyn took a deep breath. *I must make this work.* "As I said before, whoever wants to support me should find a peasant village. I want to ensure no one starves this winter, which is quickly approaching." A few knights clapped at her declaration, and Jaslyn smiled. "I also want to help the peasants find a new profession. It should not be if their father is a farmer; they must be a farmer, too. They should be allowed to become whatever they want. I am going to create a Mountain Realm that supports that." More applause filled the air, and some of the knight's faces softened at Jaslyn's words. *Is it working?* "Finally, I want to get the support of the settlements throughout the Mountain Realm. I know they are treated as horribly as the peasant villages, and I want to ensure the settlement leaders know I can help them if needed."

Applause erupted, and Jaslyn beamed with pride. *I can become a good leader for the people.* "I think that is everything," she finished awkwardly.

"Wait," someone said, pushing through the crowd, and everything stopped. An ugly man with tiny eyes peered down at Jaslyn. "What about Lady Alice?"

She gulped. *Ser Lyon had told me I shouldn't talk about Alice during the meeting, only the peasants.* Her eyes flashed to the blackened hawk with a crown on his breastplate. *A lord knight? House Osmont?* She peered at the man suspiciously. "What about my sister?"

"Everyone seems upset about the betrothal. I came to the queen's meeting to see what she had to say about it."

A few knights narrowed their eyes, frowning, and Jaslyn held an excited smile. *Are these men ready to protect their queen?*

Evergreen lightly touched Jaslyn's shoulder and leaned over. "A fight at your first meeting wouldn't be a good omen for a new queen."

She nodded with a sigh, knowing her handmaiden was right. *I must navigate this situation to make everyone take my side.* She leaned back in the chair, her arms crossed. "Why would I tell a House Osmont lord knight that?"

"Aye, and why is a House Osmont lord knight here in the first place?" Another knight question, stepping forward. The knight grabbed his embellished hilt and stood straight. "I came to this meeting to see the new queen in person, but I am now interested in her mission." He turned to Jaslyn, dropped to a knee, and placed one hand over his chest. "My queen, my name is Ser Teimothe Payne, and I pledge my allegiance to you. Please allow me to serve you and care for the peasant villages around Fairpeak."

Jaslyn's golden eyes twinkled at the young knight. *Does Ser Teimothe speak truths? Is he the first person to pledge allegiance to me? Should I look to him for counsel?* She glanced at Ser Lyon Millister, who smiled proudly. *No, Lyon was the first person to pledge allegiance to me. He must always be by my side.*

"It would be an honor to have you care for the villages near Fairpeak, Ser Teimothe," she told the knight. "We can speak later about the villages' locations and population sizes." The knight nodded, and she turned to the crowd, "Does anyone else wish to,"

"Wait!" the Osmont lord knight shouted. "You never answered my question."

Jaslyn sat straight and threaded her fingers together, placing them on the table. "Apologies, ser, but you never answered my question." There was silence causing her to groan. "Fine, what is your name? Can you at least answer that?"

The knight shifted his feet. "My name is Ser Damien Clay, but you can call me Ser Knight like the rest of the lot does."

He opened up, Jaslyn observed happily. *But does he speak truths?* "Ser Knight? What kind of stupid name is that? Your mother named you Damien, and everyone loves their mother. So, I will call you by your name."

Ser Damien gave a small smile. "Aye, everyone loves their mother," he exhaled before repositioning his stance. "Look, I understand your hesitation in speaking to a lord knight of the man who is taking your sister, but you need to understand. Alice may be in danger. I don't know what Lord Protector Osmont will do, but Alice needs someone protecting her."

Jaslyn raised an eyebrow. "So, you came all this way to tell me that my sister needs a protector while in Kingment?"

Ser Damien thought on the question for a moment before nodding. "You need someone watching her. Perhaps the Ranger? Or someone else."

She grinned, rose to her feet, and pointed directly at the strange lord knight. "I, Jaslyn Wayward, proclaim that starting today, you, Ser Damien Clay, will be the lifelong protector of Lady Alice Wayward."

ALICE

News of the betrothal spread like wildfire. House Wayward gave no reason, and rumors of the *why* fluttered around Maryere like butterflies in the early summer moons. As more highborn learned of the sudden proposal, more arrived to the Mountain Realm's capital city, hoping to see the sickly Alice Wayward leave Maryere, never to return. Even the disappearance of the Lord Protector's wife didn't stop the eyes from staring down the young Wayward girl anytime she exited the Bloody Tower.

Alice could even feel them as she walked to the courtyard, where everyone waited to say their goodbyes. She kept her pace slow, no longer wanting to leave her home. *Although Mother said she didn't try to kill Falk's children, Father believed otherwise. This was the only way.* She clutched onto her necklace. *To save my family.*

Time, unfortunately, didn't stop—the snow had finally slowed, and Alice's health hadn't plummeted. It was as if the gods desired for her to live in Kingment. Alice, however, wanted otherwise. She wanted to create a connection with her siblings and learn how to rule under her parents' leadership. But she knew her wants were a fantasy. Her siblings had forgotten about her, and constant arguing kept her parents preoccupied.

Alice Wayward was never allowed to live the life she wanted. No one would let her. Not the gods, not her family, nothing.

A crowd of highborn gathered by the wheelhouses, all shouting over each other as they tried to reach the two Lord Protectors. Lord Falk strutted around the courtyard like a peacock, laughing loudly and making everything about him. Melancholy, however, draped Lord Borin, weighing him down to an early grave.

The scene was chaotic, but silence filled the air when everyone noticed Alice. Her breath hitched at the attention, and she stepped closer, allowing everyone to return to the madness.

An ancient-looking man waddled toward her, and Alice smiled bravely. *I will get through this,* she told herself confidently.

"Hello, Lady Alice," the man started. "I'm Lord Jasper."

She noticed the onyx double battle axe, positioned to look like an X and decorated with purple and green jewels, pinned onto the man's doublet. *House Payne. What would he want from me?* "Hello, my lord. It is nice to meet you."

The old man's face shifted to concern. "How have you been feeling?"

Does it matter? Alice pressed her lips together, annoyed with the question. "Better as of late."

The Lord of the Fairpeak hummed, looking her up and down. "I will pray for a safe journey."

"Thank you so much, Lord Jasper," Alice bowed before stepping away.

She barely moved before another person called her name. A tall, burly woman approached, her smile kind. "You are more beautiful than described," the woman observed, repositioning her headband decorated with a merman crest. *Lady Hearthra Seamann*, Alice recognized. *One of only a few women who rule in the Mountain Realm.* Lady Hearthra grabbed Alice's hand and slipped her a small coin. "This is a kismet coin," she informed, grinning. "It's said to bring luck and solace. Keep it close."

Alice studied the snowflake imprinted in the metal. "Thank you," she exhaled, slipping the coin into her sleeve pocket.

The Lady of Accrid patted Alice on the shoulder comfortingly and then left without another word. *I wish I could have met all these people before I was forced to leave home forever. Maybe I could've entered into politics*, she dreamed. *The highborn here seem like reasonable people.*

Alice made her way to her wheelhouse before running into Myra. "Are you okay?" her handmaiden asked, her hands filled with bags.

She nodded and gave the girl the coin. "Put this with my things, please. I'm going to say goodbye to my family."

When Myra walked away, Alice stood motionless, again taking in the scene. *Is this how it usually is? Is this what I've been missing all this time?* Tears burned her eyes as the questions swirled in her head. *Why did I have to be so sickly? And why did I recover just to be sent away to Kingment?*

"My lady," a sultry voice called, and Alice narrowed her attention to a beautiful woman.

House Tudor, Alice recognized, taking in the woman's blue and brown eyes. "Hello, Lady Wyrra."

The woman's strange eyes widened. "Lady Alice knows my name? I feel blessed."

She blushed. "I had a lot of time to study. House Tudor was always interesting to me."

"Well, maybe you could visit one day," Lady Wyrra winked.

Alice looked away. "I will be far away in Kingment."

The Lady of Shadow's Peak gave a knowing smile. "Hm, maybe not, I believe." Wyrra Tudor then walked away before Alice could process the woman's words.

Maybe not, she repeated. *Is Lady Wyrra planning something?* She peered at the fascinating woman who had started conversing with Lady Hearthra. *Are they working together? Does my father know?*

An icy wind blew, and Alice hugged herself to stay warm. *When will I feel the cold again?* she wondered, taking slow steps to where Josef, Jaslyn, and her father stood.

"Alice!" Josef cheered, hopping from one foot to the other. "Alice, Ali," he paused, his smile fading. "Father, I thought you said Alice felt better," he said, looking up at Lord Borin. The Lord Protector looked at his three children before turning his attention to something else, not answering. Josef then rushed up to Alice, grabbing her hands. "If you don't feel good, go back inside! They cannot force you to leave! You must get rest."

She smiled at her little brother as tears streamed down her cheeks. "Thank you, but I cannot. I must leave."

"Why?"

Josef deserves the truth. Alice leaned in close. "It's the only way I can keep Mother safe. Lord Falk wants to execute her."

The boy gasped. "What do,"

Alice grabbed her brother's arm, gripping it hard to silence him. "She wanted revenge, and he found out. This was the only way." She then looked into her brother's copper eyes and patted his soft, curly hair. "Do you understand now?"

"It's not fair," he pouted.

She gave him a sad smile. "Aye, life isn't fair." She hugged her brother tightly, unable to remember the last time she had embraced him. "I will miss you."

Josef pulled away, his face wet with tears. "I will bring you back home!" he cried, grabbing everyone's attention.

Alice's heart dropped as she scanned her surroundings, noticing some in the crowd nodding at the boy's declaration. *Wait, do others feel the same?* Josef stomped off, kicking around the snow with every step until he reached Winter's Keep. *Maybe I shouldn't have told him.* Alice sighed, picking at her fingernails. *I don't know what is best.*

"He would have learned the truth anyways," Jaslyn informed as if she could read Alice's mind. "Don't worry about it."

"So, you know?"

The girl gave a grin. "Aye, they say a hawk bit a bear, but I believe some *ass* tripped a scaredy cat," she answered loudly.

"Jaslyn, enough," Lord Borin scolded before stepping away.

Jaslyn Wayward rolled her golden eyes and folded her arms. "I've got some stuff working and moving, so just stay calm and healthy."

"What do you mean?"

Her little sister got closer, almost touching Alice's nose. "I've recently gained a title that may change how everything works around here," she replied mysteriously, but Alice blinked back, confused. The short girl hugged Alice tightly as if she were the older sibling. "The peasants are revolting," Jaslyn whispered, barely audible. "They named me queen. I've got some knights. They will be watching and keeping you safe. So just endure until I can bring you home."

Alice stepped away from her little sister, her mouth agape. *Jaslyn is a queen. Jaslyn will lead a revolt against…* Her attention flickered to her father, who now spoke with Lord Falk, their conversation serious. *Is that alright?* Her mother's despondent face appeared in her mind, conflicting her feelings. She leaned toward her sister. "Promise me you will keep our family together when you take charge."

Jaslyn gave her a bright smile. "I'll try!"

The sisters then kissed each other on the cheek. "I love you," they told each other, both sobbing.

"Alright, enough with the love fest," Falk interrupted as he approached with Lord Borin behind him. "I want to leave before sunset."

"Then, you should have picked an earlier time to depart," Borin replied, his voice cold. "This is the last time they will see each other. Allow them to talk."

Falk gave an uncomfortable smile. "Well, let's get going in the next few minutes, okay Alice?"

She nodded and bowed toward her father. "I hope to make you proud and bring honor onto House Wayward."

Borin pulled her close and embraced her, forgetting his strength. "My dearest child, I haven't been the best father. I can do nothing when times get tough. I'm a coward." He paused, taking a deep breath. "Did you know that the day you were born was chaotic—just as the day of your departure?"

She lifted her head, suffocating in her father's thick beard. "You make it sound as if I'm dying," she attempted to joke.

Her father's face, however, only grew more serious. "If anything ever happens, write to me," he instructed. "Something doesn't feel right. Your mother did *something* to Falk, but she didn't threaten the lives of his children. Falk cannot give me any evidence other than his word."

"His words are shit," Alice whispered.

Borin smiled, his cheeks turning pink. "Aye, and if he treats you wrong, make sure to stick those false words right back up his ass." The two hugged again, and Alice realized how peaceful she felt in her father's arms. *I wish I could have had more of these hugs.* The tears returned. "I love you, Father. Please, keep everyone safe and remember what I asked."

"Of course, sweet girl." He kissed her forehead before giving her the saddest smile she had ever seen. "Better go to your wheelhouse before Falk says something that makes me snap."

Alice gave a small chuckle. "Yes, Father." She stepped away and began her journey toward her wheelhouse. She paused and turned around, taking in her sight of her family one last time. Her father and Jaslyn waved, both crying. Alice waved back, crying harder.

"The party is departing now," A driver called out, and horses began whinnying loudly.

Myra approached Alice and led her to the wheelhouse.

As she stepped in, the weeping from the crowd echoed around her, breaking her heart. She sat on her cushioned chair, and Myra sat beside

Alice. A knight walked awkwardly to the wheelhouse, shutting and locking the door.

The wheelhouse began moving, and Alice scooted to the window. She waved goodbye to the crowds, her family, her tower, her city, and her childhood. She waved goodbye to her happiness.

The large party of wagons and wheelhouses ventured south on the Golden Road. In a few days' ride, she would no longer be in the Mountain Realm but in a foreign place. Alice stared out the window until she could no longer see Maryere's high stone walls.

"I'm afraid," Myra whispered an hour into the journey as the wheelhouse swayed from side to side. "I've heard whispers that Falk went to see your lady mother one last time, and she attacked him again. He's been hiding it, but he's furious. I hope he doesn't take his anger out on you."

Alice blinked back at her best friend, confused. "Why would he,"

The wheelhouse halted to a stop.

Both of their eyes widened, and Alice jumped to her feet. She walked to the wheelhouse door and knocked. "Why have we stopped?" she asked frantically.

The door swung open, and Falk stepped inside—his face crazed. "Handmaiden, get out," he said, and before Myra could react, he threw her out of the carriage.

"MYRA!" Alice sobbed hysterically as Falk slammed the door shut, and the wheelhouse jerked forward. "Why would you do that to her?"

Falk slapped her so hard she fell onto her bed, "Shut up, you whore!" he yelled. "You need to be more worried about yourself!"

Alice Wayward cried, groaned, and panted for air, her face stinging.

"I said shut up!" Falk yelled again, grabbing her hair and dragging her. Alice slammed onto the floor, her hip and elbow throbbing from the fall. He kicked her in the stomach, and Alice wailed, gasping for more air. "Didn't I say to be quiet?" he asked, squeezing her cheeks before slapping her again. Another bellow echoed out of her as she crashed to the floor again, wishing the gods would kill her. "Now, if you scream out again," her uncle said crazily, "I'm really going to hurt you."

Alice looked up at him and pressed her lips together hard, preventing any noise from coming out of her mouth. *I'm no longer a child. I must protect myself.*

"Good girl," Lord Falk grinned, then kicked her directly in the shoulder.

Alice fell back and bashed her head onto the wooden corner of the seats. She tried her best to keep quiet, but the pain overwhelmed her, and she cried out loudly. *Falk will strike me whether I listen or not.* Her punishment was not for screaming but for being Lady Gloriana Wayward's daughter. Blood poured from her busted nose, and the wounds on her cheek and forehead stung terribly. Her hair was matted, and her eyes and lips swelled. *I am going to die.*

"Now, you must be a good girl from now on, okay?" Falk questioned, and Alice nodded rapidly, giving her an instant headache. The Lord Protector frowned and kicked her again in the stomach. "I expect courtesies."

"Yes, my lord," she struggled as blood dripped from her mouth.

"Good girl," he said again, smiling wide.

I am not your dog, Alice thought defiantly as she slowly stood up and tried to keep her balance on the swaying wheelhouse. She looked at her lord uncle with eyes that could kill, but the darkness in Lord Falk's eyes frightened her more than the beating.

He pulled her close and yanked off her necklace, throwing it. "You're always wearing this stupid thing, clutching it like some scared little girl. Don't you know that rubies always bring violence? Why clutch onto something like that?"

Alice's vision narrowed on the broken necklace. "It's a quartz crystal."

The slap Lord Falk responded with reminded Alice of her reality. "I don't like that tone. Sounds too much like your mother, and we don't want that, do we?"

The venom in Falk's voice melted all of Alice's defiance, and fear poured in. "No, my lord," she answered quietly.

"Good girl," he said again, patting her on the head, "You are so well-behaved. I expected much less, but you have proven me wrong, little Alice." He touched her matted hair gently, and she grunted in pain. "Did you know I lied about your mother's plans to murder my children?"

I'm sure of it, she wanted to respond, but she didn't want to be hit again. "Yes, my lord."

"Still, your mother committed grave treason," he continued. "Do you want to know what she really did?"

Her eyes stayed low. "No, my lord." *The truth doesn't matter now.*

Falk's wicked smile widened. "Well, let me tell you anyway. I fucked her so good she gave me you as my prize."

Alice spat in the Lord Protector's face in retaliation and gave a bloody grin. She was tired of her lord uncle's words and wanted him gone immediately. *If that means he hits me instead of conversing with me, then so be it.*

For a moment, the two stared at each other, her ice-blue eyes on his emerald-green ones. Lord Falk inhaled sharply through his nose and struck Alice, causing her to land on the featherbed. "You've tested me," he said, standing over her, panting. "To get the current situation through your pretty little head, I will punish you with how I pleasured your mother." He grabbed her ankles and pulled her closer, spreading her legs open.

No, she thought as Falk caressed her thighs, licking his lips. *No!* This wasn't what she wanted. She wanted to protect her family, not become a prisoner. *I never get what I want, I understand that now, but I must do something. I must be brave.* For her father, her mother, Josef, Jaslyn, and Myra. Nobody was going to come and save her. *I must be my own hero.*

A roar erupted from Alice Wayward, and she fought back.

She kicked, thrashed, scratched, and punched, but her uncle was too strong. He pulled her body closer to his and kissed her neck. "No!" She screamed. "Stop!"

I am no longer a child. She headbutted him, scratched him, and ripped out his hair. *I must protect myself.* She noticed a scar that looked like teeth on his shoulder and viciously bit him in the same place. She would fight for her purity. She would fight for her family. She would fight for her life. *I will fight until Falk's dead!*

EXODUS

Part 2

GLORIANA

Gloriana Wayward sat on the floor with her knees tucked under her chin. *This is all my fault.* She had wanted to be smarter; to be better. *I wanted to have a hold over Falk.* The tears returned. *Because of that, my family is falling apart.*

From the moment Gloriana pulled a knife to stab Falk, Borin had locked her away in her bedchamber. *At least I'm not in an unkown dungeon like I would've been in Kingment.* Her lord husband didn't believe that scheming Falk Osmont, but he didn't believe Gloriana either. *What am I going to do?*

Trumpets blared, and her attention snapped to the window, her heartbeat quickening. *No, Alice's departure couldn't be today.* Gloriana knew Borin would release her to say goodbye to their eldest daughter. *Right?*

Cheers overlapped the music, and her body turned cold. *He didn't.*

Gloriana's arms and legs jeered chaotically as she scrambled to her feet and rushed to the window. "No," she exhaled, taking in the snowy sight of the mountain people waving goodbye to the Osmont party. "No, NO!"

She dropped to the floor, her face twisted with grief. *Why would Borin do that!?* Her husband appeared in her mind, standing there, doing nothing. *He's afraid.* She gritted her teeth at the realization, her body boiling with rage. "COWARD!" she screamed, climbing back to her feet.

Outside the window, the party traveled farther away, and the crowd had begun to dissipate. "NO!" she continued at the top of her lungs while banging on the window, hoping everyone heard. "No! Bring her back, you coward! Bring our daughter back!"

Gloriana turned away from the window and flipped a table over. *Why is Borin like this?* She couldn't take it; it was all too much. A beautiful Summeran flower vase was the next victim of her rage. In one swift motion, Gloriana grabbed the vase and smashed it, causing water to splash on her legs. The water brought Gloriana a coldness to her skin that matched her heart. *I can't do this! I can't go on!* She kicked the scattered flowers, scuffing her toes.

Again, she fell to the stone floor, and finally, her screaming ceased. *What's the point?* She was the cause of her family's destruction, and the gods were punishing her. *I barely spent time with Alice. I could've at least stayed by her side as she suffered while asleep.* Gloriana reflected on the hours she wasted shopping for anything that could remind her of home. Her vision narrowed on the broken vase, and everything felt numb. *I never thought about her or any of my children, only myself. I am a selfish woman, and a terrible mother.*

Gloriana Wayward cried on the floor, her head pounding.

She closed her eyes and pictured the day she left her childhood home. The warm summer moon tingled her skin as waves crashed in the distance, and the fragrant smell of Summeran spices swirled around Gloriana Thoren as she said goodbye to Goldspire. Her father, mother, and siblings stood at the docks, speaking with Ser Rodrick Wayward as servants loaded her things on the ship. *I never saw my family again.*

Terror morphed her family's pleasant faces as the multi-colored morning sky turned black. Her brothers screamed in agony, and blood splattered throughout her consciousness. *These aren't my memories. It's the reports I read when Lord Robart told me the dreaded news.* Then, her little sister, Alice, appeared, her face fierce and determined. The young girl fought back, taking down several Osmont knights, but soon, they overwhelmed her, too, and her face turned ghostly. *Just like the Seers described.*

Gloriana forced herself out of the nightmare, unable to take it. *I named Alice after my little sister, hoping she would be like her.* Instead, Gloriana's daughter was meek, sickly, and powerless. *I should have named Alice after a Wayward like I did for Jaslyn. Maybe then Alice would've flourished.*

She sat up. *Everything is always my fault.*

A light knock came to her door, but she didn't answer. *What's the point?* She pushed her hands through her tangled hair, trying to stay sane. *Didn't Falk say Victoria had gone mad? Could the same be happening to me?*

The door opened, and the kind knight smiled, entering her bedchamber. "You're released, my lady," he informed, holding his hand for Gloriana to grab. "The Lord Protector would like to see you in his study."

She wanted to vomit. "What is your name?"

"Ser Bradberry, my lady."

Borin is more than a coward. Having one of your lord knights release me instead of doing it yourself—pathetic. Gloriana's eyes narrowed as she examined Ser Bradberry. *He is different from the other lord knights. Perhaps he could be more helpful to me than just killing that fat dumb knight.* Gloriana grabbed the man's hand and stood. "Ser Bradberry, please tell my lovely husband to kiss my ass."

"I can't, my lady," he chuckled. "I will tell him you weren't interested." Ser Bradberry bowed and left the bedchamber, keeping her door unlocked.

Alone, Gloriana clutched her stomach and dry heaved. She hated the nothingness that engulfed her. *What do I want?* She stood straight. *I want Alice home, but how can I do that?* She grinned deviously. *By becoming the next Lord Protector.*

Gloriana slipped on a casual black dress with long sleeves, and the collar stopped at her chin. *Today, I'm in mourning.* Her usually long flowy hair was tied tightly into a bun and her shoes were flat and simple.

I will uncover the knowledge that will pave my way to ruling the Mountain Realm. Gloriana strode out of Winter's Keep, her gaze fixed on the Grand Library. She avoided the prying eyes and ascended the steps to the Lord Protector's loft, where she had first seen Lord Falk, and her life turned to shit.

Gloriana scanned the bookshelves, trying to figure out where she should start. She pulled a book on the laws of the Mountain Realm and another on Queen Rayleen Wayward. *One is to see if I can come into power; the other is to learn more about the most famed leader of the Snowlands and even the Mountain Realm.*

Gloriana sat farthest away from the eyes and opened the first book.

Lord Robart mentioned that his father had written a law that changed who could rule, Gloriana tried to remember, slightly annoyed she had to think about her early years in Maryere. She flipped to the back on the book and scanned through until she found it.

The section was short but told Gloriana everything she needed to know.

Although it was customary for the firstborn son to inherit the title, Lord Protector Crimson Wayward broke the standard, causing the Third Holy War. After the war, the thought of another woman holding the title of Lord Protector seemed implausible. That was until Lord Protector Emeis Wayward demanded that his eldest daughter, Rayne Wayward, become his heir. This declaration, however, scorned his second wife, Lady Cruelle Wayward, who had just given birth to their first child, Robart. The highborn were also not pleased, citing the Third Holy War. Lord Emeis signed the First Son Clause to appease, where the firstborn son, instead of the first child, would become heir to the Lord Protector's title after Rayne Wayward's death. Lady Rayne, however, died giving birth to her fourth child and first son, never becoming Lord Protector. With Lady Rayne leaving behind three daughters, the title was passed to Robart—continuing the succession as we know it.

Gloriana's fingernails dug into the soft book cover. *It's against the law?!* She had known that the tradition in Mystos was to give the title to the first son, but she had never imagined that the Mountain Realm would outright ban women from ruling. *No wonder Borin looked at me as if I was insane when I suggested that Jaslyn become the heir because Alice was too sick. It would never go to them, but what if Josef had never been born? What then?*

Imagine when we have our boy; Borin's young, cheery voice echoed in Gloriana's head, causing her to freeze. *I hope he's big and strong like a Wayward is supposed to be.*

The pain Gloriana endured while being alone after Alice's birth swirled in her chest. *He didn't touch me for years. Then, I gave birth to another girl.* Borin's sad copper eyes flickered into her son's. *And he wanted anything but that.*

Violent nights from ten years ago filled Gloriana's head. She had begged to be left alone, but her lord husband refused. *We can't let time slip away,* he had told her.

And then, she gave birth to Josef less than a year after Jaslyn.

Tingles vibrated through Gloriana, and her stomach churned. She covered her mouth, not wanting to vomit, but the bile still crept into her throat. *Why did I never put it together? I'm so oblivious.* Memories of Borin cooing over a three-day-old Josef as Gloriana laid in pain, still breastfeeding Jaslyn, poured into her brain. Her head lowered, and she felt ashamed. *Borin never learned to love me. I should've known better. I'm just a womb who held his children.*

Gloriana opened the other book, no longer wanting to think. *Most tales of Queen Rayleen Wayward were fantastical and heroic. As the last Wayward to survive the Plague of the Arts, she lived a life of freedom, inspiring the common people. Queen Rayleen could captivate any man but her decision to remain unmarried while legitimizing her four children angered many. The queen ruthlessly crushed any opposition, even eradicating House River, her mother's family, for planning a coup. Although Rayleen's life spanned over a century, the beloved queen never stayed idle, even after retiring.*

Every aspect of Queen Rayleen Wayward's long, illustrious life stirred something deep within Gloriana. *I want to be as formidable and revered as she was.*

"Ah, Lady Wayward, so you were here," Lady Taylia Fletcher said slyly as if she were someone of importance.

Gloriana lifted her attention to the herd of women. *What are they doing here?* The frown that stretched across her face ached as her eyes were met with cold, muddy brown ones—the eyes of Joan Myster.

Lady Joan of Bear's Creek was the matriarch of House Myster, one of the oldest and wealthiest houses in the Mountain Realm. At the tired age of sixty-five, the old woman believed *she* was always right. The old woman matched Gloriana's frown, and her numerous wrinkles frowned too.

Gloriana had heard that Lady Myster was once lovely and cunning, but she never knew that woman. She only knew Joan, the old hag who insulted her, along with Lady Fallen Wayward. Gloriana had tried to stay away from Lady Joan after Fallen's death and had been generally successful. *What does she want now?*

Joan interlaced her fingers, and her frown morphed into a smile, bringing terror into Gloriana's heart. She opened her mouth to speak.

"Aye, I'm surprised that the Lord Protector didn't have you locked up in the cells for ruining the harvest dinner," Lady Allaric Cantree scoffed.

"It wasn't a harvest dinner, now stay quiet," Lady Haylise Hayward scolded.

Taylia, Allaric, Haylise. She studied each woman. *All bear their name from famous Wayward women.* A ting of jealousy struck Gloriana. *My name isn't like that. There were never any famous Glorianas.*

She felt her mother's ghostly presence. *Being named after a flower is prettier than being named after a long-dead person.* Remembering her mother's soothing voice brought a strange warmth to Gloriana's heart, melting the annoyance the flock had brought.

Her attention flickered to the other two women who stood slightly away from the rest of Joan's group, with their heads low, never meeting her eyes. *That's Lady Hearthra,* Gloriana recognized, observing the silver mermen that littered the neckline of Lady Hearthra's gown. The mountain woman lifted her eyes then, and Gloriana gave a small smile, causing Hearthra's eyes to dart back to the floor. *So that must be Lady Tamra Ward,* she deducted, taking in the trembling woman who clearly didn't want to be there.

Lady Joan moved closer to Gloriana. "Covering up does not fix," the old woman said cryptically. "Was it a bear or a hawk?" Without warning, the old woman pulled back Gloriana's sleeve, revealing five small scars curved like fingernails. *Falk.* Joan humphed and released the clothing, unimpressed. "In a moon, come to the Row of Lords alone," Lady Myster commanded, already walking away. "The highborn are gathering and have something to say that might please your unpleasable soul."

JARIN

U sually, Jarin stood behind his favorite chair, and waited patiently for the maids and servants to finish setting the dining table to his liking. Today, Jarin leaned awkwardly on the cresting rail of his chair, grunting, moaning, and complaining to the maids and servants to hurry up. His joints had ached non-stop for days now, constantly burning, throbbing, and keeping him up at night.

"The spoon, dear." Jarin pointed at the large silver spoon, and his command frightened the serving girl. She looked up at him and her lips quivered. "The spoon is crooked," he tried to say politely, but his voice was rough and full of pain. The girl looked down at the spoon and nodded, fixing her mistake. She looked back up at Jarin and slightly smiled, before curtsying and hurrying out of the room.

Jarin placed his tired, hurting hands on the long wooden dining table. He had hated the table since he was a young boy, always wanting to throw it into a fire pit. The dining hall table, however, was made from the hands of King Saline Ayers, centuries ago. He wouldn't dare move the handmade piece of furniture from its place.

Slowly, he walked to where King Saline's initials were carved into the aged wood. Jarin moved his swollen fingers over the divots, feeling the letters S, A, and I. *King Saline Ayers of Waterbrook, first of his name,* Jarin thought, feeling the tabletop. *And there would not be another king like him.*

Jarin regretted naming his sons House Osmont names to please his unpleasant lady wife. *My sons should have been named after my brother, or my grandfather, or my grandfather's lord father.* But not his own lord father, no. Jarin would make sure until the day he died that no child bore his father's name. *They don't deserve that pain.*

"Is the dining table set to your liking, my lord?"

Jarin's eyes snapped to the setup. *A few mistakes,* he critiqued, but his throbbing ankles, elbows, and fingers caused him to ignore everything. "Perfect," Jarin lied. *I'm going right back to my old ways.* He groaned before glancing around, seeing no food. "What will be served this evening?"

"Lentil soup with hard bread, the braised belly of a pig, smoked cod, and quail, with a side dish of roasted cabbage and carrots," an old servant informed. "As well as wine and ale to drink it all down with, and sweet bread with blueberry flavored cream for dessert."

"It all sounds wonderful and warm on this cold evening," Jarin responded with a forced smile. He fell into his favorite chair, and the feathered cushions gave ease on his pulsing hips. His ankles, knees, neck, and elbows felt relieved from the pain. All but his fingers which never stopped aching.

Lines of maids and servants entered the dining hall and set dishes on the long table. They placed the food around Jarin and put a hot bowl of lentil soup right in front of him to begin his meal. Jarin sat awkwardly as the servants sat more bowls, platters, and plates on the table. It was enough food to feed twenty hungry men, yet Jarin was the only one there.

Finally, the maids and servants finished, and each one stood against the wall with their hands behind their back, waiting for the Lord Protector of the Riverlands to call for them.

Jarin stared at his bowl of lentil soup and offered a brief prayer to the gods, as he always did before he ate. Last night had been the first autumn snow, an *early* one. Although it melted as it touched the ground, it was snow nonetheless. Usually, Jarin would have panicked, knowing that his people would suffer and die during the long approaching winter. But this time, he didn't. He had worked tirelessly with Hamlin and prepared the citizens of Waterbrook for this year's colder seasons. Everyone, even the peasants, had enough food and firewood to last them through the winter. *Bless the people so that no one will suffer,* he prayed. *Please bless them so the people will praise my name.*

When Jarin opened his eyes, his most trusted lord knight, Ser Bronston Hedge, stood quietly beside him. "Yes?" Jarin inquired.

"A letter has been received that you need to see," the knight informed, his voice low.

Jarin sighed heavily and lifted his hand. Ser Bronston pulled the letter from behind his back and gave it to Jarin before bowing and walking out of the dining hall.

The Lord Protector examined a moon and sun pressed into the black seal, unbroken. *It's a letter from House Ashmire, or I mean House Thoren.* Jarin broke the seal and read the letter. His eyes skimmed over the words as his smile grew bigger. *They want Terryn to marry one of their daughters.*

"Call for my sons!" Jarin yelled suddenly, his body rushing with excitement, "Tell them to have dinner with me!" He rolled the letter back up and placed it in the inside pocket of his vest. *Finally, things are falling into place.*

When his sons arrived, Jarin had eaten most of the hard bread and finished his lentil soup. Both Terryn and Dain were the age of seventeen, and many mistook them as twins. But the two boys were so different.

Terryn strolled into the room with swagger, mirroring Jarin's older brother, Domeric. His sunkissed skin, big brown eyes, and long, curly, black hair made him the perfect representation of House Ayers. Only his strong jaw mimicked House Osmont.

Dain, however, looked nothing like a member of House Ayers. Dimia had always fawned over how much the boy looked like her brother, Falk. And that's all Jarin saw too—an Osmont. Light freckles dotted Dain's pale skin, and his fiery red hair was short and barely had a curl. Sparkling emeralds glimmered in his tiny eyes, and his long, thin nose upturned to the sky. He was scrawny but his chiseled jaw was what made him handsome. Just like every Osmont.

"My sons," Jarin cooed, "Come, sit, and eat dinner with your lord father."

Terryn sat beside Jarin, but Dain hesitated. He walked to the other side of the table, sat right in front of Jarin, and gave a soft smile. "Father, you look tired," Dain began. "We lost track of time and didn't know it was dinner, we're sorry."

"What were you doing?"

Dain glanced at Terryn warily. "We were reading about battles," Dain explained, "in the library the University has started building."

The University is building a library in Waterbrook? Why didn't I know about this? Jarin kept his face emotionless and turned his attention to Terryn, and his eldest son nodded in agreeance. Jarin smiled back politely. *The University might be building a library, but that is not where they were at.*

"It is alright," he told his sons. "Go on, eat."

Terryn studied the plates of food on the table and picked up a quail leg. Dain only slurped his soup, slowly and quietly, staring at his father.

"I received a letter today," Jarin began. "House Thoren of the Black Hills has accepted the request to wed their eldest daughter, Lady Kaylien Thoren to House Ayers." He turned back to his eldest son who was unaware that Jarin was talking to him.

Their eyes met, and Terryn spit out his food. "You mean me?" he blurted, and Jarin nodded. "Father, you can't mean me. I don't want to wed this girl."

"You haven't even met her. What if you lay eyes on her and she is the most beautiful woman you have seen?"

"I already met that woman!" Terryn whined.

"Who?"

"Sophie," Dain chuckled.

Terryn gasped. "Dain!"

Jarin's eyes narrowed. "I don't know a Sophie."

"Of course, you don't!" Terryn shouted. "She's outside the castle. Somewhere you never travel."

The words struck Jarin in the chest. *I'm trying to do better. It is hard,* he wanted to confess. *The world is evil and there is so much we don't know. Wouldn't it be better to stay inside the Water Castle where it is safe?*

"She is the baker's daughter who comes and delivers goods to the castle in the mornings," Dain described, continuing the conversation.

"And what do you want from this girl?"

Terryn shrugged. "I don't know. I haven't spoken to her, yet," he replied, causing Jarin to stiffen. "I just see her lovely face, and I forget how to speak." Dain giggled and Terryn's eyes darted to his brother's. "Shut up!" he yelled, but Dain kept laughing.

"You did not expect to marry this baker's daughter, did you?" Jarin questioned, still puzzled at his son's intentions.

"Her name is Sophie!" Terryn snapped back, but then sighed, frustrated, "I don't know." he confessed. "I just want to talk to her and see if she feels the same way about me as I feel for her. And then maybe, if she does, maybe I would ask you for your blessing."

Jarin burst into laughter right along with Dain. "Thank you, my son. Thank you for making me laugh on one of my most exhausting days." Terryn only stared back, silent, causing Jarin to sit straight. "Now, no more japes. You will meet this Thoren girl, and you will marry her. I don't care if you like her or not, Terryn. I don't care if she is the ugliest woman you have ever seen. I don't care if she smells worse than the cows. You will marry her. You are at the age of seventeen now. You are a man grown. You should have a wife already. Maybe even a son, or at least a son coming. This is the first time anyone has responded to my request for a betrothal. You are going to marry her. We will make an alliance with the Summerlands, so we can trade with them, and so that they will defend us if another house gives us trouble, and us the same to them. We need this Terryn, and you will not take that away from the Riverlands just for some baker's daughter."

Terryn's eyes watered. "Mother will never approve of this," he said through his teeth.

"Your mother is not the Lord Protector of the Riverlands," Jarin reminded, "She doesn't have a say in these matters."

"Besides, Mother still hasn't awakened. The Saavant said she may never wake up, so she would never know," Dain added, spooning carrots into his mouth.

Jarin looked at his youngest son, "The Saavant said that?"

"Aye, you haven't spoken to them yet?"

"Father hasn't even gone to see Mother yet," Terryn answered angrily.

Jarin's head raced. *There is a chance Dimia would never wake up again. There is a chance that she could die.* Jarin's heart hammered in his chest, and his lips twitched. He had thought he wanted his lady wife dead, but now he wasn't too sure. She had caused him so much pain. He wanted to tell her how much she hurt him; and how much he had loved her.

"The girl is coming within the new moon, and you will treat her kindly," Jarin informed Terryn, and the boy's frown deepened. "Now, excuse me. I think I'll go to bed early," he told his sons, standing up awkwardly. His hips, knees, and ankles ached as he stood, and he made a face of discomfort, grunting in pain.

"Father, are you alright?" Dain asked worriedly.

Jarin grunted again as he pushed his chair back, "I'm fine, just tired."

"But you are moving like an old man."

"I promise, I am fine."

Dain grabbed Jarin's elbow and felt the fevered heat that radiated from it. The boy's eyes grew wide, "No you aren't," he confirmed, his tone serious. "Terryn come help."

Terryn stood, grabbing Jarin's other arm. "Father, what is wrong? Are you sick, too?"

"Shh," Jarin replied, trying to calm his sons. "I don't know, but I will be fine."

"I'm going to get Hamlin," Dain informed. "He will know what to do."

"No," Jarin said sternly. "Hamlin will insist on getting a Saavant or a priest to look at my body."

"Why do you not want that, Father?"

"Because, they are part of the Establishments. They sell your secrets to others. I don't want the other highborn knowing that there is something wrong with me, when your mother is sick, and both of you are unwed," Jarin whispered.

"It could cause a war," Dain gasped.

Terryn nodded understandingly. "Alright, Father. I will meet this girl, I will love her, and I will marry her."

"I never said you had to love her," Jarin replied, regretfully. *I want Terryn to live happily and not suffer through a loveless marriage, like the one I am in.* He pressed on a smile. "But it would be nice if you did. So, try to."

"Of course, Father," Terryn responded somberly.

"Please, help me to the Black Towers. I wish to see your mother."

"That is unwise," Dain warned. "You have not seen Mother in a long time. You will not like what you see."

Jarin wanted to scream. His entire body burned as he realized that his wife was the monster in his dreams from moons ago. *The gods warned me, and now I must face reality.* He took a deep breath. "I want to see her anyway."

Terryn and Dain slowly helped Jarin to the Black Towers. His sons' were strong, and struggled less than he imagined. *They are not my little boys anymore.*

When they reached the top of the stairs of the Black Towers, Dain knocked on the door, and an old Saavant opened it. His sons let go of Jarin when they saw that her eyes were black. *A Seer.* "My lord," the old woman said, "please come in."

Jarin walked into the bedchamber as if there was nothing wrong with him. He made his way to a chair, sat down, and sighed, holding back a wail.

Terryn walked over to Dimia, bent down by her bed, and prayed. Dain stayed by the door, his gloomy eyes on his sleeping mother. Jarin narrowed his vision on Dain, refusing to look at his wife. When Terryn finished with his prayer, he walked back to Dain and his sons silently bowed and left the room.

The Saavant closed the door, "I told that boy to not get close," she complained, smacking her teeth.

"Why?" Jarin asked. "Is it contagious?"

"Contagious?" The woman laughed. "My lord, Lady Ayers has deathskin." The confirmation caused his stomach to churn. "You turned pale, my lord," the Saavant added worriedly, and Jarin tried his best to act as if everything was fine. "I am glad you have come to see her. She needs her lord husband here, maybe then she will wake up."

Maybe I should leave, Jarin thought cruelly, keeping his eyes on the Saavant.

The old woman frowned, "You haven't looked at her, my lord. How she looks now will never go away. You need to accept that. This is deathskin we are talking about, there is no cure."

"I don't know what I can accept," he replied truthfully.

The Saavant sighed. "Fine. Then I will leave you here with her. You can look at her when you finally have the courage. I will be back in the morning to check on her. Don't touch her." The old woman grabbed her burlap sack of belongings and left the bedchamber, leaving Jarin and Dimia alone.

"I am afraid," Jarin exhaled, looking at nothing. Tears filled his eyes as he quickly glanced at Dimia. *No.* His eyes settled on her as the tears streamed down his face. *That's not Dimia. It cannot be Dimia.*

A sickly greenish color now tinted her skin, and large red wounds spotted her everywhere. Medicated sab covered her arms and legs, but still some of the wounds seeped pus onto her bed. Each ragged breath she took seemed painful, as if there was something in her chest she needed to cough out, but couldn't. All of Dimia's long red hair was gone, and her scalp had large risen blisters.

She is ugly. Dimia has never been ugly.

Jarin sat silently for hours watching his wife sleep. Pity tugged at him as she struggled right in front of him. Struggling to breath, to sleep, to live, and there was nothing Jarin could do to help her.

"Jarin," a voice whimpered. "Jarin wake up."

He awoke, grunting in pain and listening to the sound of his joints popping. *I fell asleep?* He opened his eyes and two sunken blue ones stared back.

Jarin screamed in terror.

"Shh!" Dimia hushed, grabbing for him, but Jarin stood and moved away before she could. "Darling, why am I here?"

"You are sick."

"I can tell. I keep coughing."

"No, you are truly sick, look at your skin."

"My skin hurts," she moaned. "I'm too afraid to."

Jarin bit his lip as he stared at his ugly wife. *I was forced to see her. She doesn't get to run away from her reality. I won't allow it.* "Look at your skin," he commanded, lifting his chin.

Dimia's lips quivered at Jarin's demeanor and she inhaled sharply. "Fine!" She snapped, her eyes still on Jarin. The two stared at each other for a moment before Dimia gulped, looked down at her arms, and wailed. "What's wrong with me?" she weeped, struggling to sit up. "Help me," she called for him, stretching out.

"No, I won't touch you."

"Why?" she sobbed. "What's wrong with me?"

"You have deathskin," he answered and Dimia cried hysterically. "You have been asleep for moons."

"I wish I had never woken up!" Dimia screamed. "Look at these sores! They will never go away! I am hideous!" She lifted her hand to finger through her hair, but when she felt nothing but blisters, her bawling intensified. "I want to die! Let me die! I deserve it!"

"You're acting ridiculous," Jarin replied calmly. "Your hair might grow back."

Dimia moaned, "But my skin will never look the same."

"I am sorry you are sick, my love."

"Don't!" she spat. "Don't stand there and act like you care! I bet when you found out you sang praises to the gods. I bet you wanted this to happen. I know how much you hate me. As much as I hate you, and I hate you more than anything else in this world! So just don't!" her voiced cracked. "Don't pretend. Just pray to the gods for a quick and merciful death."

Jarin sat back in his chair. "I don't hate you, I just don't like how much you have hurt me. I tried to be a good husband, and you repaid me with animosity. I gave you everything you could have wished for, but it was never enough. Nothing was ever enough for you."

"If you loved me, you would have let me return to Kingment!"

"I did! I let you visit both of your brothers plenty of times. Any time you asked, I'd let you go."

"I mean stay there forever!"

Jarin sighed. "You know I couldn't do that, Dimia. It wouldn't be right. You are my wife; you have to live here in Waterbrook with me."

"I don't want to see you anymore."

"It doesn't matter what you want. I am the Lord Protector of the Riverlands," he declared. "I had my men find your people and put them in the dungeons. All of them, even the ones that don't reside in Waterbrook."

"You didn't."

"I did."

Dimia's face twisted in anguish. "GET OUT!"

"You cannot shout commands at me, I am not one of your little whores."

Dimia whimpered defeated, too weak to fight. For a moment she looked at the ceiling, and then her bright blue eyes snapped to Jarin. "You know, when you came to Kingment, I did like you. I thought you were kind, sweet, generous, and handsome. At first, I did want to be your wife. I even dreamed of it. But then, you killed my people and burned the city. You were our guests, and you attacked us," Dimia seethed. "Even though we showed you hospitality!"

"I did not attack you," he reminded bluntly. "My lord father did."

Dimia wiped her tears, "Even that didn't make me hate you. I saw how upset you were by the sight of the violence, and when I came to comfort you, I saw how happy you were to see me. I loved you then and only then. And it was the biggest mistake of my life. After that, your father kidnapped me and made me his hostage so my lord father wouldn't fight anymore. As if my father cared. Then Alen forced me to marry you, and when I declared how much I loved you in the chapel on our wedding day, all I could think about was what would happen if I murdered you. I prayed every day that my brothers would reach Waterbrook and sacked it. And when they did, I still couldn't escape."

She paused, rubbing her temples. "When I learned I was pregnant with Terryn, I wanted to get rid of it. Every day I held the vial the Saavants made for me, and every day I was too afraid to drink it. Then Terryn was born and you didn't bother showing up." She shook her head and gripped at her scalp. "When I saw how much Terryn looked like you, I wanted him dead. To smother him with a pillow, but still I couldn't. He was my child, and it didn't matter how much he looked like the person I hated, he was *still* mine." Dimia looked back at Jarin and her smile wicked.

Inside, Jarin felt broken. *She wanted to kill Terryn.* He couldn't believe the evil that radiated from Dimia. *Has it always been there? Have I been ignoring the truth and forcing myself to only see the good?*

He clenched his teeth, refusing for his wife to win. "You know, on the night you fell ill, I went on a walk through the castle. During my stroll, I heard a woman moaning with pleasure as a man told her some joke about a giant." Jarin paused and studied Dimia's wide eyes. "There were several people in that room pleasuring the woman. It was so unusual and I couldn't help myself. I had to listen. I almost wanted to go into the room and pleasure the woman, too. But then, someone started violently throwing up, and the other people in the room scattered about. I was afraid too, and ran to my room. The next morning, I was told that you had not awaken from your sleep."

Dimia's glassy eyes settled on him before throwing up blood. Jarin jumped to his feet and took in the thick dark red puddle, his mouth agape. She dazed at him, as if she was about to fall back into a slumber. "I could feel him in my stomach," Dimia smiled, her teeth red.

"I can just imagine Jossa's pain right now, as she's crying all alone in a dungeon cell," he countered.

Dimia puked again at his words. She continued to vomit until she collapsed, hanging over the bed.

Jarin smiled at his unresponsive wife. He wanted to grab a knife and slit her throat, but he couldn't. *It would be a sin the gods wouldn't forgive.* He walked to the door, turned the knob, and his fingers burned, reminding him of his morality. *I want to die an old man, and I am not old yet.* He took a deep breath and rushed down the steps as if his body wasn't roaring in pain.

And the whole way down, Jarin screamed for the Saavant.

VICTORIA

Lady Victoria Osmont thought about throwing herself from a window. Ideas of death plagued her at almost every moment of the day, as her mind spun in circles, making her see things that were not there. Even in her dreams she could not escape from the madness that engulfed her mind. She even thought about killing herself as she sat at the table alone, waiting for her sweet children to join her; so that they could all break their fast, together as a family.

Cold hands suddenly wrapped around Victoria's arms. "My lady, you look at nothing," Saavant Enya said, grabbing her attention. "Your skin is clammy. Maybe you should go for a stroll this afternoon. It might be the last warm day of the year."

Victoria stared at Enya's leathery tan face, "I cannot live this life anymore," she whispered. "I think it is time for me to go now. Release me, for my own sanity."

Enya squeezed Victoria's hands. "The gods have not taken you yet, my lady. You mustn't give up!" she paused for a moment, squeezing harder, "I feel a dark spirit approaching the kingdom. You need to have energy to stop it. Have you been reading the book?" Victoria nodded slowly. Enya looked around the empty room, and carefully pulled out a small cup, already filled with a strange liquid. "You need more power," she breathed out. "Drink this."

"What is it?" Victoria questioned, grabbing the cup.

The old woman smiled. "You shouldn't worry too much about that."

"Mother!" her youngest son, Rosert, shouted as he entered the dining hall. "Good morning."

Victoria examined her son's unflattering garments and frowned. Everything Rosert wore were in shades of brown and green, and splattered with deep red stains. Dirt covered his pale skin and matted red-brown hair. *What was he doing to get so dirty?* Rosert was a very handsome boy when he was clean. His plush curly hair framed his face and his sparkling copper eyes always showed excitement.

Nevertheless, her son was never clean. The boy hunted, would fist fight any grown man willing, and trained his skills of battle with a war hammer. He even rode wild valley horses with no saddle. He loved chopping down trees, and swimming in the river. Her youngest son loved doing wild things, and Victoria had no interest in it—and neither did Falk.

She erased her frown and greeted him in the politest voice she could manage.

"Drink," the old woman commanded, pushing the cup towards Victoria's mouth. A thick, deep red liquid swished around inside the cup. "It will make you feel better, more like yourself." Enya added, tilting the cup so that Victoria had to drink it. "And it will ease your mind and make you stronger, so much stronger."

The liquid was thick, hot, and disgusting.

Rosert sat across from her, and she swallowed the unappetizing drink before he could notice anything. Although her son was wild, he was clever.

Victoria gagged as the strange drink slid down her throat. She quickly grabbed some cloth to wipe her mouth, afraid that the deep red liquid had stained her pale lips. Energy returned to Victoria as she reached for a pitcher of water, causing her to stop. Her bones did not ache anymore, nor did her head. She felt as if she had died and come back again; younger and healthier. *What is that liquid?*

Emeline, Catrain, and Cleric, all walked into the dining hall, giggling amongst themselves.

Emeline was Victoria's eldest daughter. She was only the tender age of twelve, but she acted older than a naïve child would. Emeline behaved like the perfect daughter, always being quiet, polite, and lovely, just as she had been taught. *She will make the perfect wife.*

A servant approached, bowing. "Breakfast is served, my lady."

Platters of food were placed around them, and her children waited no time before grabbing the food and putting it on their plates.

Victoria smiled, enjoying the time she spent with her three children. *Three? No, I have four.* "Where is Doran?" she asked. Her two daughters looked at each other, unsure whether they should answer. Victoria glanced over to Rosert, who stared back at her, a smile forming on his lips. "Where is he?" Victoria asked again, irritated.

"I do not know, Mother." Emeline replied quietly.

"I have not seen Doran since we broke our fast yesterday," Catrain added, her mouth filled with food.

Victoria turned to Rosert and noticed his smile had grown wider. "Well?"

Rosert shrugged. "Guess he didn't feel like it today."

Is that true? Is my eldest son doing nothing.

Before Victoria could ask another question, Ser Edmund was by her side. "A letter for you, my lady."

Gloriana, she thought, eager to read the response. She opened the letter and her body grew cold when she noticed the handwriting. *No, Falk.* As she read, her body grew colder and colder until she was shivering.

"Momma," Catrain called, bringing Victoria's mind back to the table. "Are you okay?"

Victoria looked at Rosert, her face serious. "Bring me your brother."

Rosert's eyes widened and he stood from the table. "Yes, Mother," he bowed, and raced from the dining hall.

"Mother, what's wrong?" Emeline asked, panicked.

"Why would anything be wrong, dear?"

Emeline opened her mouth, and then closed it, pressing her lips together.

"Because you asked Rosert to do something," Catrain innocently answered instead. "You never do that."

Victoria stared at the empty chair where Rosert had sat. Her daughters were right to worry. She grabbed her cup and took another sip. "Your cousin Alice is coming."

"Is that the one with the golden eyes Lord Borin spoke to me about?"

Borin is no uncle to my children, Victoria reminded herself. "No sweet girl, the girl coming is her sister."

"How long will she be staying?"

"Forever," Victoria replied sadly. "Alice will be frightened in this new place, so please be kind to her."

Catrain smiled and nodded, but Emeline was too quick to see that something was wrong. "Forever? Why can't she go home?"

Victoria didn't have an answer for her eldest daughter. She didn't want to break the girl's spirit with the realization that the same will happen to her one day.

"Mother!" Doran greeted, entering the room. Her eldest son raced to her side and hugged her. "You look so beautiful today. Dark green suits you, it makes your eyes shine bright, as always." He then kissed her forehead.

Catrain rolled her eyes at her older brother's actions, while Emeline giggled. Rosert sat back at the table, and filled his plate with food, ignoring them all.

"I have some news," Victoria began, her face serious. "Your father is returning to Kingment."

Rosert, Emeline, and Catrain froze in their seats, but Doran gave a fake smile. "That's wonderful! We should have a feast for his safe return."

Victoria forced a smile. "What a splendid idea." Doran nodded, and as he pulled away, she grabbed his hand. "I have more." Her son looked down at her confused. "Lady Alice Wayward is traveling with him."

"Alright," Doran responded cautiously. "For how long?"

"Forever," Catrain answered with a toothy grin, not understanding anything.

Doran glanced at his little sister, and then looked back to Victoria. "I don't understand."

"Father found you a wife while he was away," Rosert laughed.

Victoria shot a look at her wild son. *How could he have guessed that?* She almost screamed. *What all does he know? Does he know what I did to his father's bastard children? Does he know who Cleric is?* She glanced at the seemingly invisible girl who stood in the corner of the room, watching them curiously.

"No!" Doran shouted, pulling Victoria from her thoughts. "I don't want to marry her!"

"Is that what it means, Mother? When a girl leaves her home forever, she is to marry?" Emeline questioned, hugging herself.

The room spun. *Calm down. Take deep breaths and calm down.*

"That doesn't matter," Doran spat. "I don't want to marry that girl!"

"Why?" Victoria asked, trying to sound sympathetic. "You have not met her yet."

"I don't want to marry some stupid mountain girl," Doran whined.

Her other three children gasped and Victoria saw red. *Stupid mountain girl?* She took another sip of her brew, and this time, the liquid did not taste so bad. She blinked slowly, trying her best keeping her composure. "Emeline and Catrain have agreed to be nice to your cousin. I am sure Rosert will, too. Right?"

Rosert read her face and looked at his brother, shaking his head wildly. "We must always be kind to family, Brother."

"Right," Catrain added happily.

All eyes were on Doran again, but he was not backing down. "My cousin?" he asked, his lips raised in disgust.

"Aye," Victoria replied calmly. "Highborn people do it all the time, to keep the blood pure."

"Her blood is not pure. She is nothing but mountain scum!"

This time, Victoria had enough. Rage blurred her vision as she slapped her son viciously. When everything cleared, Doran laid on the floor, holding his swelling cheek and looking at her as if she had just stabbed him.

"Mother is from the Mountain Realm, you stupid boy!" Emeline croaked, tears streaming from her eyes. She puffed out her cheeks and balled her fists in anger before stomping out of the room. "Don't you know anything?!"

"Yeah!" Catrain yelled, following closely behind her sister, with Cleric at her heels. "I was told I had the blood of the bear! Does that make me scum, too?"

Doran jumped to his feet when realized what he had done. "Mother, I didn't mean that, I,"

"You have Wayward blood, too," Victoria reminded, her voice shaking.

Rosert was now behind his mother, ready to protect her. "I heard the Mountain Realm is a beautiful place. I would like to visit one day and hunt with Uncle Borin."

Victoria smiled at his words, yet her other son's eyes grew wide with fear. "But the girl, her mother; grandfather murdered her family."

"I'm sure Alice holds no ill will," Rosert answered.

Doran blinked. "Grandfather massacred them because they were not like us! Their skin was kissed a thousand times by the sun. Grandfather believed that because of this they were Wickeds who practiced the dark Arts. So, he eliminated them." He looked away. "Grandfather thought those things for a reason. There must be truth to it. Them being Wicked and all."

Victoria grabbed her son's arms and squeezed them hard, "Nonsense! Do not continue the hatred I've attempted to quell in this kingdom. You *will* be kind to Alice, do you hear me?"

Her eldest son responded by smacking his teeth and ripping his arms away from her grip. His teary green eyes studied Victoria for another moment before he stomped out of the room.

"Are you alright?" Rosert asked, touching her shoulder.

"No," Victoria confessed with a sigh, taking a seat.

Her son kneeled beside her. "I know Doran is stupid, but,"

"I think your father has done something horrible."

Rosert blinked at the interruption. "I don't understand, I thought a betrothal was a normal occasion?"

"Gloriana would have written me, too, if the betrothal was normal."

"Lady Gloriana is Alice's mother. She would have written to you before Father, because she would be so excited, if everything went normal."

"Aye, and the only time she doesn't write is when she feels threatened. There have been times where she does not write for moons, and when she does, the letter is filled with horrible events she had endured."

"What do you think happened?"

"I believe your father stole Alice." Her voice was almost inaudible.

Rosert's eyes widened. "That could start a war!"

"No," Victoria said, squeezing her son's hands reassuringly, "He is using something against House Wayward. You must stay close to Alice when she arrives. Get information from her. Find out what happened. Your brother may mistreat her, but you must gain her trust and become her friend."

"Of course, Mother," Rosert answered, kissing her on the forehead. And without another word, he left the room, leaving Victoria alone.

Maybe I've put too much pressure on him, she thought, her body growing weak. *But who else can I put my faith in?*

✳ ✳ ✳

She sat quietly in the gardens within the Black Castle, taking in the day. *What do I do with Doran? How did he become so terrible? Does he truly speak how he feels inside?*

Chain metal clacking approached and Ser Edmund stood in front of her with a sad look. "Hello, my lady," he greeted, bowing. "I have your tea."

Victoria grabbed the cup and immediately gulped a mouthful before sighing. "Thank you."

"That *tea* looks like blood," Edmund informed in disgust. "Smells like it, too."

She waved her hand, ignoring the knight's concern. "Saavant Enya told me not to worry, so I won't."

"I don't know, my lady," he continued. "I have a feeling she dabbles in the Darkness and,"

Victoria no longer wanted to hear the knight's thoughts. "Enough of this, why are you here?"

Ser Edmund frowned. "All the bastards have been sold," he whispered, reminding her of the task she had given him. "The gold has been put towards the dinner for the Lord Protector and Lady Alice Wayward's safe journey to Kingment."

Victoria nodded, her lips trembling. She had forgotten—forgotten about their wide, frightened eyes and cries as she declared they would be sold. She had made the command and never thought about it again. *Am I that evil? Do I care so little for other people? Is that why Doran acts the way he does?* The questions caused her to gasp, and she clutched the ribbon sewn onto her dress. *No, I'm not like that.* She imagined the quiet Cleric who was always a step behind Catrain. *I'm a person who shows mercy. Was I so blinded with rage that I threw out all reasoning? Is this the insanity that will kill me?*

Her green eyes flickered to Ser Edmund and sniffled. "The children," she struggled. "Bring them back."

"Excuse me?"

"Bring them back," she repeated, crazed, and gripping onto the knight's sleeve.

"It is too late." He shifted uncomfortably. "Best forget them, my lady."

Streams of tears fell down Victoria's cheeks as she silently nodded, knowing she had committed a grave sin and had no one to blame but herself. She finished her tea and placed the cup on the ground. *How could I do such a thing?*

"I have more to discuss, my lady."

"I do not wish to hear it," she cried into her lap, the children's faces swirling in her head.

Ser Edmund Archard sighed. "The Lord Protector took most of his lord knights with him, and since the lady knight has arrived, I don't know what to do with her. May I dismiss her? I don't know why Lord Falk approved her place in our elite group."

Victoria stopped crying and stared forward, her vision unfocused on the bushes before her. She knew exactly who this lady knight was. *Lady Raya Vale.* Rosert constantly gushed about the tall and gallant woman who now walked the halls of the Black Castle. *She even knocked Doran off his horse,* Rosert's voice echoed. *Do not punish her for it, though; Doran needs to get stronger anyway.* Rosert's eyes sparkled each time he spoke about the lady knight. "Bring her here," she commanded, clearing her throat.

Ser Edmund nodded and left without another word.

Victoria returned to her much-needed silence. *I'm evil. I guess I was the perfect wife for Falk. No wonder I fell in love with him so hard when I was younger.* A light snow fell in her imagination as she remembered the moment she met the young Falk Osmont. *I knew I wanted him. And he knew exactly how to get me.*

She shivered, thinking about his infidelities. *I guess he could get anyone he wanted. I was just too naïve to think he would never touch someone else.* Fictional scenes of her husband having sex with faceless women filled Victoria's head. She hugged herself and tried to think of something else, so her mind tortured her with the melancholy faces of Falk's bastards.

I need more of that tea to calm down, she realized, trembling. *I can't do this. My mind can't do this.* She gripped at her long brown hair. "I'm afraid."

"Why are you afraid, Mother?" her eldest child questioned, standing before her. She lifted her head and stared at Doran, causing the boy to sneer. "And why do you look like that?"

"I did not expect you to be in the garden," she grumbled in a low voice, not answering her son's questions.

Doran reared his head back before smiling. "Nor you," he replied and sat down beside her. "I'm here almost every day. But why are you in the garden, Mother? You don't visit much anymore."

Victoria studied her son. *Doran spends his days in the garden—is he the same when Falk walks the halls?* She didn't know the answer. *I thought I knew my children. I thought I was an excellent mother. Did I do it all wrong?* Again, she didn't know. *Am I hopeless?*

She sniffled again and rubbed her sweaty palms against her dress. "I am waiting for someone," she finally answered.

"Who?"

"You may find out if you stay a while. Please, stay, and let's chat."

Her son hesitated before nodding and relaxing on the stone bench. "I don't usually sit while I'm out here," he confessed, clearly uncomfortable.

He's telling me something about himself. Maybe if I can open him up, I can retry how I mothered him. Perhaps it's not too late. Victoria gave her son a small smile. "Oh, what do you prefer to do?"

"I like to smell," Doran paused. "It doesn't matter."

"Yes, it does."

He turned away. "I don't want to talk about it."

"Well, have you been preparing?"

Doran gave her a confused look. "Preparing for what?"

"Alice Wayward's arrival."

The boy's face darkened. "I don't want to talk about that either."

She buzzed her lips. "Please, be kind to her, my son."

Doran looked back at Victoria and took in her debilitated presence. He inhaled sharply, puffing out his chest. "Fine," he groaned, still unwilling.

"My lady."

Her attention turned to a towering woman who shaded her from the sun. Doran groaned, but Victoria could do nothing but smile. *Rosert didn't do this lady knight justice when describing her. This woman is beautiful.* "Hello, my lady."

The woman's cheeks turned dark pink as she shook her hands, "Oh no, you do not have to use courtesies with me."

Victoria nodded, her smile never fading. *She is no older than Doran.*

"My name is Raya of House Vale," the young woman introduced, her almond-shaped eyes sparkling.

"I'm happy to welcome you to Kingment officially, and I apologize for taking so long."

"Please don't apologize, my lady. I'm not worthy."

Why does Raya think she isn't worthy? Her smile twitched, and she placed her chin in her hand to hold her head up. "Please, tell me about yourself."

"Of course," she bowed. "I'm well-versed in the duties of a knight, but I'm mainly a fighter. My weapon of choice is a great sword, but my father also taught me to dual wield."

"And she's a Solamar," Doran added.

"Who cares?" Victoria questioned, not looking at her eldest child. "I heard that you spar with Rosert," she continued.

The girl smiled wide, showing her big and bright teeth. "Yes, my lady, and Doran, too," she added, pointing.

"Don't point at me, Solamar scum," Doran seethed.

I will regret what I do if I move, Victoria thought, forcing herself to stay still. "Doran," she exhaled, her voice too calm. "You need to leave before I knock you the fuck out."

"What?" her son shrieked, standing.

"You need to leave. You're a cruel person with cruel ideals. Fix it before someone fixes it for you," she threatened, still calm. Doran stomped away without a word, leaving Victoria and the lady knight. "Please excuse my son," Victoria told the knight, exhausted.

Lady Raya gave a kind smile. "Do not worry, my lady, Doran does that often. I'm used to it now."

She frowned. "The next time that little brat spews hate, punch him square in the jaw and let him know that's how his lady mother will fix that Wicked soul."

ALICE

Her fingertips lightly rubbed against her busted knuckles, and she sucked in through her teeth. The unbearable pain reminded Alice that she was alive, but that wasn't enough. *Nothing will ever be enough.* She gritted her teeth, pulling off a scab. *I want Falk's head on a platter.*

Lord Falk Osmont had tried. He tried to hurt her. He tried to break her. He tried to dehumanize her.

Yet, Alice Wayward prevailed.

She grinned so hard, imagining the strikes she had delivered to Falk, that she split her top lip open for the fifth time. *I'm not healed.* She swiped the wound and examined the bright red blood that lightly covered her fingers. *Will I ever heal?* She wasn't sure.

I'm going to punish you like how I pleasured your mother, Falk's venomous words echoed. Alice clutched the strange coin Lady Hearthra Seamann had given her. *I wonder if this coin saved me from that hell.*

Her father's bloodshot copper eyes appeared in her mind. *Something doesn't feel right. Your mother did something.* Her stomach jumped, just as it did when Falk kicked her, and she wailed in agony.

Mother is a selfish woman.

She curled into a ball, lying on the wheelhouse floor as she pictured her beautiful mother. Her dark blue eyes, shiny black hair, and sultry smile swirled in Alice's head. The woman's Summeran features made her different in the Mountain Realm, and the confidence exuding from Gloriana influenced Alice. *I wanted to be like her,* she remembered, as continuous tears flowed freely.

"Alice!"

She lifted her head at her best friend's voice. "Myra," she exhaled, picturing the girl's terrified face as Falk threw her out of the wheelhouse. Alice scampered to the door. "Myra," she said again, breathlessly. "I miss you."

On the other side, there was silence.

Her heartbeat quickened, and she pressed her face against the wood. "Myra, are you,"

"I'm here," the handmaiden interrupted. "I just came to tell you that we've exited the Silverwood Forest. We were going to pass the Gulflake River, but the river flooded the bridge, so we stopped."

The resentment in the handmaiden's voice ripped at Alice. *Is Myra mad at me?* Her lip trembled. "Uh, how long have we been traveling?"

"I don't know, I think a moon has turned."

"And we haven't stopped?"

Myra buzzed her lips. "We stopped plenty of times."

Alice lowered her eyes. *Falk hasn't let me out of here in weeks.* "Apologies," she croaked. "I lost track of the days."

"Some knight wanted to speak with you," Myra added, her voice fading. "Bye."

Silence once again surrounded Alice. "Um, hello?"

"I didn't think he would do that to you," a rough voice responded, "He's gone crazier than Victoria."

Alice blinked at the statement. *Aunt Victoria is going crazy?* She didn't understand. Locks jingled on the other side before she could question the voice. *Falk locked me in here.* The realization hit Alice harder than Falk's strikes. *I assaulted the Lord Protector of the Northern Kingdom of Valley Pines.* She scampered to the other side of the wheelhouse and curled up defensively. *He's not just locked me in here. I'm under arrest, and now they are letting me out of my cell. Am I going to be executed?*

Memories of House Osmont's knights harshly tossing Alice off their Lord Protector flooded her mind. She was so proud to see the blood and bruises she had given Falk. *How stupid can I be? I did nothing but guarantee my death.*

The door opened, and sunlight flooded the dim interiors of the wheelhouse. Alice shielded her eyes, prepared to be yanked out and placed in chains. A shadow obstructed the exit, and Alice prayed to the gods one last time.

But then, nothing happened.

"Get out," the voice commanded harshly, but Alice didn't move; she couldn't—fear froze her. The knight groaned and stepped into the wheelhouse, revealing an ugly, hairless face. "I said get out."

"Please," she cried. "Have mercy. I was only trying to protect myself."

The man moved closer, and Alice could smell the dirt and sweat radiating from his body. "The Lord Protector wants to see you."

"No," Alice replied, remembering the ugly man's beady eyes glaring down at Gloriana Wayward as he pinned her to the floor. "You hurt my mother."

"I had no choice. She attacked the Lord Protector."

"That's because he was lying!"

The knight sighed as if he had heard the argument before. "The Lord Protector wants to see you."

Alice sat up, knowing she was just like the knight. She had no choice. *If I'm going to survive, I need to make friends, not enemies.* She outstretched her hand, and the knight helped her, showing kindness. *It will start with this man.* "What is your name?"

"Ser Damien Clay, but most call me Ser Knight."

"You don't like courtesies?" she questioned, stepping into the outside world for the first time in weeks. She scanned the campsite, noticing all eyes were on her. "Oh, um,"

A damp cloth swiped across her face. "No, and I'm sure you don't either," Ser Damien answered, placing the rag in her hand. "Don't worry about the eyes. They stare no matter what you do."

Alice nodded and continued cleaning off the dirt that had caked onto her skin. "You had mentioned my aunt had gone crazy. What do you mean?"

"She's okay, just slowly losing her mind, as we all do," the knight explained, "but ask your uncle when you speak to him. Learn when lies are spewed."

She peered at Ser Damien Clay. "Why are you helping me?"

"Some snotty little girl with golden eyes proclaimed that I was your lifelong protector," he shrugged. "The child queen was right about Falk. I didn't take her seriously, and now you have scars on your face. I promise you won't have to deal with anything like that again."

Alice thought about the little girl the knight described. *My sister is the Queen of the Mountain Realm.*

And she was so pleased with that.

"Your handmaiden has set up a tent over there," Ser Damien pointed. "Maybe wash up a bit more before speaking to the Lord Protector."

She nodded and shuffled to the tent with her eyes on the green grass beneath her feet. *I must stay calm and healthy until Jaslyn can rescue me. I can't have anyone know what's going on.* She pushed through the tent flap and walked into the enormous tent, where her handmaiden sat in a mirror, combing through her short hair.

"I've been sleeping in the castle tent alone," Myra grumbled, not looking at Alice.

She pressed her lips together. "You say that as if it's my fault."

The young woman jumped to her feet and strutted over to Alice. She intently studied the girl, her cheeks puffed with agitation. "I imagined you looking different. With how you beat Falk," she exhaled, relaxing. "I'm glad he looked much worse than you do. He forced me to tend to his wounds, and his scars look just like yours, yet no one treated you." She gave a small smile. "You beat him good."

"So you're not mad at me?"

"No, of course not! I was worried about you, duh, but being near these Valley people has sucked the life out of me. So, I'm sorry if I seemed off."

Alice jumped into Myra's arms, embracing her tightly. Touching another human brought so much strength into Alice's hopes and dreams. She pulled away, smiling brightly. "Jaslyn is the Queen of the Mountain Realm."

Myra's eyes widened. "Just a rumor, along with all the others."

"No," Alice confirmed. "She's serious."

"So, we might be able to return to Maryere?" Myra inquired, her excitement infectious. "This nightmare might end?"

Alice brought her best friend close. "Aye, but we must stay calm and healthy."

Myra gave a toothy grin and walked to a tub. "When I heard Falk wanted to speak with you, I went ahead and filled the bath." She added soap to bubble the steaming water. "Now, let's get you washed up and add that shimmering strength that always radiates from Lady Gloriana. Maybe that will frighten Lord Osmont even more."

Her face darkened, and she stripped naked, not hiding the healing bruises that littered her thighs and ribs. She turned to the mirror to examine herself and picked at a scab. "Don't mention my mother ever again."

The Summeran handmaiden reared her head back. "But why?"

Alice wiped the tears that constantly flowed from her eyes. "My mother didn't threaten to murder children. My mother had sex with Falk."

"Lies!" Myra gasped. "All lies and rumors!" But when Myra studied Alice's emotionless face, she nodded, not asking any more questions. The handmaiden moved around the tent, quietly performing her duties as Alice continued to stand naked in the middle, doing nothing. "Your water will get cold," Myra informed after a few silent minutes. "And I'm sure the Lord Protector won't wait much longer."

Alice's eyes stayed on her reflection. She didn't want to be compared to Lady Gloriana Thoren of Goldspire because she wasn't her. She was Alice Wayward, and a bear was pacing inside. *Where is her strength?* Alice wanted to scream. *Is it where Falk punched me? Or maybe where he slapped me and pushed me onto the floor? Is her strength in the bruises I received? Or in the beating I endured?* Alice felt like a child, wanting to scream, cry, and punch the air.

Instead, she took a deep breath and stepped into the steaming tub. She sat with only her nose and eyes above the water. *I can soak in here forever.* She dunked her head underneath, and stayed under the water until her lungs were ready to burst.

When Alice reached the surface, Myra was there with a brush, soap, and a sad smile. She sighed and turned so her handmaiden could clean her. Slowly, Myra scrubbed the grime and old blood. The brush's bristles scraped Alice's skin clean, making it sore. After her handmaiden finished washing her hair, Alice again dunked herself underwater. *I'm so tired,* she thought, opening her eyes under the water. *What if I went to sleep?*

Myra wrapped her tiny hands around Alice's arms and pulled her out of the water. Air forced itself into Alice's lungs, and she realized that she had been drowning. *I cannot die, no matter how badly I want to.*

The two girls stared at each other silently for a moment before Alice stood and exited the tub. "You shouldn't do that," Myra whispered, wrapping a towel around Alice. "My older sister accidentally drowned playing under the water like that."

Alice frowned. "I'm sorry."

"Don't worry about it," Myra replied quickly, grabbing a comb. "She died before I was born, but I'm worried about you."

"I worry about myself too," Alice confessed, sitting at the vanity.

Silence washed over the girls again as Myra methodically attempted to untangle the knots. After sectioning a piece of Alice's hair, the young handmaiden paused. Her fingertip grazed against a gash hidden in Alice's hair, causing Alice to grunt in pain. "Sorry!" Myra squealed, her face jumping from the sound. "It's just, I'm just,"

"It's okay," she exhaled. "Let's finish up. I'm growing tired."

Myra nodded and slipped Alice into an intricate burnt orange gown. *An Osmont dress,* Alice frowned, pulling on the black feathers stitched onto the shoulders. Her handmaiden then concealed the cuts and bruises that still lingered on Alice's face, and every so often, Alice whimpered.

After over an hour, Myra Nores was finally finished. "Come now, Lord Osmont has been waiting for your presence."

Alice nodded, lowered her head, and followed Myra outside. They crossed the campsite to a tent twice as large as hers.

Inside, Lord Falk Osmont sat alone, eating his dinner. He looked up from his plate at the disturbance and smiled sweetly, but Alice gave him a cold stare. "Alice!" he practically cheered. "How long has it been? A moon's turn?" Alice pressed her lips harshly together. "Bring Lady Alice some supper; she's nothing but bones," he commanded. People moved throughout the tent, setting up a place for Alice across from the Lord Protector.

Alice Wayward sat at the table, her face unchanged.

"I see you've cleaned up nicely," Falk began, his eyes on her.

She gave a shit-eating grin. "As have you, my lord," she replied, nodding toward him.

Falk straightened in his chair, his green eyes wide. "Yes, well, please eat your dinner. The food isn't poisonous."

Alice turned her attention to the disgusting slop of grey gloop. A list of insults filled Alice's mind before she inhaled deeply and attempted to shake the anxiety out before taking a giant bite of her supper.

It was disgusting.

The chef needed to learn what salt was; the pork was entirely too fatty, and Alice knew people had broken their teeth on the hard bread. She held in a gag as coughs erupted from her chest. Ser Damien placed a mug of ale in front of her, and she downed the contents in response. *At least the ale is good.* When the coughing subsided, she wiped her mouth and smiled dainty. "Delicious."

"Is this your sickness?" he questioned, his lip curled in disgust. "All that."

Yes, she wanted to respond with a bite, but she wiped her mouth again instead. "Not sure; this has never happened while I ate, but it *could* be the sickness."

An awkward silence draped over the dining table, and Lord Falk cleared his throat. "The trip started a bit rough, but let's put the past behind us and learn to trust one another."

A bit rough. Put the past behind us. Learn to trust one another. Alice Wayward wanted to laugh hysterically at every suggestion that tumbled out of the dumb Lord Protector's mouth. She gave Lord Falk the face she knew he wanted to see. "Yes, my lord, of course. Thank you for your mercy."

Falk frowned. "You're nothing like your mother. I should have known. That's a Wayward soul sparkling in your eyes. Just like Victoria."

"Will I go mad like your lady wife, too?"

The Lord Protector stared at her, his face growing angrier. "Who told you that?"

"When you're locked in a tower, you hear a lot of rumors," she lied.

"That's exactly what they are: rumors."

Alice shrugged. "We will see when we reach Kingment."

The tent grew tense, and Lord Falk repositioned himself. "Careful now, girl. You said I have shown you mercy once before, but I am not known as a merciful lord. I punish without a second thought," Falk threatened. *I can tell,* Alice wanted to respond, lowering her head to act ashamed. "That snarky attitude will annoy Doran quickly. You better fix that before he dismisses you."

"If I'm dismissed, I can go home," she grumbled.

Falk grinned. "If that's what you want to think, then sure."

Alice shot to her feet and stared down her lord uncle. *What does he mean by that?* She raged before going emotionless. *No, he wants this reaction. I must stay calm.* "May I be excused?"

The Lord Protector threaded his fingers and leaned back. "Of course," he replied, pointing toward the exit. "Have a nice night, Lady Alice."

"Good night, my lord," she said through her teeth before grabbing Myra and marching out of the tent. Outside, she let go of her best friend and clutched at her chest, seething. *I see why Mother attacked that asshole. I cannot take another minute with that wretched, ugly,*

A cold metal hand landed on Alice's shoulder. "Let me escort you to your tent, my lady," Ser Damien offered, his voice soft.

She studied the knight before releasing the hatred in her heart. *I must stay calm and healthy.* The emptiness inside told Alice she was doing neither. *I must do better.* "Aye, thank you."

Ser Damien walked with Alice and Myra across the campsite. Servants whispered amongst each other as they passed by and Alice quickened her pace. *I want to go home.* When the trio reached the tent, Ser Damien stayed outside. "It wouldn't be polite to step inside."

"Thank you for walking with me," Alice sighed, exhausted. "I think I will," she paused as a letter suddenly appeared in her hands. She eyed the knight before turning to Myra, who looked just as confused. "Wha,"

"The Golden Eyes will protect you," he told her cryptically before walking away.

Myra scanned their surroundings and pushed Alice deep into the tent. "What the heck is that?"

Alice studied the unsealed letter, frowning, "It's from the Queen of the Mountain Realm."

JASLYN

Jaslyn Wayward slipped through the outdoor hallways of Winter's Keep, trying her best to stay unseen. The bowstring rubbed irritatingly against the soft skin of her chest, and her wooden bow, decorated with colorful little flowers and white lion heads, bounced on her back as she ran. *Father got this for me as a present. I guess it's his way of apologizing for the situation, but nothing will be enough until Alice returns home.*

Her gigantic lion trotted alongside, his long pale-yellow mane bobbing up and down as he walked. His mouth and paws were still stained from his hunting prize, a sizeable fluffy rabbit he had eaten earlier. Kai always received an award from Jaslyn every time they went hunting together. She gave him treats like rabbits, birds, frogs, squirrels, beavers, and pieces of deer and bear carcasses she found. Kai loved his prizes and refused to eat them until he was ready to.

Jaslyn slowed when she reached the icy walkway leading to the Bloody Tower. She repositioned her bow and checked her tattered sack to ensure her treasure remained inside.

Strange clacking caught Jaslyn's ears. *Someone is here.* She sprinted to a large marble column, her breathing now heavy. *It's forbidden to be in this area now.* Jaslyn pressed her hands against the bowstring. *I can't be caught.* She had to escape from the footsteps.

"Come here, Kai," she whispered harshly, and the lion lazily walked to her. Kai sat on his haunches, and Jaslyn noticed they were the same height. *Will he get even bigger?* Kai roared a yawn that echoed through the walkway, and her golden eyes darted to Kai's fiery ones. The lion looked back at her carelessly and put his large white head down to nap in the pale sunshine that shone down in between the columns.

Why haven't the footsteps responded? Bravery filled Jaslyn as she swung her head into the open walkway to see the situation, to see the knights, to see her fate.

It was empty.

She slowly backed into the thicket where Kai napped. *Where did they go?* "Kai," she whispered, shaking the lion's shaggy mane. Kai peeked his eyes and then closed them back shut. "Stop playing around, you silly thing." Kai opened his mouth wide in Jaslyn's face for another yawn. "Ew!" Jaslyn giggled. "Your breath smells like Maiden Barda's farts!"

The lion happily licked Jaslyn, and a cold wind blew, freezing her wet cheek. The sensation reminded Jaslyn Wayward where she was—a place where she was forbidden to be.

"We must get into the Bloody Tower now. No more playing around." She softly grabbed his face and looked into his dark red eyes, "I mean it."

Without warning, Kai's enormous head was in between Jaslyn's legs. She slid backward and straddled her lion's back as her feet lifted off the ground. She held on tightly to his mane, trying her best not to pull too hard. She had never ridden Kai before, and her heart jumped in her chest as Kai galloped to the Bloody Tower.

The lion stopped in front of the boarded door, and Jaslyn slid off Kai's back. "We got here so fast!" she squealed, petting Kai. "That was fantastic! You were great!" Kai licked her face in response, and Jaslyn hugged him, feeling the companionship that only Kai could provide. The lion's warmth radiated, comforting her in the cold.

A fierce wind whipped around the pair, forcing Jaslyn's attention to the tall Bloody Tower. Grey clouds covered the sky and light snowflakes fell, making everything colder. She walked to the tower's side, where a few loose bricks exposed an opening where Jaslyn could sneak in. *Alice had told me about the entrance years ago, but I always allowed the locked door to stop me from visiting. Alice wanted someone to be with her, and I was selfish, but now she's gone.* Tears filled Jaslyn's eyes. *How can I be queen when I didn't treat my sister with the love and kindness she sought?*

Jaslyn slipped into the tower and sat on the freezing stone steps. *I don't want to be selfish as queen, but is making the mission of bringing Alice back a priority a sign of selfishness? The peasants don't care about my older sister. They want food and warmth. If I bring them what they want, would they be more willing to assist with my needs?* The thoughts tormented Jaslyn.

Kai started up the stairs, pulling Jaslyn out of her mind. She moved to her feet, dusted off her clothes, and scaled the curved stairs leading to the tower's only bedchamber. *The tower's first resident was Obediah Wayward.* Jaslyn turned the doorknob to open the room, imagining the young boy confined to the tower, only to still die from the Plague of the Arts, a mysterious illness that had struck Mystos centuries ago.

Rhythmic banging of nails on wood, sealing away the Bloody Tower, rang in Jaslyn's head. *And Alice was the tower's last.* Her skin burned with embarrassment as she thought about her sister's erasure. *Why didn't my mother and father care about Alice? Why were they okay with getting rid of her when she was so clearly unwell? I get that Falk meant to endanger the family, but a Wayward never faulters to threats. Everyone knows that. And yet...*

She stepped into her sister's old bedchamber, her eyes focused on the little presents she had previously left. A wide range of orange, red, yellow, green, purple, and brown leaves scattered throughout the floor. *These are Alice's favorite colors.* Pinecones and pineneedles were intricately placed to spell *Alice* and *I love you.* Around the room, obscurely shaped sticks sat in little piles and sporadically placed rocks sparkled to give everything more life. Deer, rabbit, beaver, and wolf pelts circled the magnificent unlit fireplace originally decorated by Queen Lyra, Obediah's mother. *I want everyone to have a soft place to sit when Alice returns.*

Kai walked past Jaslyn and sat on the furs, yawning.

"Get off those pelts before your fur is out there, too!" Jaslyn scolded, but Kai ignored her and licked his paws.

Jaslyn rolled her eyes at her insolent lion and reached into her sack, pulling out Alice's latest present. She studied the small strip of bear fur she had found and gleamed with pride. *Alice loves bears.* Bears were the beauty of the Mountain Realm and were known to always protect House Wayward.

She placed the fur near the other pelts, and Kai growled lazily as if she were disturbing his nap. The bitter iciness that lingered around the unlit fireplace gave Jaslyn goose prickles. Her attention focused on Kai, who now trembled as he slept. *It's too cold here.* She frowned and turned to the door. *We should go where it is warm.*

"Come on, Kai, let's get out of here!"

The lion reluctantly got up, and the pair rushed out of the Bloody Tower.

Outside, Jaslyn's lungs burned with every breath, and her insides felt like ice. *It's chillier than usual,* she realized, hugging herself as Kai stopped her. He pushed his damp nose onto hers, and she took in the warmth that radiated from the lion. "May I ride?" Kai answered by laying on the snow so Jaslyn could get on his back. She slid onto the lion and positioned herself to be comfortable. "To the Grand Library," she whispered, and her lion galloped to the destination.

Jaslyn patted Kai's side to slow when she saw the snow-covered glass dome roof of the Grand Library. She slid off the lion and examined the emptiness around her. Alone in the snow, all Jaslyn could think about was her sister. *Is Alice happy?* Jaslyn exhaled, remembering the only proper command she had made since becoming queen. *At least Alice has someone watching over her. She should be okay. Right?*

Jaslyn jumped up the front steps and pushed open the door, and the ice on her skin melted away from the library's warmth. Before she could sigh with relief, she felt them. She felt the eyes staring at her and Kai standing at the entrance.

The Seers are venomous. Her mother's warning echoed in Jaslyn's head. *They feed off secrets, so you must starve them like a pest.* Jaslyn walked through the library with her back straight and head held high. *Don't let them know your secrets.*

But it didn't matter, they already knew. The Seers were aware of her biggest secret, and that frightened Jaslyn more than anything in the world.

She approached a tall bookshelf filled with histories and lore from every place she could imagine. She returned to the book she had last been reading: *Lore of the Region North of the Northern Peaks.*

Jaslyn held the thousand-page book against her chest, and the heaviness crushed her until she shifted her feet. She hobbled and dropped the book onto the table as Kai plopped down near the fireplace and rested. Her attention shifted around, and the black eyes casually stared back. *Don't let them know your secrets.* She took a deep breath, sat down, flipped the book open, and began reading.

Jaslyn was drawn into the captivating tales of Larkyn, Pirate of the Great White Sea, a human slave turned pirate from the Empyrean Ascendancy Era. Having just finished the chapter on Larkyn's journey to the White Abyss, where they sailed through the White Sea and earned their name, Jaslyn was eager to delve into the next adventure—*Larkyn's Journey to the Black Ice Tribe.*

She paused. *Asterin is a member of the Black Ice Tribe.* The young handmaiden's fierce blue-green eyes lingered in Jaslyn's mind. *What revelations await in this story?*

Regrettably, the story was penned by Saavant Rike, Jaslyn's least favorite author in the book. His narratives lacked the depth Jaslyn craved, and she could almost hear his exasperated sighs as he wrote. *Why bother writing when you lack the passion?* She muttered internally, turning the page disappointedly. It never made sense to Jaslyn why people pursued jobs they hated.

She stopped reading, and her attention narrowing on the flames that danced in the hearth. *Wait, the peasants don't get to choose.* She clutched her shirt, remembering the predicament she was in. *Does anyone get to choose what they want to be?*

Saavant Rike's uninspiring story turned for the worse, ending with Larkyn's tragic death at the hands of Rosalind the Hero from the Black Ice Tribe. Jaslyn turned to the next chapter, her vision blurred by tears. *Larkyn would've given Rosalind anything, yet she betrayed them, stabbing them at her father's command. How could she even become a Hero after that?* More tears welled in Jaslyn's eyes. *Could one truly betray someone they love and still be a Hero for all to love?*

The story of Queen Allaric of the Trident flashed in Jaslyn's mind, and her frown deepened. *Allaric Wayward and her half-brother, Leander, supported and loved each other, and yet, Leander murdered her. How often does betrayal like that happen?*

She lifted her head and studied her napping lion, still taking in the heat radiating from the fireplace. *Could Kai bite the hand that feeds him?* She didn't know the answer, and her heart ached at realizing she knew very little of anyone's intentions.

Jaslyn Wayward sighed then and glanced around the library until something caught her eye. It was a boy. Her cheeks grew warm as her interest piqued. *He's beautiful,* she observed wistfully as the boy pushed his light brown hair away from his face and looked up.

Jaslyn darted back to the book. *Did he catch me staring?* Slowly, she lifted her eyes back to the boy and noticed the purple and green shirt he wore. *Those are House Payne's colors.* She thought about Ser Teimothe Payne then. *He did say he was the third grandson.* Jaslyn looked the boy up and down again. *But he is younger than Ser Teimothe.*

Jaslyn noticed the boy's spotless clothes, freshly washed face, and plush, clean hair. She tugged on the dirty sleeve of her blouse and understood that the highborn boy would never notice a plain-looking girl like her. *People like me because of my eyes,* she thought resentfully, flipping to another chapter in the book—*the Divine Queen Zera's Quest to the White Gate Fort.*

Her eyebrows raised in interest as she read the introduction. *It is said the White Gate Fort, one of the oldest structures in the Mountain Realm, was built at the end of the Exordium Era by the Valkans, who used the blood of enslaved Lower Arcs to construct the fort. Divine Queen Zera, the Arc's last monarch, traveled to the White Gate Fort to learn the secrets of its construction in hopes of building something similar in Lismure. There she found the blade of,*

A book shutting brought Jaslyn's attention back to the boy. He stood from the table, holding the book he read close to his chest, and his hazel-colored eyes snapped to Jaslyn. The two stared at each other momentarily, and the boy smiled, forcing her to look away and blush. She twisted in her chair from embarrassment as she tried not to squeal.

A sudden shadow cast over her, and Jaslyn's heart was in her throat. *Is it the boy? Does he want to talk to me?* Her face burned at the possibilities.

"Jaslyn?"

Her eyebrows furrowed. *Josef.* Her excitement faded as she stared into her little brother's bright copper eyes, noticing the boy was already gone.

"What are you doing here?"

"I'm reading just like you and everyone else."

Josef wrinkled his nose. "You didn't bathe first?"

"I don't have all the time in the world like you, oh!" Jaslyn gasped, reading the title of the book her brother was carrying. She slammed her hand, covering the title from the wretched Seers. "What you are doing, stupid?" she whispered angrily, and her brother stared back at her with terrified eyes. Jaslyn sighed and forcefully sat Josef down. "You shouldn't be reading this here. People will see you!"

She slid the book into his lap, and Jaslyn re-read the title. *The Complete History of Wars in the Kingdom of Valley Pines.*

The little boy grinned. "I want them to see."

Her heart throbbed as she understood what Josef was undoubtedly planning. *He is only ten. He has no business preparing for war.* But Jaslyn knew she couldn't stop her little brother from whatever he was planning. *Josef is more hardheaded than I am.*

GLORIANA

L ord Borin had built the Row of Lords over ten years ago, so the high-born visiting the capital city had a place to stay after he abandoned the much larger Sun Keep. Gloriana, however, knew the truth. *Borin wanted their prying eyes out of Winter's Keep.*

And Lady Joan Myster was his biggest concern of them all, yet the old woman lived in Crimson's Quarters just down the hall from the Lord Protector's bedchamber.

Should I be doing this? Her knuckles hovered over the wooden door as a wave of rowdiness roared on the other side. Gloriana vigorously pushed the door open, and everyone quieted, staring at the invader. She scanned the room, immediately recognizing the sigils from House Fletcher, House Ward, and House Blackmour. *Do the highborn meet here regularly?*

"Lady Wayward, you made it," Joan Myster said, stepping out of the crowd. The old woman's ease caused the room to continue their conversations as if Gloriana wasn't there. "Come, come, let's chat."

Is this a trap? Gloriana followed Lady Myster, her hands sweating as conversations grew louder and she recognized more faces.

"Apparently, the Warrior Raiders are back in Valley Pines," Lord Ward exhaled, sitting with a few other older lords.

"That's frightening," Lord Mason replied, his eyes wide. "I'm telling you, something is coming. Kikisi is building an obelisk. I traveled all the way up the Brightwater River and saw it with my own eyes. Those sneaky Grasslandi, taking our land and then,"

"That's not frightening, that's interesting," Lord Jasper Payne interrupted, sitting forward. "I heard a city sunk in Nempur, now that story brings me cold sweats at night."

Gloriana's gaze met with Lady Hearthra Seamann for a moment as the woman sat with the other ladies of the Mountain Realm, and strangely, she relaxed. *Stay confident. Don't let them rattle you. You got this.* Gloriana repeated the mantra, trying to quell the fear and uncertainty swishing inside her.

Lady Joan led them to the back of the main room, slightly away from the others. Gloriana pressed her wet palms against her dress as she sat, trying to calm the remaining anxiety built up in her. *I may be safe inside this chalet, but I'm unprepared for a meeting with the old hag.*

Joan cleared her throat, and her tired eyes landed on Gloriana. "So, tell me, what happened?"

She blinked, sitting straighter. "W-what do you mean?"

"Falk extorted House Wayward, didn't he?"

A cold chill vibrated through Gloriana as memories flashed in her mind. She lightly touched her forehead, a headache already brewing. "Why do you want confirmation on something you already know?"

The old woman grinned at the question. "By your looks, no offense, it's clear you didn't want Alice to leave. I mean, by the gods, Borin wouldn't even let you say goodbye. Now, you don't have to tell me what he bribed Borin with, because personally, I don't care. But House Wayward ignored coercion for centuries, my family should know. So, what happened?"

Tears filled Gloriana's eyes for many reasons, all too much to process. "Aye, I wanted Alice to stay. She had only recently awoken from a three-week sleep. And Falk took her," Gloriana explained, her anger growing. "Borin locked me away because I tried to stab Falk. If I had it my way, Falk would no longer be breathing, and I would explain to Victoria how he fell from his horse."

"Enlightening," Lady Joan's smile widened, "I knew Borin was apathetic, lazy, and dull. That's why he's gotten away with barely ever holding court or doing any of the Lord Protector's duties. He ignores everything like that dumb Lord Protector in the Riverlands, and I would rather throw my husband's ashes into Bear's Creek than sit here and watch the Mountain Realm crumble. So, I kept things afloat, I'm sure you've noticed," Joan explained, pointing to the conversations around the crowded room. "But, Gloriana," she exhaled, dragging out the name. "This weakness Borin has shown; it's unacceptable. People are talking. Divisions are growing. Things are changing. Personally, I'd endorse the Lush Bear as the next leader. Just so you know."

Is Joan warning me of an uprising? Gloriana's heartbeat quickened. *Are these people against Borin or House Wayward?* Her attention moved around the room before returning to the tiny old woman who sat across from her. *Joan rules the highborn and confessed that she would support Josef if anything were to happen.* Gloriana thought back on the laws of the realm, a smile appearing. "Have there been any movements to make this adjustment?"

Joan's beady eyes narrowed. "Oh, so you didn't fill little Josef's head with,"

The door burst open, and Borin Wayward, the Lord Protector of the Mountain Realm, entered the chalet. His entrance brought a heavy silence over the room, each highborn's face a mask of unreadable emotions. Gloriana's stomach dropped. *What is he doing here?* She glared at her lord husband, clinching her teeth. *After all this time, Borin has done nothing, and now, when I'm ready to make a move, he appears.*

"What in the hells is going on here?" Borin's voice boomed through the room, and no one moved. Her lord husband's fiery copper eyes landed on her, and she lowered her head, unable to stare back. The Lord Protector smacked his teeth. "Is no one going to respond?"

"We are meeting based on recent events, my lord," the old Lord Jasper Payne answered.

He frowned. "Why are you all meeting here instead of waiting until court is held?"

"And when would that be?" Joan spat, standing. "If I remember correctly, the last time you held court was in the spring of last year. Would you've preferred we waited another year to have a discussion? By then, Alice could already be pregnant."

Borin's face turned bright red. "HOW DARE,"

"Don't raise your voice at Lady Myster!" Lady Allaric Cantree shrieked as she gripped at her cheeks. "Show some respect!"

The Lord Protector peered at the peculiar woman, uninterested. "And you would be?"

Shouting filled the air, all directed at the Lord Protector. Gloriana had never seen such a glorious sight. *Why are they so serious about getting Alice back or making Josef the Lord Protector? Why keep House Wayward in power?*

"I don't care what you all have to say!" Borin yelled over everyone. "Alice will be marrying Doran Osmont, and that is that! No more discussion about it!" He then turned on his heels to exit.

Lady Joan crossed her arms. "Inform your children of that when you return to your ugly keep."

Borin's angry eyes fixated on the Matriarch of the Mountain Realm. "What did you just say, woman?"

Joan laughed. "You say *woman* as if that is supposed to offend me."

"Excuse me, Lord Protector," Lord Milton Ward said, drawing Borin's attention. "Your son, Lord Josef, he uh, approached me."

"Approached?"

"Said I was to gather my men," the Lord of Goldharbor coughed, not looking at Borin.

"Why?"

Joan stepped forward. "He's creating an army to get his sister back, you fool!"

The room erupted into multiple conversations, causing Borin to roll his eyes. "Ignore the child because he is a child. There will be no army."

"Lady Alice did not seem like a girl excited to go to a new place, and Lady Gloriana doesn't look like a mother pleased with her daughter becoming a woman," Wyrra Tudor observed, her voice hoarse.

Gloriana's attention landed on the woman with mismatched eyes. *House Tudor rarely bothers themselves to leave their secluded island. Why is Lady Wyrra here? What does she want?*

"We are mountain people, strong and proud! That didn't feel like a proper goodbye at all. My lord, you didn't even press snow between Alice's eyebrows to say good luck on her journey. Who knows the horrors she's experienced?" the young Lord Asten Dawphrey yelled, his voice high-pitched, and the room erupted again.

Gloriana focused on the young teenage boy whose face twisted with displeasure as he was quietly scolded by his grandfather, Lord Jasper. She frowned, remembering the young lord's tragic past. *Lady Klissa learned of her husband's infidelities and threw herself from a tower. Then, instead of taking responsibility, Lord Cayle Dawphrey gave up his rights as lord and ran off with his lover to Ihphy's Archipelago, leaving his twelve-year-old son, Asten, alone to become the new Lord of Snow Creek.* Gloriana took a deep breath, her heart aching. *The boy's family was ripped apart, just like mine.*

"I don't feel like hearing this nonsense," Borin waved off. "Return to your home keeps and rule peacefully in your domain. That is all I ask."

"Aye, but what about your daughter?" Lord Cyrus Caster questioned.

The Lord Protector groaned. "I'm pretty sure I just said,"

"Not Alice, my lord, Jaslyn."

Gloriana's heart sank. *What does Lord Caster want with Jaslyn?*

"That conversation is unnecessary," Borin answered uncomfortably. "She is still too young for marriage."

"No," Cyrus repeated, his annoyance clear, "Jaslyn has crowned herself Queen of the Mountain Realm."

No, Gloriana's breath escaped her as the room erupted once more. *What are my children thinking?* Both were too young to do anything politically, yet they had entered that world anyway. *How could they do this without my knowledge?* She felt so stupid.

"I am aware of what my youngest daughter has declared," Borin lied, placing his hand on his forehead. "Jaslyn is simply pretending. No one honestly believes that she is the queen. This is only a game to her," he laughed, but the room stayed quiet. "I can see Jaslyn's smug face now if she knew that the highborn of the Mountain Realm took her claim seriously. She would laugh aloud that she was able to fool you all." When the silence continued, Borin sighed. "Jaslyn is eleven with a vivid imagination. She knows the Mountain Realm has no kings nor queens."

"I heard she's gathering Maras," Lord Rallor Fletcher informed, causing some to gasp. "So, she doesn't seem to care about the Mountain Realm's traditions."

"Maras?!" Lady Allaric squealed. "We must contact the Harbingers!"

"Having Maras could be helpful," Lord Jasper countered. "Maybe we should contact the Rangers instead."

Lady Haylise Hayward sneered at the old man. "Are you suggesting we side with Wickeds and cambions?"

"It is a bit aggressive to call all Maras Wicked," Lady Hearthra Seamann attempted to reason.

"Silence!" Borin yelled over the audience. "You lords and ladies come together, scheming behind my back, thinking I don't know what my children are doing. They are children! My children are of no concern to you nor the realm," again he turned away. "Wife, come with me."

Gloriana jumped to her feet, her body trembling, "but,"

"Come with me!"

She lowered her head and shamefully walked across the room as the lords and ladies of the Mountain Realm stared at her, following her lord husband's demands.

Outside, Borin grabbed her by the wrist and pulled her close. "What in the hells were you doing in there?" he growled through his teeth, squeezing tighter.

Before Gloriana could respond, Borin slapped her as hard as he could. Her face stung, and she tried to move away, but he yanked her back. *Borin hasn't hit me in so long*, she realized, clutching her cheek. *It almost feels new to me. Like the first time he ever hit me.*

The Lord Protector pressed his lips together. "No one told you to,"

"Lady Joan invited me," she interrupted.

The answer caused Borin to release Gloriana, and she stumbled back. "What did the old woman want?"

She looked away, her face still throbbing. "I don't know. I had just sat down when you showed up. I think she was going to tell me about Josef."

Borin Wayward crossed his arms. "Do you agree with our children?"

The frosted wind stiffened Gloriana as she repeated her husband's question. *I tried to stab Falk. Of course, I agree with them!* She cleared her throat, knowing she couldn't respond how she wanted. "I think our children have been touched by the gods."

Lord Borin chuckled and shook his head. "Don't say that."

"It's true! What sane child declares herself queen? The gods are having a great laugh, cursing us like this."

The smile melted off Borin's face, and he started his trek back to Winter's Keep. "Don't go back into the Row of Lords again. You must stay inside the keep," he commanded, his voice trailing. "And don't do anything stupid!"

Alone, Gloriana hugged herself in comfort. Light snowflakes started to fall around her, yet Gloriana felt warm. *The highborn want him gone. My children want him gone. I want him gone.* A smile spread across her face. *It's time for Borin to be exiled.*

"Psst," a voice called from behind.

She turned to see Lady Hearthra Seamann hiding behind a corner, motioning towards her. *Since when did Lady Joan's flock speak without her present?* Gloriana ensured no one was watching before dashing into the shadows with the Lady of Accrid.

Gloriana took in the magnificence of Lady Hearthra up close. Her high cheekbones, red-brown hair, and broad shoulders matched the description of the perfect mountain woman. *She has little freckles on her nose, too*, Gloriana observed, suppressing a smile. The woman's plump lips upturned, revealing a beautiful smile, causing her hazel eyes to sparkle.

"Hello, my lady. Apologies, we've never spoken before. I don't travel to Maryere much. I know you don't know me, and unfortunately, I associate with Joan for my House's safety, so I'm sure you don't trust me either. Sorry, I'm rambling," The woman then pushed a coin into Gloriana's hands. "For good luck."

She studied the strange pyrite coin, confused. "Thank you, but why?"

"Everyone in your family wants something different. When that happens, death will come," Lady Hearthra frowned and turned away. "I wish you nothing but luck, my lady."

JARIN

H e stared into his lady wife's cold blue eyes. *Why is she alive?* He questioned angrily, studying her sly grin. He had thought he was rid of her, but of course, she proved him wrong. *I wanted her to suffer.*

Dimia was ugly now.

The deathskin had affected everything that was once so beautiful about her. It ruined her. Pink scars littered her skin from the boils that had once covered her. Her curvy body was now nothing more than skin and bones, matching her bald head and lifeless eyes. Yet she stood confidently before him, undisturbed by his lingering glare. She held her head high with her hands on her hips. *That attitude.* It infuriated him.

"Why are you here?"

She smiled. "What do you mean? I am cured. I can do what I please."

"Why are you here?" he asked again.

"Can I not see my husband?"

"I was planning for a meeting, and you interrupted my thoughts," he replied, his voice cold.

"And what will your meeting be about?"

He grinned. "Discussing Lady Kaylien's arrival."

"Who is that, and why are they coming here?"

His smile widened. "She is Lord Bryce Thoren's daughter, of course. She will be betrothed to Terryn." Dimia's face darkened, and Jarin held in a fit of laughter. *Yes, be in despair! Your precious son will be betrothed by the end of the year.* "Is it not wonderful?" he continued. "I was finally able to betroth our eldest son to someone with value."

Dimia took a ragged breath, and coughed, "Why was this not discussed with me?"

"You were dying. What would have been the point in discussing a marriage you would not see?" he questioned cruelly.

"What did Terryn say?"

"He accepted. Of course, not without some complaining. He is my son after all," Jarin chuckled.

She crossed her arms, and tapped her foot against the stone floor. "Who convinced him?"

"I did."

"And how did you do that?"

He stared at Dimia, unable to answer. He couldn't tell her the truth. He couldn't tell her how his body burned, and his joints ached with every move he made. He couldn't tell her about the look on Terryn's face and her sons fearing for their future. He couldn't tell her any of it. *I want her to suffer in every way possible*, he thought, still mulling over Dimia's question. *She cannot know the truth.*

"I spoke to him," he finally answered.

Dimia took in the answer. "What about Sophie?"

"Oh, you knew about the girl?"

"Of course!" she scoffed. "I constantly talk to my sons, unlike you."

Yes, but they don't tell you everything, he wanted to counter. *If they did, then you would know about the betrothal.* Dimia had been awake for longer than a fortnight now, and Jarin knew their sons had visited her. *Yet they told her nothing.*

"You did not expect our eldest son to marry the baker's daughter, did you?" he asked Dimia.

"Why not? He loves her! He might have to give up his claims to the Riverlands, but I am sure he would be willing to do that for Sophie."

"You cannot be serious when you say this. He has never spoken to the girl! He is our eldest son and must do what is right for the kingdom. He knows this, and has accepted it."

She pressed her lips together, unable to argue. "So, what about Sophie?"

"I advised him that when I die and he becomes the Lord Protector of the Riverlands, to make her one of his most trusted advisors like Hamlin is to me."

Dimia blinked, confused. "Why can she not just be his whore now and be his advisor later? Terryn must keep her close."

Jarin matched his wife's face, "He can keep her in other ways. Women are more than their body."

She sneered at his comment. "So, that's what this is? You neglected my intelligence for years, and now when I cannot help, you see how important women can be. Is that what that little mouse is doing scurrying beside Hamlin? Or is that your new wife in training for when I die?"

Lysane. How has she already noticed? "Why are you so angry? Is it because she is pretty and now," he eyed his wife, "you are not."

"Don't," Dimia pointed, her face morphing into frowns and wrinkles. "Don't talk about my looks." A stray tear fell down her cheek, and she wiped it away as quickly as possible.

Jarin sighed at his wife's behavior. "Why are you here?"

More tears fell. "I told you, I just wanted to see you. Am I not allowed to see you?"

"I am not a fool, Dimia. I know how much you hate me." He shifted in the chair, and his body screamed in response. He pressed his lips together, refusing to show the pain he felt. "Just tell me why you are here so we can be on our way."

"I don't hate you anymore," she mumbled.

"Oh?" He smiled, slightly amused. "When did this happen?"

"While I was locked away in the tower, with almost nobody visiting me. I had time to think. I thought about everything that had happened, but I found myself thinking about you most of all. I realized that none of this is your fault. You were a child, just like me. You suffered more. All I did was lose my home although it still stands. You lost everything. And yet, you continued to be kind. Not just to me, but to everyone. You have a gentle soul. You offered me so much, and I took it for granted. You gave me two boys whom I love so much, and I never thanked you for it. I am sorry. I want us to move on and try to be friends. We cannot love, but we should tolerate each other. For the boys, for our people."

"No."

"Jarin."

"No," he repeated. He did not want her apologies. *For so long, she has made my life a living hell. She is not allowed to say sorry and act like none of it ever happened.* He refused. Finally, he was over her; she couldn't slither back into his life. "Do you know what you've done? If I were a madman, I would have shipped you off to Ihphy's Archipelago years ago. No, better yet, I would have sent you to the dark abyss that is Eeccess." He paused, studying Dimia's horrified face and his fingertips lightly tapped against his forehead. "My children needed their mother. My people needed their lady. At least you did that right. Regardless, I can't forgive you as if I was unaware of what you did behind closed doors."

"Is that why you are upset with me? Because I slept with others? Did you not do the same?"

"NO!" he shouted a bit too loudly. "I have never touched another woman. Never!"

Dimia's clear blue eyes narrowed, and Jarin's heart sunk to his knees. *She has something clever to say, she always does. Even now when she should be humbled with grief for what the gods did to her, she is cockier than both of our sons combined.* And it drove Jarin insane.

"So, that girl really is here to be your advisor, what a waste."

"What do you mean?"

Dimia bent forward with her hands on her hips, and a smile plastered on her face, "That girl is so gorgeous. She should be wedded to Dain, not become an old ugly advisor like Hamlin. Who is she anyway?"

"She will be wed to no one."

Dimia stood straight at Jarin's blunt statement. "So, you do like her?"

"She is a child," he scoffed, disgusted. He couldn't bear the thought of his old hands on Lysane's soft skin. "I'm not like you."

She bowed her head. "You hurt me, dear husband."

"Not as much as you've hurt me."

"I have apologized for it."

"Doesn't make it right," he pouted with his arms crossed.

The childish feeling reminded him of Brea. *Because you are my little brother, and I love you so,* her words echoed in his mind. Arguing with Dimia reminded him that he was truly alone. He wanted to confide in his sister. He wanted to cry in her arms like he did when he was an angry little boy. But he couldn't. *She's gone.*

"I will make it right. I swear it by all the gods. I will make you trust me again so that we can be friendly. I really will."

Jarin sighed. "You don't have to. Actually, I don't want you to."

"Sometimes it doesn't matter what you want. I am going to do it anyway. By the time we are old and wrinkled you may even love me again."

Jarin laughed sarcastically, "We shall see."

Dimia gave him a curt nod and moved to leave the room. Finally, their conversation was over. *I didn't realize how tired I was,* he thought watching her leave, imagining his soft bed.

Then, his wife stopped and turned on her heels, smiling. "By the way, I went to the dungeons and Jossa wasn't there. Where is she?"

Jarin frowned at her question. *Just when I thought the conversation was over, Dimia finally expresses what she really wanted.* He did not want to talk to his wife about her handmaiden, he wanted to sleep. He had grown tired of her mocking laughs and smiles. "I told you, the only people inside the castle will be people I can trust. Not your little stoolpigeons that will bring destruction on the Ayers Dynasty."

"Where is Jossa?"

He wanted his wife to know that she was alone now, too. Just as he once was. "She's gone."

Dimia stiffened. "Where?"

"Away."

"What did you do to her?"

His jaw throbbed from at all the talking, "I'm not a cruel man, I'm a sane man. A man who must make important decisions. Especially when my family is concerned. But she is gone now, I sent her away. No harm was made onto her. I promise."

"Where is she?"

"Gone like I said," he repeated, but the answer was not good enough for his lady wife. No answer but the one she wanted would be good enough. He sighed his thousandth sigh, and shifted again, "She sobbed when I approached her," he began, and Dimia's eyes lit up with the story that she wanted, "She asked if she would be locked away forever and I told her no, but that I could not trust her, and that I would have to banish her from Waterbrook. Then the poor girl wailed and told me that she could be trustworthy. She was just a maiden and a friend that you so *desperately* needed. She cried on her knees and begged to stay." He smiled watching Dimia try to hide her horror, "So, I told her that if she went to receive Lady Kaylien for me, then I would trust her and she could stay."

Dimia's green face turned bright red. "You sent a lowborn hand-maiden to receive the eldest daughter of the Lord Protector of the Summer-lands? Jossa is not capable of that!"

"Oh, she is very capable. I see her potential. Maybe you should, too." He rubbed his pulsing hands together. "I did not send her alone. A caravan of knights went with her. *My* knights. No harm will come to her or the Thoren girl. Jossa is simply the messenger and a new friend for the poor girl who must travel to this new and strange land. She should be back within the fortnight, and with her, your new daughter by marriage."

Dimia crossed her arms, "I do not want that girl to see me. She will scream, cry, and run back to the Black Hills."

"Maybe she will accept and love you as if you were her own mother. You always wanted a daughter, right? But you are not allowed to take her under your wing. You will not influence her."

Dimia bowed, "Yes, my lord."

Is she being honest? Jarin wondered, staring at his wife's ugly face. "Anything else?" He was so miserably tired, and just wanted Dimia to go away.

She shook her head and left the throne room without another word.

When he was finally alone, he allowed himself to grimace in pain. "Hamlin!" he called, and the old monk shuffled into the room, with Lysane at his heels.

"Yes?" Hamlin called, as Lysane stared silently at the floor, trying her best to seem invisible.

"Lysane, what is wrong?" Jarin asked.

She chewed at her lip. "We listened to the conversation you had with Lady Dimia. I am sorry, my lord."

Jarin smiled. "Dear girl, that's alright. Hamlin knows what Lady Dimia is. If he believed it was important to listen, then I am not one to question it."

"I haven't found an alchemist to help with the pain," Hamlin informed. "You know, since it's illegal and all."

Jarin pointed a limp finger at Hamlin. "Make sure Dimia doesn't find out about this. You know how she feels about alchemists," and the monk nodded.

Lysane's eyes grew wide. "How does Lady Dimia feel about alchemists?"

"The Lady of the Riverlands believes that alchemists are Wickeds who perform the dark Arts," Hamlin explained simply, and Lysane nodded, immediately understanding Dimia's distaste.

Differing ways of medicine are not the dark Arts, Jarin thought, rolling his eyes. "Give me something for the pain; anything."

"Of course." Hamlin slipped a small bottle out of his sleeve and gave it to Jarin. "You will no longer feel pain, but you will be smiling like a wild man as the medicine works."

"Good," Jarin sighed. "I need to be happy one way or another." Jarin brought the bottle to his lips and drank the potion. He gagged at the taste and gave Hamlin back the bottle.

"You are not happy, my lord?" Lysane asked, her voice soft.

"Lysane," he exhaled. "No more courtesies."

She lowered her sunset-colored eyes. "Of course."

"Do you feel better now?" Hamlin asked, and Jarin nodded. "Come now, Lysane. Let us discuss the conversation between the Lord Protector and his lady wife in the Shadow Tower." The monk then turned to Jarin. "You should get some rest now."

Hamlin and Lysane exited the room, leaving Jarin alone in his thoughts. *I need to get rid of Dimia*, he decided, as the potion warmed his body. *First, I need to worry about the Thoren girl's arrival. Everything must be perfect.*

He examined his swollen joints and clenched his fingers. *It doesn't hurt.* He jumped to his feet, deciding to go for a walk. *I should walk now before my body gives up.* He wanted to stroll through the castle. The Water Castle's halls had memories; good, kind memories. Memories that did not involve Dimia. *Maybe I can forget her there.*

ALICE

S he had been given some freedom by Lord Falk Osmont's standards, but it wasn't enough. *It will never be enough. I had more freedom trapped in my bed in the Bloody Tower*. The stops during the journey grew inconsistent, even though Alice's entire body ached, and her episodes of sickness came and went more frequently than before. Falk's solution was to give Alice more handmaidens when camped, but she didn't want that.

She wanted to go home.

Even though Alice was stuck in the wheelhouse most of the day, she stayed awake and now had time to spend with Myra. The young Summeran woman had always been Alice's best friend, but as the days passed, they found comfort within each other. Then, Myra became more. She became Alice's voice of reason, her sanity, her last piece of home.

The wheelhouse halted, pushing a sleeping Myra on top of Alice. She giggled, soaking in the warmth that radiated. Alice hesitated before lightly touching the curve of Myra's side. Her fingertips grazed against the Summeran's smooth, sunkissed skin, completely mesmerized.

Myra shifted from the touch before fluttering her eyes open. "We've stopped moving," she yawned, her nose touching Alice's.

She grinned. "I know."

The two girls continued to lay together, unmoving, taking in each other's touch. It had become their morning routine for the last seventeen days, but the sudden stop threatened all of it.

Please don't take away my little piece of happiness.

Movement outside forced Myra out of bed. As the handmaiden looked through a pile of clothes, Alice's eyes lingered on Myra's bare body, wanting her best friend back in bed. Myra slipped on her undergarments before putting on her blue-grey wool dress. She exhaled and returned her attention to Alice. "I guess I should see what's going on outside."

"I preferred how you were about five minutes ago," Alice replied, making Myra blush. "Come back to bed."

Myra moved around the wheelhouse, tidying up as if it were second nature. "I can't. These servants are nosy, so I'll see you later." The handmaiden gave a soft smile and stepped outside.

The sun brightened the wheelhouse momentarily, and Alice squinted before laying back down and staring at the ceiling. *I should probably get out and stretch.* Now that Alice wasn't confined to a bed, she always wanted to be out breathing in nature.

Alice dressed quickly and escaped the confines of the wheelhouse, immediately surprised by how set up the camp was already. *How long will we be stopping?* She searched the blur of faces to find Myra or Ser Damien. *I want to be near someone I love.* She paused. *Do I love Ser Damien?* She realized then that her love for Myra differed from Ser Damien's. *I would never want to sleep in the same bed as the old knight, but I wouldn't know what to do if something happened to him.*

She noticed Myra rushing behind a barrier with a basket of clothing, and a grin spread across Alice's face. She walked across the campsite and snuck behind the enormous sheet that covered them from everyone else. On the other side, Myra furiously washed alone. *Perfect.* Alice tiptoed toward the handmaiden before poking at her side.

Myra squealed. "What the? Alice!"

She covered Myra's mouth, causing her eyes to widen. "I don't want people to know I'm here," she whispered, closing the space between them.

"Why?"

"Like you said, the servants are nosy," Alice replied, moving closer and breathing in her best friend's air. She tucked a piece of hair behind Myra's ear. "You look pretty today."

Myra's attention darted around before she attempted to pull away, but Alice kept her close. "We shouldn't seem so intimate."

"You're my handmaiden," she replied, buzzing her lips. "It's not intimacy. It's friendship!"

The handmaiden grabbed Alice's hands, her face serious. "You know what I mean."

But Alice Wayward didn't know what her best friend meant.

Shifting caused them to pause, and the girls turned to see a young maiden standing beside the sheet, staring. Myra separated and opened her mouth to speak, but the other handmaiden was faster. "I didn't see anything," she whispered, trembling, before rushing away.

Myra looked back at Alice. "See, now we will probably get in trouble."

"I don't fear Falk."

The handmaiden tossed the clothing. "Well, I do!" she shouted, her eyes glassy. "Gods, Alice, just because you feel a little better doesn't mean you cannot face punishment!" Myra puffed her cheeks as she looked Alice up and down. "Just stay away from me while we're camped, okay?" She added before stomping away.

Alone, the iciness of the outdoors encased Alice. *Stay away.* Tears filled her eyes at the idea. *Am I putting Myra in danger by just being her friend?* She didn't know if she should be worried or not. *I suppose I will stay away like Myra requested. I can have more time with her in the wheelhouse when we depart.*

Alice somberly walked to where her tent was usually staked when camp was made and entered. The emptiness surprised her before Myra's nervous voice filled her head. *Stay away.* She took a seat on a decorative plush chair and exhaled heavily. *Where are we?* Contemplation stirred within her to get back up, but her bones denied her. *What can I do while staying away from Myra?* She groaned, listening to the constant commotion outside.

Across the tent, Alice noticed a stack of books she had never seen before. *What's that?* She forced herself to her feet, walked to the table, and read the title of one of the books. *Current Histories on the City of Easthaven.* She pressed her lips together, confused. *Current histories, what does that mean?* Her eyes traced the intricate inscription. *I didn't bring any books with me.*

Alice flipped the book open to a folded page. *Chapter Fifteen: Discoveries Underneath Easthaven's Obelisk.* Scribbles covered the sides of the text like little notes. *Someone was reading this before*, she realized. *Was this book placed here by accident?*

Curiosity rained over Alice, and she sat at the table, immersing herself in the chapter; barely understanding a word. *What the heck is an oubliette, and why is it underneath a densely populated city like Easthaven!?* Alice continued reading, ignoring the random servants who walked in and out to complete their chores. *Horrible man-eating monsters dwell in these oubliettes.* Her head shot up at the thought. *Is there an oubliette at home?* She flipped back the previous page and studied the illustration of a black obelisk stretching into the clouds. *No, Maryere doesn't have that anywhere.*

"Alice," Ser Damien called, rushing into the tent. "You need to come with me."

The panic in the knight's voice caused Alice to jump to her feet and race to his side. *It's nighttime*, she realized as she stepped outside, the icy cold air burning her lungs. *How much time has passed?*

Ser Damien didn't wait for Alice, still marching ahead. *What happened?* She wanted to ask but stayed quiet and followed the knight to a different side of the campsite. *This is where the servants sleep, right? Why did he take me here?*

"This way," a voice called, directing the pair. Ser Damien shifted and headed for the tent. "She's over there."

She. Alice stepped into the tent to see an unconscious woman. "MYRA!" she recognized, racing to her best friend and dropping to her knees. Her eyes bounced from Myra's shallow breaths to the bandages now stained with blood. She grabbed Myra's freezing hand, hyperventilating. "WHAT HAPPENED TO HER?"

Large hands grabbed Alice's shoulders. "Calm down."

"Don't tell me to calm down!" she raged, pushing Ser Damien away. "What happened?"

"We found her like that behind some bushes," a man responded from behind. "Seems she was struck in the head."

No! Alice fell to her knees, her body weakening. *Someone attacked*

Myra. She placed her head on Myra's hip and stared at the girl's tranquil sleeping face. *I must be strong. I must get justice.* "Who did this to her?" she questioned to no one in particular.

"Lord Osmont's knights," a little voice answered.

She snapped her head toward the young servant. "Which ones?"

"Alice," Ser Damien tried to call.

"Which ones?" she repeated through her teeth.

The young servant's body shook, her eyes on Myra. "I-I don't know. They were all wearing helmets, and it was dark."

"How many were there?" Ser Damien inquired, the tone in his voice shifting.

"Um, four."

The knight looked at Alice with a sad face and shook his head. "It could be anyone, my lady."

Alice Wayward refused that answer.

She marched out of the tent with Ser Damien shouting from behind. *Something must be done about this,* she thought, her skin pulsing with adrenaline. *I cannot stay calm as everyone wants. Not when my beloved friend is in danger. Not while I feel okay. Not while I'm conscious.*

She approached the Lord Protector's tent and stared at the ties, closing off visitors. *I must get justice,* she decided, using her nails to untie the strings.

"Al," Ser Damien called from afar, but it was too late.

Alice stepped inside the Lord Protector's tent, where Falk Osmont bedded some unknown woman. *All men are the same, aren't they?* She questioned, watching the pair. The two didn't notice Alice's entrance, so she took a deep breath. "Why did your men beat my handmaiden?" she questioned, her voice loud, startling the couple.

The woman rolled off Falk and covered herself with the blankets as Falk sat up. He studied the angry girl before chuckling, his face flushed. "You are constantly reminding me that you are a Wayward. I suppose that is my punishment from the gods for believing you were a Thoren."

"Why did your men beat my handmaiden?"

"Lyla," Falk cooed, and the woman shifted off the bed, still covered with the blanket, and rushed out of the tent. The Lord Protector's smile widened. "Do you know what you've just done? You've violated,"

She didn't care about the man's words. "Don't talk to me about violation! Myra is unconscious because of your men!"

He gave a puzzled face. "Who is Myra?"

Alice let out an ear-piercing scream she had been holding the moment she stepped out of the Bloody Tower for the last time. She rushed to the naked man, frightening him. "You are going to find the people who assaulted Myra, or you are going to regret ever messing with my family!"

Cockiness refreshed the man's nervous face. "Oh yeah, and what are you going to do?" Alice jumped at him to attack, but large hands held her back. She kicked, thrashed, and roared—delighting Lord Falk Osmont. "There is the savagery I knew was within you," he laughed, stepping out of the bed and exposing himself.

Alice shut her eyes tightly as the person continued to hold her, pushing her against chainmail. *Oh no, I didn't stay calm like Jaslyn said. I tried to attack Falk, just as Mother did.*

Warmth breathed down her neck. "You're not going to do shit. Your family isn't going to do shit. No one is going to do shit," Falk whispered through his teeth. Alice squeezed her eyes harder as she felt the man step away. "But, you already know this, sweet Alice. Don't you?"

Tears streamed down her cheeks. "Myra is a highborn."

"Oh, please! No Summeran are true highborn. Arcan blood flows through their veins," Falk replied, now on the other side of the tent. "Ser Knight, take Alice to her tent and find her a new handmaiden."

Alice slightly opened her eyes to see Falk covered in a decorative silk robe, his face twisted with annoyance. *He's letting me go. He isn't going to arrest me.*

The knight shifted his feet. "Of course, my lord, and I will also search for the assailants."

"What for?"

The question ripped at Alice as silence filled the tent. *Falk doesn't care.* She should have known, but surprise still swirled within her. *Someone attacked an innocent, and the Lord Protector turned a blind eye. How many times has my father done the same?* Borin Wayward's cold copper eyes stared at Alice, and she realized she didn't know the answer.

I know nothing at all.

Ser Knight left the tent without another word, still carrying a sullen Alice Wayward. *Myra,* she cried, picturing her beautiful handmaiden whom she loved so much. Her head ached as she tried to process what had happened. *What if Myra never wakes?* Alice blamed herself for her best friend's misfortunes, bringing a terrible cold sweat. *I must do something.*

Ser Damien carried a weakening Alice inside her tent, no longer showing the nervousness he showed before. He placed her on the feather bed and observed her silently. "Calm down," he hushed, patting her damp black hair.

Her eyes grew wide as breathing became difficult. "I cannot," she struggled. "He did this. I know he did."

"What would be his gain?"

Falk would do anything to see me cry, she realized, panting. *He will hurt me mentally now since he can't do it physically.* She attempted to sit up, but her body was too heavy. *I must do something. I cannot be Falk's toy.*

She returned her attention to the knight, understanding that he treated her differently. *He is my protector, but that protection isn't extended to Myra.* She wanted to scream and cry and curse at that. *I must do something.* "Write to my sister."

The knight made a face. "Let's think about this."
"Write to her."
"And say what?" Ser Damien questioned, worried.
"Tell her to be the Queen of Valley Pines, too."

JASLYN

Her father's copper eyes shined as he stared down at her. Jaslyn sat uncomfortably and looked at anything but her father. He had been scolding her for an hour straight, but now he was silent, leaning against his dark mahogany desk, staring at her.

Finally, the Lord Protector of the Mountain Realm sighed heavily, and Jaslyn did the same. "You mustn't involve yourself in politics," he said once again after repeating it to her over a hundred times. "It only brings death."

Each time, Jaslyn had nodded silently, although internally, she protested every word her father spoke. This time she grunted under her breath as a response.

"What was that, young lady?"

You let them starve, Jaslyn wanted to tell her father. *What else was I supposed to do?* Instead, she quietly chewed her lip. *I have to respond,* she thought, knowing that her father would sit there until the next moon turned waiting for a response. She looked at him and crossed her arms defiantly. "What do you know about the peasants and smallfolk?"

It was not exactly what she wanted to say, but it was a start.

Lord Borin Wayward repositioned the way he stood, and mirrored Jaslyn's crossed arms. She had forgotten that she got her hardheadedness from her father. Her behavior would not affect him the way it did others. "What do you mean?"

"What do you know about the peasants and smallfolk?" she repeated with a quick roll of the eye.

And he laughed at her.

Borin's laugh bellowed through his library, and Jaslyn sat there with her mouth agape. Of course, he was laughing at her. He was a man grown, and she was a child. *A stupid useless child.* "They are people just like us," he answered, tears strolling from his hard laughing, "They are born, they live, and they die. Just like us."

"No," Jaslyn said bluntly, not waiting for her father's answer to settle. "That is not what I meant. You know that is not what I meant. Why must you pretend I am an idiot when I am not?"

"I know that pretty girl."

Pretty. The word repeated in Jaslyn's mind. *I'm not pretty.* She knew that. No one ever called her pretty. They called her strong, intelligent, willful, and clever; but never pretty. She studied her father's stern face and held back the tears that were attempting to betray her.

"What are you trying to tell me, Jaslyn? That your treason is for a good reason?"

Treason. The word made her head spin. She was committing treason. Finally, someone said it.

"Yes!" she managed to choke out. She placed a hand on her chest and tried her best to stay calm as the room roared. Kai snored loudly by the fire that crackled in the hearth. The chair constantly creaked underneath her and every nervous swallow echoed in her ears. "You have let them starve for years!"

Weakness is a woman's weapon. Her mother echoed in her mind as she watched her father's face soften to her tears. *Mother sobbed when Alice was betrothed. Alice had cried, too. So many people were filled with grief.* She looked at her father with determination. *Their tears did not stop evil from happening. I must be strong.*

"You knew that they were starving, and did nothing about it. The peasants know this and are aware that you don't care for them. It is no secret, Father. They want to rebel against House Wayward, and they want a proper leader for the rebellion."

"So, they elected an eleven-year-old girl to be that leader?"

"They just want food," Jaslyn replied overwhelmed. Her father made it seem so ridiculous that people had faith in her. She could be strong. *Stronger than any boy or man.*

Borin gave half a laugh. "They have food."

"No, what they harvest is taken from them and brought to Maryere for us to eat. What are they supposed to eat when everything is taken from them?"

"Who told you that?"

"The peasants," she mumbled.

"What are their names?"

Now, Jaslyn was the one who laughed. "You believe me to be an idiot." She continued to laugh as her father reposition himself again. "You truly do."

"Jaslyn, you know that is not true," Borin began, but his words only made Jaslyn laugh harder. "Stop it Jaslyn, I am only trying to help."

But she did not stop, she could not stop. Behind her laughter, Jaslyn was crying. Her smile twitched into a frown as she thought about all the dead bodies she had seen. No one cared for them. *Only me.*

Jaslyn finally calmed, and her father pulled out a chair. He sat beside her, sighing and groaning as if the conversation was slowly killing him. He looked deep into Jaslyn's golden-colored eyes. "How were you going to handle this?"

"What do you mean?"

"The rebellion," he replied. "How were you going to handle a peasant rebellion?"

"Well, I would lead."

Borin sighed sadly, and grabbed her hands, his large ones swallowing hers. "Sweet girl," he said as if she was a toddler, "How would an eleven-year-old girl lead?"

Jaslyn pulled her hands away furiously. Her anxiety awoke Kai from his nap, and he sat at Jaslyn's feet. His bright red eyes watched Lord Borin, but Borin ignored the lion, only looking at her. "You underestimate me, Father," she told him rubbing her hands, "when you think of leaders you only think of war."

"Do you think that won't happen if you led a rebellion?"

Jaslyn scoffed. "You are just like Jojo."

Her father laughed at that, "Yes, I heard about what my son has been doing as well."

"I do not mean to start a war. I just want to help the people you refuse to help."

Borin fell silent for a moment, thinking.

The silence allowed Jaslyn to think, too. *Can I lead?* she wondered, staring at Kai. *He wants you to doubt yourself,* her consciousness screamed back at her. She did not know what to do. She had to defend the defenseless. *But against my own family?*

Wariness made Jaslyn buzz her lips. *Can I lead?* The ugly knight who traveled with Alice appeared in her head. She remembered when she approached him. *He already knew who I was. The other knights had told him.* She had forgotten. *It's not just the peasants who support me, but the knights, too.* Jaslyn placed a hand on her chin. *Father can never find out.*

"This village under your control, Queen's Cove. You realize it is extremely close to Maryere, right?"

"Nothing is under my control, Father," she tried to reassure, waving her hands frantically. "Everything belongs to the realm."

"The peasants are certainly under your control," he replied sitting back in his chair.

She shook her head. "No one is under my control."

"They call you queen."

She smiled at that, "Being called a queen, and demanding for people to be under my control are two different things. I did not ask for this, you must know that. But when I saw the helpless peasants I knew something must be done."

"You are a smart girl," Borin replied. "I almost believed you when you said you had nothing to do with any of this, that you were completely oblivious. I'm not a fool either child, nor would it be wise to cross me again."

She rose her eyebrows. *Was that a threat?* She loved her father so much, and he threatened her like some sort of criminal. *Am I a criminal?* She was his perfect little girl. *Did becoming a queen ruined that?* Her mouth twitched downward. She did not want to live in a world where her father did not love her.

"What would you do to me?" Jaslyn questioned. "Would you throw me in a dungeon? Would you cut off my head and put in on a spike?" Her sadness and anger fueled the fire within her as she stood up. She wanted her father to love her, of course, but she also wanted him to be the proper ruler he was supposed to be. *And if he can't, then I will have to go against him.* She stared down at Lord Borin, feeling taller. The sight of her father having to look up at her made Jaslyn tingle. "I committed treason," she grinned manically, "What are you going to do to me? To your youngest daughter?" she sounded mad; maybe she was. "I heard about the things you like to do. How you like to torture. Are you going to do that to me, too?"

Borin jumped to his feet, towering over her. "Shut up!" he yelled, slapping Jaslyn so hard that she fell to the floor. "If you were not my daughter, I would have you hung for what you have done to the Mountain Realm!"

Jaslyn laid on the floor and held her face, completely stunned. *What did he say?* She had heard the rumors, but her lord father never showed any signs of bloodlust. He was always kind, sweet, and gentle. *I wasn't being serious about the torture. Is he going to kill me?*

A flash of white jumped over Jaslyn and screams filled her ears.

"Get this beast off me!" Borin wailed as Kai ripped at his flesh.

"Kai," Jaslyn cried helplessly, "Kai stop it!"

Finally, Kai stopped.

"I should have that white monstrosity skinned! That thing should not be allowed within Winter's Keep!" Borin yelled.

Jaslyn rose to her feet as Kai walked behind her growling the entire time. "You will not touch Kai," she told her father boldly. Her voice now had power, it had strength. "You will not touch me," she added, frowning as hard as she could. "You will not touch anyone!"

Borin grinned, "Is this what they see?" he asked, clutching his wounded arm. "Empty threats in a big voice?"

"Lord Wayward," she began cautiously, "your reign will end. It will end and you will fall."

"Aye, but not by you."

The somber response melted Jaslyn's strength and anger. *What does he mean by that?* Her father continued to sit on the floor, moaning in pain from what Kai did to him. "Do I need to be wary of you, Father?"

Borin's face softened, and once again, he looked like the father she knew and loved. "No, sweet girl, but you must end this nonsense. I will handle the peasants so this can all go away." He looked away from her then. "I should not have lost my temper. I should not have said those things. I should not have hit you. What you heard were rumors. I do not torture others."

Her father's words meant nothing. She did not care about his temper, or his threats, or his abuse. Those things would not stop her. She had been declared queen, and a queen she would be. *You slapped me, Father. I will not forget that.*

Borin stood and walked to the door. "I'm going to go find someone to fix this up. Remember Jaslyn, you mustn't do this again. You're not a queen," he added, leaving Jaslyn alone in his library.

No, Father, I am the *queen.*

When the door to the library clicked shut, Jaslyn bounced out of her chair and rushed to the other side, where another room was hidden. Jaslyn pushed one of the bookshelves, remembering when she accidentally found the secret room as a child, moving, smashing, and banging anything she could find. *Father doesn't know that I know about this place. I wonder if anyone else knows.*

Jaslyn slipped through the bookshelf, and her eyes widened at the little room covered with papers. *What is all this?* She stepped forward carefully, trying not to slip on anything that littered the room. Her eyes scanned every inch, searching for the decorated chest that had been stored there before. *Where is it?* She looked behind a shelf, and her eyes widened. *Found it!*

She dropped to her knees and opened the chest, and coins shimmered before her. *Yes!* She pulled out her sack and filled it with gold coins, repositioning the jewels so that her father couldn't tell anything was missing. *I've run out of money; I must do this for the peasants. Father wouldn't understand. He showed that by hitting me. But I will not let him stop me from helping those in need.*

When the sack couldn't take another coin, Jaslyn Wayward slipped out of the secret room and exited the library.

Kai followed closely as Jaslyn raced through Winter's Keep. *I must be smarter,* she thought practically scolding herself, *I have been so stupid, so childish. Lives are at risk.* She needed to do something. *The situation is bigger than it was before.* In her father's eyes, the situation was over, but Jaslyn understood that it had only begun.

She needed help. She needed *real* help. *Ser Lyon will just agree with everything I say and do.* He was her sworn shield, the leader of her knights, and her friend. She trusted him, but he did not counsel her. Evergreen and Violet were her most trusted friends that would guide her. *But they have no wealth and authority.* Jaslyn needed someone else. She needed Alice.

Alice would have scolded Jaslyn for her rash decisions, while swaying the highborn to Jaslyn's side. *Alice isn't here, she is hundreds of leagues away. I must find someone else.*

Her mother could help, but that day would come when the sun went black, Jaslyn knew. *Should I ask Jojo?* She sighed as she exited the keep and into the blistering cold. Fresh snow crunched underneath her muddy boots as she contemplated what to do. *Would he run back and tell Father?* She was not sure, and it made her feel horrible. *Why can't I trust my little brother?*

Suddenly, she stood in front of the Grand Library. *Maybe I should read. But then again, I will be watched.* She was always being watched. Those shadowy black eyes seemed to be watching her increasingly as the days went by.

Waiting.

For what?

She wondered who they reported to. *Father? Mother? The other high-born?* Jaslyn understood now that she was a threat to everyone within the Mountain Realm. She laughed at that. *A girl of eleven is a threat to some of the strongest houses in the realm.* She looked at the grey sky, frowning. *I sound like Father.*

She paused then. *Mother.* Jaslyn didn't know how her mother felt about this. *Is she proud? Angry? Was she planning to do something similar?* Jaslyn did not know, nor did she want to know. Her mother was unpredictable and unforgiving. If Gloriana believed someone crossed her, they would find out eventually. *That's why Father locked her away until Falk left.*

Jaslyn decided to take a chance, and entered the library. She wanted to do something, she needed to do something; she felt so helpless. She silently walked around the library, making sure that she did not wear an emotion on her face. *The Seers would report that, too.*

She picked up a meaningless book and examined it. She smiled, knowing no one would run off to tell her parents she was reading a children's story.

Jaslyn sat alone in a quiet corner of the library. She placed her sack on the table, opened the book, and stared at the words, but she didn't read. She couldn't. Instead, she thought about the large array of houses that *could possibly* go against Lord Borin for her cause. *What is my cause?* If she wanted to approach a highborn for help, she would have to know the specifics. *Would my cause be for the people?* Her answer was yes, but she knew that the lords and ladies of the Mountain Realm was just like her father. They did not care particularly about the people.

Jaslyn had heard from some knights, that the highborn complained about her lord father's leadership. *I need to know everything.* She could not just sit and wait for information to come to her as she had before, she needed to act like the queen she claimed to be. *I will have Evergreen get information,* she thought as she flipped through the pages of the book, *and I will have Violet continue giving food back to every peasant in the realm.*

Then, she felt someone standing over her.

She slowly lifted her head and was pleasantly surprised to see the pretty boy in purple and green standing in front her. *It's him!* She beamed towards the boy and put the book down as her hands began to shake. *I must seem mad smiling like this,* she thought as the two stared at each other silently. *Is this what the maids felt like in those silly stories Maiden Barda would read to me when I was younger?*

"Hello," he said with a friendly smile.

Jaslyn was not sure what the boy wanted, but nonetheless, she was happy that he had approached her. "Hello."

The two were silent for a moment, staring only at each other. *What do I do?* Words failed her as she smiled at the boy. *What could he want with me?*

The boy cleared his throat. "You are Lady Jaslyn, correct?"

"Yes," she replied, straightening her back. "Please sit down. Do you wish to speak with me about something?" Jaslyn tried her best to sound older than she was, but her voice betrayed her. *I am a child.*

"No need," he told her, shaking his hands. "Would you please walk with me, my lady?"

"I'm sorry, I do not know who you are," she admitted shamefully.

His eyes grew wide, "You don't?" Jaslyn shook her head, and the boy sighed in disappointment, "I am Lord Asten Dawphrey, my lady."

"The Little Lord?"

Asten laughed at that, "I don't like the nickname my elders have given me."

Jaslyn looked down. "Apologies, my lord."

The boy laughed again, "No need for apologies, and you don't have to call me *my lord*. We are almost the same age."

"But you called me *my lady*," Jaslyn rebutted.

"Should I call you *my queen* then?"

Jaslyn gasped and shot up from her seat. *Who does this boy lord think he is?!* She questioned with fury. *Oh,* she relaxed. *I'm a girl queen, I am no different.* She had forgotten.

"Please don't," she begged, her voice barely a whisper. She scoped the library waiting for the black eyes to meet hers. *No one is looking.* She nodded to the boy, and tied the sack of gold coins to her hips. "We can go for a walk."

She took a step forward before pausing. She turned to Kai who still slept by the fireplace. "Stay here, I will be back." And her lion yawned in reply.

Asten smiled widely and grabbed her hand to lead her out of the library. The cold air kissed her fiery hot cheeks as she walked with Lord Asten through Maryere. He said nothing at first, he just walked quickly and refused to let go. Even in the cold, Jaslyn's hand sweated entangled in his, but Asten said nothing about it.

When the two reached the lively market area of Maryere, Asten finally slowed down. "I wanted to speak with you about you being a queen."

"I am not a queen anymore," Jaslyn lied. "My lord father ended that."

Asten burst into laughter. His laughs were bright, beautiful, and lively. "Lies are not useful, my queen," he whispered, leaning in.

He is so close. Her thoughts paused as she took in the warmth of his breath on her ear. A small smile appeared on her lips. "Please don't call me that," she replied, trying her best to hide her blushing cheeks with her too short hair.

"Well it's true. Lies are not useful. And you are a queen."

Jaslyn crossed her arms, "Do you wish to get killed?"

"I know you will not allow anyone to kill me."

"You don't know me."

"You're funny, I like that."

Jaslyn sighed, slightly exhausted from the previous conversation with her father. "What do you want from me?"

"I wish to help you."

"You are only a kid."

Asten rolled his eyes, "That didn't stop me from being named the Lord of Snow Creek. Besides, age clearly doesn't matter, my *queen*."

She stopped walking. "If you wish to mock me, please join my lord father in that. Do not do it in front of my face."

Asten touched her shoulder gently. "I would never mock you, it was a small joke. My apologies if it seemed otherwise."

His eyes are so sincere. "No need to apologize," she whispered, glancing at his lingering hand on her shoulder. "But, how can you help me?"

Asten resumed their journey. "Everyone in Snow Creek loves me as if I am their own son, but they respect me, too. My people would never belittle me. When I heard of this girl queen with a white lion, I rode to Maryere as fast as my horse could take me. I had to meet you. I have been watching you for a while."

Jaslyn stared at him longingly while they walked through Maryere, but Asten continued forward. He looked like a lord as he walked and talked, and Jaslyn saw why his people loved him.

"I was so angry when Lord Caster told your secret to the Lord Protector. I wanted to yell and scream, but my grandfather told me to wait. To be patient." *His grandfather?* "He likes you, too," he added with a smile, finally looking at her.

Jaslyn matched his smile. *Does he mean Lord Prestan Dawphrey?* She thought the old man had died. *His mother,* she remembered, *her father is Lord Jasper Payne.* Her grin transformed into a wide smile. *That's why he was wearing House Payne colors last time I saw him. House Payne is a major Mountain Realm house! If I could get his support... I wouldn't have to steal anymore coins to pay for what I need.*

"When I saw you reading in the library today, you looked so sad. I had to speak to you," Asten finished, leaving Jaslyn stunned.

I looked sad. She hadn't noticed. "How will you help me?" she asked again. She did not want a story about how Asten knew of her. She wanted to know how he could help her become Queen of the Mountain Realm.

"My knights, they support me. They told me about you, too. I admit, at first I was jealous that a little girl whom I knew nothing about could get the respect of even my toughest knights."

"How can they respect me?" Jaslyn had to know. "I have never met your knights before."

"You care for the weak. You defend the honor of the Mountain Realm. You're attempting to destroy a system that has been in place for centuries. Talks of destroying the Lord Protector are nothing new, but no one has ever rose up when the weak called upon them. My knights informed me that you did that without hesitation. You saw the flaws and decided to act, even though it didn't affect you. You could have cried and told them how sorry you were and that you would pray for their poor souls like so many highborn had before. But you didn't. You said okay. You said you would help them." He took a long breath then. "I know about Queen's Cove. I know how you have been smuggling food back into the village from Maryere."

Jaslyn looked at her feet. "They were starving."

"Aye, but *you* were not starving," Asten explained. "You have a sweet heart."

"They're people, too."

"Many forget that," he told her, lifting a finger. "My grandfather always told me to remember who they are—people."

"Your grandfather sounds intelligent."

"Oh, he is. He told me to help you, but I will be honest; I didn't want to. I wanted to keep an eye on you and see what you did. I didn't want to put my people in danger. My grandfather, however, insisted that I helped you."

"You still haven't told me how you were going to do this," she noted, giggling.

Asten laughed, too, "That is because I am not sure myself. My grandfather told me I must help you, but not how. He just says things but does not explain afterwards. He wants everything to be a learning lesson."

"And your grandfather supports me?"

"Of course! We are just trying to figure out how to go about this. The Lord Protector is not the right leader for the realm. Every highborn knows this, but they still will not go against him."

"He is afraid of war."

"Apparently not anymore. He is mobilizing to get your sister back."

Jaslyn wanted to scream. *Father is nothing but a liar.* Borin didn't respect her; he practically lied to her. *He is mobilizing? Is that why Jojo is not in trouble, because Father agrees with him?* She was seething now; of course her lord father agreed with his only son, and not his youngest daughter. *He is too late. Alice is gone.* Hot tears welled-up in her eyes at the thought. *Ser Damien told me that Falk would burn down his entire kingdom before giving Alice back.*

Jaslyn wondered if her mother knew about the plan. *Of course, she does.* Her lady mother probably jumped with joy when she found out. *She probably thinks that Father is her knight in shining armor.* He was bringing Alice back. *Idiots,* Jaslyn thought, her body growing tense, *they are all idiots.*

Snow lightly fell around them. "Let's go to someplace warm."

"A tavern," she suggested.

"No, this way."

Jaslyn raised her eyebrows when they approached the Sun Keep, but decided not to question it. She had never visited the keep's ruins before; Lord Borin would never allow it. *Many of the dead walk in there,* her lord father's warning bounced around in her head.

They entered the ruins of the Sun Keep, and Jaslyn was disappointed by the lack of warmth. The Sun Keep had been abandoned for too long. The weather had worn the ceiling, and there were holes allowing snow to fall inside the keep. *A fire had been lit here recently,* Jaslyn noticed.

Asten hugged himself in comfort, "It is much colder than I imagined," he said and Jaslyn noticed his breath in the cold. "And I don't know how to start a fire," he admitted, his hazel eyes no longer smiling.

Jaslyn pressed her lips together and marched to the fireplace. In the hearth, there were a few usable pieces of wood to make a fire. She piled up the sticks, and rubbed two dry ones together. *Two dry sticks,* she remembered, creating friction until smoke appeared. As the fire grew, the snowy room glowed orange. Jaslyn sat on a fallen beam, happily feeling the warmth on her face, and Asten quietly settled himself beside her.

"Lord Osmont is not going to give Alice up," she whispered, breaking the silence that surrounded them.

Asten nodded. "I know, and my grandfather does too. Somehow the Lord Protector doesn't."

"He means to murder half of the kingdom to get my sister back."

"And you don't wish the same?"

She sat there quietly, trying her best to think of an answer. "No, I would not go to war. I want to kill Falk first, with my own hands. Then, I plan on rescuing Alice."

"That still means war, right?" he asked doubtingly.

"Aye, it does. Lives must be lost to get what I want, but I am different from my lord father. He wants to go to war to get my sister back and then march home. No, I mean to march to Kingment and execute that bastard for his crimes."

"Then the Northern Kingdom would be in disarray."

She shrugged, "I guess I will have to be a conqueror too, not just a queen."

"That sounds like the Mad King Alen Ayers."

"No," Jaslyn replied looking directly into Asten's eyes. She had to be serious now. *He's right. What I am suggesting seems crazy.* Only the King of the Riverlands tried to unite the Five Great Lands of Mystos, and in doing so, he grew insane and cruel, and was executed when his plan failed. Jaslyn knew she could do it and do it right. She could be a queen and a conqueror, and she wanted Asten to know that, too. "I mean to free the people. That stupid old king just wanted to murder them all. The Lord Protectors are oppressing everyone, and when I die, I want the world to be better than the one I was born in. If that means war for this generation, then so be it. Cruel men will no longer rule the lands. I will become queen, I will get my sister back, and I will kill Falk. And no one is going to stop me."

Asten smiled at that. "I knew I liked you for a reason."

HADRIAN

S pray from the rain slapped Hadrian Osmont as he tried to keep up with the fast-moving traveler. He kept forward, afraid of what might be lurking. Anything could be behind him, but at least Hadrian knew what was ahead—trees. Bare branches filled with pinecones smacked him so suddenly he screamed in pain and terror. "I think we're far enough from the Raiders now," he exhaled, but Raynese ignored him and continued running. "The smoke is gone, and all I hear is silence. We are alone."

"It's not silent," Raynese replied, her voice tense. "I hear the forest; she is screaming." The woman's strange nature captivated Hadrian. "She tells me to move left, right, down the hills and through the stream. She tells me where to go."

Hadrian, however, tripped over the roots and smacked into more branches. "The forest can't talk," he grumbled, "It says nothing, it wants nothing, and it knows nothing."

"She knows everything!" Raynese shouted, abruptly stopping.

Hadrian collided with Raynese and fell to the ground. He rubbed his bottom and looked up at the young woman. Her chest rose and collapsed quickly as she put a hand on her dagger. Hadrian's eyes widened, and he scooted backward, completely terrified.

Raynese's eyes widened at the reaction before she finally relaxed. "Warrior Raiders are savages. They live off pillaging and killing. Although the Establishments tried to abolish them, most Raiders are too egotistical to hide from danger. No, they face danger and kill it. They are monsters."

"But my father and Lord Falk got rid of them."

She chuckled. "No, they successfully banished them from the kingdom. The Establishments still deal with them in Unmosis. If they got rid of the Raiders, we wouldn't be running from them right now."

She's right, Hadrian realized, his cheeks burning with embarrassment. "Well, instead of running, we could just walk?"

Raynese considered the suggestion for a minute. "We can move slower," she agreed, "but we still need to be careful."

She then took a deep breath before looking toward the sky. Raynese seemed so mesmerized by how the forest worked, and it was something Hadrian couldn't understand. *I was raised as a lord, not a traveler.* When Raynese saw the forest, her eyes lit up. It was as if she saw birth, life, death, and rebirth all at once. However, when Hadrian looked around the same forest, all he saw were bugs that bit, branches that smacked, and birds that never shut up.

Raynese closed her eyes and gently touched a tree beside her, causing the bark to glow green.

What's that? Hadrian carefully watched the young woman. "Um, what are you,"

That's when the birds quit chirping, the wind stopped howling, and the sound of rain ceased. Everything was quiet. *What's going on?* Suddenly, differing screams filled Hadrian Osmont's head all at once. The Warrior Raiders howling their taunts. Colvic shouting to run. And Patty. Patty's wail was the loudest of all. Hadrian dropped to his knees and covered his ears, but it only became more deafening. *Oh gods, make it end!*

And then everything was silent.

When he opened his eyes, he saw Raynese leaning against a tree, silently staring. He put his arms down and waited for the young woman to speak. *Please*, he begged, *say something. Say something!* He always felt so stupid in front of Raynese. He knew she now thought of him as only a child while he now believed she was someone blessed by the gods. *I want to know what you did. I want to know more about the world. Please.*

"We will continue east," Raynese informed rigidly. As she walked past, she glanced at him curiously, leaving Hadrian with more questions.

Is she going to explain the glow? He watched the woman continue ahead, leaving him behind. *No, she isn't. Raynese believes my screams were from childish terror. She thinks I'm afraid of her. So she isn't going to talk about it, so she doesn't scare me further.* Hadrian stood, shook out his anxiety, and headed east. *I need to grow up. Then maybe she will teach me the truth.*

Walking through the Great Forest was much better than running. Every tree looked so different from the blurs Hadrian had seen before. Some were tall, some weren't, and some were skinnier than Hadrian's arms. Wildflowers, the color of the sun and sky, grew in little tufts near tree trunks, while ivy and honeysuckle clung to the tree bark. Everything looked as if it had lived for over a hundred years.

It's beautiful.

Dusk broke when Hadrian grew tired. The aching in his head and feet made everything burn, and he wanted to sit, but Raynese showed no signs of stopping. Hadrian grew slower and slower, no longer able to keep up. "Uh," he called out, breathless, "could we,"

But Raynese was gone.

He stopped and scanned his surroundings, yet every direction looked the same. *What do I do?* He took a deep breath and started running straight. *I must find her. I can't be alone.* He ran as the rain picked up, and branches kept slapping him.

"You must return to where you are running from," something whispered. "To escape." The voice sounded as if it was the wind that whipped around him.

Tears filled his eyes. *I must be strong. An adult wouldn't cry, but a child would.* Hadrian stopped again and looked into the trees. "Who are you? Come out!"

"You must become weak to grow strong."

Did the voice read my mind? "S-show yourself!" he commanded, his courage waning.

"And your faith shall kill you." The voice filled Hadrian's head, repeating the same phrases louder and louder. "You must return to where you are running from to escape. You must become weak to grow strong. And your faith shall kill you."

Hadrian clenched and pulled at his hair. He leaned over, hyperventilating, as the once whispery voice now blared in his head. The loudness mimicked when he saw Raynese's strange power. *What is going on? I didn't see the green glow this time.* He dropped to his knees, covered his ears, and screamed along with the voice, "STOP IT! LEAVE ME BE!"

But the voice continued, "You must return to where you are running from to escape. You must become weak to grow strong. And your faith shall kill you."

I've heard this voice before. Blood-red eyes flashed in his head. *The woman I spoke to the day before my birthday!* He had no idea who she was. *Did she curse me? Is that what this is?*

The agony lasted for what seemed like hours. *Where is Raynese? Why hasn't she saved me yet?* After a while, Hadrian laid in the dirt, repeating the phrases aloud along with the voice. "I must return to where I am running from to escape," he struggled, tears streaming down his face. He held his ears as he rocked back and forth for comfort. "I must become weak to grow strong." Each word was implanted into Hadrian's brain, no matter how hard he tried to fight it. "And my faith shall kill me."

"HADRIAN!" Arms wrapped around him.

Hadrian, however, didn't move or smile or say anything. He stayed on his knees, rocking back and forth with his ears covered, repeating the phrases.

"Hadrian, stop it. You're scaring me."

But Hadrian didn't stop. He wanted to, but he didn't. He couldn't. The omniscient voice controlled him and he could no longer hear Raynese's pleas. He felt a light kiss on his ear, and the warmth made Hadrian's head spring up. The two stared at each other for a moment. "And your faith shall kill you," his voice trembled.

"What?"

His eyes grew wide with embarrassment. *No, that's not what I wanted to say!* "And your faith shall kill you," he croaked.

Raynese embraced Hadrian and kissed his forehead lovingly, as he sobbed. She was so warm, and her dirty hair smelled like rain. He pushed his head deeper into her arms, taking in her comfort.

After a few moments, Hadrian finally calmed down.

The young woman moved to pull away, but Hadrian grabbed her sleeve, refusing to let her leave. "Don't worry, I'm not going anywhere."

Thank you, he tried to say. Instead, "And your faith shall kill you," tumbled out of his mouth.

* * *

While running for his life and away from the prophesied words, Hadrian had put him and Raynese off course by weeks. He had taken the pair to a part of the forest unknown to the traveler woman so they could do nothing but continue their journey toward the Northern Kingdom of Valley Pines.

But their journey felt like circles.

Hadrian Osmont was tired. Cuts, bruises, and scabs littered his skin; every breath was ragged, and his dry throat kept him constantly thirsty. Walking through the Great Forest had become exhausting, and all Hadrian wanted to do was lay in his plush bed back at the High Castle in King's Berth. Instead, he continued silently walking, allowing the traveler woman to guide him.

Raynese stayed a few steps ahead, with a frown constantly spread across her face as they trekked. For days, the lush green that usually filled the Great Forest was now a barren wasteland. It wasn't a type of barren that winter brought, but something that had stripped life from every piece of nature. Dead flowers, dead trees, dead animals—nothing survived around them, and Hadrian could feel the death that stalked the forest creeping into his soul.

When will we get out of here?

He bumped into Raynese, who knelt over, scooping handfuls of parched dirt. "The Darkness lives here," she exhaled, her eyes still on the ground. "Day and night."

Hadrian inhaled to question the woman's words before pausing. *And your faith shall kill you.* He knew those were the only words he could say, so instead, he sighed and waited for Raynese to continue.

The woman stood, walked to a dead pine tree, and touched the broken bark. "Some kind of beast created these gashes."

Beast. Images of twisted Wicked animals filled Hadrian's head, matching the descriptions of the monsters in the stories his mother would tell him. *Unmos, the god of Darkness, bitter with his sister-goddess, Axone, created things that looked like animals, but none could be tamed like a dog or an oxen. All they wanted to do was kill.*

Raynese's eyes flashed toward him, seemingly more green than brown. "We should finally reach some foliage in a few hours." He stepped back and nodded silently, causing the young woman to smile, and the scar that stretched across her face smiled too. "You look exhausted, cutie. Come here."

Hadrian found himself stumbling into Raynese's arms, taking in her embrace. Warmth radiated from her hands to his head, and Hadrian could see a strange green glow from the corner of his eyes, so he pushed her away. *What the heck are you doing?!* He wanted to question, yet the continuous phrase escaped his lips.

Raynese gave the boy a sad smile and hugged him again. "Look, you have been stuck in shock for some time now. My Art soothes, so please accept my help."

Her Art, Hadrian repeated, not understanding but allowing the woman to hug him again. *What is an Art, and how does it soothe me?*

He focused on a strange sparrow on a bare branch, staring directly at him. *This world is much stranger than I initially believed, but how much do I want to learn?* Hadrian just wanted to go home. He frowned. *I also want to know the truth… about who my mother is.*

Finally, Raynese released him. "Is that better?"

I do feel lighter. That might be good for the continuous journey. Hadrian nodded, pressing on a smile. *Thank you.*

She gave him a genuine smile. "I felt that, thank you."

The two continued on through the lifeless piece of the Great Forest, and every once in a while, Hadrian could hear the caws of a bird song, causing him to sigh.

Even though Hadrian now lived in silence, his mind was never quiet. If he was not pondering the idea of another woman being his mother or thinking about the prophesied words that trapped his voice, then cawings screeched in his head. At first, he thought that killing himself would be better than constantly hearing those birds, but he could not do that.

That would mean Mother won.

A berry bush appeared before them, and Raynese leaped toward it. "Something is growing!" She swiped at the fruit and tasted it before grinning. "Finally!" Raynese plucked a few more and handed them to Hadrian. "Here, eat some." She then returned to the bush, and it glowed green. "The River Lilia is still far."

Hadrian nodded and popped a few berries into his mouth. He loved to squeeze the fruit in his mouth and let the sweet juice slide down his throat, quenching his thirst. The berry was sweet and tangy, like the lemon drops he ate back at the High Castle.

Leo and Wynn would love these berries, too.

The pair continued their silent journey for another few hours until Hadrian followed Raynese out of the barren wasteland, into a field, and up a grassy hill.

Raynese skipped around with glee. "Humans made this, can you tell?"

Hadrian observed his surroundings, nodding. *The Forestland Hill Tribes,* he wanted to answer, remembering the lessons an old Saavant used to teach. *The River Lilia is named after the creators of the hill tribes' daughter. Same with the River Aimil, named after their son.*

He climbed up the first hill as Raynese continued, laughing beautifully in the sunshine. *We've been traveling north, so these must be Alnor's Hills. Where is Alnor's Fortress?* He turned to his left, and a small stone keep was in the distance between some hills. *Smaller than the one at Seascape.*

Hadrian noticed a flicker near the top of the fortress, causing his heartbeat to quicken. *A scope reflection. Someone is watching.* He rushed to Raynese and tugged on her sleeve, pointing toward Alnor's Fortress.

The woman's hazel eyes narrowed on the old small castle, and she smiled before waving, causing Hadrian's mouth to drop open. "Don't worry," she told him, patting his curly hair. "As long as we don't approach, they won't bother us. Let's keep going. We will be at the river once we pass the hills to the east!"

Then, Raynese was tumbling down the green hill, her arms and legs wiggling around with a child-like excitement. Hadrian scrunched his face and ran after the traveler woman. As he ran, butterflies fluttered all around. Each was beautiful, with their brightly colored wings splashed in pinks, greens, and yellows.

The cool breeze kissed his face as he ran faster, stumbling as he tried to keep pace with Raynese. *Why is she so fast? It's like she has infinite stamina or something. Can she fight against the beasts that damage the land like she did with the Warrior Raiders?* Hadrian could feel the strength that radiated from Raynese, but Ser Colvic was right. He knew nothing about the woman. *She used some light to calm my body. What is the Arts? Why have I never seen anyone else use something like that before? Is it illegal?*

Hadrian Osmont wished he could ask the endless questions that filled his mind, yet the exact same terrible words escaped his lips like always. "And your faith shall kill you."

He paused and opened his eyes, realizing Raynese didn't respond. *She always says something when I try to speak.* He looked around, but the strange traveler woman was nowhere to be found. *Wait, where did she go?* His attention snapped from the hills to the forest before him, and he sighed. *Raynese is just ahead,* he told himself, dashing forward.

Thick vines and trees surrounded him, and he knew he wasn't in the field anymore. *How many leagues have I ran since I last saw Raynese?* He ran as fast as he could, unable to see anything. A low branch slapped Hadrian, and he fell to the ground, holding his face. He screamed, hoping Raynese would find him.

The woman came without warning, hugging Hadrian comfortingly, "Shh! Let me see," she commanded in a tone Hadrian's mother used when he wasn't listening. Raynese tugged at his hands, and he relaxed. His eyes narrowed on the blood that stained Raynese's already dirty skin, and he cried out loudly. "Shh!" Raynese hushed again, looking at his wound, "You didn't duck?"

His face twitched into a frown as the birds in his mind squawked louder. He winced from all the pain and fell to his knees, sobbing. *I can't do this. We barely know where we are, and it's my fault. Everything hurts, and I can't speak. I hate my life. Why couldn't I have just been my mother's child?* Hadrian's frown deepened. *How does that even happen? How didn't she know I was her child?*

Lady Arla Osmont's kind brown eyes smiled in Hadrian's mind. *When I first gave birth to you, I thought I had lost you.*

The airiness in his mother's words calmed him, yet the tears continued. *Was Mother tricked?*

"Let's keep walking to the river, and we will clean your wound there," Raynese decided, grabbing Hadrian's hand and forcing him to his feet. "You will feel better when you dip into the water."

He still pictured his mother, who wasn't his mother, feeling completely lost. *Why did Mother decide that I needed to be killed? I could have helped her find the people who did this instead. We could've still worked together. We could've still loved each other. Why did she turn on me? It's not like I was the one who tricked her.*

The sun had set, and Hadrian continued behind Raynese for another hour before the sound of rushing water caused him to grin. *We're here!* He had grown tired of the blood running down his face and the constant stinging from sweat touching his wound.

Raynese said nothing and swung her arm out for Hadrian to stop. She backed away in a different direction silently, her hazel eyes glittering murderously as she clutched onto two of her daggers. Her attention moved to the tops of the trees, and she started climbing without a word of explanation, disappearing into the darkness.

Hadrian pressed his back into a tree, not sure what was happening. *Raynese must have seen something. What kind of predators lurk in the Great Forest?*

A small grey-brown sparrow flapped above Hadrian, hopping from this tree to that, chirping an annoying high-pitched song. Another bird chirped, then another, and then thousands of birds screeched around Hadrian, but he could still only see the one sparrow hopping from tree to tree. *Wait.* He watched the bird cautiously, noticing the animal attempting to sound like there were more birds than just one. *It feels threatened.* The bird's wings flapped wildly, and when its beak opened wide, thousands of bird caws came loudly from it. *What is it afraid of?*

Slowly, Hadrian turned his head to see an enormous animal resembling a forest leopard. The wild cat was a beautiful creature perched up in the trees, but something was wrong. *It doesn't look right. It's twice as big, and it's coloring.* Hadrian exhaled, taking in the leopard's peculiar jade fur blending perfectly with the green leaves that refused to change from the cool autumn air. The beast's brown-yellow eyes glinted as it stared directly at Hadrian. It growled momentarily, and its ivory-colored fangs bared fear into Hadrian's soul. *What do I do?*

He knew the leopard would leap from the tree if he ran. If he screamed, the leopard would jump and attack. Hadrian gulped and decided to pray aloud. "Citia, this jaded beast bears its fangs, but I wish it no harm. I beg for your grace and assisting this animal in finding another prey to stalk," he prayed, his eyes never leaving the leopard. "Axone, please hear," he continued, but the squawking from the frightened sparrow drowned the boy's prayer, bringing tears to his eyes. *I'm going to die. Not from the hands of the Warrior Raiders as my mother wanted, but regardless, she won.*

He looked into the animal's yellow-colored eyes, and the sparrow's fearful caws transitioned into the beautiful singing voice of his mother. *Far, far. Far the wind blows. Far, far, away. Far, far. Far the wind blows. To sweep you through the day.* Tears streamed as he sang along with his mother's chore song, wishing for a better day. "Far, far. Far the wind blows,"

The leopard responded by roaring before jumping from the branch with its claws out, ready to rip Hadrian into shreds. He dropped to the ground, preparing to die.

Instead of meeting death, the chilly wind kissed his wet cheeks. Hadrian opened his eyes to find himself in Raynese's arms as she hopped from tree to tree, farther away from the strange leopard. Her movements were unnatural as she held Hadrian, swung off one branch, and sprung from another.

Although Raynese swiftly moved through the trees, she couldn't distance them from the beast. The leopard roared, causing Hadrian to shriek, but Raynese held him tighter and continued through the forest. The traveler woman's fast pace quickened, and everything blurred.

Is this why I would lose Raynese so often during our journey? Hadrian wondered, his eyes still on the unnatural movements of the leopard behind them. *Raynese moves are weird, too. How is she doing this? What is going on?*

"Oh shit, we're at the river!" the young woman cursed, still flying through the trees. "Don't let go!"

Before Raynese could say anything else, they dropped into the water.

The river's current swept Hadrian away from Raynese's grasp, and in a single moment, she was gone. "Help!" he screamed when he resurfaced. "Help!" he shouted again, spitting water as more poured into his mouth.

Gods, I talked! No, wait,

Hadrian Osmont sunk in the rushing water, and when he reached the river's floor, he prayed to every god and goddess he knew by name. *Axone. Aros. Varva. Citia. Obum. Please save me.* His lungs constricted, and the feeling of sharp knives digging into his chest overwhelmed him. All he saw was darkness; after a moment, he felt nothing. *You've won, Mother, the bastard is dead. Your once son is dead. I am dead.*

And the birds screamed in anguish as Hadrian drowned.

ALICE

O ver a fortnight had passed since Myra's attack, but the handmaiden's condition didn't improve. Alice stared at her best friend, sniffling. Even as the journey continued, she stayed by Myra's side. Alice gave her friend sponge baths, washed her hair, and changed her clothes. *It's like we switched places,* Alice realized, imagining her handmaiden working hard as Alice slept. *I wish we could switch again. At least then, you would be awake.*

Lady Myra Nores didn't look like a girl who slept day and night. Her glowing tan skin, shiny black hair, and cute little face matched an energetic person who lived happily. *I wish I could've given her happiness,* Alice thought longingly. "I only gave you sorrow," she whispered, lightly patting Myra's head, laying beside her.

It didn't matter if they were in the wheelhouse or the tent; Alice laid beside Myra. She didn't want to be in any other place. *I don't even want to look at Falk.* Just the thought of the Lord Protector of the Northern Kingdom of Valley Pines made her seethe with rage. *If I'm near him again, I might just kill him.*

Myra shifted, and Alice hovered over the girl, waiting for Myra to open her eyes and smile, but it never came. *What am I going to do if she never wakes up?*

A knight marched in, and Alice shielded Myra like a mother bear. "Why are you here? Where is Ser Damien?"

"The Lord Protector wants you."

She blinked back at the man, thinking of the different ways she could murder Lord Falk Osmont. *What does he need?* She hadn't spoken to Falk since Ser Damien carried her out of his tent. *What do I do? I can't deny him.*

Alice moved off the bed and leaned over to say goodbye to her handmaiden. She placed the lucky kismet coin in Myra's hands and kissed the handmaiden's cheek, still not wanting to leave. "I'll be back."

A cold metal hand gripped her wrist and pulled her out of the tent.

"Hey, wait! Let go of me! I didn't even get to dress. Do you know who I am?"

Alice's protests went unheard as the knight dragged her across the campsite. When they reached the tent, he pushed Alice in harshly, and she landed on her knees, now breathless. Her attention focused on Falk, who sat on his throne with his feet resting on a body lying on the floor. *What's going on?* She scanned inside, and the emptiness frightened her. *What happened?*

She stood straight. "You needed me?"

The body lifted its head at Alice's voice and wiggled around, making muffled sounds. Alice stared at the body, her eyes wide as Lord Falk kicked it silent.

The Lord Protector's eyes snapped to her as he fingered through his fiery-colored hair. "Alice, there you are," he started, motioning to come closer. "I have a present for you."

Alice stepped toward to her lord uncle, and the body started squirming again. "W-what is it?"

Falk Osmont grinned his terrible grin and yanked the bag off of the body's head.

Alice's world went dark. *No.*

It had happened again. A person Alice loved so dear was once again in trouble, and it was all her fault. She clutched her chest as she tried to process what was in front of her. Her mouth attempted to make words, but nothing came out.

"Do you like what you see?" Falk questioned, chuckling.

"No!" she screamed, backing away.

The cold, dark eyes of Ser Damien Clay stared at her, sad and defeated. A knight pushed past Alice, grabbed a chair, and placed it beside Falk Osmont. "Sit," the Lord Protector commanded, his excitement growing.

She did as she was told without speaking a word. *Falk arrested Ser Damien.* Her big eyes stayed on the knight as her entire body shook in the chair. A black eye, a busted lip, and bruises littered Ser Damien's skin. The proud knight had been beaten, branded, and emasculated. *And it's all my fault.*

"Ser Knight," Lord Falk began before lowering his eyes and clearing his throat. "I mean, Ser Damien Clay, you've been arrested with charges of treason. How do you plead?"

Ser Damien coughed, and blood trickled down his chin. "I've committed no treason."

"You mean the letter you planned to send to the Lord Protector of the Mountain Realm wasn't treason?"

Her heart dropped. *Oh shit.*

"I did not write to the Lord Protector," the knight replied, his voice hoarse.

Falk tapped on his short beard. "Oh, yes, that's right," he said, almost pleased with the answer. "You thought you were so clever, writing to Lady Jaslyn Wayward as a cover. Who were you really writing to?"

And Ser Damien Clay stayed silent.

"I asked a damned question," Lord Falk screamed, throwing a tantrum. The Lord Protector jumped from his seat, kicked the knight in the face, and stomped on his chest. "Answer me, you traitor!"

The knight's eyes stayed on the floor as Falk continued striking, and Alice could only stare. *I failed Ser Damien. I failed Myra. I failed everyone.* She gripped the handrests of the chair, trying her best not to wail. *There is nothing I can do. I'm a naïve, stupid girl. It will be my downfall.*

"Answer me!" Falk shouted, bringing Alice back to her terrible reality. "Now, knight!"

"I've committed no treason."

Falk roared in reaction before stomping toward a display sword and unsheathing the blade. *He's going to kill Ser Damien!*

Alice Wayward leapt from her chair and slid between the knight and lord. "Stop, please!" she cried, but Falk only stared at her wildly.

Lord Falk Osmont gritted his teeth into a smile and lifted the sword, unfazed by Alice's intervention. *Oh, he's going to kill me too.* She stared at the sparkling blade as it swooped down on her, and she prepared to die. *I guess I tried,* she thought solemnly. *Just not my best.*

Before the sword could hit her, Ser Damien pushed Alice aside and held up his arm as Falk connected with the knight's flesh. The weight behind the strike caused the sword to stick into Ser Damien's arm. He roared in agony before falling onto the ground, unconscious.

"What did you do?!" Alice wailed, laying over the knight as a shield. *I don't care if he kills me, but I cannot allow him to hurt the people I love anymore.* She clutched at the knight's tunic and attempted to calm her breathing. *I must do something.* Her attention focused on the disgraceful Lord Protector, yet her anger only brewed. "Call for someone to tend to him," she commanded, her voice strained.

"Who do you think you are!?" Falk shrieked. "I warned you I wasn't a merciful lord! You didn't think my threats were real, but this will bring you to reality. You're stuck in hell now."

Alice sneered. "Wickedness reeks from you."

The man's eyes widened at the insult. "Go to your tent! I don't want to see you again for the rest of the trip."

She slowly rose to her feet, ignoring her aching body. Her eyes never leaving her lord uncle. "You *will* have someone tend to him."

"I'm not afraid of you," he scoffed.

"I'm not trying to frighten you," Alice replied, her voice calm. She stepped forward, but Falk stepped back. "I want you to do what is right, but it seems you are incapable of that. I guess that is because you're an Osmont," she insulted, finally looking away. She studied her protector, feeling useless. "You will leave Ser Damien and me alone starting now. I'm tired of playing these games with you."

A glimmer of life sparkled in Falk's green eyes, and he got into Alice's face. "You think you can command me, little girl? Let me teach you another life lesson."

Another, Alice frowned. *What is he going to do?*

"Let this scar be a reminder of your disobedience," Falk threatened, but the words were only whispers.

Before Alice could react, Ser Damien tossed her, once again protecting her from one of Lord Falk's strikes. "You will not hit Alice," Ser Damien slurred, and Falk replied by kicking the knight in the face.

"Guards!" Falk called, and six men rushed in. "Take the prisoner to the holding carriage," he commanded. "And lock Lady Wayward in her wheelhouse."

Alice sat on her knees, the spirit to fight melting. *Lock me in the wheelhouse.* The knights moved to grab her. "No!" she shouted, pulling away. "No, please!"

"Oh, and put her little sleeping friend in the wheelhouse, too," Falk added with a grin, and Alice silenced. "Yeah, I thought that would shut the bear up!"

GLORIANA

Her tired blue eyes stayed on the old woman as the two sat in Gloriana's bedchamber. Lady Joan Myster relentlessly stared back while nibbling on some bread. The tension caused Gloriana to grit her teeth, unsure of the conversation she was about to have. For almost a moon, Gloriana locked herself away in Winter's Keep just as Borin commanded, constantly in a state of anxiety. She would tiptoe through the halls, listen to the servants' gossip, and eye her children suspiciously. *Who is going to make the first move?*

Lady Joan Myster swallowed and wiped her mouth clean before sipping her drink. "So, you've stayed in here the whole time?" Gloriana nodded, looking away. "Are you that afraid of Borin?"

"*You* don't have to worry about his animosity."

The old woman's eyebrows raised. "Does he show that side often?"

"Only when I do or say something he doesn't like," she answered with tears to her eyes. "I love him, but his volatility is why I spend most of my time away. So, since he wants me in Winter's Keep, I'll do that. I've simply stayed in this area and minded my business as a woman should."

Joan Myster buzzed her lips. "No point in lying to me, dear. What's the Lord Protector planning?"

"Nothing," she replied. "From what I've gathered, he's been overeating, drinking until he passes out, and listening to no one but his thoughts. There are even some whispers that Jaslyn's lion attacked him."

"Oh, please! That lion wouldn't hurt a fly unless Jaslyn commanded it or," Joan paused, her eyes widening. "Have you seen Jaslyn recently?"

Gloriana's lip twitched. "About a week ago, rushing out of the keep."

"Do you hate your children, Gloriana?" Lady Myster inquired, interlacing her fingers together.

"Of course not!" she gasped.

"So, why do you ignore them?"

Gloriana shrugged. "That's just how I was raised, I guess."

Lady Joan repositioned herself in the seat. "Well, your mother should've done better."

Gloriana closed her eyes and took a deep breath, trying her best not to attack the old woman. "I meant how I was raised *here* in the Mountain Realm. Lady Fallen allowed me to figure things out myself, so I did the same for my children."

"What about your actual mother?"

Gloriana Wayward reflected on her childhood, but much was just a blur. "I treat my children with love and care as my mother did."

"Sure," the old woman exhaled. "So, the Lord Protector has not moved to bring his daughter back?"

She frowned. "No."

"Well, he's running out of time."

"Is that supposed to bother me?" Gloriana questioned, crossing her arms. "I thought we agreed upon the Lush Bear and exiling Borin."

Joan grinned. "Very optimistic. I thought I would have to convince you further to go along with my plan. I even found his whore to sway you."

Her heart dropped at the woman's words. "You found... his whore."

Lady Joan's beady eyes narrowed onto Gloriana. "It seems you already know. Do you want to meet her?"

Gloriana shook her head. "I won't be able to take it."

"You may want to. It might increase your hatred for him."

"I don't hate him," she cried.

"Exactly. You still have love for the man, and we cannot proceed with your murky feelings. Meet the whore, and you might find yourself hating him." Gloriana's attention snapped back to Joan and she wiped her tears, allowing the woman to continue. "Her name is Esme, and she lives by the chapel in the Merchant's District. A purple candle burns outside her door."

"I don't want to meet her."

"Aye, you do," the old woman insisted, not caring about the tears. "And you might want to do it now. I'm sure Borin will be eating his dinner soon. It will give you time to sneak out."

"You're not giving me a choice, are you?"

Lady Joan smiled. "Finally, you're getting it! Now, go on and meet the whore. Learn about what she's experienced, and then let's talk again about eliminating Borin."

Eliminate Borin. The words didn't make sense to Gloriana. *I didn't want Borin dead; maybe just banish him.* She rubbed her hands together, conflict filling within her. *He could have arrested me, but he didn't. I can at least repay that favor, right? Does he deserve that kindness?*

Gloriana relented and grabbed a cloak before sticking her small dagger into her ankle holster. "I'll go see the woman now." She then exited the room, leaving Lady Joan behind.

Her heels clacked loudly against the stone floors as she briskly approached the keep's exit. *Why would meeting Borin's whore make me hate him?* An aching headache appeared, just as it did when Gloriana realized Alice was leaving without them saying goodbye. *What am I to do?* Terrible memories of abuse from her husband filtered through her mind. *I might dislike the man, but I don't hate him. I don't know if I can hate him.*

Gloriana had been taught to love Borin Wayward more than she loved herself. *My son only deserves the best, and I know Summeran women do what-ever they want.* Lady Fallen Wayward's toxic words swirled around, height-ening her anxiety. *Don't talk back. Respond with 'Yes, dear husband.' Never make Borin repeat himself. Always allow him into your bed. You can never tell him no.* The woman's mocking grin appeared in Gloriana's mind. *If you don't do those things, he might punish you, and you know he enjoys exterminating the rats.*

She paused, hyperventilating. *Please leave me alone.* She was tired of the dreadful memories that replayed in her head. *Why can I never remember the good times?*

"Gloriana," Borin's voice echoed, and she turned toward her husband, meeting him at a hallway intersection. The Lord Protector looked her up and down. "Where are you going?"

She covered herself with the cloak. "To the garden."

"At night?" he questioned, unconvinced. "During a snowstorm?"

Finally, Gloriana looked right into her husband's shining copper eyes. "I've lived in Maryere much longer than Goldpsire. I know the cold," she lied. "And Alice enjoyed spending time in the garden. I miss her since you took away my opportunity to say goodbye."

"You took that away from yourself," Borin grumbled, frowning. "Any-way, I need you to do something for me."

She could feel her heart beating in her ears. *Borin rarely asks for my assistance.* The Lord Protector only allowed Gloriana to play the happy lady wife his mother molded her to be. *He needs me.* She stepped forward, placing her hands behind her back. "What do you need, dear husband?"

Borin rolled his eyes. "Write to Lord Ayers or Lord Thoren,"

"Ashmire," Gloriana corrected, her voice cold. "Why?"

"We must send Jaslyn away as a ward, creating an economic pact, especially since those two kingdoms never recovered from the war. We have the upper hand."

He's trying to be a Lord Protector, she realized. "Write them yourself."

Borin slapped Gloriana, causing her to stumble back. "Don't talk back to me!"

Lady Fallen Wayward echoed in Gloriana's head, repeating Borin's words. She gritted her teeth and lifted her eyes, her entire body shaking an-grily. "Apologies, I will write to them immediately."

No, I'll write to Borin's older sister, Sable. I'll even have Asterin deliver the letter and request that she work in the Lion's Den Castle so someone I trust will walk through the halls. Gloriana suppressed a grin. *The Grasslands is the saf-est place in the world anyway.*

"Your performance today isn't the same," he stepped into Gloriana's personal space, causing her to shrink within herself. "It hasn't been the same since I returned." Again, Borin looked her up and down, taking her all in. "Maybe I shouldn't have let you taste power. I thought acting as Lord Protector while I was away would be a passive task for you since you rarely cared about ruling anyway, but I was wrong." He turned and walked toward the dining hall. "I don't like hitting you, so stop being stupid."

Alone, Gloriana exhaled, not realizing she had been holding her breath. *Borin is more violent than usual.* Her head pulsed. *Wait, is that why Kai attacked Borin? Did he hit Jaslyn?* Fury brewed inside. *Fallen never said anything about hitting children.* She started her march to Jaslyn's room when she paused. *Oh gods, is that what Joan meant?*

Gloriana dashed out of Winter's Keep and into the never-ending snowstorm. Icicles and bitterly cold wind burned any exposed skin, forcing her to pull the cloak closer. She entered the Merchant's District and headed straight to the chapel.

The Chapel of the Sun never held a close place in Gloriana's heart. As a girl, she had asked Ser Rodrick and Lord Robart where she could find solace; their answers were always the same: the chapel. Gloriana, however, found no comfort, no peace, nothing. Just some old priests, monks, and canonesses whispering amongst each other or doing secular deeds.

Instead, she found her haven in the shops, where she convinced merchants to bring more Summeran products to Maryere. As years passed, the Merchant's District slowly began to smell, taste, and look like the fading memories of Gloriana's past. The district became her second home, and Borin knew that.

She paused. *And so he houses his whore here instead of in the residential district.* She saw it at the end of a street, and a frown spread across her face. *I didn't realize Borin hated me so much.*

Gloriana slowly approached the cottage, the purple candle burning outside the front door. *What will I see when I get inside?* She knocked, and her heartbeat quickened as footsteps approached.

The door swung open, revealing a healthy-looking young woman. "Hello, what do you need?"

"Hello, the storm made me lose my way, and I'm terribly cold. May I stay here for a bit to warm up?" Gloriana introduced, trying her best to sound feeble.

The woman smiled and stepped aside for her to enter. "Of course, please come in."

Gloriana shuffled into the cottage, pulled the cloak from her head, and quickly took in her surroundings. *It's a quaint cottage, like the one the Borin gave to Maiden Barda when she retired.*

Esme stood with a smile plastered on her face.

Gloriana suppressed a look of disgust, not understanding what the purpose of all of this was. *I would've preferred to have never met you.* Curly, bright-orange, and luscious hair tumbled down the woman's shoulders, causing her green-grey eyes to glitter. *Esme is a Valley woman.* She was taller than Gloriana, and her hips and waist hadn't yet experienced motherhood. The woman's smooth, ivory skin contrasted greatly with Gloriana, who had started to age from all the stress. *Does Joan think I would hate Borin because he picked a beautiful woman?*

"You have a charming cottage, miss." Gloriana complimented, trying to start a conversation.

"Thank you!" Esme beamed. "Why were you out in a snowstorm?"

"I had spent my day in the chapel praying, and when I tried to go home, I got lost, seeing the chapel repeatedly. They've put out the fire in the congregation room to deter the peasants from sleeping there. Then, the snow became unbearable, and I was so cold."

"Oh, you pitiful thing," the woman said, walking towards Gloriana. "My name is Esme. It is nice to meet you."

She nodded. *If Esme told Borin about her strange interaction, he might want names. I must be careful.*

"Would you like some hot tea, Lady Gloriana?" Esme questioned, moving away.

The moment Gloriana heard her name, she pulled out her small knife and held it to the woman's throat. "How do you know who I am?"

Esme tried to separate from Gloriana's grasp. "Apologies, my lady, but the only highborn Summeran woman who walks through Maryere is you."

Stupidity looked Gloriana right in the eyes. *Of course, everyone knows who I am. I don't blend in with the rest of the mountain people.* She released Esme and took several steps back. "Well, I just wanted to,"

"Did you come here to help me?"

Lady Gloriana looked at the young woman, perplexed. "Why would I help you?"

"Oh, I thought you knew," Esme frowned, reaching for the buttons of her shirt. Gloriana lifted the dagger, but Esme only stared at the blade as she undressed.

When the woman began to slip her shirt off, Gloriana wanted to look away, but something stopped her—something sinister.

Her gaze moved to a gash that sat underneath Esme's collarbone, close to where Gloriana had held her dagger. The blade slipped from Gloriana's grip as she took in the purple, blue, green, and yellow bruises that colored the woman's arms. More scapes, scratches, and scars littered Esme's chest, and the woman turned her head from Gloriana, but Gloriana couldn't look away. "Who did this to you?"

Esme's green eyes lowered, examining the marks. "The Lord Protector of the Mountain Realm, Borin Wayward."

"No," Gloriana whispered, backing away. "You're his whore. Who tortured you?"

A strange smile crept across Esme's face. "I thought I was going to be his whore as well when I saw him for the first time. I thought he was so handsome, such a burly and strong man. He told me how much he loved his wife and would never break his promise by sleeping with someone else." Tears streamed, causing Esme to cover her face. "He said he had other pleasures, too, and that he would use me to fulfill them because he didn't want to continue hurting you. He wanted to be a better husband and father."

You might find yourself hating him after meeting his whore. Lady Joan echoed in her head.

Gloriana Wayward intertwined her fingers together and took a deep breath. *I thought Borin only struck me. He has a better relationship with our children than I do, but does he beat them, too?* She imagined all the times Borin slapped, punched, or kicked her throughout their relationship.

I'm married to a Wicked. And it was her worst nightmare.

For years, Gloriana had noticed the darkness that slipped out of her lord husband anytime his anger grew out of control. *Is he uncontrollable now? Did he get Esme so he wouldn't end up killing me?* More questions swirled in her head, but it didn't matter. She understood one thing now. *I must get Borin deposed before someone sticks a knife through his heart.*

Esme looked up at Gloriana, her eyes shining brightly from the tears. "After one of his beatings, I secretly went to a Saavant who deals with whores, and he stitched my wounds together. He pressed me about who did it, but I am not stupid. I know the black eyes talk. I was hoping, however, that the information would get to you without too much being exposed so the Lord Protector would not find out."

Her head spun as Esme spoke in a single breath. "I,"

"So, will you help me, my lady?"

Pity stung Gloriana's heart. "I,"

Esme frowned. "You see this scar?" she questioned, pointing at her neck. "He slashed my neck after Lady Alice's betrothal. I suppose he thought if he killed me, all of it would go away. But I did not die, and his problems did not go away. Another time, he whipped and thrashed me until he left scars on my back. The Lord Protector told me it was because he could not control his life anymore, but could control me."

"Please, Esme," Gloriana called, unable to take the woman's experiences. She then exhaled heavily. "Does he come to you any time he is upset?" Gloriana questioned, and the young woman nodded. *Borin still hits me. Does anything quell his rage?* Bile crept up Gloriana's throat as she realized she didn't know her lord husband. Her eyes scanned Esme's chest and arms. *I am married to a monster.* Unwanted tears burst from Gloriana. She was so tired and hurt and confused and lonely. *I wish my family could go back to how it was.* She missed constantly staring at the grey clouds with nothing to do. She missed the uneventful moons she spent, hoping for something to happen. *Something did happen, and now my life will never be the same.*

"My lady, I want your permission to kill the Lord Protector."

Gloriana hiccupped. "What?"

"Give me permission to kill Lord Borin," Esme repeated, her smile bright. "I will do it and take the blame."

"Why do you need my permission?"

"I need to know that you agree with my intentions. If you do not, and you want him to live, then I will let him live. I do not wish to rip apart a family."

Gloriana peered at Esme's hopeful expression, her heart breaking. *I can't do it. I can't give the orders.* Shame burned Gloriana's cheeks, and she turned her eyes to the wooden floor. *Why?* She wanted to scream to herself. *Why can you not do it!? Borin is a horrible person who made many lives terrible, especially mine. This is the perfect chance to get rid of him and take control of the Mountain Realm.*

Joyful smiles flashed in Gloriana's eyes. She felt the warmth of her husband's embrace and heard the soothing voice that had helped her sleep on freezing nights. *Was it all a fantasy?* Her heart broke. *Why do I not want him to die? He's an abusive lunatic! Why do I still love him?* She paused. *I'm pathetic.*

Gloriana lifted her head to meet Esme's sad eyes, and regret filled her. "Let me see what I can do to take you away from Borin."

Esme frowned. "You rescue me from the Lord Protector, and then what? I will not be able to afford this cottage. Where will I go? What will I do?"

Gloriana thought for a moment. *I need someone I'm friendly with to always be near Lady Joan Myster. Could that person be Esme?* "That question will be answered the closer we get you out of this situation."

The young woman rolled her eyes impatiently. "Fine, I will wait and will continue to endure."

She gave Esme the dagger. "If he ever tries to whip you or slash at your neck, don't hesitate."

"Yes, my lady, thank you."

Gloriana then turned to the door, knowing she was running out of time. "We will speak again soon, but please, for now, act like nothing has happened."

Esme gave a wide smile and opened the door, revealing the icy hell awaiting outside. "No worries, my lady. The Mothers at Bordella's Parish taught me how to be a better actress than the ones at the troupe."

HADRIAN

Screams rippled through the water, and Hadrian's eyes snapped open. He thrashed until he reached the surface of the raging water, taking a deep breath. The water splashed in his eyes and nose, and the current pulled him under again. Underneath, Raynese's screams continued, but they were now faint.

I must find her.

The rushing river continued to carry him down, and something grabbed onto his ankle, forcing him down again. "Help!" he screamed in between breaths, but the grip tightened. "Stop!"

Again, he was under the water, and he looked down to see the traveler woman holding onto his leg, her face twisted in agony. *It's Raynese, but what's wrong with her?* He repositioned himself to reach down and bring her close. He noticed her consciousness slipping as he wrapped his arms around the woman. *I must get her to some air.*

Hadrian swam them to the surface, and Raynese's first breath was filled with coughs and screams as she convulsed in his arms. "What's wrong?"

The woman gasped, and her eyes shot open. "You spoke."

"Aye, and I have a lot of questions."

"The Unmen on the surface," Raynese groaned and lifted her hand from the water to touch Hadrian. "You saw too much."

The boy slapped Raynese's hand away. "Stop, what are you doing?"

She responded by screaming, her body seizing in Hadrian's arms. He looked the woman up and down, unsure of what to do. *Is she truly hurt, or is she avoiding my question?* He swam to the riverbank as Raynese continued her cries and struggled onto the shore.

He then looked down at the woman, who continued to shriek. "Raynese," he exhaled, pointing at a mangled, broken, and bruised leg.

Her eyes narrowed on Hadrian. "Please," she whispered, "Help me."

Hadrian panicked. *Raynese is asking for my help. She needs me.* The careless traveler who ventured to places Hadrian didn't know existed was in trouble. He admired her so much, but the journey with her had brought so many questions that his faith in her waned. *I must help her.*

The roar of the strange green leopard rang in his head, along with the wretched squawking from the sparrow. *Raynese called the beast an Unmen.*

What is that?

Raynese sprung forward and headbutted Hadrian, causing him to see a flash of light. "Ow, why would you do that?"

"Do what?" she groaned, lying down again. "I only asked for your help."

"No, you," he paused. *What did Raynese do?* He touched the slight tingling in the middle of his forehead, unable to remember. The sparrow once again started to sing, but something felt off. *Wasn't there another animal? Something more frightening than a bird.*

"Hadrian, please don't go into shock like before. My leg hurts so much."

His attention focused on the woman's leg bent into pieces. *Okay, yeah, Raynese's injury. That's what I was worrying about before, right?*

He couldn't remember.

Hadrian Osmont bit his lip viciously as he examined the young woman's body. *Raynese broke her leg, and I must do something about it, but how? What all can I do?*

Raynese screamed, and the pain in her voice brought Hadrian back to when his little brother, Leo, had broken his arm. The boy had screamed and cried and thrashed as Lady Arla Osmont hurried around the child's bedroom, gathering supplies.

Hadrian stepped forward in his memories as Raynese's agonizing cries faded. *Mother.* The woman moved with grace as she now hovered over her youngest son. She wrapped her chubby fingers around the broken limb before setting it into place with a content smile on her face, causing Leonidas to wail, his other body parts flailing around.

I must do the same, Hadrian realized, his attention now on the woman drenched in sweat. He repositioned Raynese to lay on her back. "I'm so sorry for this," he whispered, placing his hands on her mangled leg.

"It's okay," she whispered, lightly touching his cheek. "Do your best." She smiled bravely and then closed her eyes.

Hadrian took a deep breath and twisted her leg. *Something doesn't feel right.* Raynese's bones cracked, and her wails mimicked his brother's before she passed out. *Leo did the same,* he recalled, staring at her straightened leg. *But still, something feels so off.*

Lady Arla's smiling brown eyes appeared in his mind. *We must keep the leg straight so it can heal correctly. We can't have a bent arm, can we?* His mother's kind voice echoed, and he frowned, feeling empty.

Hadrian stood and took in his surroundings, noticing another sparrow in a willow tree. *Is it the same one from before?* His mind went blank. *Was there something else there it was afraid of?*

His eyes flickered to the shivering Raynese, his frown deepening, and the long gash on his cheek stung terribly. *The willow tree's bark should be flexible enough to support Raynese's leg.* He walked closer to the tree, and the bird didn't move or make any noise.

It just stared.

"Hi, little bird," Hadrian waved weakly, moving some flowy branches out of the way. He moved deeper into the middle of the tree, but the sparrow's attention never left him. *Does it want something from me?* He grabbed a piece of bark and stripped it off the tree, and the bird squawked in panic, reminding him of his prayer. *Citia, this jaded beast bears its fangs, but I wish it no harm.* He ripped another piece off. *A bird doesn't have fangs. What is going on?*

Hadrian returned to Raynese with a handful of sticks and then went to find more robust, less flexible branches. He observed several trees and decided on two branches resembling planks. Again, he snapped the branches with ease. *When did I become so strong?* He studied his arms, barely recognizing the muscles that popped out. He had been such a weak boy, coddled by his mother, and disinterested in anything relating to violence. He couldn't hunt, he couldn't fight, and he couldn't take care of himself. He couldn't do anything.

Maybe I'm not who I was before.

The sun had set behind the trees when Hadrian finished making the brace for Raynese. Afterward, Hadrian sat with Raynese's head on his lap for hours. He stroked her hair gently, watching the rushing waters before them. "Do you remember when you kissed me?" he asked the unconscious woman. "It felt like ages ago."

Raynese, of course, stayed quiet, but that didn't bother Hadrian. He didn't want her to say anything at all. *Sometimes, Raynese says too much, and it gets me second-guessing myself. I prefer this silence where I can talk without wondering.*

A breeze picked up around them, and the birds replied with a delicate song that didn't bring Hadrian the usual headaches he endured. *There was another sound*, he told himself, squeezing his eyes shut. Raynese shifted, groaning, and Hadrian waited until she rested again, but she continued to move, and sweat droplets began beading at her hairline.

"You know, sometimes I think about the stories my mother used to tell me to help me sleep. Do you want me to tell you some?" Raynese stilled, bringing a smile to Hadrian's face. "The story goes that when the evil Sakal the Conqueror looked death in the eyes, he gave his soul to Unmos, the god of Darkness. For many years, no one believed the ancient king lurked with the monsters, but one day, Nozel the Valiant delved under the surface and stood face to face with the corpse of Sakal, still alive and more powerful than ever. Then, a huge green leopard sat in a tree," he paused. "Wait, that's not right. Apologies, I don't know where that came from."

Hadrian attempted to steady his breathing, and Raynese grew restless again. He pressed his hand against the woman's short hair and felt strange heat radiating from her. He stared at Raynese's visibly pale face, her skin growing more feverish by the minute. He had fixed her leg but did not account for the fever that would come. *What should I do?*

He looked at the multicolored sky, thinking about the remedies his mother used. "I need Colvic," he sighed, completely unsure of everything. His attention settled on a bird who flapped its wings intensely. *It's acting like it's afraid.* His entire body grew cold. *I've experienced this before, right?* His eyes snapped to the trees, waiting to see a predator staring back at him, but nothing was there—just the bird.

Raynese stirred again, and Hadrian hesitated, everything overwhelming him. *I need ale and elderflower.* Arla's voice surrounded the pair, bringing Hadrian a sense of calm. *This is a peasant's secret to cure a fever. Don't tell your father.* He pictured his mother winking at that with a slight giggle. He missed his mother's humor, warmth, and kindness. *I will never receive that from her again.*

"Hadrian," Raynese struggled. "Hadrian, please don't let me die. Please. I love you. Save me. Please."

His entire body shook from the confession. *Raynese loves me.* A part of him didn't believe her. *She is just in agony and saying anything, not making any sense.* He relaxed and patted her hair again. "Don't worry. I'm going to find you some remedies to break the fever."

Raynese stayed silent, and Hadrian's vision narrowed on the River Lilia. *I need to put her somewhere safe and find a place where I can buy something to help her.* It was the best option Hadrian could come up with, and he knew he didn't have much more time to think of anything else. *The fever must break soon before she becomes even sicker.*

Hadrian carefully wrapped his cloak around the young woman, picked her up gently, and smiled when he realized how light she felt. *I'm so much stronger now. Father would be proud, and Colvic would insist on sparring to prove it. I miss them all so much. I miss home.*

He found a giant oak tree with a hollow large enough to hide Raynese. Slowly, he laid her inside it. "Just stay here and be comfortable." He untied the small sack of coins hanging from her hip and snatched one of the two additional daggers strapped to her back. *She's so prepared. I guess that's what it takes to be a traveler.* He paused and took in the sight of the usually unbeatable woman now struggling just to breathe. He pulled the honeysuckle that grew off the tree and placed them around her before lightly kissing her forehead, frowning from the woman's cold sweat. "I'll be back soon," he whispered, his eyes warm with tears.

Hadrian traveled north along the river, his mind racing, making him more exhausted. *I don't even know where I am. There must be a town somewhere or an inn. What am I going to do if I can't find anything? Or if I can't remember how to find Raynese? Or what if she's dead by the time I return?*

All the questions made Hadrian dizzy, and he paused, clearing his mind as he stared at the rushing river. Hadrian pulled at his shirt as he tried to understand his feelings about Raynese, and everything became overwhelming once more. Raynese was older, wiser, stronger, beautiful, courageous, engaging, and everything Hadrian was not. He liked her, yet she also frustrated him with the unnecessary lies. *I never want Raynese to leave my side, but I also want her to leave me alone.*

A trail of patchy grass appeared before Hadrian, and he smiled. *When you find a natural trail, that means people have traveled there. You should see a village or settlement soon,* Colvic's voice explained. A false image of the knight pointed toward the trail. Hadrian stepped forward before pausing, picturing Leonidas rushing ahead, more enthusiastic to learn about survival. Sighs slipped out of Hadrian, wishing he was like his little brother.

A sparrow sat on a branch above and cawed, causing him to trudge forward, ignoring the bird. *That must be the same bird as before. Is it following me?* He knew there was no reason to question further. *It's not like I can stop a wild animal.*

As Hadrian traveled down the small path, the route transitioned into a road, and he grinned, taking in the small plumes of smoke just ahead of him, indicating civilization. His pace quickened, and his heartbeat pulsed in his ears. *I did it!* He dragged his heels into the gravel, gasping as he saw his salvation—an inn. He raced toward the building, noticed a stable boy tending to the horses, and stopped. He looked into the sack of coins and smiled. *Maybe I can purchase a horse, too, so we can stop walking during our journey.*

Hadrian approached the inn and opened the wooden doors.

Inside, candlelight danced as people drank and ate their meal around the main room. Everything smelled of fruit, meat, and musk. He stepped in, and eyes connected with his, causing Hadrian's heart to sink. *Do they know who I am?* He shook his head, remembering that he had changed after moons of journeying. He no longer looked like Hadrian Osmont, heir to the title of Lord Protector of the Southern Kingdom of Valley Pines.

Now, he was just some boy.

Hadrian was bulkier; his curled hair had become matted, and cuts spotted his skin along with a thin layer of dirt. *My parents would not be able to recognize me now, so how could anyone else?* He gripped at his side as another realization filled his head. *How will Ser Colvic recognize me?*

He approached the innkeeper and stared at the shadowy black in her eyes, which was supposed to be white. *A Seer.* He had believed Seers were only in large cities. *Why would one work at a random inn? They wouldn't recognize me either, right?*

"What you want, boy?" The old woman asked in a ragged voice.

"You got ale?" he questioned, trying not to sound too highborn.

The old woman raised an eyebrow, "a copper."

"You got elderflower?"

"What do you think this is, the Citadel? I'll give you a pint of ale, but no elderflower."

Hadrian held his breath, faltering. "Please, my friend is sick. I need to help her. Anything you have that would break a fever would be greatly appreciated," he said, placing the sack of coins on the counter. "Anything, please."

The old woman laughed. "You must be an idiot pulling out a bag like that. Bring the friend to the inn for some good rest and a meal. You are no doctor. More harm than good."

She waved to dismiss him, but he grabbed the old woman's hand, startling her, "Please, if you have it, give it to me."

The old woman studied Hadrian, her expressions growing suspicious. "Bring the friend here. That sack looks heavy. I'm sure we can find a doctor to care for her."

He groaned, and pulled out one of the coins. "Fine, I'll buy the ale."

The old innkeeper grabbed the coin and examined it. "This is worth nothing," she scoffed, tossing it back to him.

"What do you mean? It's a gold coin."

"Ain't never seen a coin like that before," she explained, pointing at the snowflake imprint. "And it's too dull to be gold. Either give me a copper or get out of my inn."

He studied the strange coins filled in the sack. *I can't even buy anything.* Tears filled his eyes. *I came all this way for nothing.*

"Next," the old woman huffed impatiently.

He snapped his attention to the innkeeper, gasping. "Please, wait!"

"I'll pay for his things," a voice said from behind.

Hadrian whipped around to see Ser Colvic Rames towering over him. He grinned eagerly, but Colvic's stern face made his smile disappear. *I can't act like I know him. The Seers would be able to recognize him.* Hadrian realized, bowing his head.

You must become an actor under pressure, his mother instructed inside Hadrian's head, and he was unsure if it was a memory or something he was only imagining. He gave a smile. "Really? Thank you!"

"You're not getting it for free, boy. Gotta be my squire for a while."

Hadrian bit down on a laugh. *That's an awful accent!* "A squire? My father would be so proud!" he replied instead, and Colvic's face grew soft.

"Three coppers for the boy's things," the old woman groaned, interrupting their fake conversation.

"Three? I heard you tell the boy one."

"I changed my mind," she replied simply. The knight smacked his teeth and gave the woman a silver, which, in return, she gave him seven coppers and a glass jar of ale with a lid. "Since the sick friend isn't here."

Colvic looked at Hadrian curiously before turning back to the innkeeper. "Thanks."

They left the inn without another word, and Colvic hobbled to the stable boy. "Bring me my horses," he commanded.

"But you said you were going to stay for the night. I haven't tended to them yet," the boy replied quickly.

"Doesn't matter, bring them," Ser Colvic commanded, and the boy rushed into the stable and came back out with three horses Hadrian did not recognize. "Get on," Colvic instructed, giving Hadrian the reins. Hadrian did as he was told. The knight then mounted his horse and held onto the third by its reins. "We aren't going fast."

They traveled silently, with Hadrian leading his pair. When they reached the small path, he decided to talk. "How did you know it was me?"

"Your voice," Colvic replied bluntly, his eyes scanning Hadrian, "Although I was not quite sure, you have changed since I last saw you."

"Aye," he exhaled, and silence weighed over them once again.

When they were beside the River Lilia, Ser Colvic trotted beside Hadrian. "Where is she?" he interrogated, his voice cold.

Hadrian stared at the horse's mane. *Does he think she abandoned me?* "I hid her in a tree," he replied awkwardly. "I didn't know what to do. She broke her leg and caught a fever. I did what my mother had done when,"

"She is not your mother."

"Right," Hadrian hesitated, and the birds around him screeched. His attention then snapped to the famed knight. "I was thinking, what if I found the person who tricked Lady Arla into thinking I was her child? Do you think that would rebuild our relationship?"

"She wants no relationship with you," the knight responded harshly. "She wants you dead. Even if you found the person who deceived her, she would question why you were still breathing. She believes her time was wasted loving a child who wasn't hers. She hasn't been thinking rationally for a long time. You must've realized that."

Hadrian frowned, turning away. He had noticed his mother's impulsive actions, but never believed she would take her anger out on him. *I didn't do anything. How could she blame me?*

They continued silently until they reached the hollowed tree. "Raynese is in there," Hadrian informed, pointing, and Ser Colvic Rames leaned into the tree. "Will the ale help?"

Colvic touched Raynese's burning cheeks, not answering the question. The knight then stuck his head into the tree and whispered, causing the woman to stir. Hadrian watched uncomfortably, trying to peek inside.

"Wait," Raynese said to Ser Colvic, trying to stay quiet, but Hadrian could hear. "Please, hide me from him. He will worry."

The knight obliged by shifting, but Hadrian could still see a green glow radiate from the woman's body. *Raynese is using that ability again.* Flashes of a jade-colored leopard springing toward him appeared in his mind, and a bird started a song from the branches above.

You must become an actor under pressure, Lady Arla Osmont's voice echoed as Raynese jumped from the tree, completely healed.

Impossible. Hadrian then jumped from foot to foot, behaving like the fool that once visited the High Castle long ago. "A miracle! A miracle!" he clapped and cheered, blinking away the tears that filled his eyes. "A miracle!" His happy smile twitched into a frown. *No, this cannot be. Raynese is a Wicked!*

DUSK

Part 3

VICTORIA

V ictoria stood on the Black Castle's balcony that overlooked the entire city of Kingment. She stood uneasily, watching the crowd below cheer. She placed her hands on the stone railing, and tried her best to control her breathing. *They are coming today, I must be prepared.* Victoria's dark green eyes scanned the balcony. To her right stood Catrain, Emeline, and Doran. To her left stood Ser Edmund and Lady Raya, with Cleric hiding away in the shadows behind Catrain. Her other son, however, was nowhere in sight. "Where is Rosert?"

Everyone stared back silently.

Farthest away, Doran had a stupid look on his face. "How should I know?" he asked, shifting his weight onto one hip and shrugging carelessly.

If I could beat him right now...

"Um," Catrain whispered, her golden eyes shining. "Rosert went hunting today."

Hunting!? Rosert shouldn't be hunting at a time like this; he needs to gain Alice's trust. Victoria didn't know how to feel. "When did he leave?"

"Before the sun rose," Emeline answered with her head high, still staring at the crowd. "He said he didn't want to see the mess Father was bringing to Kingment."

"He sounds like me," Doran replied, laughing.

Emeline shot a look towards her eldest brother. "Rosert did not mean cousin Alice when he said that. You know *exactly* what he means."

And what is that? Victoria wondered, not understanding. Emeline snapped her head back forward, and Doran stared at his sister with his mouth wide open. Victoria glanced at Catrain who held herself, terrified. *Why have I never noticed their broken relationship with Falk? Do they feel the same about me?* She clutched her chest as she continued to stare at her children. *No, they couldn't. I know I've been acting strange for a while, but still, I've never done anything to hurt them; right?* Her mind raced. *I want my children to love me.*

The roar from the crowd brought Victoria's attention back to what was in front of her. In the distance, the faint sight of horses and wheelhouses appeared.

Emeline hugged Catrain as the young girl whimpered and Doran watched the interaction between sisters, staying quiet. *Maybe I should send them all away. If I do, maybe they could find some solace.*

"Children," Victoria called, and three pairs of eyes set on her. "If your lord father frightens you that much, then maybe you should run away," she told them with a cold smile.

NO! She screamed internally. *That was not what I wanted to say, I wanted to comfort my children.* As Catrain's whimper grew louder, Victoria's smile grew more malicious. *What is wrong with me?*

"My lady," Ser Edmund whispered from behind. "Perhaps you should stay quiet?"

Victoria put her head down in shame. She tried to steady her breathing, but Catrain's cries grew louder than the cheering crowd. *I must leave before I say something else I will regret.* Slowly, Victoria turned to swiftly take her leave.

"Mother!" Doran yelled and she stopped moving. "You must be seen from the balcony when they approach the gates."

Victoria closed her eyes and thought for a moment. *I don't care where I'm supposed to be seen.* At the door, stood two knights with their faces covered. "Let me out," she commanded.

The knights opened the door, and Catrain wailed. *You are supposed to be my home, Catrain,* Victoria thought, walking out of the balcony and down the hallway. *And bears do not wail.*

She quickened her pace to the throne room. *That's where Falk will go first.*

A horrible eerie quiet stilled the air in the throne room. Victoria tiptoed deeper, and walked quickly to the throne that sat above everyone else. It was Victoria's favorite place to sit. *I'm going to miss sitting here.*

As she stared at her lap, she noticed something that surprised her—she was not wearing green. Victoria always wore green. Her father had told her how pretty she looked in green, and when he died that was the only color she ever wanted to wear. *So, why am I wearing black? It's as if I am attending a funeral.* She paused, her skin cold. *Am I?*

She stood from the Lord Protector's high throne, and shifted to the chair that she was supposed to sit in. *A seat for a nobody.*

The door to the throne room swung open, and Lord Falk Osmont strutted in, smiling as if he was actually happy to see Victoria. "My lovely wife, you're feeling better again," he greeted. "I'm just so pleased to see that. You will survive another year. Bless the gods!"

Victoria stayed silent. *Incredible how those kind words are laced with venom.*

Falk took his seat. "I did not see you waiting for me at the balcony when I approached the gates, why?" he whined with a fake pout.

As if he cares. Victoria rolled her eyes. She refused for Falk to steer the conversation the way he wanted. "Where is Alice?"

Her lord husband's eyes widened.

The reaction made Victoria realize that she had never attempted to control their conversations. She always answered his questions without hesitation. *Is that what makes him so powerful? No. Falk's power is nothing but a title. A made up title because Peyton didn't want to drag the kingdom into a civil war.*

Lord Falk Osmont wasn't powerful at all.

"She's preparing for her entrance before court," Falk finally answered.

"Preparing?" Victoria repeated. "What is there to be prepared?"

"Alice has been traveling for more than a moon, she needs a bath."

"Had she not bathed the entire time she traveled?"

Falk's face reddened. "Of course, she has! She needs to look as best as possible. When the audience comes, then she will arrive. But I need you to do something for me, dear wife," Falk exhaled and Victoria met his eyes. There was a pause that choked the air from the room. "Sentence Ser Damien Clay to death."

"Ser Damien!? You mean Ser Knight?" she shrieked and Falk nodded. Victoria shook her head, not understanding. "He is one of our most trusted and loyal knight in the kingdom. Why is he on trial? What happened?"

"He tried to help Alice escape," Falk grumbled, crossing his arms.

Victoria leaned back in her chair. *I was right,* she realized, *Falk kidnapped her.* "Why would Alice want to escape?"

"Just do it woman!"

"What if the trial concludes that he has done no wrong?"

Falk sat up again. "He committed treason! You are the judge of this trial, not some priest or Saavant. And you will judge him guilty!"

"Why am I the judge when you are the one deciding the sentence?"

"Just do it," he spat.

"Will an audience be here for the trial?" she asked, her body stiffening.

Falk smiled his gorgeous smile, bringing Victoria cold sweats. "Aye, and that little bitch, Alice, too."

Victoria's mouth dropped open. *I must stop this,* she realized, but no plan came to mind. *What happened during Falk's visit to the Mountain Realm?*

"Oh, you don't mean that," she said, trying her best to sound in distress. "You don't mean for your most trusted knight to be butchered like an animal." Lord Falk's cold green eyes met hers and she understood then—he did mean it. *He means for me to be the villain. I must come up with an excuse.* "I cannot," she exhaled with a sob. "I'm a woman. A woman cannot sentence an anointed knight to death."

Falk chuckled. "We aren't in the Mountain Realm. That's not written anywhere in the law here in the Kingdom of Valley Pines. Women can do whatever they want. The law does not stop them from obtaining power."

She studied her lord husband. *Could I dispose of Falk and run the kingdom myself?* Internally, Victoria smiled with glee. Externally, however, her frown only grew deeper. "Tell me true. Why are you doing this?"

"Alice isn't a little Saint like everyone thinks. She plots wickedly and doesn't care who gets hurt."

That sounds more like you. Victoria wanted to reply. *Borin and Gloriana wouldn't raise a Wicked. They would raise a kind and trusting child, probably one who is unfamiliar with the true evils of life.*

"Why do you care? You've never questioned me."

She narrowed her eyes. "Alice is my blood. I have a deeper connection with her, than you do. If we work together, maybe I could convince the girl not to escape." She paused and rolled her eyes at Falk's smug face. "I'm not doing it for you," she added, wiping the smile off her lord husband's face. "I don't want a war. If I can have Alice submit to her fate, maybe the Mountain Realm will see that we are treating her kindly and that she is truly happy here."

Falk's face twisted. "I couldn't care less if she's happy."

The throne room doors opened and people quickly filled the room, ending the couple's conversation.

"Remember; do what I told you," he spat before looking towards the audience with a smile.

Victoria's mind and face were blank. She didn't know what to do, say, nor how to act. She could only sit there. *Will I be Falk's next target to torment? Is that how he operates now?*

She glanced at a small table, where a teacup was filled with her special drink. *When did this get here?* She had not seen Enya approach. *Is it just my imagination?* She reached over, picked up the cup, and quickly took a small sip of the brew. *No, it's real. Thank the gods.*

Immediately, the distinct metal taste of her tea filled her mouth. The overbearing taste used to make her gag, but it did not bother her much anymore. She took another sip and placed the cup down. *I must be prepared,* she thought as she forced a pleasant face. *Falk gave me the task of being the villain.* And she could do nothing but abide.

"Highborn of Valley Pines," Lord Falk called, standing from his throne. "I've returned from the Mountain Realm and brought a gift that will bring prosperity to our kingdom. I'm quite tired so my lady wife will be the one holding court." He turned towards a knight. "Bring in the girl."

"Now presenting, Lady Alice Wayward of Maryere."

Maryere, Victoria thought as the doors opened and the crowd parted ways, *home.*

Alice Wayward awkwardly shuffled into the room and the audience whispered. Victoria's mouth gaped open as her niece walked deeper into the throne room. *Falk Osmont, what did you do, you piece of filth!?*

Alice was nothing but skin and bones.

As the girl walked, Victoria noticed the scars that littered her skin. *Borin said Alice was sickly and always stayed inside. So how did she receive those scars?* Victoria's anger continued to increase, as Alice stopped and forced a smile.

"Hello, Aunt Victoria," the girl greeted weakly with a wave. "I'm very pleased to finally meet you."

Victoria was appalled. *What did he do to you?* She knew that when word spread of how Alice looked; the Mountain Realm would seek vengeance. *Why must Falk be so arrogant? He thinks nothing of the consequences. He just hope someone else will clean it up for you.* She sighed. *I don't want that someone to be me.*

"Thank you for my necklace," Alice added, sounding a bit more alive. "Unfortunately, it broke."

Victoria placed her fisted hand under her chin and kept her attention on Alice, not caring about the stupid gift from moons ago. Her eyes lingered on Alice's body, scanning it up and down. Her niece was truly only skin and bones. *Why?* "Did you starve yourself to be skinnier for my son? I promise Doran does not like skinny girls."

Alice lifted her head and stared directly at Victoria. For a moment, she saw the House Wayward spirit the girl had, but it quickly disappeared. "I have always been skinny," Alice confessed. "I suppose I have lost a little bit more weight during the journey."

Victoria nodded. "I heard that traveling cause stress, was this journey stressful for you, my dear?"

Alice's bright blue eyes flashed to Falk. "No, it's just, my handmaiden was attacked and hasn't woken up. I wish for her health and my prayers have been draining."

"Has the girl been attended to?"

Alice Wayward looked away. "No, my lady, she hasn't." The answer brought mumbles into the room, frightening the girl. "But, Lord Falk made the journey a relaxing experience otherwise," she added, her voice trembling.

"Well then," Victoria smiled. "Let's have a Saavant look over her. I suppose my lord husband is a Saint otherwise, huh?" The room erupted in a peculiar form of laughter, making Victoria uncomfortable. *Their joy feels dark.* She turned towards the small table, grabbed her teacup, and took another sip.

"Enough of this nonsense," Falk growled, upset with the joke. "It's time for the trial. Guards bring in prisoner."

"No!" Alice shouted, tears already streaming down her cheeks. "Please, spare him! Have mercy! Spare him!" The young woman stepped forward, but knights were already behind her, holding her back.

What happened during this journey?

Finally, the knights pulled a sobbing Alice into the crowd as the doors opened again. Chains clacked rhythmically against the polished stone floor as Ser Knight entered the throne room. The accused no longer dressed in chainmail; instead wearing a brown rough spun shirt and breeches. *He's skin and bones, too.*

Two knights pushed the man's shoulders, and Ser Knight dropped to his knees. His hands and feet were bound by chains, reminding Victoria of the bastard children she sold into slavery. *Is this how they looked?*

Lady Victoria shifted in her chair, unsure how to begin. "Ser Knight, you have been charged with treason against the Northern Kingdom of Valley Pines," she declared. "How do you plea?"

"I've committed no treason," the knight whispered. "So, I plead innocence."

"Liar!" Falk shouted, standing from his chair.

For a moment, Victoria thought it would be best to get up and leave, ending the trial. *If I did that, I would never hear the end of it.* "Quiet," she instructed, forgetting all courtesies. "If I'm going to judge, I need no outbursts."

Her husband slowly returned to his seat with a knowing smile.

Victoria swallowed her guilt and turned back to Ser Knight. "Why have you been arrested for treason if you claim to have committed none?"

The knight smiled. "What I did could be seen as treason by the laws created by man, but not by the eyes of the gods."

Gooseprickles littered Victoria's skin. *That's not good,* she thought as the crowd murmured again. *Ser Knight is bringing the judgment of the gods into this.* A cold sweat dotted her hairline. "What did you do?"

"I've committed no treason."

"Yes, yes, but that is not answering my question. What did you do to be arrested?"

Before the knight could answer, Victoria scanned the audience. Alice, stood in the back corner with her mouth covered, silently crying. Several knights had their heads bowed as if they were in prayer, and many of the simple servants who made the journey were either crying or praying. *They all know,* Victoria realized. *Was what Ser Knight did seen as a chivalrous act?*

Ser Knight smiled again. "Please ensure Lady Alice no longer cries."

"EXECUTE HIM!" Lord Falk screamed. "NOW!"

Victoria snapped her head towards her husband who once again stood from his chair. His face was as red as his hair, and his bulging eyes and gaping mouth made him look crazed. Many of the highborn gasped at the way their Lord Protector acted. *This man is a fool. Why is he doing a public execution in the middle of our throne room in front of all the highborn who barely trust us? What happened to this just being a trial? Was it ever a trial?*

As the guards approached, Victoria looked back over to where Alice had stood and noticed that the girl was gone. She was not sure if Alice was attempting to make her escape, but that didn't matter to Victoria right now. She had bigger problems to deal with, and it started with the man who stood on the balls of his feet continuously screaming for someone to execute Ser Knight. *There is nothing I can do but watch.* Victoria relaxed in her chair and grabbed for her teacup again. The entire room roared, but it all sounded so muffled to Victoria as she drank.

A hooded man approached Ser Knight, and the accused bent his head down without a fight. *Please ensure that Lady Alice no longer cries.* She held her breath as the hooded man was given his execution weapon—the long-sword.

"It's over, Damien!" Falk declared, lifting his arm before swinging it down. "This is what you get!"

In one swift movement, Ser Knight's head laid on the floor and blood puddled all around him.

The crowd screamed in terror, but Victoria's face stayed emotionless. Seeing the decapitated body of the man who had protected her family for many years was too much for her to bare. *I'm so sorry, Ser Knight.*

"I'll be in my room. Don't bother me," Falk announced before stomping away, and leaving Victoria to clean up the mess.

Figures he would do this to me. Victoria studied her husband as he disappeared from of the throne room, her head throbbing. *I don't want to, but I must.* She took a deep breath. "Clear the crowd!"

Quickly, knights shoved the uneased highborn out of the throne room.

How did my life turn out like this? Victoria didn't know the answer, but she knew the spectacle her lord husband had created needed to end, now. Victoria studied Ser Knight's decapitated body, her heart breaking. *I will never let Falk get his way again.*

JARIN

Kaylien Thoren presented herself before the court, waiting for the Lord Protector of the Riverlands to speak. Golden moon hairpins were tucked in her light brown hair, matching her dress. Pink dusted her pale olive toned skin, reminding Jarin of the war that ruined his family. *Will this work?*

He sat straight and cleared his throat. "Lady Kaylien Thoren, I welcome you to Waterbrook."

The girl curtsied. "Thank you for inviting me, my lord. I am pleased you decided that I was fit to wed your son."

Jarin pressed his lips together anxiously. *Why wouldn't she be fit to wed Terryn?* In the letter, Lord Thoren had promised that his daughter was one of the most beautiful girls in the Summerlands; but Jarin couldn't understand why the man agreed to the arrangement. *Something is off.*

He thought about the situation. *Does House Thoren genuinely want an alliance? What are they planning?* Jarin's head spun, and he redirected his attention to the girl. "How was your journey?" Jarin inquired, trying to sound kind. He wanted Kaylien to feel welcomed and loved, although the Riverlands had a reputation of being unlovable and unwelcoming.

"Your knights and messenger treated me kindly," she answered, her voice still little. "Traveling is a pleasant experience for me, my lord, and the gods treated the river roads kindly."

Messenger, does she mean Jossa? Is that what the handmaiden told her? Jarin took a deep breath and decided to ignore it. He had to ignore a great deal of things so he wouldn't go insane. "How do you like the Riverlands so far?"

"It is not like how my lord father described."

Jarin rose his eyebrows at that, and the crowd murmured. *Not how Lord Thoren described it; and how would he describe my kingdom?* Internally, Jarin seethed with anger. Externally, Jarin smiled wide like a crazed animal, because of the medicine Hamlin gave him. "So, what is it like then, my lady?"

"Um," she began, clearly in distress.

"Child," Jarin interrupted. "You are safe here, please speak freely."

"Oh no," Kaylien waved her left hand in front of her face, embarrassed. "I mean, that, um..." her voice trailed off again.

Jarin examined the young girl's demeanor. *Kaylien isn't showing her right arm,* he realized. *Why?*

"The Riverlands are beautiful!" the Thoren girl shouted, bringing the room's attention back to her. "Saavants taught me that the Riverlands is like a desert, but it is not. The Riverlands are an oasis."

Dain chuckled, and Kaylien's eyes ripped away from Jarin to the boy. "An oasis?" he grinned. "Lady Kaylien this is the Riverlands, not the Summerlands. To compare it to an oasis would give the idea that this kingdom is warm, which it is not. Better to compare this place to a gross, musky swamp." Dain lightly teased and much to Jarin's surprise, a small smile formed on Kaylien's lips.

Terryn jumped to his feet at the interaction, bringing everyone's eyes to him. "Hello," he squeaked. "I'm Terryn Ayers."

Jarin rolled his eyes, and he could hear Dimia sighing heavily from the shadows.

Kaylien smiled. "I am very pleased to meet you, I'm Kaylien Thoren." *Oh, great,* Jarin thought, *they seem perfect for each other.* The girl then turned back to Jarin, "Please, my lord, call me Kaylien. I am not a lady yet, merely a girl of sixteen."

Jarin nodded, lifted his hand, and Ser Bronston stepped forward on command. "The introductions are over," the knight announced. "Please, exit the throne room." The audience shuffled out, leaving the members of House Ayers, his small council, Daya, Jossa, and Kaylien.

When the room emptied, Jarin smiled again. "I will be your father-by-marriage, so please do the same," he said, causing Kaylien to smile. "But you look so stiff. Take your cloak off and relax."

"Uh, my lord," Jossa spoke up, and Jarin's eyes darted to her, causing the young woman to stiffen. "Uh,"

"I don't think the Lord Protector allowed you to speak," Ser Bronston reminded, his voice quiet but stern.

Jarin lowered his head. *What could Jossa have to say that would give her the courage to put eyes on her? Should I let her finish?* He pressed his lips together. "What is it?"

Jossa's face lit up at the question before her eyes flickered in realization. "My lord, thank you for allowing me to speak," she paused and inhaled sharply. "I don't think asking Kaylien to remove her cloak is appropriate."

"Who do you think you are?" Dain snapped. "What you just said could be punishable by death!"

Jarin sighed. "Dain, calm." His vision then narrowed on Jossa, causing the handmaiden to tremble. "What makes you speak so boldly?"

"I, uh, I,"

"Excuse me!" Kaylien squeaked. She took a deep breath and removed her cloak, revealing her right arm stopping at the elbow. "Jossa was trying to protect me. Please, don't get upset with her."

Jarin's eyes stayed on the stump, understanding why Lord Thoren agreed to the marriage. *She is just like us. No one wants her.* His medicated grin tensed as his attention steadied on Kaylien. "I'm not upset with Jossa. I'm pleased she attempted to shield you from harm," he glanced at the handmaiden whose face continued to shine brightly. *Jossa may be of further use to me.* "And you will not be ridiculed," he promised the young Thoren girl. "If anyone does, come to me."

"Thank you," Kaylien bowed. "I feel more at peace."

"Wait, so that means she's like me," Dimia exhaled, stumbling out of the shadows.

"My lady, you shouldn't," Jossa attempted to tell the woman.

Dimia snapped her head to the handmaiden. "Don't speak," she commanded, and Jossa stopped following the Osmont woman. "Jarin, you didn't tell me the girl was afflicted." She then looked at Kaylien. "Sweet girl, I caught the wretched deathskin and survived. What happened to you?"

Kaylien's eyes grew wide, and she stepped away from the woman. "Uh, I was attacked." Dimia gasped and reached to touch Kaylien, but the girl pulled away. "I'm sorry, but who are you?"

The sickly woman stood straight. "I'm Dimia Ayers, the Lord Protector of the Riverlands' wife," she introduced, lifting her chin with pride.

"I'm pleased to meet you," Kaylien replied, bowing and forcing a smile.

"You don't have to be so formal with Mother," Dain explained casually. "She doesn't know what formalities are."

Chuckles erupted in the room, and conversations overlapped. *Is this it?* Jarin wondered, feeling warm. *Is this what I always wanted?* He peeked at Hamlin and Lysane, who stood in the corner, away from everyone. *This is it! Everything I've ever wanted will happen. I will be a great lord.*

"Stop talking, all of you!" Terryn shouted, forcing everyone to silence. "You're laughing and getting along great. You're becoming a family right before my eyes," he seethed. "Yet you didn't even ask me how I feel about it!"

"About what, my son?"

"About that," he shrieked, pointing at Kaylien's stump. "I don't want to marry that!"

"What?" Kaylien questioned, shielding her arm. "What do you mean?"

Terryn puffed his chest. "You're ugly."

Kaylien burst into tears, and Dimia stomped to her eldest son and slapped him as harshly as she could. "What the hell is wrong with you?!" In one swift motion, she grabbed Terryn by the ear and marched him out of the throne room with Jossa closely at her heels.

"Daya, follow them," Jarin instructed, and Daya disappeared in response. He then sighed, thinking about his eldest son's words. *I didn't know I had raised a human like that.* He shivered as his past flashed in his head. *Well, I didn't raise Terryn at all.* "Kaylien, apologies,"

"I'm used to it," she interrupted, wiping away tears. "I just didn't expect my betrothed to be so blunt. But I will show him that I'm lovable."

"My brother is an idiot," Dain confessed, walking down the dais. "Please, ignore him. You are far from ugly." Kaylien blushed, and Dain snapped. "Maidens, please take Kaylien to her room so she can settle." He flipped his attention back to Kaylien, and his face softened. "Let's try again tonight at dinner. I promise Terryn will come around."

The girl nodded and exited the room. When the door clicked shut, Hamlin and Lysane exited from the shadows, joining the group.

Jarin studied the everyone around him. "Dain, what do you think of Kaylien?"

"The girl is smarter than how she is acting," he replied, crossing his arms.

Lysane nodded in agreement, "She has been taught well."

"We need to plan," Dain mumbled, his body tense.

He turned to his son. "Why are we planning? Is the girl a threat?"

Dain Osmont pressed his lips together. "No, but Mother is. She has changed since recovering from her illness. I see now why you always stayed away from her. She is a pretender, too. She pretends to be nice when, really, she is a cruel woman. I see that now. I always blamed you for the distance in our family, but I understand that you were just trying not to get hurt. Mother is particularly good at hurting people." Now Dain was the one looking down, and Lysane stared at the boy with compassion. "I don't believe Terryn has realized this. He is so stupid! Kaylien isn't malicious, but I will not put aside the thought that she could manipulate him. I think Mother will manipulate Kaylien, and Kaylien will manipulate Terryn."

"Why will that matter when I have all the power?" Jarin asked.

His youngest son stayed silent, and his silence made Lysane's entire body shift as if someone was in the room watching. "You mean Lord Jarin's life is in danger?" she whispered.

Dain stayed quiet and Lysane covered her gaping mouth with her hands. Jarin's eyes widened as he understood what was happening. "I don't know for sure," Dain began, his voice still low, "But I have heard whispers. We must act."

Jarin's mind raced. *I did not think Dimia would act so quickly.* It scared Jarin to know his wife was so heartless, but he should not have expected any less. *I need to see the world differently. I need to see* her *differently.* He knew the truth. He was still in love with Dimia. The gods cursed him to love her forever, and he could do nothing but see the best in her. *Of course she would try to kill me, even as she smiles in my face.*

"We can't do anything until we foil an assassination plot," Ser Bronston informed.

"What if Jarin dies before we can uncover the plot?" Lysane questioned, her eyes watery.

Jarin's chest stung as he took in Lysane's distraught face. He never wanted to see her hurt. He then looked at Dain who tried his best not to stare at Lysane. *I will protect everyone.*

He leaned in and spoke in a hushed voice, as a plan unraveled in his mind. "If I die, and Dimia takes control through Terryn, then Lysane, I need you to take Dain and go to the Grasslands. Ask for Lord Gardener's presence and explain to him what has happened here. I've heard that he is an honest and trusting man. I think he will harbor you both." He stopped then. *Would Lord Gardener truly harbor them?*

Dain sucked his teeth, "Father that is a terrible plan. We need to act now!"

"Where did you hear the whispers from, boy?" Hamlin inquired.

Dain glanced at Jarin before taking a deep breath. "I heard some kitchen maids whispering about a knight approaching them and asked if anyone knew of an Art that poisons," he mumbled.

Hamlin and Lysane exchanged glances. "Food and drink," they said simultaneously.

Dimia already has people working for her again? Jarin seethed. A small piece of him hoped that Dimia had changed. However, his wife was Dimia Osmont, the wicked witch of the Riverlands. *Stupid! Stupid! Stupid!* He scolded. *Dimia is nothing! Quit making her something. Giving her something will ruin everything.*

He wished that she had died from the deathskin.

"We will have Lord Jarinns food cooked outside of the kitchens from now on. No one will know about this, except for the people in this room. I know a trusted cook who will make your food," Hamlin decided.

"When we believe Dimia is carrying out her plan, give the food that is presented to me to someone else," Jarin added.

"Why?"

"I made a promise with someone and they did not fulfill their end. Death from Dimia's hands will be their punishment."

"Then we will have whoever you want to eat the food. We will also have extra guards, trusted by me, by your side at all times just in case the assassination attempt changes. Hopefully, Dimia carries on with her plan and does not assume anything is array," Hamlin decided while rubbing his hands.

"If everything goes to plan, we can convict Dimia of attempted murder," Ser Bronston added, smiling wide.

Everyone silently nodded in agreeance.

"Dain, I need you to take up all of Terryn's time," Jarin commanded, and Dain rolled his eyes in defiance. "You could either do that, or you could take up all of your mother's time."

Dain's face morphed into a happy smile. "I can spend more time with Terryn, no problem."

Lysane chuckled at Dain's reaction and Jarin turned to her. "Lysane, I need you to become Kaylien's friend. Make sure that no one other than you, Terryn, Dain, or me is around her, understood?"

The girl nodded. "What happens if Lady Dimia approaches and wishes to speak with Kaylien alone?"

Jarin thought for a moment. "Allow the woman to do as she pleases, but immediately report it to Hamlin and me. Then report it to Dain, and he will take up his mother's time." Jarin smiled, as Dain groaned.

This is a test, my son, he wanted to tell Dain. *If everything is true, I will be able to trust you with my life.* Jarin was disappointed in himself that he could not trust his own son. Truthfully, he could not trust either of his sons. Not because they were liars or anything like that, but because they lived in a world where Dimia was their mother. They grew up around her, and broke their fast with her. Dimia had bathed them, and fed them from her own breast. When Jarin separated himself from his wife and sons, Dimia became closer to the boys. She knew their secrets, their dreams, and their favorite foods to eat. All Jarin knew was the boys' name, and that they were his sons.

It made Jarin feel uneasy.

"We do not usually communicate as a group," Hamlin informed. "We need to behave inconspicuously. We cannot tip off to Lady Dimia's rats that we are together. We need to act like strangers to each other, as we have been this entire time. Even though Lady Dimia acts like a beast, she plans like a deer. At the first sight of her plan unravelling, she will run off." The entire time Hamlin spoke, he only looked at Dain.

Dain gave Hamlin a challenging stare. "Your counsellors seem wary of me, Father."

Jarin smiled. *Everyone is wary of you, Dain.* "Hamlin is just old. He is wary of the dust."

Hamlin pressed on a smile and bowed. "You are correct. My apologies young Dain, if I have seemed unkind to you."

The boy waved his hand, not really accepting the old monk's apology. "Don't worry, I hold no ill will. At the end of this, you will *all* see that I'm telling the truth. I care about what happens to the Riverlands, and *all* the people who live in it. I only want what is best."

I only want what is best too, Jarin agreed, his attention shifting to the raindrops splashing on the windows. He thought about his past, the good and bad, immediately creating a headache. *And I will do what is best, because I am the Lord Protector of the Riverlands.*

HADRIAN

Hadrian Osmont now realized how much of a child he was. Only a few hours after Raynese awoke from her fevered sleep, the trio was back on their journey, traveling toward the northern kingdom. Most of the time, everyone was quiet, and a nipping insanity visited Hadrian daily, along with the same stupid sparrow with its same dumb songs.

He frowned and buzzed his lips, trying his best to stay calm.

Hadrian had attempted to ask the millions of questions in his head to pass the time, but of course, he was just a child. *Ser Colvic, why are you walking like that? Did you get hurt? Did you ever see a strange green wildcat while traveling through the forest?* Hadrian inhaled sharply. *Raynese, do you know anything about strangely colored beasts in the Great Forest? What about the Arts? How are you even walking again?* His companions conveniently ignored the most straightforward questions and always found something else to do. Even now, as he sat on the frost-stiffened grass, Ser Colvic and Raynese moved around their small campsite, doing tedious tasks.

He was over their shit. He was over everyone's shit.

"The water is warm now," Ser Colvic informed, not looking at anyone as he moved to tinker with something else. "Go wash up."

Hadrian stood, not responding, and walked into the thicket toward a small bubbling watering hole. He untied his laces, ready to wash himself. A rip tingled his ear as he repositioned himself, causing him to groan. *Not my shirt.*

Raynese jumped on his back, hanging over his shoulder. "What's wrong, my love?" she questioned, her lips lightly touching his ear.

He shook her off and covered himself. "My shirt ripped," he grumbled, not understanding the young woman's demeanor.

Although Raynese refused to answer his questions, she never wanted to stop talking to him and expected responses. Hadrian wanted to scoff at that. *Does she think I'm too childish to know the truth? How can I prove to her that I've grown up?* All Raynese wanted to do was hold Hadrian's hand, hug him from behind, or invade his personal space. Even a few nights, she slipped into his sleeping bag and cuddled him.

Now, Raynese acted nothing like she did before. Her mysterious nature had been replaced with a giddy love, which conflicted Hadrian. Everything about Raynese made Hadrian unsure. *I do like her, but she is a Wicked.*

I saw it with my own eyes. Is she doing this to stay near me? Should I push her away?

His attention narrowed on the traveler woman who now slowly slipped off her clothing. Hadrian covered his eyes. "What are you doing?"

Raynese pulled Hadrian's hands away, but he refused to take in her naked body. "You didn't want to bathe with me?"

He turned his head. "The watering hole isn't big enough."

Raynese took Hadrian's hands and pressed them against her body before leaning in to kiss him. Hadrian grew rigid and moved his face, forcing the woman to pull away. "It's getting cold, isn't it?" she questioned, their noses touching.

"Aye."

"You said you loved me. You really do, right?"

There was a millisecond of hesitation. *I must be an actor.* "Aye."

The traveler woman's beautiful face brightened. "Okay, you go bathe, and I'll speak with Colvic about getting you a new shirt."

He pressed on a smile. "Thank you!" He accepted an embrace from her, and she slipped back on her clothes and skipped away happily. *She does whatever she wants without the thought of consequences.* He gasped at the description. *She's sort of like my mother.*

Hadrian halfway cleaned himself, not in the mood. He slipped back on his freezing clothing and retreated to the campsite where Raynese and Ser Colvic were still conversing, both of their faces serious. "It's too cold to bathe," he informed his companions, forcing their attention.

The famed knight nodded. "Fine, we will go. Let's pack up."

"What town are we going to?" Raynese questioned, balancing on a fallen log.

I must know more about her Art. Is she some kind of healer, so fixing her leg is easy? However, the abilities she used also helped me when I was overwhelmed, and she seemed to look through trees leagues away. It was all too complicated for Hadrian's ignorant mind, yet he knew one thing for sure. Her leg was broken, and she healed it, yet when Ser Colvic struggles to walk, she doesn't offer to help. *Can she?*

"If it's true that you passed Alnor's Fortress, then we will head to Eldersgate," Colvic answered, pointing to Raynese. "You lead, and I'll be in the back." The woman saluted the knight and rushed to her horse as Ser Colvic gave Hadrian a cloak. "Here is one of my extras. You'll freeze if you don't wear it."

"Thank you," he exhaled, and Colvic smiled a little before struggling forward. "Are you okay? Do you need help?"

The knight pressed his lips together. "I'm alright. Just stiff."

"Raynese might be able to help you."

He gave Hadrian a suspicious look. "What do you mean?"

"Will we chat all day or head to Eldersgate?" Raynese questioned, already mounted on her horse. "Come on, let's go."

Hadrian rushed to his horse, grinning, knowing he never answered the knight's question.

By the time Hadrian settled on his steed, Raynese and Colvic were gone. He sighed, kicked his horse's sides, and began the game of catch-up. "Come on, Oak, go faster," he pleaded to his horse as she galloped through the thick forest. His long hair practically covered his eyesight as he bounced on the saddle. He felt like an idiot, but then again, Hadrian felt like an idiot most of the time.

Finally, he saw Colvic and Raynese's horses walking calmly ahead of him.

"Took you long enough," Colvic said, facing ahead.

Raynese giggled. "Don't pretend, Colvic." She then turned to Hadrian. "You caught up much faster than usual," she told him, boosting his confidence. "You have been teaching your horse well."

"How much farther?"

Colvic still looked forward. "Some way to go."

Hadrian looked down, defeated. He wanted to be in Eldersgate now and see the people who inhabited the town in the middle of the Great Forest.

"Why must you bother Hadrian so much, you old knight?" Raynese inquired, her eyebrows raised, grabbing Hadrian's attention. She then smiled, her hazel eyes on his. "We should be there soon, my sweet."

Eldersgate was underwhelming.

An old, weathered, wooden fence encased the town to protect the citizens. Towers were posted at the four corners of the wall, the fire still lit from the night watch. *This town is truly in the middle of the forest.* Ser Colvic Rames stood at the gate, speaking with other knights as Hadrian and Raynese stayed back, waiting for a signal. Hadrian blocked his eyes from the harsh morning sunlight and noticed the sharp points at the end of each wooden stake. *Was this fence built to keep out the Warrior Raiders or wild animals?* Ivory-white fangs filled his mind. *Like a leopard?*

"You see, this is why I hate the northern kingdom," Raynese complained, crossing her arms.

"What do you mean?"

She walked toward the gate, and Hadrian followed behind. "It's all trees; so ugly!"

The trio stepped into Eldersgate, each observing the highly populated city. Children played loudly, blacksmiths and butchers worked outside their shacks so others could watch, and women walked around with large baskets, shopping. The people were living simply, yet contently with their regular lives.

Hadrian frowned as he continued to take in the sight. His eyes snapped from the residential houses to the shops and the surrounding fence. *Everything is wooden.* He tugged on Ser Colvic Rames' sleeve. "Cities shouldn't be made of wood. It's too dangerous. Why is this allowed?"

Raynese beamed at the question. "My beloved has a brain!"

"Cut it out," Colvic snapped. "It's allowed because they can afford nothing else."

"I'm sure with years of work, the city could transition to stone. Don't they know what happened to Tealoch a hundred years ago?"

Colvic placed his hands on his hips and looked down at Hadrian. "It was a little more than a century ago, and of course not. They don't have tutors like you did." Hadrian pouted at the response and looked away, causing the knight to pat him on the head. "But seeing you care brings me joy. You would've been a great Lord Protector."

Hadrian frowned harder, not finding any comfort in Ser Colvic's words. "Thanks."

Colvic shifted his footing. "Alright, listen up, you both need new clothes and better weapons."

"I do just fine with what I have," Raynese replied, turning away.

The knight sighed. "Fine, then get what you think you need because you need *something*. And no playing around. I want to be in and out of the town in an hour. And try to find women to do these tasks. They ask less important questions." He handed Raynese a small sack, and the two stared at each other. "Take care of Hadrian."

Brightness returned to Raynese's face, and her tiny hand closed around the coin sack. "Of course!"

Hadrian moved away from the pair as they continued their conversation, which he didn't care much about. *They both keep secrets from me and treat me like a child. I don't need to listen to their conversation.*

He continued onward, knowing Raynese would catch up eventually. *Can I find a female tailor or blacksmith?* He had never considered such a thing. *I can't be so naïve.* He pictured the traveler woman stepping out of the tree, fully healed. *I've seen stranger things.*

A woman younger than Raynese approached him not three minutes into his journey. "You are a pretty boy," she told him, her breast practically spilling out of her dress.

The girl's stench reached Hadrian's nose, and he turned his head. "Thank you."

"The name is Willa. What's yours?"

"Uh, I must find a tailor. Would you mind pointing me to where one resides?"

Willa licked her lips, her eyes lowering to stare at Hadrian's body. "No, but I could point you to somewhere nice and moist," she replied, reaching to grab his hand.

Hadrian backed away. *This woman is just like,*

"My sweet, why did you leave?" Raynese questioned from behind, interrupting his thoughts. He turned to the traveler woman whose face was twisted in anger. "My sweet," she called again, cautiously, staring only at the big-breasted woman. "Who is this?"

"Your *sweet* was just about to pay me to receive some of *my* sweets," Willa chuckled, revealing a missing front tooth.

"Ew," Hadrian said childishly, causing the woman's smile to fade while Raynese's widened. "All I asked you was where a tailor resided. Don't put words in my mouth. Please, point me to where the tailors are."

"Go west," Willa mumbled, her brown eyes teary.

Hadrian hurriedly walked away, with his head lowered, embarrassed.

"Can you believe that woman?" Raynese asked, catching up. "To think that I would believe you would pay an ugly wench to do something you are too scared to do to me," she snorted and smacked Hadrian on the back. "Ridiculous, right?"

Hadrian's face heated up. *She thinks I am a child.* "I'm not afraid. I'm cautious."

"Of what?"

He thought for a moment, "The Warrior Raiders."

"Don't worry." Raynese stopped and pulled out one of her many daggers. "I will kill every last one of those Raiders to get a kiss from you," she declared, and Hadrian rolled his eyes.

He was tired of watching one of the strongest people he knew pretend she was nothing more than a carefree traveler. *I guess she's being an actor, too.* The darkness of the world engulfed Hadrian as he understood one truth. *Everyone must become actors to get through life.*

Hadrian Osmont wished he could tell his younger siblings that.

Eyes followed Hadrian and Raynese as they walked through Eldersgate. "Why do people keep staring at us?"

Raynese smiled—her smile mesmerizing. "Well," she began, trying to catch the eyes that stared, "it is either because they find you stunning or they have never seen a woman like me. Either way, we both stand out and maybe they want to know more." While Raynese spoke, her smile never faltered, but Hadrian saw her eyes showing concern. "Don't worry about them."

Hadrian forced himself to swallow the bile that climbed up his throat as his mind raced. *No. Something is wrong.* He continued west, and the birds in his head began to squawk. *Not now,* he begged, noticing a sparrow perched on a sign above a tailor shop. He quickened his pace toward the bird, wanting to get his materials and leave Eldersgate.

"We're here," Raynese announced, opening the door to the tailor's shop.

The shack was dark, dusty, and empty.

"Well, hello there," an old man hooted, rubbing his long, hooked nose. Skin flakes dotted the old man's grey, bushy eyebrows, and there were too many age spots to count. "What do you need?"

Raynese stepped forward and placed her hands behind her back. "Hello there," she greeted cheerfully, matching the man's hooting. "Mind making some clothes for us?"

The old man bowed his head. "Of course, who shall I measure first?"

"Actually," Hadrian spoke up, "Is there a woman here who could make my clothes? My mother always made my clothes, but a fever took her. I want mine to have a woman's touch." His lie was convincing; he knew that when he saw the old man think for a minute, and Raynese smiled widely.

"My wife can measure you, but I would have to make the clothes," the old man replied, and Hadrian nodded. *That should be close enough.*

"We are in a bit of a hurry; would you be able to make the clothes within the hour?" Raynese asked.

"Of course. You two have been the only people to come to my shop all day, and I have pre-fits, so half the job is done already. Just need to alter." He smiled and rubbed his hands together, and turned toward another room. "Wife!" he called before returning his attention to the pair. "So, just an outfit for the two of you?"

"He needs two outfits with two extra shirts," Raynese answered. "I don't know what I need."

"How about two outfits and an extra pair of pants?" the old man asked.

Raynese grinned. "You don't mind making pants for a woman?"

The old man shrugged. "Why should I care? None of my business. Nope, my business is the needle, thread, and cloth. Nothing else."

Raynese leaned over to Hadrian. "I like this old tailor."

Hadrian smiled and nodded, still closely watching the man as his wife entered the main room noisily. "Took you long enough," the old man huffed, and his wife responded by waving her hand. "Measure the boy. I will measure the girl. Don't question. It's what they asked."

The old woman took Hadrian by the arm and led him into another room. "Stand here," she said, her voice sharp. She then pulled out her measuring tools and observed Hadrian. "You're tall. I would have preferred to measure the girl." *What does she mean? I'm shorter than Raynese.* The old woman wobbled away, grabbed a stool, and placed it in front of him before she started measuring. "Please undress."

"I requested for you," Hadrian replied, his voice shaking as he took off her clothes down to his underwear.

"Why? I know no information."

He gulped at the statement. "No, it is just that my mother used to make my clothes for me. So, I wanted a woman to do it."

"My husband believed that lie? Typical."

His mouth gaped open in surprise, thinking about Colvic's words. *Of course, women ask less important questions; they can already figure things out without saying a single word.* "Why did you truly want me?"

Hadrian sighed, defeated. "I was told to."

"By who? I know no information, child."

"I do not know why," Hadrian said, not answering her question. "I was just told it would be preferred to have a female tailor."

"Well, I'm not a tailor, just his wife. So, you have failed in your task."

"It was not a task, more like a suggestion."

The old tailor's wife laughed and placed a pin in her mouth. "Sounded more like a demand to me."

"Well, I guess you're right, and I guess I failed."

Hadrian stayed rigid as the tailor's wife finished measuring and wrote down her findings. "I will give these measurements to my husband."

He followed the old woman back into the main room, where the old tailor chatted with Raynese.

"Within the hour," Raynese reminded the old man, and the tailor smiled, nodding. The traveler woman turned to Hadrian and grabbed his arms. "What should we do while we wait?"

"I'm starving."

"Let's eat then!" Her hazel eyes flickered back to the tailor. "Within the hour," she said once more, and the old man replied by starting on the outfits. Raynese led Hadrian out of the shop, still smiling. "I love that feisty couple!"

Hadrian smiled. "Aye, they were nice."

A tavern by the tailor's shop sold beef stew for lunch. Hadrian tried to enjoy himself as he ate, but he couldn't. The unrelenting eyes burned into him.

Raynese's once carefree demeanor had soured by the end of lunch, and she sat quietly at the table, observing the people around them. "The hour is almost up. Let's go," she informed, sounding like the woman Hadrian had grown to enjoy.

There is the real Raynese.

The pair left the tavern and traveled back to the tailor's shop. As they walked, the eyes seemed to follow. Raynese moved with swiftness as they approached the small shack.

"Wonderful timing," the old man greeted, standing up. "I just finished."

"Wow," Raynese cheered, her fake persona returning. "You did an amazing job!"

The tailor smiled wide. "Well, thank you. I see that neither of you have bags, so here is a satchel to carry your clothes in, free of charge."

"You're amazing!" Raynese stripped into her under clothes in front of the old man and changed into her new clothes, so Hadrian did the same.

She's rushing. It's like we are running out of time. His new clothes slipped on perfectly, and he smiled, finally looking presentable. *At least I was able to get some new clothes.*

"For all of this," the old man pointed, "three silvers."

"That is a steal!" Raynese yelled, twirling towards the door as Hadrian opened the coin sack to pay. "We will only be coming to you from now,"

Suddenly, everything became eerily quiet.

Hadrian turned on his heels, terrified by the traveler woman's silence.

Raynese stood at the wide-open door, still facing inside, her body trembling. Tears filled her eyes as she stared past Hadrian, causing his heart to sink. Slowly, he returned his attention to the tailor, whose face mirrored Raynese's.

Then, the tailor coughed blood.

Hadrian's once silent world now rang with roars and squawking and screams and shouting. He hyperventilated while the birds in his head continued, louder and louder. His eyes shifted away from the ghostly face, only to see the end of an arrow sticking out of the old man's throat.

JASLYN

An excruciating pain ripped through Jaslyn, forcing her from her sleep. *What's going on?* She tried her best to sit up in bed, and she gripped at her lower belly—the part that hurt the most. *What is this pain?* She laid back down and groaned, holding back tears. *Has someone poisoned me?*

The question frightened Jaslyn, and she shot herself out of bed with all her might. Her stomach and legs burned from the movements, causing her to grunt. The nightdress stuck to her skin, soaked. *What the heck?* She lightly touched her gown and examined her red-stained fingertips. *No,* she panicked and turned to her sheets, her entire body aching. *NO!*

She was bleeding.

No, not now, she cried. *I cannot become a woman now!* Her head spun as another sharp pain vibrated through her abdomen. Jaslyn fell to her knees and screamed so loud that her ears rang. *This cannot be happening to me.* She shivered, and bile crept up her throat as she stared at the stone floor. *What do I do?* Again, agonizing pain overwhelmed Jaslyn, forcing her to lie on the floor, clutching at the bottom of her stomach. *Can you die from something like this?*

The sudden sensation of a liquid trickling down her thighs caused her body to run cold, and she vomited on the floor. *I feel so weak. How can I be a queen to the people like this?* She wondered if her father was right all along. *I have no idea what I'm doing.*

Jaslyn's twin handmaidens rushed into the bedchamber, both completely breathless.

"What," Violet started before pausing, her mouth agape. Tears streamed down her face as she took in the sight of Jaslyn Wayward on the floor, covered in her blood.

Evergreen pushed past her sister and scooped Jaslyn into her arms, her big eyes studying the queen. "Are you okay?" Jaslyn answered by sobbing loudly, and Evergreen turned to Violet. "Go find someone to clean the room while I run a bath." Violet nodded at the direction, while Evergreen placed Jaslyn back on the floor.

She felt the wet, coldness of her dress stick to her skin, causing her to hurl again. "I'm sorry," she gagged, suppressing more vomit. "It just hurts." No one responded as the twin girls hurried throughout the room.

Jaslyn focused on the anxious footsteps that pattered around her, taking deep breaths. She attempted to sit up, but the heaviness in her body was too much. Jaslyn fell again, and Evergreen surrounded her. "It hurts."

"Sh, I know, try not to move," Evergreen exhaled, grabbing Jaslyn's shoulders. "The gods torture the strongest. Now, take this," the handmaiden said, and she opened her mouth in response.

Jaslyn tasted a tablet on her tongue and swallowed it quickly. "What was that?"

"It's medicine to stop the bleeding for a moment while I clean you. Luckily, mine just finished, so I had some on hand."

"Ever, I can barely open my eyes," Jaslyn complained. "My entire body hurts."

The handmaiden nodded, slipping Jaslyn into the warm bath water. "Like I said, the gods torture the strongest."

"I am not strong," Jaslyn whispered, laying her head on the lip of the bathtub.

Evergreen's violet-colored eyes burned into Jaslyn's. "Don't say that. You are one of the strongest people I know."

"How?"

The handmaiden puckered her lips fiercely. "Because I said so."

Jaslyn widened her eyes to roll them forcefully. "That is not a true answer," she exhaled as the handmaiden scrubbed Jaslyn's skin clean.

"You're strong because you are the queen," Evergreen explained, gripping Jaslyn's shoulders and making her shiver. "I believe you're a queen. So do Violet, Ser Lyon, the knights, and the peasants. Even that pretty young lord believes you're a queen."

"Asten," Jaslyn blushed.

Evergreen nodded at that. "Don't allow your father's words and this experience with moonblood drag you down. You are strong. You are stronger than your father, mother, Josef, and Alice."

"No," Jaslyn replied. "I am not stronger than Alice. Alice is the strongest woman in the Mountain Realm. Maybe even the entire world."

"Aye, but you must tell your lady mother of this."

Jaslyn moved away from her friend and covered her budding breasts. "Why must I tell her? She won't care." In truth, she did not want to tell anyone. *Only Evergreen and Violet. Men require strong leaders. How can I be strong when this hurts so much? If the men who support me find out about my moonblood, would their support waiver?*

"You must tell her," Evergreen repeated. "Your mother will explain what is happening."

"I already know what is happening! Moonblood appears once every new moon until I get old, like Lady Myster old. Then it ends. From now until I am almost twenty, I will grow taller, my hips will get wider, and my breasts will get bigger. I will turn into a woman."

"Tell her," the handmaiden insisted, standing up from the side of the tub. "Hurry and get out of the water and get dressed. The medicine should be wearing off soon."

"Can I not take another tablet?"

"No," Evergreen told her sternly. "You must only take it when you wish to bathe. This is a natural part of life. You cannot stop it."

Jaslyn stood and stepped from the tub, catching a glimpse of her naked, childish body as Evergreen wrapped a towel around her. *Now, I will start looking different, like Evergreen and Violet have been experiencing the past few years.* She pictured her captivating mother's lustrous curves and compared them to her father's stocky body. *Who's appearance will I mimic when I finish my adolescence? What will the people's queen look like in adulthood?*

"You are a beautiful girl," Evergreen said as if she could read Jaslyn's thoughts. "You need to stop thinking otherwise."

Jaslyn spat out a laugh. *Beautiful?* Her mouth twitched into a frown, and tears streamed down her face. *I'm not beautiful—just a regular girl.* Nothing was funny, and everything hurt.

Evergreen stroked Jaslyn's hair comfortingly. "It is just the pain coming back." Jaslyn quietly followed her handmaiden to some clean clothes and stared at the ugly padded underwear beside her trousers. "You must wear this until you stop bleeding," Evergreen explained, helping Jaslyn get dressed.

Jaslyn's trousers did not fit right, and she looked down uncomfortably. "I guess I should not wear trousers with this type of underwear," she said halfheartedly.

"Aye, but you'll wear them anyway." Evergreen gave a sad smile. "Now, go and tell your lady mother. She is breaking her fast in the dining hall," the handmaiden informed, pushing Jaslyn out of her bedchamber.

Jaslyn struggled to get where her mother was; each step intensified her pain. *Why must women go through this hell? Men do not get to experience this pain. They get to rule and die bravely in battle.* It all angered Jaslyn, but she could not do anything about it. *The gods made humans this way.*

She paused at the dining hall door and calmed her breathing before turning the brass handle. Inside, Lady Gloriana sat at the table, ignoring the food before her and writing fiercely.

"Good morning," Jaslyn greeted as kindly as possible. Gloriana, however, ignored her youngest daughter and continued writing, forcing Jaslyn to clear her throat loudly. "Mother, good morning."

Gloriana stopped and sighed. "Morning. Do you need something?"

Jaslyn blinked, surprised by her mother's tone. "I wanted to break my fast with you."

"Don't pretend like I don't know," she replied coldly, looking down at Jaslyn. "You know, although you were the child Borin wanted the least, he ended up loving you the most. When he learned of your treason, the hurt that struck his face was unbearable. I understand if you don't care about me, but your father, I,"

"I don't care what you think!" Jaslyn cried, refusing to listen to her mother's hurtful words. "The peasants are dying, selling everything they have to taxes, and you do nothing about it!"

"Oh please, you don't think I've disagreed with the tax harvest implemented over two hundred years ago? Your father refuses to get rid of the tax because he hates change. But Jaslyn, why didn't you tell me? Do you hate me?"

Her eyes flickered to the floor. "No, I-I didn't know what to do. The peasants were asking for my help and saying they had asked you already. It felt like they were asking the last person they could think of, so I was hesitant to come to you. Plus, we never talk… about anything. I thought you had no interest in me."

Gloriana held Jaslyn's cheeks, smiling. "My wonderful child, of course, I have interest in you," she paused, her face transitioning into a frown, as she released her youngest daughter. "Your skin is slick with cold sweat. Are you sick?"

Embarrassment swirled within. "It seems I started my moonblood."

The Summeran woman's dark blue eyes shimmered with awe. "You speak truths?" Jaslyn nodded, and the small smile reappeared on Gloriana's lips. "My heart beats with happiness, but please, tell no one but your handmaidens. Your father speaks of sending you away."

"What?"

Gloriana grabbed Jaslyn's wrist. "As a warden via an economic pact, not a marriage proposal. Regardless, if he ships you away, you can't be queen, and he will want a pact to be completed even quicker if he learns of your moonblood. Although he will be pleased that you're not like Alice."

"Don't say that," Jaslyn snapped, frowning. She did not want to bring Alice into the conversation. *When it was realized that Alice would never receive her moonblood, everyone called her cursed and used it as another excuse to force her to stay in the Bloody Tower forever. Alice was never supposed to marry, and everyone knew that.* She took a deep breath. "I never wanted Father to know anyway."

"I guess I do know my daughter a little bit," Gloriana joked, and Jaslyn gave an uncomfortable smile. "So, what do you plan on doing now?"

Her heart dropped. "What do you mean?"

Gloriana repositioned in the chair. "Well, your father is earnest about sending you away. He wants you to go to the Black Hills or Waterbrook, but the best I can do is Griffon's Den. If you don't want any of that, you might as well be queen elsewhere."

Jaslyn stepped back. "You want me to runaway?"

"The moment you opened those big, bright golden eyes, I knew you would rise above the rest of your siblings. Josef may have your father's eyes, but you have the eyes of House Wayward. That will always determine your destiny for you. I don't want you to leave home, but your father no longer wants you here." Jaslyn stayed quiet, frozen by her mother's words, causing

Gloriana to sigh. "I really didn't think my first daughter would be shipped away to a hawk's nest while my other daughter declares herself queen."

"Well, Alice wouldn't have been shipped anywhere if you didn't threaten to kill Falk's children!"

The light in Gloriana's expression dimmed, and her attention narrowed to the cold plate of food before her. She scooped a mouthful of eggs and groaned. "Thank you, Korta, for blessing me with this food," she prayed before taking a bite. "It seems everyone thinks I'm a Wicked who would murder innocent children."

"I didn't believe it, but why did Father?"

Her mother peered back at Jaslyn before taking another bite. "Because your father is a fool."

Jaslyn stepped back. "But you are not."

Gloriana smiled and returned to her writing. "No, my daughter, I am not a fool. I am a woman with a different way of doing things and have been cursed with living in a place that thinks of me as an outcast. If you want to be queen, go and be queen, but think long and hard because you cannot take it back once you truly commit treason against the Lord Protector."

Jaslyn stepped back again, and it was clear that Lady Gloriana Wayward was finished with the conversation. *What does Mother mean?* Jaslyn's heart drummed in her chest as her mother continued writing. *Is she warning me?* Her entire body ached as horrible thoughts ran through her mind.

"Thank you, Mother, for the advice," Jaslyn uttered, and Gloriana gave a single nod.

She stumbled out of the dining hall and into the hallway, her mind racing. *What am I going to do? I don't want to leave Maryere. I don't want to betray my family.* Jaslyn hugged herself in comfort. *I don't even know if I want to be queen. I just want to save Alice. And I want to be free.*

Then she ran.

She rushed through the hallways, out of Winter's Keep, and into the busy afternoon streets of Maryere. *I want to do whatever I want. I want to grow up to become a pirate or Ranger and spend my days hunting beasts that rival the monsters in my bedtime stories.* Everything around Jaslyn turned into a blur, and the stabbing pain continued, but she ignored it all. *I must be strong. But why? Who am I being strong for? Myself. The peasants. Alice.*

Jaslyn Wayward didn't know.

She rushed past the Northgate and stopped, her short hair blowing around her face. She took a deep breath to calm herself, but it only brought another sharp pain. *I hate this.*

"Jaslyn," Asten called, already grabbing for her hand. "You're as pale as a ghost. What's wrong?"

"Everything," she answered, clutching her stomach.

The young Lord of Snow Creek lightly touched her cheek. "Is it your stomach? Do you have snowworm? You're sweating. Should I call a Saavant?"

"No!" She said forcefully to shut him up.

It angered Jaslyn that Asten cared so much. She wanted everyone to think that she was untouchable, like a goddess. *Like how the peasants see me.* That's all Jaslyn Wayward wanted—to be loved and depended on.

"Then what's wrong?"

Jaslyn focused on Asten, who again wore purple and green, slightly annoying her. *Those aren't House Dawphrey colors. Why does the Lord of Snow Creek continue wearing House Payne's colors? Does he not hold pride in his house?* She wanted to yell and scream at the boy, but since she had no real reason to be upset, she cried. She fell to her knees, the gravel scraping the skin underneath her pants. *All of this is stupid.*

Now, Asten's hands wrapped around Jaslyn's scrawny shoulders. "Please, tell me what is bothering you."

She lifted her head, and the pair's noses almost touched. She swayed at the sweet scent that radiated from the teenage boy. "I'm afraid."

Lord Asten Dawphrey's hazel-colored eyes widened. "What are you afraid of?"

"My father thinks he holds no control of the Mountain Realm, and wants to send me to the Summerlands or the Riverlands. I cannot leave."

Asten nodded and pulled Jaslyn into his arms, embracing her warmly. "My grandfather warned something like this might happen," he whispered, bringing a tingling sensation to Jaslyn's skin, weakening her knees. The young Lord of Snow Creek then pushed a small scroll into her hands. "Don't break the seal," he warned, turning the paper over to show an owl imprinted on brown wax from the Citadel of the Owl.

She stared at the seal with amazement. *Things are getting too serious, and I am barely queen. Am I ready for the challenges this world will bring? I don't know if I want to commit to this fully. Before too much happens, I must figure out what to do. I can't take back the decisions once I make them.*

"You must keep this on you at all times. Do not put it down anywhere. If you do, it will get stolen. When ready, take the scroll to one of your most trusted knights. He will know what to do when he breaks the seal, but only he can break it. When the seal is broken, you will have to disappear. Once that happens, I will say I am returning to Snow Creek, but instead, I will go and find you. Now, I need to speak to my grandfather. Will you be okay?"

Jaslyn nodded, and more tears rolled down her cheeks as the young lord rushed away in a different direction. She was terrified. Jaslyn remembered the times she had visited Queen's Cove. She pictured the little boys and girls running around the village in rags, yet they were optimistic whenever they saw Jaslyn. Everyone in Queen's Cove looked at her with pride. *They chose me.*

Jaslyn Wayward took a deep breath. *I must do what I can for the people. My life will mean little if I can't save them.* She didn't semi-accept the title of queen to aggravate her parents. Nor to become powerful, as many others believed. She did it to save the mountain people from an inevitable death the highborn had structured for them.

She thought about Alice then. She pictured her older sister's bright blue eyes and raven-black hair. She imagined the young woman's paleness and how the constant cold brought a tinge of pink to Alice's nose and cheeks. She thought about Alice's warmth and kindness. *Many in distress need a hero. I want to be that for them. Not a queen, but a hero. Like Rosalind.*

The story of Rosalind the Hero replayed in Jaslyn's mind. *After murdering her love to save her people from possible persecution, Rosalind realized she wanted to be a fighter, but her father forbade it and sold her off to a rival tribe for a decade of fishing hole rights. Instead, Rosalind made a pilgrimage to Nephele in Eeccess and learned to fight like the Titan warriors of the past. After saving many during excursions to monster nests, High Priestess Anahita, recognized Rosalind's bravery and declared her a Saint of the People, giving her the more known title, Rosalind the Hero.*

Jaslyn clutched her lower belly at the tale. *Like how Queen Sahasha Gardener was known as the Peasant Saint, I'll be like that. I will live for myself while helping the people.* She gave a small smile then. *I guess I'm more like Rosalind than I initially thought.*

HADRIAN

Blood dripped from the wound as the old tailor coughed, speaking inaudible words. Hadrian's face twisted from the sight, and he began hyperventilating. *What's happening?* His panicked eyes stayed on the arrow that stuck through the man's throat. Hadrian stumbled back, and everything around him grew dark as the birds screamed. *What's happening?*

"Get down!"

Before Hadrian could move, another arrow flew through the shop, whizzing past and striking the tailor's wife in the chest. *What's happening?* The old woman fell to her knees and silently died, never realizing that she had been hit.

Hadrian clutched onto the bag the old man gifted him and raced toward the exit, where Raynese threw arrowheads at the approaching attackers. She hit one in the chest, one in the eye, and another in the throat. *More violence. More death,* Hadrian thought, rushing out of the tailor's shop.

Bright orange flames flickered in the evening sky, and Hadrian coughed violently, remembering the feeling of smoke filling his lungs from moons ago. Shrill horse screams from the stables overlapped the cries of the townspeople. The birds in Hadrian's head squawked so loudly his ears rung, and he fell to his knees. *Oh no! Eldersgate is burning to the ground!* Hadrian hugged himself, preparing for certain death. *Patty. I'll get to see you again. I've missed you.*

Raynese lifted him off the ground. "What the hell are you doing? You're not fucking dying on me!" She let go, picked up a sword from the dirt, and examined it briefly before tossing it to Hadrian. "You know how to kill, right?"

Hadrian made a face, not answering, and Raynese raced ahead. He followed behind, tugging the sword along with him. *It's so heavy.* A giant, rugged man stepped in front of Hadrian with an enormous battle axe, causing the teenage boy to gasp.

A Warrior Raider. They've found me.

The burly man grinned and swung. Hadrian lifted his sword to block, and his arms vibrated from the strike. He squealed from the pain, stumbled backward, and landed on his backside, already crying.

I can't give up! I can't die yet! Again, the Raider swung his battle axe, but this time, Hadrian ducked and thrust the sword into the man's stomach. Blood poured from the wound and covered Hadrian's hands as the man's face went pale. Hadrian slid the sword out, and the Raider dropped to his knees. *I did it. I killed someone.* He scrambled to his feet and started running toward the gate. *I can't stop. I must leave Eldersgate.*

Then, he was in the air.

Hadrian struggled against the bulky arm wrapped around his waist. *Who has me?* He kicked and thrashed as Eldersgate burned all around.

"Stop it! I'm going to drop you!" Ser Colvic Rames roared, and Hadrian immediately calmed.

I thought the stables burned. How did he grab a horse in time? The knight's arm squeezed tighter, trying to pull Hadrian up. He climbed onto the horse and Colvic held him tightly as they galloped through the city toward the gate. *We can escape!* They neared the wall, and his heart dropped. *Raynese.* "Wait! She's missing!"

Colvic's horse didn't slow down, and he smacked his teeth. "I don't know where she went, and we don't have time to look."

Hadrian scanned the death and destruction, noticing a figure leap into the air. His eyes narrowed as the figure twirled into a strike, stabbing one Raider in the forehead while slicing another in the throat. *There she is!* Raynese then spun on one foot and cut down three Warrior Raiders simultaneously. *She's incredible!*

"There!" Hadrian pointed.

Ser Colvic sighed and redirected the horse from the open gate. In one swift movement, Colvic scooped Raynese into his arms before she could murder another Warrior Raider.

"Put me down! Put me down!" Raynese screamed, thrashing wildly.

"Oi, calm yourself! We need to leave Eldersgate now!" Colvic shouted, and the traveler woman quieted, sliding onto the horse and sitting behind the famed knight. *Colvic is fantastic too! I wish I could be more like them. Yet, they want to hide everything from me.*

Arrows whizzed past, and Colvic maneuvered the horse, trying to escape. Ahead, several Warrior Raiders were on the towers, cutting the ropes to shut the gate. "Oh, all the hells," Ser Colvic groaned, exasperated. "How did they say it? Um, *Pack Animal Skill*, oh fuck, I don't know!"

"You have the Arts and don't know how to incant?" Raynese inquired, her face filled with surprise, and the knight shook his head. "What are you trying to do with the horse?"

Colvic frowned. "Go faster so we can escape."

Raynese thought for a moment. "You seem to be a more natural Mara, so just think about the horse speeding up, and it should happen in reality."

The man's frown deepened, but he nodded and closed his eyes. Hadrian gripped tighter as the horse's speed increased. *Amazing! How is Colvic able to do this?* The horse galloped faster, and they slipped through the gate, successfully making it outside the city.

Ser Colvic Rames rode the horse hard for an hour before stopping.

"This should be far enough," he informed, jumping off. "Bonnie needs a break."

Hadrian slid off the horse, and his knees wobbled when his feet hit the ground. *I killed someone.* He retched as the old tailor's face appeared in his mind. *This was not supposed to happen. The tailors were good people, kind people.*

He vomited again, and Colvic groaned. "Are you done?"

"Colvic, leave him alone," Raynese replied. "He killed someone. Let him cope."

Hadrian shivered and stared at his hands. Both were dirty and cracked with scabs and underneath his nails, there was blood. *Is it my blood, the old tailor's, or the Warrior Raider's?* His stomach churned as he imagined their faces. *This is too much.*

"You speak too casually with me, *Wicked*," Ser Colvic Rames grumbled.

Hadrian's attention snapped to the two as tension filled the air.

"You call me Wicked as if that is supposed to make me afraid. Say what's actually in your heart, knight!" Raynese shouted back, and Colvic made a face, opening his mouth, but gave no rebuttal. "What? Are you mad that I know about the Arts? You're a Mara too! What are you, a self-hater like the Harbingers?"

In an instant, Ser Colvic Rames had Raynese in a chokehold with a knife to her throat. "I'm tired of your antics. All you do is lie and make people feel bad for distrusting you. You are no traveler. Who are you?"

The young woman grinned. "To think I would be in a position like this. Good job, fair knight," she complimented, contorting her body out of Colvic's grip and holding onto the blade, smiling. "But you do not fear me."

Colvic responded by swinging the knife and connecting with Raynese's throat. "I know you fear nothing. Not even death."

Raynese stumbled back, her eyes wide, clutching her throat as more blood slipped through her fingers. A green glow appeared as her breathing slowed, and the blood stopped. She released her throat, showing that the wound had perfectly healed. "Ta-da! Is that what you wanted; to see me use my Art? Is this what a Wicked is to you?"

So, she's not a Wicked. Hadrian's mouth became agape, and he could do nothing but stare. "W-what are you?"

The woman turned to Hadrian and grinned. "Well, I'm a person, of course!"

Again, Ser Colvic pounced on the woman, but this time, Raynese was ready and threw the man off, pulling out one of her daggers. "I don't want to fight. Calm yourself, knight. I want what you want: Hadrian safe."

"How can I know that?"

Raynese chuckled. "I've proven plenty of times that I care for Hadrian deeply and will slaughter any person who wants to cause him harm. Isn't that enough?"

"No." The knight peered at the woman, his stance relaxing. "So, what were those fake gold coins? And why do you dabble in the Darkness?"

"What?" She questioned, and when Colvic didn't back down, she sighed. "Fine, I'm not a traveler, but most things I have told you are true. I am a Grasslandi woman who has traveled this vast and interesting world."

Raynese didn't answer his questions.

Colvic crossed his arms. "Why were you in Seascape? Were you following us? Did you already know about Hadrian?"

"Fine, fine. There is no reason to hide it now." Raynese waved her hand as if this was just a big inconvenience to her. "Take a good look."

She lifted her shirt, and Hadrian's eyes snapped shut on instinct. *Wait.* He peeked, realizing he had never seen the young woman naked before. *She is always hiding important information, even under her clothes.* Between her breasts was a small tattooed lion's head.

"A Zaiku," Colvic recognized.

Re'ins. Hadrian held in a gasp. *The regional assassins of Mystos.*

"Not just any Zaiku," Raynese grinned and turned around, exposing a decorative coiling snake inked in red onto her back. "I'm the Red Cobra."

Colvic rolled his eyes. "Aye, sure, sure, and I'm a Titan warrior," he replied, and Raynese's cheeks puffed in agitation. "Why would the Lord Protector of the Grasslands allow one of his trusted guards to leave his side?"

"The Red Cobra is a free spirit, didn't you know? Lord Merrick couldn't confine me to the Lion's Den Castle, so he sent me to the Summerlands to get some funds back that House Thoren owed House Gardener." Raynese then leaned forward. "I was going to kill that stupid lord for messing with my precious Lord Protector, but when I got to the Black Hills, he was nowhere to be found, and Lady Riya didn't have what House Thoren owed. I wrote to Merrick, who told me to keep looking for the man, so I traveled to Seascape, where I ran into you, the Austere Ram of Craven Hill."

Colvic's eyes narrowed at the moniker. "Why Seascape?"

"I was actually on my way to King's Berth because I learned that Lord Osmont the Elder might know Lord Bryce's whereabouts."

Ser Colvic Rames scoffed. "That name is ridiculous and Peyton knows nothing about that man. Those rumors were false."

"I don't know. The Black Mamba is always right."

Hadrian stepped forward. "Well, it doesn't seem like you've been looking for Lord Thoren for several moons now. Does Lord Gardener know you've abandoned your post? Or are you lying?"

She studied the pair for a moment with pain in her hazel eyes before her face transformed into a smile. "I'm not lying, and I haven't abandoned my quest. When we were in Eldersgate, I wrote to Merrick and updated him on what happened. When we reach a good point, I will return to Griffon's Den. Just not yet."

Hadrian looked at her with wide, confused eyes. *I was with her the entire time we were in Eldersgate, right? I never saw her write anything.*

"Not many women would get a red snake tattooed on their back for fun, so I cannot take that from you. You're the infamous Red Cobra," Colvic decided.

Hadrian peered at the woman. "Why are you infamous? Are you known for more than the downfall of Mikos?"

Raynese opened her mouth, but Colvic was quicker. "What?" the knight laughed, "You mean the Destruction of Mikos?"

"Aye," Hadrian replied cautiously, "Raynese wiped out the entire population because they made fun of her," he paused, realizing how ridiculous he sounded.

"No, the story is that when Ihphy, the goddess of the Sea's tear fell into the Cold Mountain, a volcano erupted and wiped out the Mikosi. They were gone thousands of years ago," Ser Colvic informed. "The name *Red Cobra* itself is infamous, not Raynese. There have been many Red Cobras, but I didn't know the Red Cobra was a young woman now."

"Aye, for about five years."

"You started young, huh?"

"Don't we all?"

The pair chuckled, once again acting friendly.

Their laughs boiled Hadrian from inside. *So Raynese lies and lies and lies and lies and I'm supposed to accept it. Oh, she lied about this but not that, so it's okay. What the hell? How can I trust her at all? I don't even know if I can continue acting around these people. It's all too much.*

"Well, it seems the Warrior Raiders have found us again, so we aren't safe," Colvic said, moving the conversation along. "We need to think of a new plan."

"We should continue north, so they think I'm going to Kingment," Hadrian suggested.

"That's a good idea. The Raiders seemed anxious to kill this time," Raynese analyzed. "It seems someone gave them a timer."

"Lady Arla is an impatient woman. She will want results soon," Colvic replied, turning to Hadrian. "You killed one of them, good, but you may have to kill many more next time."

Hadrian shifted his footing. "Could I do it using the Arts like you and Raynese?"

The pair looked at each other, and Colvic frowned. "Highborn don't usually have the Arts."

"But you do."

"Aye, and I had to hide it for years and learned nothing about it. But I know about the Warrior Raiders. I will teach you how to fight them and turn you into one of the greatest fighters this world has ever seen!"

ALICE

S he gazed at the endlessness of the Sapphire Sea. *Back home, all we had was a lake.* Myra's voice echoed, being carried by the sea breeze. Alice inhaled the salty air, wishing her handmaiden was by her side. *I want Myra to see the Sapphire Sea, too.*

Her aunt Victoria had kept her word, and an elderly Saavant named Enya cared for Myra daily. Everyone hoped the handmaiden would awaken —well, almost everyone.

Restless waves crashed against the King's Cliffs below, mirroring the turmoil in Alice's chest. *What am I going to do?* Her protector was beheaded, and it was her fault. Her best friend was incapacitated, and she was sure it was her fault, too.

Well, none of this would've happened if my mother wasn't impulsive. Alice reasoned, attempting to push the blame elsewhere. *I agreed to leave though. It's still my fault, even if it was to save my family.* She groaned, knowing there was no point in scolding herself about it. *What's done is done.*

Lady Alice Wayward closed her eyes, inviting the nippiness that swirled around her. *Kingment's winter feels like the late summer moons in Maryere.* She wrapped her fingers around the stone railing that separated her from the spiky black rocks below and exhaled, her body growing heavy. *I've stood for too long*, she realized, shifting toward a bench. She sat and closed her eyes again, wanting to disappear. *At least I'm left alone in the Black Castle.*

It had become the only positive in her life.

Her betrothed refused to meet, her uncle pretended she didn't exist, and her aunt sometimes acted like Alice was a nuisance. Everything made her feel like an outcast.

Alice continued to sit on the bench with an emotionless face as her little sister appeared in her head. She had tried so hard not to think about her family, but their faces appeared anyway. *I wonder what Jaslyn is doing.* She wanted her sister to continue running, hunting, playing, and laughing.

Her heart throbbed imagining Jaslyn, so she decided to think about something else while she rested, but the only other thing that came to her mind was Josef. Alice looked at her hands and squeezed them into fists. *Why must I think about Josef and Jaslyn?* She thought about their childish yells, hugs, and smiles. When she thought about her siblings, she felt warm—the good kind of warmth Myra brought into Alice's soul any time the two girls lay together.

But thinking about her siblings also hurt.

For one minute, I will think about Jojo. Alice closed her eyes and panicked. In her mind, Josef was just a name. He had no body and face. Her hands shook. *Why can't I remember what Josef looked like?* When Alice thought about Jaslyn, she pictured her little sister with a dirty face, laughing like always. Jaslyn wore trousers and tucked her short brown hair behind her large ears. Jaslyn's golden eyes sparked in Alice's mind as she smiled and waved her stubby little fingers. Alice even imagined Kai's white-yellow fur and fiery red eyes. *How can I picture Kai and not Jojo?*

She imagined her brother again. *I will bring you back home!* Josef's words bounced around in her head.

I can't remember. She couldn't remember his favorite weapon or what he liked to study during lessons. She couldn't remember his favorite thing to eat or his favorite story. She couldn't remember anything about her little brother, only the last words he had said to her. Her heart beat rapidly in her chest as she tried to remember how Josef looked. *He has lightly tanned skin with curly brown hair, and eyes like Father.*

Still, no face appeared.

"Hello!"

Alice lifted her attention to a boy with copper eyes smiling down on her. *Just like Jojo.* She had never seen the boy before, but she could tell they were almost the same age. *Wait, is he my betrothed?* Her eyes narrowed, taking in the boy's dirt-caked skin and matted hair—matching the wildness of House Wayward. *Looking at him reminds me of home, but the glint in his eyes.*

Those were Falk Osmont's eyes.

"Uh, hello," she finally greeted, and the boy smiled harder. *He smiles like Falk, too.* Alice gulped, a cold sweat already dotting her forehead.

"I sincerely apologize for missing your arrival," he bowed. "There was a lot that I had to do that day."

"That's alright, but," she looked away. "I don't know who you are."

His eyebrows furrowed before relaxing. "I'm Rosert Osmont."

Alice suppressed a frown. *Rosert, not Doran.* She didn't know when she would finally meet her betrothed. *Is it normal to go this long? He should have been in the throne room when I arrived.* Her screams echoed as memories of Ser Damien's execution flooded her mind. *That's right. None of the Osmont children were there. Falk wouldn't want them to see the evil behind those fake smiles.*

"Why were you crying?"

The question startled Alice, and she wiped her wet cheeks. *I didn't realize I was crying.*

It felt like Alice Wayward was always crying.

"Did my stupid brother say something to you?" Rosert questioned, placing his hands on his hips.

More tears filled her eyes. "I haven't met Lord Doran yet."

The teenage boy's face reddened. "I'm sorry if you feel slighted by my brother's ignorance. And he's not a lord yet, so he doesn't deserve the title."

She lowered her head. "I don't feel slighted, but thank you for your apologies."

Rosert shook his head, and his matted red-brown hair barely moved. "He just doesn't have a brain. Don't fault him for it. Would you like to meet him? I'm sure we can find him."

He turned to move, and Alice grabbed his wrist. "No," she exhaled as Rosert's attention landed on her hand. She released the Osmont boy and cleared her throat. "I mean, that's okay. I don't want to disturb him."

Rosert relaxed again and took a seat beside Alice. "Understandable," he groaned as he sat, sounding like an old man. "So, why were you crying?"

Why is he acting like he cares? Alice studied Rosert for a moment. *He's intense like Jaslyn,* she realized, breaking eye contact. *He seems sincere, but I can't tell him the truth. I don't want Falk to learn that I'm missing my family. He will use that against me.* Another person she missed dearly appeared in her mind. "My friend, Myra, was attacked during the journey to Kingment. Nothing was done about it, and the Saavant says that even with treatment, she might never fully recover."

"Oh, Alice, I'm sorry to hear that! Surely my father will find the culprit and,"

"I *said* nothing was done about it," she interrupted, her voice cold. "No culprit will be found."

He gave a sad smile. "Then my mother will find them."

Alice's eyes widened. *Lady Victoria said she would find someone to care for Myra, and she has done that. She never mentioned anything about finding the person who assaulted Myra.* Alice wondered if Rosert was just as naïve as she was or if he knew something she didn't.

Rosert frowned. "I heard about Ser Knight."

Unexpected tears filled Alice's eyes. *No, don't cry,* she begged, but the tears fell anyway. *No, stupid, stupid, stupid!* Rosert leaned in to hug her, but she moved away.

The teenage boy inhaled sharply. "I do not blame you for being cautious with whom you trust, but you must have a friend that walks through these Black Castle halls."

"I have a friend," she replied, wiping her cheeks dry.

"Aye, but is she walking through the Black Castle halls?"

Alice Wayward jumped to her feet, her entire body shaking. *House Osmont slings insults around like it's their natural way of speaking.* She stared at the boy, trying to make sense of her anger. *I never told him Myra was asleep, just that she was attacked. Rosert already knew about Myra and her condition. He just pretended to be clueless.*

She hated people like that, but she knew that to live in this godforsaken world, she would have to behave the same way. *I must stay clueless and helpless—playing the Alice Wayward they expect to see.* But she didn't want to be that person anymore. *I will grow strong.* Her head pulsed, reminding her of the grim reality. *If my sickness allows it.*

Alice stepped back, her body weak, and the desire for her bed heightened. "I'm sorry, but I just met you. I know you are being nice, but your father taught me better than that." She then bowed. "Have a nice rest of your day, Rosert."

"One day, you will learn to trust me!" he shouted as Alice walked away. And all she could do was roll her eyes.

She started her journey to her bedchamber, daydreaming that Myra would be awake, smiling at her. *That will never happen.* A pain in her chest made her stumble, and she caught her footing by leaning against the wall. Suddenly, she was breathless, and every movement felt like her last. *I must get to the room and lie down.* The hallway seemed to extend forever, increasing Alice's anxiety. *I have overexerted myself*, she realized, barely taking a step before gagging. *I need my bed now.*

"Hello, Miss. Do you need assistance?"

Alice lifted her head to see a beautiful woman clad in armor beside her. "No, I'm okay."

She attempted to move, stumbling again, but this time, the woman caught her. "Doesn't seem like you're okay. Please, let me help you."

Alice studied the woman. *Does she know who I am?* The question caused Alice to pull away, but the sickness had taken over, making her limp. *I can't get sick again,* she cried, hanging onto the woman, now unable to speak. *I must protect Myra.*

"Let's take you to the garden for a moment to calm down," the armored woman suggested. "The sun always makes me feel better."

Alice wanted to protest, but she could do nothing but continue along.

The pair entered the garden, and the woman laid Alice on a bench. She kneeled close, giving Alice a small smile. "Will you be okay alone, or would you like me to stay?"

The question invigorated Alice. *Who is this woman? Her kindness and chivalry are nothing like I've seen.* "Please," she struggled to reply. "Stay."

The woman's smile widened, and she sat on the bench and placed Alice's head on her lap. "Is it okay to rub your hair as you soak up the sun? My mother used to do that anytime I didn't feel well."

Alice nodded, and the woman began stroking her hair, just as Myra had done during their days in the wheelhouse.

For the first time in over a moon, Alice felt bliss.

"My name is Lady Raya Vale," the woman introduced. "I would ask for your name, but I think you should try to rest for now."

Alice closed her eyes in response, taking in the woman's name. *Lady Raya Vale. She is a highborn, too.* Alice pictured Raya's bronzed skin and shiny black hair. *She looks almost like Myra and Mother. Is House Vale from the Summerlands?*

"I haven't seen you before. Are you new here?" Raya asked, and Alice nodded. "Ah, so you might be suffering from homesickness. It will go away soon."

Tears filled Alice's eyes. *I hope so. It hurts too much.*

"When I first left Steephorn, I was homesick for almost a fortnight. It wasn't until I started sparring with Lord Rosert that I found a new home. Perhaps you can find one here, too."

Steephorn. Alice pictured the coastal city, surrounded by the North-western Range. *Lady Raya isn't a Summeran. She's a Solamar.*

"Why are you touching Lady Alice Wayward so casually, you scum?" a boy questioned with a twisted face.

Lady Raya's big brown eyes landed on Alice. "Oh gods, you're not a servant?"

Alice shook her head, and Raya shifted away before Alice stopped her. "I want you here," she struggled.

"Didn't you hear what I said, knight?"

Raya returned her attention to the annoying boy. "Your mother told me to slap you the next time you spoke like that, but I won't because I'm busy ensuring Lady Alice feels better since that's what she wants."

The boy grabbed Alice's hand and yanked her off Raya. "She doesn't want to touch you, scum," he started, but when Alice fell to the ground instead of standing, he paused. "Ew, what's wrong with you?" He turned to Lady Raya, and Alice lifted her head. "This is who I'm supposed to marry?"

Alice's eyes widened. *He is Doran Osmont.* She should've known the cocky teenage boy with reddish hair and dark green eyes was the person she was engaged to marry. *He looks more like Falk than Rosert does.* Annoyance filled Alice as she moved to her knees. "This little boy is who I'm supposed to marry?" she questioned with a grin, and Lady Raya matched her face. "I thought I was marrying someone with," she paused and looked him up and down, "more."

Doran Osmont's face turned bright red. "Now listen here, you bitch,"

"Don't," Lady Raya started, standing.

"My lady," a servant interrupted.

Alice turned to the woman, no longer wanting to conversate with the Osmont boy. "Yes," she responded pleasantly, trying not to seem so sickly.

"Your handmaiden, uh, Lady Myra Nores. She's woken up."

JARIN

His wife's ghastly face awoke him from his sleep. "What in the hells are you doing here?" he screamed, sitting up and grabbing his blankets. Dimia eyed him from across the room, unfazed by his outburst.

The woman quietly sat in his lounge chair with a wicked smile etched into her face, causing Jarin to hyperventilate. *Does she know? Is that why she is here? Did her plans change?* Each short and shallow breath seemed to choke him as he studied his wife. *I need to calm down,* he thought, clutching harder onto his blanket.

His wife shifted. "You overslept, so I came to wake you."

"Why does it matter to you when I wake?"

Dimia sighed at Jarin's tenseness and stood. "So, you have forgotten."

"Forgot about what?" he questioned, slipping out of bed. He shuffled to the window and pulled back the curtains, hoping for sunshine to pour in. But it was another rainy day. *Thank the gods for the rain, I guess.*

Sticky sounding footsteps approached Jarin from behind. "The feast you were so excited about moons ago," Dimia reminded.

Jarin gasped. *Life got so hectic, I forgot.* The past few moons flashed in his mind, and Jarin smiled, strangely proud of his growth. *I've expanded my council while creating alliances. The rain has reinvigorated the economy, making this the perfect time to be the lord Hamlin would be proud of.* His eyes snapped back to his ailing wife. *Dimia was right. The feast is useless, I need to center my focus on,*

"I assumed you had forgotten, so I planned it myself," Dimia informed, interrupting Jarin's thoughts. "The dinner is tonight. I've announced that the dinner is for Kaylien's safe journey to Waterbrook, but you can add its original purpose when you give a speech."

He turned to stare at his wife's smug face, completely dumbfounded. *Tonight... this is her chance to kill me. This is what Dain warned about.*

"Thank you, Dimia," she encouraged, trying to get some appreciation out of him.

"You planned it all yourself?" he asked instead.

Dimia placed her hands on her hips. "Aye, when it was apparent that you had forgotten and Hamlin didn't care, I took the reins on the entire project."

He hugged his wife, and when he saw a seductive smile on her face, it made him want to vomit. She puckered her lips, and he kissed her without hesitation; but in his head, he screamed. "Thank you, my wife. What would I do without you?"

"Drink yourself to an early grave," she quipped.

He frowned. "I don't drink."

Now, Dimia was frowning, too. "You know what I mean, Jarin. It was a joke." He burst into laughter, and grabbed Dimia's arms. Dimia attempted to laugh along with him, but his laugh muffled hers. "Jarin you are squeezing me," she whispered under his laugh.

He stopped and studied the aggressive grip he had on Dimia's arms, before shifting his attention to her uncomfortable face and wide, terrified eyes. *Why am I even touching her?* He released his wife, leaving a grey-green handprint on her skin. "I am sorry, beloved, I lost control of myself," he explained forcing a smile. Dimia forced a smile, too. *We are both just pretending.* "Are the boys prepared for the dinner?"

"They are always ready for anything."

"The Riverlands aren't that boring," he replied, laughing loudly again, but this time, Dimia did not react. Quickly, he went silent. "Allow me to get dressed for the day and have my daily meeting with Hamlin. Then I will find you and we can talk more about the feast."

"No need," Dimia replied, walking away. "Just prepare a speech and show up in the dining hall when the sun begins to fall."

"Of course, my wife, thank you."

Dimia smiled. It was not pretty, nor a goofy one, but a smile that he saw in his nightmares. "No Jarin, thank you," she exhaled and slipped from his bedchamber.

The Lord Protector of the Riverlands inhaled sharply, his body pulsing, and said a prayer to as many gods as possible. *It is time.*

He marched to the most inconspicuous place possible within the castle—the observation room. He grabbed the carved marble handles of the great oak door and took a deep breath. *I must update the council on what Dimia is planning.*

Jarin opened the door to the observation room where Hamlin, Lysane, and Dain sat at an enormous cherry wood table, all silently staring at Jarin. He walked to his chair and sat, his hips burning from the trek.

"My lord," Lysane and Hamlin each said, and he nodded in recognition.

Jarin then turned to his son who stared back, still silent. "Dain," he said, nodding his head once.

"Father," his youngest son responded, mimicking Jarin.

He smiled at that. *Dain is like me*, he realized, breaking eye contact with his son. "I am in agony, Hamlin."

The old monk frowned. "You need to be examined. The medicine is a quick fix, not a long term one."

Jarin waved his hand in dismissal. "Please, Hamlin, spare me your lecture. You have yet to find anyone you trust. It is your fault I have yet to be examined, not mine." Hamlin huffed and reached into his sleeve, retrieving the vial that Jarin so desperately needed. "Thank you, Hamlin. You are a true friend."

"Father, why can't you just be examined by a Saavant?"

"You are asking a question your lady mother would ask," Jarin replied with a bite to his tone, and Dain's mouth dropped open.

"Saavants cannot be trusted," Lysane answered instead. "If Lord Jarin is truly ill, the Saavant who examined him will tell the Seers at the Citadel of the Raven. Then, every person with power would know that the Lord Protector of the Riverlands is sick."

"That sounds like a lot of trouble," Dain whined.

Jarin chuckled, "It is." He held up the vial for Dain to see. "That is why I take this, and that is that." He opened the vial and swallowed the contents from within.

"What if you are truly sick?"

Jarin's nose scrunched from the medicine's lackluster taste. "Well, we won't know until *Hamlin* finds me someone," he replied glancing at the unbothered monk before sighing. "Now, enough about all this. I have disturbing news."

Hamlin sat straight in his chair. "Lysane has informed us about the dinner tonight." He groaned. "That is why Ser Bronston isn't here. I had forgotten about your plan. Dimia is extremely clever."

"Aye," Dain nodded. "I heard some maidens talking about it in the gardens this morning."

"How can no one know about this dinner yesterday, yet today everyone gossips about it?" Jarin questioned his council, slightly upset.

Lysane bit her lip and glanced to Dain who only shrugged. Hamlin was the one to speak first. "That is how assassinations work. No one knows and then everyone knows. It makes it harder for a counterattack."

"We already have a counterattack." Jarin rebutted, trying not to show any emotion. *If Hamlin sees any doubt, he will cancel the entire ordeal.* And Jarin would have none of that. *The plan must succeed so that Dimia understands exactly who she is dealing with.* Jarin smiled, matching his son's toothy grin.

Hamlin sighed loudly. "Jarin, answer this, is someone dying from the poisoned food what is best for the kingdom?"

The question swirled in Jarin's head. *What does Hamlin mean?*

"We are putting Lady Dimia in her place," Lysane interjected. "She is attempting to murder the Lord Protector. Any way to stop it would be for the betterment of the Riverlands."

"I think Lysane is right," Dain spoke up. "My mother thinks too highly of herself. I have been near her all my life, and have seen what she is capable of. We should *all* be extremely afraid of her. Killing her beloved handmaiden will let her know that she is not so cunning after all."

"How will that benefit us?" Hamlin interrupted, practically shouting. "This will only anger Dimia more."

Jarin buzzed his lips, tired of the argument. "No matter, the plan has been set regardless and there is no backing out now. The dinner is only in a few hours, we must go and prepare."

❋ ❋ ❋

Aromas of sweet wine, sweat, and smog filled the candle-lit dining room, as music played underneath everyone's conversations.

Jarin sat at the end of the dining table, and like normal, everyone ignored him. Usually, depression crushed Jarin at the thought of being over-looked, but not today. *Wait and watch.* He scanned the faces who sat around the table. *I don't know many of the guests*, he realized, disappointed. *Dimia wanted me to die around strangers.*

Closer to Jarin, Dain and Lysane sat beside one another, and on the other side of the table sat Terryn and Kaylien. Dimia sat farthest away, with Jossa at her side. Jarin watched his wife and handmaiden talk, and Dimia's happy and content face brought a smile to Jarin's lips—he couldn't wait for it all to go away. *Dimia doesn't deserve happiness. Even the gods know this.*

Beautiful crystal blue eyes settled on Jarin Ayers, making his heart sink. Dimia grinned, resting her head on her hand. Jossa turned and waved to Jarin, and he waved back, trying not to seem too anxious. *They must not know what is happening until it has happened.*

Jarin looked away, noticing something strange. *Hamlin is not here.* His attention snapped to Lysane. *Look at me. Look at me, please.* Lysane, how-ever, happily paid attention to Dain, nodding, smiling, and replying when she needed to. *Look at me, Lysane!* He screamed internally, and then her orange eyes met his, relaxing him. He smiled and motioned for Lysane to come. The young woman nodded and stood from the table.

Dain and Dimia watched Lysane as she walked toward Jarin. Lysane bent down and turned from the prying eyes. "Yes, my lord?"

"Where is Hamlin?"

Lysane's face twisted with concern. "I was going to speak with you after the feast, but Hamlin fell extremely ill about an hour ago. I checked on him before the dinner," Tears filled her eyes. "He doesn't look good."

Jarin's body tensed. *No! It's too soon! I haven't become a lord Hamlin would be proud of. He can't die! What will I do when he dies? How can I go on?* The news caused his head to pulse and he returned his attention to Lysane. "He was fine earlier today."

"Age is taking him," she answered, almost inaudibly. "It won't be long now."

He studied the girl's sad face, holding back tears of his own. *Hamlin can't die.* He took a deep breath. "Fine, let the servants know dinner can begin."

Lysane's eyebrows raised at the command. "My lord, I am a guest." His umber-brown eyes glared at her, and he stayed silent. "Uh, of course," she corrected, her voice quivering. Lysane stood straight, bowed, and marched to the servants who stood along the wall.

When the servants moved, Jarin stood, and the room grew eerily quiet at the sight of the Lord Protector. *I must give a speech that brings hope. A speech declaring everything I've ever wanted for the Riverlands.*

He took a deep breath and faced the crowd. "My esteemed guests, welcome and thank you for spending time with House Ayers on the last night of the eleventh moon. Tonight, we are celebrating new beginnings. First, we celebrate the safe arrival of Lady Kaylien Thoren of the Black Hills and her betrothal to my son, Terryn." The crowd applauded, causing Kaylien to blush while Terryn rolled his eyes. "We also celebrate Obum for giving us the rain the Riverlands desperately needed this autumn season. This rain has brought a revival in the Riverlands; we will not let this opportunity slip through our fingers. We must continue building wealth, so each house will receive specific supplies based on your needs. Please see my son, Dain, before you leave for more information." Bright smiles filled the room as Dain smacked his teeth. "I hope this will continue our pleasantries and serve as a starting point to strengthen our relationship. As I said, we are celebrating new beginnings, including our budding alliances. So, please take this seriously as the rain does not last long. The Riverlands will thrive for centuries, starting here and now." Jarin lifted his flagon. "To the Riverlands!"

"To the Riverlands!" The room cheered before drinking their wine.

Servants scattered with meals in their hands as Lysane appeared beside him once again. She placed a plate in front of him. "This is what Hamlin had prepared for you," she whispered. "Jossa will now get the contaminated plate."

Jarin grabbed Lysane's wrist, stopping her from walking away. *Wait,* he took a deep breath. *Should I go through with killing Jossa?* Hamlin's pale face frowned in his head. *Will her death really help the Riverlands? Or just my ego?*

His attention flickered to his wife as she continued to chat and drink, unaware that he held Jossa's fate in his hands. *I could tell Lysane to throw the plate away. Would that be wiser?* He watched as Jossa quickly kissed Dimia's shoulder and Dimia replied by cupping the handmaiden's face, reminding Jarin of two lovebirds. His heart sank. *It should be Terryn and Kaylien behaving like that.* He turned to eldest son who completely ignored the girl he was to marry.

Finally, Jarin released Lysane. *No, it must be this way.*

"My lord?" Lysane questioned, confused.

"Nothing," Jarin waved off and Lysane walked away.

Everyone begun their meal, and practically no one paid attention to Jarin; expect Dimia. His wife now watched him closely, her attention moving along with the fork as Jarin scooped some potatoes and took a bite. Dimia's bright blue eyes burned into him. *She won't look away.* Finally, Jarin swallowed and Dimia turned to begin her meal. *Is she that impatient?* He wondered, taking another bite.

Thud.

Screams and wails echoed throughout the dining room, and there sat Jossa, her head smashed into her plate of food—dead. The sight of the dead handmaiden made Jarin feel uneasy. He wondered if that was what he would have looked like if Dimia's plan had worked. Dead and stupid.

Dimia shrieked for a Saavant and wailed as she came to terms with the fact that her handmaiden, her best friend, was dead. As she screamed, she clawed at her grey-green face, making her cheeks bleed.

Others rushed to Dimia's side, but Lysane, Dain, and Kaylien stayed in their seats. Lysane and Dain watched the ordeal with contentment etched into their faces. Kaylien's sweating pale face, however, tore at Jarin's heart. *She wasn't prepared for this,* he realized, tracking, his oldest son. Terryn had rushed to his mother's side just like the others, leaving his wife-to-be alone. *My eldest needs to get his priorities in order,* Jarin thought unhappily, *Kaylien will remember this for the rest of her life.*

Before Jarin could stand, his knights surrounded him. "My lord, some monks are on their way to take the body," Ser Bronston informed, taking his spot beside Jarin.

Jarin nodded as Dimia screamed and cursed at every person in the room. *I shouldn't stare.* The scene his wife made reminded him too much of his father. "Find a Saavant and make sure they give her a sedative."

"Of course, my lord."

"Also," Jarin pointed at the frightened Kaylien who still sat alone, hugging herself. "Bring the girl to me so I can comfort her. She looks absolutely terrified."

"Ser Nolan, Ser Mealer, bring Lady Kaylien to us," Ser Bronston commanded, and the two knights walked over to Kaylien. Jarin watched as the knights approached the frightened girl and smiled at her sweetly, allowing Kaylien to relax. "Those two have the kindest faces I have ever seen in a knight," Ser Bronston explained as Kaylien smiled slightly and grabbed one of the knight's hands.

Jarin nodded. "You are very good at making decisions in a hard situation. You think about everyone involved and try to make the best decision possible for each person. That is why you are my head lord knight."

Ser Bronston smile grew wider. "Thank you," he said as Kaylien approached them. "You have given me a lot of trust. I am glad to know that you believe it was a good decision."

Jarin pressed on a wide smile as Kaylien stood in front of him. "Kaylien, are you alright?"

The girl frowned and wiped her eyes that had no tears. "Jossa sat right beside me. One minute she was telling me about the food, and the next she was dead." Finally, after rubbing her eyes as hard as she could, Kaylien cried.

"Everything is alright. How about I walk you to your bedchamber?"

The girl nodded, but then stopped. "Could," she began, pressing her fingers together. "Could Lysane sleep with me tonight?"

Jarin's eyes widened. He was happy to know that his trusted advisor had completed another task with ease. *When did Lysane get a chance to create a relationship with Kaylien? And why does Kaylien know to ask me?* He suppressed more questions. "Of course, little star," he replied sweetly. "I am sure Lysane will be pleased to comfort you."

His peered to Lysane who still sat beside his youngest son, both covering small smiles with their hands. Lysane's sunset-colored eyes showed an accomplished satisfaction that frightened Jarin. *Dimia will notice Lysane's attitude. Dimia will target her. Lysane is not safe in Waterbrook.*

His lady wife's echoing screams told Jarin that.

Lysane's attention snapped to the Lord Protector and she stood, already knowing he needed her. When she approached, she hugged a sobbing Kaylien, before turning to Jarin. "It's so horrible what happened," she sniffled, still holding Kaylien.

"Aye," Jarin agreed. "Terrible. *Horrible.* Poor Jossa. Anyway, Kaylien has requested that you sleep with her tonight for comfort. The handmaiden who died sat right beside her."

"Of course," she replied, pulling away from Kaylien. "I had already planned to do that anyway, Kay. Remember our sleepover?"

And Kaylien nodded in reply.

Although they were similar in age, it was clear that Lysane was much older mentally. *Or is that what Kaylien wants me to think?* He knew she was smarter than she was letting on. *But how much?*

"Would it be okay if we take our leave now, my lord?" Lysane asked.

Jarin squinted at the young woman. *I must do something about Lysane's safety.* "Aye, go ahead, but be careful."

Lysane matched Jarin's face. "Aye. I am always careful." She then grabbed Kaylien's hand and left the dining room.

Now, all Jarin could hear was Dimia's endless screams. Many of the guests had already slipped out of the room so that an investigation could begin, but Dimia refused to leave the dead woman's side.

Jarin took a deep breath. "Ser Bronston, write to Lord Gardener."

His head lord knight bowed at the command. "What would you like the letter to say, my lord?"

Dimia's screams echoed in Jarin's head and his ears rung. He wanted to ask where the Saavant was to shut her up, but he had to keep his composure. *I must act like a Lord Protector worthy of loyalty.*

He cleared his throat and studied the enormous knight. "We need to send Lysane to the safest place in the world."

Ser Bronston shifted his feet. "Not Dain?"

"No, Dain will stay here. Dimia would never target her son."

VICTORIA

Victoria walked through the hallways alone, her mind completely blank. She had regressed again, her mind slowly slipping from reality. *What do I do?* She didn't know why she was walking or where she was going, but she continued her unnecessary journey. *What do I need?*

"My lady," a voice called. Victoria shivered as Saavant Enya walked beside her, holding the newest brew. "What are you doing?"

Yes! Victoria took the cup and immediately drunk it. "Walking," she replied, as the liquids warmed her insides. *I need more of this.* She took another sip, and the red-colored tea caused her mind to race. *But what's in it?* She looked forward, now knowing what she wanted to do. *I will get to the bottom of this strange tea Enya brews. It makes me rational and gives me empathy. I become a regular person again when I drink it. I must know more.* She took a deep breath. "Where do you make this tea?"

The old woman smiled. "In the castle, of course."

"Where?"

Enya thought for a moment. "You don't need to know that, my lady. If you see where I make the tea it might cause you to panic."

Victoria's eyes narrowed and she gave the Saavant back her cup. "I don't care. Show me, now."

The wrinkly old woman sighed and shifted directions. A few minutes passed before the two stood in front of a giant red door. *I've never seen this door before*, Victoria realized. *And I can barely remember how we got here. What is this Saavant doing?*

"This is the door to my laboratory. Does that please, my lady?"

"No," she replied, her voice shaky. "I want to see the inside as well."

"You really should not," Saavant Enya warned.

Victoria shook her head, so that her mind was clear from any doubts. "Take me inside."

Enya nodded and hobbled to open the door. "This may take a moment," the woman chuckled. From top to bottom Enya unlocked the knobs on the door. *Seems a bit inefficient.* Victoria observed as the Saavant finally opened the door. "Enter quickly, my lady."

Victoria lifted her skirts and rushed into the secret room. The old woman closed the door, and for a moment, they both stood in darkness. Enya lit a candle and moved closer to Victoria.

"I want to see," she whispered.

Enya made a face, but obliged, taking Victoria's hand, and leading her through the room. The old woman stopped and lifted the candle up to show what was before them.

Chains tapped against the floor, as a figure reacted to the light. *Someone's imprisoned here*, Victoria realized, examining the naked woman. A shiver ran down her spine. *Ser Edmund was right.* She noticed a recent cut on the woman's ribcage. *Is it her blood that I am drinking?*

The woman struggled to lift her head. "Please," she managed to say, "help me."

Enya giggled nervously. "Please, do not pay attention to her, my lady."

"What is the meaning of this? You bring me a tea and tell me not to worry so I trusted you. I would've ended this madness if I knew."

"That's exactly why I didn't tell you. I promise, this person means nothing to anyone. They have no family, no friends. No one will miss them."

"What is your name?" Victoria questioned the prisoner.

The woman's eyes fluttered open. "Varva," she breathed out, and then her eyes snapped back shut.

The goddess of Peace. Victoria stepped back. "She has a name. She is a human being. I will not allow this."

"She was brought to me from some peasant village," Enya explained. "I bought her legally, and now I use her blood to make you stronger."

Victoria took another step back, hyperventilating. "Are there others?"

Enya nodded and led Victoria deeper into the chambers.

In an isolated room, four girls sat on the ground, all chained. "Are these all the rest?" she asked and Enya nodded again. Victoria walked closer to the Saavant's prisoners. *They are much younger than the one chained to the wall.* The four girls stared at Victoria, all completely terrified. "What are your names?"

The four girls looked amongst each other.

"Veilia," one said.

"Veriya," said another.

"I am Vanadey, and this is my little sister, Valkyrie."

"Valkyrie?" Victoria repeated.

The little girl named Valkyrie nodded. "After the Divine queens of long ago; the Highest Arcs."

Victoria turned to Enya. "Why do all of your prisoners names all start with a V?"

The old Saavant sighed heavily. "These girls still have their maidenhood intact and their names start with the same letter as yours; all going according to the ancient text."

"What text?"

Enya grabbed her hands. "The ones the Arcs left behind. I follow the text, and the gods grant you sanity, strength, and power."

Victoria chewed her lip. "Yeah, but," she looked back at the girls and their eyes shifted around the room as if they weren't listening. "This is wrong. I want all those things, Enya, but not like this."

The old woman rolled her beady eyes. "I knew I never should have let you enter." Victoria continued backing away, terrified. "Forget you ever saw this"

Enya snapped her fingers, and Victoria was no longer in the old woman's secretive laboratory. Instead, she found herself in a hallway that lead to the courtyard. *This is not where I entered,* she realized, looking at her surroundings. *What did that Saavant do to me?*

"My lady!" Ser Edmund yelled, running to her.

Victoria's eyes widened. *I must tell him. I cannot be an accomplice to the crimes Enya has committed.* "Ser Edmund, I found something that,"

"The Lord Protector needs your presence in court."

The interruption startled Victoria. "What's wrong?"

"I am sorry, my lady, but the Lord Protector should be the one to tell you."

Victoria's heart sunk. *Has Borin decided to attack the Northern Kingdom to get Alice back?* The young knight rushed ahead, bringing Victoria back to reality. "Ser Edmund, I," she paused, clutching her forehead. *What did I want to tell him? I don't remember. Why? What happened?*

"Yes, my lady," the knight exhaled, clearly exhausted with her antics.

"I-I don't know."

Ser Edmund turned away. "Then we should get going. Lord Falk needs you."

Falk needs me. Victoria raced to the throne room, and opened the door, breathless. She scanned the familiar faces. *What's happened?* She plowed through the crowd and took her seat beside her lord husband.

"The Warrior Raiders are back," Falk spat.

"What do you mean? We eliminated them from our lands years ago."

"Messenger!" Falk yelled. "Tell my wife what has happened. I can't bear to repeat the words."

A young man ran towards the dais. "My lady," the messenger bowed. "Less than a fortnight ago, Eldersgate was attacked by the Warrior Raiders. The entire town was destroyed."

What? Victoria didn't understand. *How could this have happened? I worked so hard to eradicate them.* Her eyes burned as she stared at the young man. "Why?"

"Your stupid sister-by-marriage," Falk informed through his teeth.

Victoria blinked, confused. "What does Gloriana know about the Warrior Raiders?"

"No, not her, the other one!"

"Arla?" she questioned and Falk's bright green eyes pierced into hers. "Does Peyton know?"

"Who knows? For moons now, the Warrior Raiders have pillaged the countryside of the Southern Kingdom, destroying everything. All because

Arla told them too, and now they have expanded to the Northern Kingdom."

"Why would she do that? The common folk and the highborn will not like this."

"Rumors are spreading that Hadrian is a bastard," The messenger answered. "Stangely, he is Lord Peyton's son but not Lady Arla's. The boy ran away, and she hired the Raiders to capture and kill him."

Victoria's eyes grew wide. "Little Hadrian isn't Arla's son? He looks just like her." She placed a hand on her chin. *Why didn't Arla hire the Cotyledon? They can complete her wishes without destroying the countryside.* She gasped. "That must mean Hadrian has made it to the Northern Kingdom and the Warrior Raiders have followed him."

Falk nodded at her deduction. "I have no idea how Peyton feels about this, but if he felt any sort of way for Hadrian, he would have stopped this madness. I'm not going to start a war with my brother for some bastard son of his." The Lord Protector declared, causing Victoria to raise an eyebrow. She remembered a time when Falk enjoyed picking fights with Peyton. *Now things have changed.* "Moreover, Hadrian isn't alone. Reports say that he was accompanied by Ser Colvic Rames while in Eldersgate."

"Ser Colvic," Victoria repeated. "Well, then that means Peyton doesn't wish for Hadrian to die. Ser Colvic is one of the best knights to ever live in Valley Pines. If Peyton is willing to let him go to protect Hadrian, it means that Peyton is aware of Arla's doing and wishes for his son to live."

Falk shook his head. "Well, have him stop this madness. Not me!"

"Fine, then send your men to protect our kingdom. There is no reason why our people had to die or lose their homes because of these *paid* Warrior Raiders!"

"Whatever," Lord Falk waved off. "Send knights to the different provinces and dominant cities to bulk up defenses. Messenger, how many died in the attack?"

"Reports say the casualities total seventy percent of the population. The Raiders are mainly to blame, but also because most structures were made of wood." the young man responded.

Victoria sat straighter. "I thought we offered to give the city fifty gold coins a year for ten years to rebuild into stone. What happened to the gold?"

Falk shrugged. "Corruption probably."

"Who runs Eldersgate?"

"Don't know," he replied carelessly. "After my father removed House Knotley from power, he never created another."

Removed. She wanted to laugh. *More like they were all put to the sword.*

"My lady, it's rumored the Marketeers secretly took control of Eldersgate a year ago," the messenger informed.

A year ago! Why does Falk care so little for his kingdom? The black market rules Eldersgate, one of our biggest cities, and are stealing from the Lord Protector. She studied her husband's slightly bored face. *Falk just doesn't care.*

We should be arresting the Marketeers and executing them. Not allowing them to do whatever they please. This isn't Lismure.

She sighed, knowing her lord husband would never do anything. "Ser Knight," she called, and the crowed murmured, causing Victoria to frown. *Damn it, I forgot.* "Can a knight with some leadership skills gather a group, send them to Eldersgate, and arrest every Marketeer there?"

A knight stepped forward and knelt. "My lady, the lord knights will collaborate immediately to assist Eldersgate."

"Send the criminals to the labor camps in Bordertown," Falk added excitedly.

Labor camps? Bordertown? She frowned. "Husband, what are you talking about?"

Falk's bright green eyes flashed to Victoria. "Easthaven Pines Prison is at max capacity. House Rainwood requested a town outside the city to help with population control, so I sent the funds for them to create Bordertown earlier this year. Apparently, labor camps make good coin. More humane than slaves." His attention returned to the knight. "Don't execute a single Marketeer. Send them *all* to Bordertown."

"Yes, my lord," the knight replied.

Why did Falk never tell me this? Is a labor camp really a good idea? Maybe I should write to House Rainwood and get more information. She held in a groan, not wanting to make a scene. "Knight, take two hundred gold coins and help rebuild Eldersgate while you're there. It's not the commoners fault their city was destroyed."

"Of course, my lady."

The crowd murmured again, and some even clapped for Victoria's generosity. She smiled, but in her mind, she saw the four little faces. *Who are they?* The faces morphed from happy to sad, ripping at Victoria's emotions. *Have I met them before? Are those the faces of the dead in Eldersgate?*

"Is there anymore news?" Victoria questioned the sea of people, and no one stepped forward. "Fine, court is dismissed, thank you for your presence."

And with that, she ended court without Falk saying a word. The men and women quickly dispersed and soon the throne room was empty except for Falk and herself. Falk continued sitting there, wearing an emotionless face. Victoria stared at him, wishing she had exited when everyone else did. The Lord Protector inhaled, and switched arms for his head to rest on, refusing to look at her. *Were my commands so strange that it left Falk speechless?* Her entire body turned toward Falk and stared at him. *I will stare forever if I must.*

After five minutes of silence, however, Victoria had had enough. "Speak," she commanded. Falk ignored her and switched hands again. He sighed, and then sighed again, and by the third sigh, his attention finally shifted to Victoria. She crossed her arms in defiance. "Speak."

Falk sighed once more, and Victoria felt as if she might kill him. "I don't know what to say."

"Why?"

The Lord Protector frowned. "You want to protect our people, even sending gold to rebuilt a city that's been rebuilt a dozen times. You act all kind and charitable, but you're not. You're a Wicked." Falk's eyes then narrowed. "You murdered all my women. I mean, you could've at least enslaved them, but no. You wanted to behave like my father."

Victoria's heart dropped. *What all does he know?* She frowned and stared at her lord husband, refusing to tell him about the children she did sell into slavery. *He might put me in a labor camp if he learns the truth.* She inhaled deeply before looking away. "I was angry."

"So, instead of punishing me, you punished my women?"

Something snapped within Victoria. "Just like you did with Alice?"

"What are you talking about? Alice is here because she is betrothed to Doran."

"Don't play with me," Victoria growled, "How are you threatening my brother?"

Falk's frown turned frightening. "You know, I wish you were dead," he confessed, ignoring Victoria's question and causing her to gasp. "When I first learned that you were going insane I couldn't believe it. Not you; not Victoria Wayward. Then, the insanity didn't kill you. You kept on living, and rarely had manic episodes. Originally, when I learned of your condition, I thought I would finally be free from you, so after being told repeatedly that you were going to die but didn't, I got angry. I wanted you to die."

"W-what do you mean?"

"I visited the Mountain Realm in hopes that you would be dead by the time I returned. Unfortunately, I've returned to see you better and stronger than ever, ready to keep on living. Enya was supposed to kill you not heal you." *Enya was supposed to kill me.* "Everyone will be perfectly fine without you, Victoria, please be aware," Falk informed. "Yet, you won't disappear. You're like a pimple that I can't pop. You've been like that from the moment I fucked you all those years ago."

She looked at her trembling hands. "What do you want me to do?"

"Kill yourself."

Her entire body buzzed. *Falk wants me to commit suicide. Does he hate me that much?* "No," she exhaled, not realizing she had been holding her breath. "I will continue to live and thrive. With or without you."

"Do you think I care?" he asked, unimpressed. "You're already sick. One day, you will die and I will finally be free."

Victoria stood slowly. *He's a problem,* she decided, walking away, without a word. *I must get rid of him. If I don't, he will get rid of me. He's already tried before.*

She moved quickly through the castle before entering the kitchens. "Please," she begged one of the cooks. "I need my tea."

"Saavant Enya isn't here, my lady," they informed, "but I'll give you the rest from yesterday."

Victoria buzzed her lips as she waited. *Enya was supposed to kill me, but she didn't.* Victoria thought about the old Saavant. *Is she protecting me?* The man placed the teacup before her, and she quickly took a sip. *Or is the woman still trying to kill me?* As the tea slid down her throat, Victoria pictured the four faces who had now transitioned into little girls. *Who are they?* A red door appeared in her head. *I don't remember that door. Wait! That same thought has crossed my mind before, but when?* She imagined Saavant Enya opening the door and forcing Victoria into the darkness.

My name is Varva.

"She had prisoners!" Victoria shouted, and the cooks stopped what they were doing and stared. "I mean, uh, nevermind."

Victoria raced out the kitchens, before noticing Lady Raya Vale standing guard with her eyes closed. "Raya," she called out desperately, catching the lady knight's attention.

"Hello, my lady, are you alright?"

Victoria stepped forward. *How do I word this to get the least amount of blood on my hands?* She looked into the young woman's dark brown eyes. "I've heard an unsettling rumor that somewhere in the castle is a strange red door that hides an unknown dungeon where people are being held. Please, look into it."

Raya gasped loudly. "My lady, if that is true, then the information needs to be brought to the Lord Protector immediately."

"No," Victoria said, grabbing the lady knight's hand. "I don't know who is behind this. I need *you* to look for the dungeon. If you find any prisoners, release them immediately, and be careful."

Lady Raya nodded at the directions, turned on her heels, and quickly went off to complete her duty.

Victoria Osmont stood alone in the hallway, her mind racing. *It was the right thing to do, even if I betrayed Enya.* She turned on her heels and walked in a different direction. *That old hag was supposed to kill me anyway. Why should I be worried about betraying her?* Victoria paused, her chest tightening. *I'm not going to let her kill me, nor Falk. I'll live to spite them all.*

JARIN

Hamlin's weak coughs made Jarin feel miserable. The old monk laid on his feathered bed, his chest slowly rising and falling as he struggled to breathe. Hamlin kept his beady eyes on the ceiling—the Clouds—waiting for his time to go.

I must inform the Chapel about Hamlin's condition, Jarin notated, adding another thing to his endless list. He pressed his hands against his face and sighed, feeling overwhelmed. He sat straight in the chair beside the old man and cleared his thoughts. *I need to stop worrying about other things and focus on Hamlin.*

His eyes settled back onto the monk, who stared into the nothingness. *What do I do?* He chewed at his lip. *Hamlin is the person I can depend on the most.* Memories of his time with the monk flashed through his mind. *I allowed depression to consume me, and Hamlin oversaw the kingdom the best he could so everything didn't fall apart. Countless times, he protected me—against my father, against Dimia.*

Imaginary destructive flames nipped at Jarin's cheeks, bringing a shiver to his spine. He touched his face gently as his father's furious expression flickered in his mind, creating pain from the phantom bruises his father had once brought. *Happiness filled my spirit when my father died,* Jarin Ayers remembered, frowning. *And when I learned of Dimia's illness,* he added, rubbing his arms as he pictured his ailing wife with her disgusting attitude.

He lowered his head, disappointed in how much joy he found in death. *What is wrong with me?* The moment his mother died on the birthing bed, Jarin had related death to loneliness. Yet, when he watched steel blades repeatedly pierced into his sister as she cried out for mercy, Jarin wondered if death might be better than being alive. *That day, the day of Brea's death. I wanted to die with her.* Inch by inch, he had stepped closer to the bloodbath, hoping that one of the enemies noticed him. *Please,* he had begged. *Kill me, too. I don't want to be here alone. I can't do this alone.*

Jarin closed his eyes. *And then, Hamlin saved me.* Jarin couldn't thank his old friend enough for that. *It's silly, life didn't get better, but I want to live now. I want to live happily with my sons and to have a peaceful kingdom.* He lifted his head and focused on the old monk. *I can't lose Hamlin. Not when I am finally becoming the leader I was meant to be. He must see this through.*

Coughs violently erupted from Hamlin, bringing a sickening ache to Jarin's stomach. *If anyone should be on their deathbed, it should be Dimia, not you,* he thought scornfully, staring at his friend and mentor.

"The tonic, please," Hamlin croaked, and Jarin passed the vial to the monk. Hamlin chugged the contents and sighed, sitting up. "How is Dain?"

The question startled Jarin and he thought about his broody teenage son. "Still upset," he confessed, sighing. "It's been a few days since Lysane left, but everyone believes I moved too quickly in whisking her away. Maybe I should have thought on it more."

More coughs rumbled from the monk, who shook his head while wiping the blood spittle that stained his lips. "You were smart to be so wary," Hamlin complimented. "It was the smartest thing you've done since you decided to wake up and be a lord."

"Thanks," he exhaled. "But why do you say that?"

Hamlin pulled out a small scroll. "Dimia started looking into Lysane and learned about the girl's mother, Lady Vera Withers. I don't know who this Vera woman is, but Dimia apparently does and she wants Vera's precious child, Lysane, dead."

Jarin scanned the notes, breaking down everything Dimia knew about House Withers. *This could be useful.* "May I keep this?"

Hamlin nodded. "You are a smart man, Jarin. Never forget that. Hardships have filled your life, and although everything beat you down, you rose from the ashes. I'm so proud to see you becoming the phoenix you are. Don't stop. Don't let her win. Don't let anyone win. *You* win." Hamlin clasped his hands over Jarin's and gave a small smile. "As time passes, you will see I was not a good ruler. I shuffled things around and quelled any descent, but it was all bandages. The dams will break. I'm sorry."

"You were a wonderful leader," Jarin corrected. "You were never supposed to be in that situation anyway. I put you there because I was too afraid to be a man."

"No, you saw that the Darkness ruled this world at a young age and didn't want to deal with it. Dimia, however, taught you that dealing with the Darkness was inevitable, and you've finally accepted that."

Jarin Ayers grinned, but Hamlin's wet and ragged cough wiped it away. "You should get some sleep," he told his friend, moving to stand.

Hamlin grabbed Jarin's hand. "Please listen," the monk began soberly, and Jarin's full attention went to his friend. "Today, I am going to die," he announced, and Jarin suppressed a gasp. "Every day is painful, and I do not want that anymore. I want to see your father again."

A stray tear fell down Jarin's face. "I understand."

Hamlin handed him another scroll. "Give this to Ser Bronston," the monk instructed. "Dimia has learned that Daya is a Dykon. She has hired another to deal with her."

Jarin jumped to his feet, gripping the scroll. *Dimia hired another Dykon!* He wanted to scream and curse at that. *She can't be left alone for one* moment. *She must be dealt with, now!* He turned on his heels to leave when a wet and ragged cough caused him to pause.

He returned to Hamlin's side and kissed the old man on the forehead. "Thank you, Hamlin, for everything. I would have been dead long ago if it weren't for you. I'm sorry I was a failure for so long, but I promise I will never be like that again. I will continue to rule in your name. I love you so much."

Hamlin gave Jarin a toothless smile. "Thank you, Jarin. I love you too, and I will miss you."

More tears streamed down Jarin's face. "I will miss you too, friend."

"Ser Bronston and Daya are waiting in the mirror room. Go to them and plan. There is no need to sit beside me and wait for the Divine to take me to the Clouds."

Jarin frowned. "Won't you be alone?"

The old man's grin widened. "I'm never alone," he assured. "Now, go be the Lord Protector of the Riverlands. For me. For everyone."

Jarin Ayers bowed and took in the sight of his friend one last time. "Aye, I will."

He marched to the mirror room, trying to remember the last time he had visited. *Hamlin took me here years ago,* he reminisced, picturing a younger Hamlin walking through the Water Castle halls. *This is perfect. No one enters the mirror room.* He slipped into a darkened hall and pressed his hand against the wall, revealing a handle. He pulled, and the wall shifted before opening, allowing Jarin inside. He entered the mirror room where Daya and Ser Bronston observed the enormous strange mirror in the middle of the room.

"Does this work?" Daya questioned, poking at the brass frame.

"I don't know," Jarin replied with a sigh, before handing Ser Bronston the scroll.

The knight quickly unraveled the paper and scanned the letter. "Did you read this?"

He shook his head. "I don't want to."

"What's it say?" Daya inquired.

"Dimia learned you're a Dykon," Ser Bronston mumbled, and Daya's animated face straightened. "She hired a Dykon to take you out."

"Who?"

"Ashton the Fraxinus of the Derich Family," Ser Bronston read before lifting his eyes. "Your family."

"She paid my mentor to take me out," Daya shrieked. "How sick can she be?"

"I find myself asking that question constantly," Jarin replied. "So, what does the letter say we do?"

Bronston frowned. "Go to Widow's Dale."

"Huh?"

"It says we go to Widow's Dale and shelter there with House Withers until it is safe to return," the knight explained. "Hamlin seems to believe Dimia will defeat herself if she is left alone."

"How is Hamlin?" Daya asked, her voice soft.

Jarin studied the girl quietly, unsure how to answer. "Old."

"The gods will take him soon," Bronston confirmed. "Just pray for a painless passing into the Clouds."

Tears brimmed Daya's eyes. "How sad."

The attention returned to Jarin, who was now deep in his thoughts. *Hamlin wants me to go to Widow's Dale. What will happen in Waterbrook while I'm gone? Does he want Terryn to rule? That can't be it. Does he want it to be... Dain?* His eyes glimmered at the thought. *Dain can rule while I plot to take down Dimia from afar. It's the perfect plan.*

"So, what are we doing?"

"Exactly as the letter says," Jarin answered, turning away from his companions. "Come, let's update Dain on the plan and get the hell out of Waterbook."

ALICE

Her fingers ached from the meticulous needlework she had been working on all morning. Bundles of blue thread littered her lap as she recreated her daily landscape—a castle on a tall cliff on the Sapphire Sea. She paused and examined her artwork, slightly pleased. *I should've done needlework at home when I was alone. It would've passed the time better than reading.*

Alice then turned the needlework to show her best friend. "Look, Myra!" she called brightly, but her handmaiden only looked past her.

Even though Myra Nores had finally woken up, she wasn't the same vibrant girl. The Summeran usually sat quietly, staring at nothing. She never responded or reacted to anything. It was as if Myra wasn't even there. *I don't know if the girl will ever recover,* the Saavant's voice echoed. *The trauma was extreme.*

Alice's attention narrowed on the lucky coin she had turned into a necklace for her best friend. *The attackers still haven't been found. What do I do?*

Shivers tingled Alice's spine as she turned to the other person in the room. *Doran Osmont.* She didn't understand it. Their first conversation was negative, but when the servant informed Alice that Myra had awakened and she begged Lady Raya to help her to her room, Doran tagged along. As the old Saavant explained the situation, Doran listened, his eyes occasionally flickering to Alice.

Even though her betrothed was always there, Alice pretended like he wasn't. *Doran was rude and never apologized,* she reasoned. *Why is he even here? What does he want?*

She preferred when Rosert came to visit. He always had something to talk about, which made the tension in the room disappear. He never said anything discouraging and even offered to help Alice wash Myra's hair.

Even though Rosert brought life to the bedroom, Doran stayed silent. He just sat and stared.

Alice Wayward took a deep breath and turned her work toward her betrothed. *If we are getting married, we should build a friendship.* "Do you like it?"

Doran's eyes widened at the question before he sat straight. "It's, uh, pretty," he responded, rubbing the back of his head nervously. "You make nice work."

She gave the boy a sincere smile. "Thank you." *This could work. Maybe we can get along.* Alice stood and pulled her chair over to Doran, causing the boy to stiffen. "Is it okay if I'm near you?"

"Uh, yeah, that's fine," Doran answered, looking away and Alice sat. "Is it Kingment?" he inquired, continuing the conversation.

Alice's smile widened. "Aye, Myra always said she wanted to see the sea."

Doran nervously glanced at the girl who had her eyes open but was practically asleep. "What happened to her?"

"She was struck in the head," Alice responded, a bit confused. "Her brain probably bled, and she won't recover. I'm sure you heard the Saavant say that."

The Osmont boy shook his head. "I don't believe that nasty old woman."

"You don't? Why?"

"The darkness that radiates from her is worse than my father," he grumbled. "I thought you would have that darkness too if Father thought you were suitable to be my wife, but you don't." Doran paused, studying Alice. "You're perfect, more perfect than Emeline. I'm sorry for ever treating you any differently."

Her heart skipped a beat, and pink dusted her cheeks. "Thank you."

Doran Osmont grabbed her hands. "No, thank you. My mother has scolded me for my idiocy before, but I thought she was just being annoying. You've taught me so much, even without speaking."

Movement caught the pair's attention. "Al-lice," a voice struggled.

Alice gasped and rushed to her friend. "Myra! Myra!" she shouted, touching the girl's face as she examined it. "Myra!"

Finally, her best friend looked back in recognition. "Al-lice," Myra said again, and Alice replied by jumping into her friend's arms. "Alice," her hand-maiden said once more, her voice smoother. She pulled away from Myra and studied the girl's teary eyes. "Alice."

Can Myra say nothing else? She turned to move. "Wait, right here, I'll get Saavant Enya."

Myra grabbed onto her wrist, refusing to let go. "Alice," her hand-maiden continued, panicked. "Alice."

She doesn't want me to go. Does Myra think the Saavant is evil like Doran does? Alice turned to her betrothed, who watched intently. "Doran, I,"

"Take her to my mother. I'm sure she's in the art room," he declared, standing. "I'm going to get Rosert, and I'll meet you there."

"Aye, I will," she replied, pulling Myra to her feet as Doran exited the room. "Can you walk?" she questioned, and her best friend nodded. "Good, let's go."

The girls hurried to the art room, where Catrain and Emeline sat silently, completing some needlework while Lady Victoria read from a titleless black book. Alice's attention focused on her cousins. *You're more perfect than Emeline,* Doran's voice repeated, and Alice felt her cheeks warming again. *I didn't know Emeline was perfect.*

"Alice, hello," her aunt greeted, standing as she placed the book on the chair. The beautiful woman glided across the room and examined the handmaiden. "Your friend is walking around now. What a blessing, but why are you sweating? Has she been examined by,"

"Al-lice," Myra interrupted, hiding behind her. "Alice."

Lady Victoria gave a questioning look. "What's going on?"

"She can only say my name, and she doesn't want to see Saavant Enya," Alice responded, still breathless.

The woman's green eyes widened, and she focused on Myra. "What did she do?" Victoria inquired, crazed. "Did she touch you?"

Tears streamed down Myra's face. "Alice."

"Mother," Emeline called. "What's going on?"

Victoria's attention returned to Alice, her face serious. "Stay by your friend's side. Don't let anyone near her without you being there. Especially Saavant Enya."

"Yes, my lady," Alice replied, ready to protect her best friend. "What happened? I thought Saavant Enya was a good person."

"Remember this, Alice, no one is a good person. If someone tells you they are, they're probably one of the most evil people you've ever met."

The door opened, with Rosert and Doran flooding in. "Is everything okay?" Rosert asked, taking in the emotions of the room. "Mother, what do I need to do?"

"Doran, could you take Alice and Myra to the courtyard," Victoria requested, not answering her youngest son's question. "They both need some sun."

Doran bowed, and his behavior completely changed. "Of course, Mother."

He then directed Alice to the door when Emeline stood rigidly, gathering courage. "May I come, too?"

"Of course, sweet sister."

"Me too! Me too!" Catrian chanted, jumping from one foot to another, causing Doran to roll his eyes.

"Aye, you go too," Victoria shooed. "Cleric, go with them." The handmaiden bowed and followed everyone out of the room. Alice was the last to exit, pushing her friend forward, when she heard her lady aunt finally answer her youngest son. "I need you to protect Alice with every fiber of your being."

The group traveled to the courtyard with Catrain and her handmaiden in front, with Alice and Myra sandwiched between Emeline and Doran. "I don't feel like going to the courtyard anymore!" Catrain declared, spinning. "Come on, Cleric, let's go have fun elsewhere!" Before anyone could respond, Catrain raced away, with Cleric rushing to follow behind.

When the girl was gone, Emeline groaned. "That girl is so wild!"

"She acts like my sister, like a Wayward," Alice replied, smiling. "You'll get used to it."

"I'm used to it. It's just," Emeline looked away. "I could never act like that."

"Do you want to?" Alice questioned, causing the girl to stop walking. "I mean, if you don't, then don't, but if you want to act wild like a Wayward, then do it."

The four teenagers entered the courtyard, the sun beating down on them.

"I'm going to practice my swings while we wait for Rosert," Doran informed the girls with a sword already in his hands.

Alice beamed toward her betrothed. "Do your best! We will be watching over here!"

Doran blushed, nodded, and began his swings.

"Wow, I've never seen my big brother act like that," Emeline observed, her green eyes twinkling. "You've changed him. Thank you!"

"I didn't do anything," she confessed, still staring at Doran. "I was too busy being selfish. He changed himself." She stepped closer to Myra and grabbed the girl's hand comfortingly. "I'm happy for it, though. I'd prefer to marry someone nice."

Emeline tried to cover her smile. "Aye, Doran is a kind person."

Footsteps rushed from behind, forcing Alice to turn around. "Rosert," she exhaled, her demeanor excited. *Rosert is going to be my protector.* She took in his bulking muscles and Wayward spirit. *He will always be by my side.*

"Hi Alice," Rosert greeted, stepping close and cupping Alice's face. "How are you feeling? How's Myra?"

"When did you become a gentleman?" Emeline teased, but when her brother blushed, her eyes widened. "Oh."

"Rosert move; I can't see Doran practice," Alice said, playfully pushing the boy out of her way.

Rosert stood straight and walked toward his brother. "I'll show you what a real swing is!"

When the Osmont boy left, Emeline scooted closer. "How did you do it?" she whispered with a goofy smile.

"What did you mean?"

"How did you get both of my crazy brothers to fall in love with you?"

Alice gasped at the question, but Myra leaned forward. "Alice," she told Emeline as if she were agreeing. Alice stared at the girls before her eyes narrowed on the two boys vying for attention. *They both like me.*

Her attention focused on her betrothed. She barely knew the boy, but his innocence reminded Alice of herself, while the brightness in his eyes mirrored a future she could see with him. *I should feel that way, right?*

Alice's eyes then landed on the youngest son. Rosert swung at the target with his smug smile, his copper eyes glittering. *He's so different than*

Doran. Rosert smiled like her mother and teased like Jaslyn. His hearty laughs echoed like her father's, and his overconfidence matched Josef.

Rosert reminded Alice of home.

Why? She couldn't understand it. *Rosert is not home.* He reminded Alice of her family, but not the thick stones that made up Winter's Keep. Nor the tall tower where she spent most of her days. He wasn't like the fluffy summer snow, the bitter coldness that always lingered in the air, nor the sea of grey clouds that covered Maryere. If anything, Rosert made Alice feel warm. It was the kind of warmth that she had longed for when she was in the Bloody Tower. *Does he make me happy, too?* Rosert did not remind her of the hell that was Kingment. When she looked at him, she forgot where she was. She forgot the terrors that she had endured—she forgot everything. *Only he can make me forget everything.*

Her heart sank. *Oh, gods.* Her eyes flashed from boy to boy as the brothers began to interact. *Do I like Rosert, too?*

"Hey Alice," Rosert called. "Who swung it better? Doran seems to think he even grips the sword right."

She stared back, panicked. *Oh, gods.* Her body grew cold, and her face buzzed with anxiety. *No, I can't.* A violent cough erupted from Alice Wayward, forcing her to hack into her sleeve. She pulled her arm away and examined the blood splatters now staining the fabric. *What?*

Then she fell into the dirt.

"Alice!" Myra screamed, crying, as blood ran from Alice's nose and ears. "ALICE!"

"Move, move," Rosert commanded, pushing Myra away. He scooped Alice into his arms and dashed toward the castle. "We must find Mother!"

"I agree!" Emeline said from behind. "Doran, go get Father too. He will want to know about this."

"You sure?"

"She bleeding from the ears! Yes, I'm sure!"

The siblings continued their panicked conversation, as Alice Wayward rocked in and out of consciousness. *I'm bleeding; this has never happened before! What's going on with me?*

"Wait, where is that Myra girl?" Doran questioned.

"What do you mean? She's right behind," Emeline paused. "Um,"

Rosert planted his feet, stopping. "Emeline, go back to the courtyard and search for Myra. Doran, find Father and bring him to the art room. I'm sure Mother is still there." And then, Rosert resumed his mad dash to Lady Victoria.

Alice attempted to lift her head. "What's happened,"

"Sh, just try your best to stay calm," he cooed, moving her hair out of her face. "Everything is going to be okay."

Her consciousness slipped. "You promise?"

"Of course. I promise," Rosert replied, and everything became dark.

GLORIANA

E ven during the last moon of the year, the Summerlands were warm. Ivies and wildflowers covered the columns throughout the Sun Castle in Goldspire. Scents of cinnamon constantly lingered in the air, mixing with the foods continually being pushed out of the castle's many kitchens. Toucans cawed from the jungles, and ruby doves responded with their songs, creating a beautiful harmony. Everything about Gloriana's childhood home was the exact opposite of Winter's Keep.

A young Gloriana leaned against her mother's arm as they sat in one of the many gardens that overwhelmed every courtyard in the castle, thriving yearlong from the constant rain showers. She took long, deep breaths, hoping this dream was a memory. *Did I ever spend time with my mother in the gardens?*

Gloriana Wayward didn't know.

"The twelfth moon of the year started this week," Lady Popealia Thoren informed. "Soon, the year will end, and a new one will begin."

"What year?"

"Four-hundred and seventy-five."

Gloriana repeated the number, her eyes sparkling wonderfully. "And this year will stop?"

Her mother nodded, looking at the cloudless sky. "Did you know the Arcs called the twelfth moon the Old Moon?" Gloriana shook her head, absorbing her mother's words. "Aye, they said, 'Shed the old and look forward to the new.' The Arcs always had sayings for everything."

"So, would the first moon of the year be called the New Moon?"

Popealia Thoren turned to Gloriana and patted her daughter on the head, causing the girl to smile. "You're so smart, Gloriana! You're going to be a wonderful person when you grow up."

Brightness from the sun awoke Gloriana Wayward from her precious dream. *No,* she groaned, shifting in the bed, *wait.* She sat up and looked at the window. *The sun is out—it's rarely out during the winter.* A chill vibrated throughout Gloriana's body. *What does that mean?* She shook her bedhead, yawning, wishing to return to her dream. *It was nice seeing my mother again.*

For the last moon, Gloriana had been busy. She wrote to Lord Protector Merrick Gardener and Lady Sable Wayward, then sent Asterin to Griffon's Den. She informed Lady Joan of her meeting with Esme and her hesitancy in killing Borin. She even spoke to Jaslyn, trying to understand her hardheaded daughter.

And now, she waited.

Gloriana Wayward didn't know what she was waiting for, but the stress strained her heart to the point that she could no longer take it. *Why can't Borin get on a ship to Ihphy's Archipelago and disappear like Cayle Dawphrey?*

It would make everything in her life a lot easier.

Gloriana shifted out of bed and stretched, wondering how she could waste another day. She strode to the window and soaked in the sun that her skin so missed. *This is nice, but will the clouds and snow return later?*

Her bedchamber door swung open, and Borin stomped into her room. "What the fuck is this?" he questioned, gripping a piece of paper.

Gloriana studied her husband's bright red face before turning away. *He's aged so quickly.* She hadn't been in the same room as the Lord Protector since she met Esme. She then pictured the abuse Esme endured. *Borin thought about stabbing and slashing me. Did he imagine Esme was me when he abused her? Why does he want to hurt me like that? Thank the gods that something stopped him from causing me more harm.* It was a selfish statement, but it swirled in her mind daily. *How could he want to do that to someone he loves?*

Gloriana inhaled sharply as anger, disgust, and fright filled her. *How could my life turn out this way?* She was supposed to marry the prince in her dreams, the enchanting and gallant Lord Protector, but Borin was never that kind of person. *No, Rodrick better fits that description.*

Finally, their eyes met: husband and wife.

"You've crumpled the paper, so how am I supposed to know what you're holding?" she inquired, crossing her arms.

Borin squeezed the paper tighter before balling it up and throwing it at her. Slowly, Gloriana lifted the letter and flattened it out. As soon as she read the first few words, her heart sank. She knew that scribble anywhere. *Sable.* Gloriana scanned the rest of the letter. *This was written to Borin, not me. That damned Sable!*

"What is it, Gloriana? Tell me!"

"It's a letter from your sister," she whispered, blinking away tears.

"Why did I receive a letter from Sable? Why is she thanking me, saying she cannot wait to meet her niece?"

Gloriana took a deep breath. "I did what you asked of me. I wrote to Sable as a courtesy. I also wrote to Lord Gardener, requesting Jaslyn stay there as a ward. Isn't that what you wanted?"

Her husband exhaled heavily through his nose, trying to stay calm. "I said to write to Bryce Thoren!"

"Ekon Ashmire," she corrected.

Borin Wayward responded by backhanding Gloriana so hard she fell to the floor. Intense stinging radiated from her cheek as she glared at her husband. *I mean nothing to this man. I've always meant nothing. Fallen was right; I am just a nuisance to him. He never loved me.*

The realization broke Gloriana's heart, and unwanted tears fell freely.

"I don't give a fuck what his real name is. You know who I was talking about. I even said you could write to Jarin Ayers! Yet you did whatever you wanted to do. It seems you've been doing that a lot recently, and it's starting to piss me off."

"Starting," she scoffed.

Borin lifted his foot and kicked Gloriana's shoulder, forcing her to lay on the floor. "It's time I teach you a lesson!" he shouted, standing over her. "I'm the Lord Protector, and you're the lady wife!" he stomped on her abdomen. "Know your place!"

Gloriana cried and grabbed her throbbing stomach as she focused on the man towering above her. Slowly, Borin morphed into Falk Osmont. Fervent strikes of punches and kicks reverberated through Gloriana's body, and she couldn't tell if the feeling was current or just a memory.

"I protected you so our family could stay together. Now, you want to send my other daughter to that lunatic!"

You didn't protect me; Alice did. Scorn fluttered through Gloriana as she lay motionlessly on the floor. *And here you are, taking all the credit.* Another kick forced her back to reality. *No more.*

For the first time in almost twenty years, Gloriana fought back.

A weak punch landed on Borin's thigh, and the two stared at the touch. The Lord Protector of the Mountain Realm responded by hitting her with full force. Everything spun, and Gloriana's arms fell to the side, defeated. Instead of pulling back, Borin continued his assault, stomping on her fingers, crushing them.

Extreme pain pulsed through Gloriana Wayward, and she wailed in reaction. Her husband pounced on her, his heaviness squishing her underneath. His large, thick hands covered her mouth and nose, suffocating her. Gloriana kicked, punched, and bit as she tried her best to get from under him, but he wouldn't move. *Am I going to die?*

"For years, you held your head high even when everyone else treated you like an outcast. I thought it was endearing, but my mother always warned that it was nothing but arrogance. I suppose she was right. She was right about everything," he paused and slid off Gloriana. "I wish she were here now. She would know what to do. She would get Alice back peacefully. She would deal with you. She would've saved our family." He shook his head. "I'll never understand why my mother jumped to her death. Everything has been a disaster since then."

Gloriana continued to lie on the floor, not caring about Borin's soliloquy. *I'm glad Fallen Wayward fell from that tower, her body breaking beyond recognition from the impact.*

It was one of the best days of Gloriana's life.

"Are you even listening?"

"Yes," she whispered, barely audible. "You wish I had died in your mother's place." Her vision narrowed on her husband's shocked face, but his silence let her know she was right. *What do I wish for?*

Every inch of her body burned and throbbed, just as it did when Falk beat her. *I wish for peace. I wish for happiness.* She lifted herself from the floor, but her eyes never left her husband. *I wish to be rid of you.* As she studied Borin, she only felt complacent. *I have no use for you now.*

"You won't be sending Jaslyn to Griffon's Den. I'll write to Lord Ayers and finish the job since you're incompetent," Lord Borin informed, not responding to Gloriana's answer. "You will stay in your chambers for another moon. You are not to leave. Do you understand?"

I hate you, she resented. *I hate you. I hate you.* The time had come. The Lord Protector of the Mountain Realm needed to change. *I hate you, I hate you, I hate you.* Those three words repeated endlessly, and her body tensed.

At last, she hated him.

Gloriana Wayward had tried her best not to come to this point, but as she caught a glimpse of herself in the mirror, her wounds matching Esme's, she knew it could not be helped. *He must die.* Desire to hear Borin's agonizing screams bloomed in her chest, and she suppressed a smile. *I wonder if he can die the same way his mother did.* Imagines of blood, broken bones, and innards splattered in her mind, and she could only see the mangled body of Lady Fallen Wayward. *I don't know if I can take another grisly sight like that.*

Lord Borin walked to the door before pausing. "I still love you," he confessed with a sigh. "Even though you became everything my mother warned me about, I still love you." He turned around, and Gloriana stepped back. He frowned at her reaction, and he looked at his hands. "Although you're pretending now, at one point, it felt like you loved me, too."

I did, she wanted to respond. Her attention lowered to her mangled fingers. "Who beats someone they love?"

"I was always told to respond to you with my instinct, even if it was violent. But when I visited Kingment, I spoke to my sister, and she couldn't believe I would ever raise my hand against you. 'That's not the Borin I adore,' she had told me. So when I returned, I tried my hardest not to hit you. That time you caught an attitude at the Grand Library or yelled at me during the feast. I saw red, but I didn't physically retaliate. I told you to get away from me. I had hoped it would be enough, but no. You thought you were clever and got cocky. Ruined everything we had built together in a matter of moons. Then, when I saw you at the Row of Lords, my patience broke. I could feel my mother telling me to bring you back to reality." He paused. "Do you see me as a monster?"

Gloriana frowned. "No, you are Unmos reborn."

The Lord Protector gave a sad face. "I'm sorry."

"Fuck your sorries," she spat before standing straight, her entire body aching. *Soon, you will be dead, and I will be rid of you. I will help lead this realm and bring my daughter back home.*

Borin Wayward burst into laughter, allowing Gloriana the moment to grab a cloak and slip out of her bedchamber. "Where did you go?" She could hear him asking as she raced down the hall. "Gloriana, get back here! I commanded you to return and stay in your bedroom! You have no reason to walk through the keep. Gloriana, are you listening to me? Gloriana!"

She walked briskly through Winter's Keep, ignoring the lingering eyes. No one said a word to her; deep down, Gloriana appreciated that. *Don't worry,* she wanted to tell those who stared. *I will never look like this again.*

Before she knew it, she was outside. *Borin must die.*

Outside, the clouds had already covered the sun, and the snow had returned. The freezing wind burned Gloriana's wounds, reminding her of everything she had endured. *I must let go.* Then, she was running. Gloriana could not remember the last time she ran, but she felt free as her legs moved underneath and the wind whipped through her wavy hair.

She raced to the Merchant's District, pleased to see a sea of people all merrily shopping. It was everything Gloriana worked for the last few years, and now, she couldn't even enjoy it. *This is nothing when an entire realm must be ruled.*

She bumped into someone in front of her. "Apologies." When she noticed Esme's glassy green eyes staring back at her, she grabbed the girl's wrist and led her out of the Merchant's District.

"Uh, my lady,"

"Not right now," Gloriana interrupted, leading Esme to the only place Borin would never visit—the Sun Keep.

The two women entered the abandoned keep, and Gloriana took in her surroundings. *Falk found me here,* she remembered, shivering. She noticed imprints on the snow-covered floor. *Do people still sneak around?* Esme walked towards the fallen beam where Gloriana and Falk shared their first kiss.

Gloriana wanted to vomit.

Esme sat and motioned for Gloriana to follow. She collapsed onto the beam and burst into tears. She squeezed her fingers as she cried, reminding herself how broken she was. *He broke me, and he will pay for it.*

"My lady," Esme said, pulling Gloriana back inside the snowy Sun Keep. "What's going on?"

Gloriana wiped her tears. "How were you planning to kill him?"

A small grin appeared. "There is a poison that rots the brain," Esme answered, reaching into her bag and pulling out a small vial. "It hits the two checks we need. It doesn't have a taste and it's incurable. The poison brings a slow and painful death, one that he deserves."

An evil smile crept across Gloriana's lips, and she accepted the vial. "A slow death?" The tortured woman nodded. "I'd like to be the one who gives it to him."

"It's too risky," Esme disagreed. "You'll want someone like me to do it."

Gloriana shook her head. "I must be the one to do it. You will pretend to be a servant and slip into Crimson's Quarters, where Lady Joan resides.

You will become her attendant."

"What if I'm recognizable?"

"Lady Joan said she has a solution, so not to worry."

Esme jumped to her feet. "Let me prepare a few things, and then I will go to Lady Myster."

The young woman rushed out of the abandoned keep, leaving Gloriana behind. She lifted her head, and soft snowflakes melted against her warm skin. Her attention lowered to the vial, studying the strange clear liquid. *It doesn't have a taste and it's incurable.* She rose to her feet. "It's time."

Lady Gloriana Wayward trekked back to Winter's Keep, her face emotionless. *I must do this quickly before Borin realizes something is amiss.* As she walked, she grabbed a flagon of wine and two glasses, sitting on a cart in the hallway. Gloriana strolled to her lord husband's study and entered without knocking.

No one was inside, causing Gloriana to sigh. *He should be here soon.* She placed the flagon and glasses on the desk before opening the vial of poison. She sniffed to ensure of no scent before pouring it into the wine. She used one of her smashed fingers to stir the liquid and wiped her hands clean. *Perfect.*

The door clicked open, and the Lord Protector of the Mountain Realm slipped into his study, exhaling heavily. When he noticed his lady wife standing in the room, smiling, he frowned. "Where did you go earlier?"

"I needed to go for a walk."

"I'm sure I told you to stay in your bedchamber."

She grinned, pouring the wine into the cups. "I will later, but not right now."

He gave a questioning look as she handed him a glass. "Why?"

"I want to celebrate with you."

Borin's copper eyes examined the wine. "What are you celebrating?"

"Well, this week is the start of the Old Moon. Did you know the Arcs had a saying for when the last moon arrived? 'Shed the old and look forward to the new.' That's why the first moon of the year is called the New Moon." Gloriana lifted her cup. "Cheers!"

Borin clicked the glass and watched Gloriana take a sip. "What are you shedding?"

Gloriana pretended to take another gulp, but instead she spat her first sip back into the drink and watched as her lord husband actually swallowed the poisoned wine. *You.* "My old self," she answered, and a genuine smile spread across her lips.

DAWN

Part 4

JARIN

H e had left in the midst of the night, so that Dimia would never know which direction he went. It was exactly as Hamlin had instructed, and Jarin was content that he was able to complete everything. Only Ser Bronston, Daya, and Dain knew of Jarin's location; and they were the only people he could trust. Jarin's confidence in his youngest son had grown recently and he wondered if he gave the boy too much credit. *Well, he does hate Dimia.*

He left Waterbrook in Dain's hands over a fortnight ago. Although Terryn was the true Lord Protector of the Riverlands while Jarin was absent, Dain understood his position. *Dain must protect everyone and everything from Dimia, even if that means undermining important people in the process.* Jarin had explained all of this to his youngest son, and he could tell by the determination in Dain's bright green eyes that everything should be fine. Jarin had prayed to all the gods that Dain would stay safe; he continuously prayed, not just for Dain, but for everyone and everything.

Jarin stared at the cloudless night sky as the stars twinkle brightly. Wood crackled from the campfire in front of him, and the fire warmed his exposed skin.

A strange silence filled Jarin's surroundings. *It's always like this in the worst region in the Wetlands—the Creepmurk,* he groaned, turning to his traveling companions, who ate their dinner. Daya nibbled quickly and quietly, her eyes darting around the campfire while Ser Bronston savored his meal, taking deep breaths between each bite.

"The long drought didn't seem to affect the Creepmurk," Bronston observed, striking up a conversation.

Jarin lifted his eyebrows curiously. "We have passed dry floodplains, so the Wetlands were affected," he informed. "All the recent rain was a gift for this region. It needs the flooding."

Daya grinned. "Oh, so the southern Wetlands are wetter now."

Ser Bronston chuckled at the girl's response, bringing a smile to Jarin's face. *Pairing Bronston and Daya was genius,* Jarin praised, taking in the lively campfire. *I wish I had more time to witness Hamlin's strategic mind.* He returned his attention to the sky, refusing to pity himself. *That didn't happen, and it's my fault, but I can't regret my decisions anymore.* He inhaled sharply. *I must move forward.*

"My lord, you should eat your dinner."

Jarin's eyes lowered to the crackling meat skewered above the flames. *Snakes*, he complained, dragging out the word. Every species of those reptilian stomach crawlers made Jarin's skin tingle. *I hate snakes.*

Owls and hawks roamed the skies in Waterbrook, lowering the snake population and allowing Jarin to forget the animal even existed. *I'm not in Waterbrook anymore*, he thought, rubbing his hands together nervously.

In the Wetlands, snakes were the primary meat to hunt, forcing Jarin to starve. Daya ensured to hunt for vegetation, so that Jarin could eat *something*, but in the Creepmurk, there was no vegetation—just murky water, trees, and snakes.

For three days, Jarin had went without food and yet, the skewered meat didn't make his mouth water; only nauseous. He glanced to his head lord knight. "I cannot eat that," he said, his voice low and whiny.

Ser Bronston Hedge sighed heavily and repositioned his legs. "Why not, my lord? You have been starving yourself, and now your cheeks are gaunt."

"Aye," Daya mumbled, her arms crossed, "I risked my life getting those vials from Hamlin's study before Dimia had her people burn the Shadow Tower. Starving yourself is going to be counterproductive to the treatment."

She's right. He picked up the skewer, making Daya and Ser Bronston smile. The smoking pinkish meat made Jarin's stomach turn, and his companions' eyes watching and waiting for him to take a bite only brought anxiety. *I must eat.* Jarin swiftly chomped on the food and chewed as the slimy meat moved around in his mouth. *Oh,* he thought, and immediately vomited. Ser Bronston and Daya's wide eyes stayed on Jarin as he slowly placed the snake meat back over the fire.

No one asked Jarin to eat again.

After a few hours, long fluffy clouds littered the sky and Jarin stared at the darkness above him, repeating a list in his head. *Destroy Dimia. Trust Dain. Ally with Kaylien. Influence Terryn. Protect Daya.* He glanced at the young girl. *In a moon, I will complete my first task. No one will touch Daya in Widow's Dale.*

"Let's share stories," Daya suggested, bouncing. Bronston shrugged in response and Lord Jarin nodded. "Yay! Okay, my story is about Lismure," she explained. Ser Bronston smacked his teeth, and Daya giggled. "You cannot retell stories, knight." And Bronston smacked his teeth again.

At first, interest swirled inside Jarin. *Lismure is the city that knows all, and the only place in Mystos where the Arts are decriminalized.* The Arts were a mystery to Jarin. *If I want to defeat Dimia, I may need to learn about the Arts.* Hamlin had been against the Arts and Maras, claiming their very existence was a sin against the gods. But Jarin thought differently. *I must become stronger, and the Arts could be the answer. If it were really so sinful, the gods would have destroyed it.*

The story, however, was not about the mysteries of Lismure. The story was not about the Arts or its independence, like Jarin had wanted.

Daya's story was about the gods.

"One day, Axone, the goddess of Life, started building a continent for the Arcs on the terrafield called Mystos. The other gods were interested in the project, and Axone decided that only five gods could help create Mystos. Axone had Krella, the child-goddess of Revelry, created a dice game for the gods to play. Unmos, the god of Darkness, lost miserably and wasn't selected. When the gods completed Mystos, Unmos went behind their backs and dropped a black hole in the middle of the new continent, creating the Lake of Shadows. It is said that thousands of years later after the gods had long disappeared, the cambions, more well known as the Wickeds, Unmos' children, used the Darkness to create Lismure, the floating city."

Quietness surrounded the campsite, and Jarin narrowed his attention to Daya. "Very good," he yawned.

She crossed her arms, "Bronston fell asleep."

Jarin shifted his eyes to the knight. "It's fine, we need our sleep," he replied, patting her head before laying on the squishy dirt. Jarin seeped into the darkness of his dreams and last thing Jarin could hear before sleep took him, was the snakes hissing.

❋ ❋ ❋

House Withers' holdfast was ancient.

Jarin observed the water rocks stacked against one another to create the enormous holdfast. *No one has used these rocks in Riverlands architecture for several centuries.* A deep moat circled the structure, so that no one could enter without using the drawbridge. Jarin stared at the moat strangely. *That is the old way to keep people out.*

Ser Bronston Hedge stopped his horse beside Jarin, pulling him from his thoughts. "By the looks of it, it seems that Widow's Dale is one of the oldest holdfasts in the Riverlands, but I've never heard of a House Withers."

"Aye, the holdfast used to belong to House Boulder, but they committed treason, so my grandmother eradicated them according to Hamlin's notes," Jarin replied, clearing his throat.

"Hm, my lord father told me Lady Wisteria Ayers was a quiet woman, that must be why this place has been lost to history," Bronston responded. "Widow's Dale is a vassal of House Hedge, but we have no information on House Withers prior to Lady Vera, so they're hiding how they got this holdfast. It's also strange that my father never looked into it."

Daya rode up to the pair and took in the structure, breathless and amazed. "I have never seen something so old before."

Jarin tilted his head at the girl's statement. *Daya lived in one of the oldest cities to exist. Is there nothing old in Lismure?* Imaginary flames danced in Jarin's mind. *I forgot a quarter of Lismure is always burning. They're the ones who taught the Five Great Lands how to build with other materials instead of wood.*

The drawbridge lowered and the unbearable creaking forced Jarin to cover his ears. The noise grew louder; screaming to the world that the bridge was lowering. *No one can sneak in or out*, he realized, noticing the murky water in the moat rumble. *Lysane said she's ran away twice.* His eyebrows furrowed. *How; and why?*

Finally, the drawbridge hit the ground, and a small dust cloud swirled in the air.

A tiny figure raced toward them. "Hello! Hello!" a girl squealed, jumping with excitement. She wore a flowing white dress that stopped at her calf, with matching flowers pinned in her long black wavy hair. The girl suddenly sprinted forward causing Jarin and Ser Bronston to exchange concerned looks. They quietly dismounted their horses and Daya hesitantly did the same. "Oh, my lord, my lord," the girl sang and clapped, approaching. She grabbed both of Jarin's hands and smiled widely. "Hello! Hello!"

Jarin cleared his throat and brought some space in between them, but the girl's grip was strong. "Ah, hello."

"My name is Penelopei Withers," she introduced, squeezing his hands excitedly.

"Well, hello Penelopei," he replied, still uncomfortable. He turned to his companions, and luckily, the girl loosened her grip. "This is Ser Bronston, my lord knight, and this is Daya."

"Pei!" a voice called from behind the walls. "Pei, you can't just start skipping and singing without telling me where you are going first!"

That's a motherly scold. Is it Lady Vera?

Penelopei released Jarin and resumed hopping. "Let us go inside, my lord!" She suggested, her eyes shifting to Bronston and Daya, "Come, come, you too!" She added, never losing her cheery demeanor. Penelopei then turned on her heels and ran across the drawbridge, her barefeet smacking against the old wood.

Jarin sighed, already exhausted. He started the trek and Ser Bronston and Daya followed along, staying quiet. When Jarin crossed the drawbridge, he approached a second girl who raised her head, elongating her thick neck and double chin.

"Nelia! Nelia!" Penelopei shouted, twirling around.

Everyone entered the courtyard, and the drawbridge resumed its screaming, shutting them out from the rest of the world. Jarin gulped nervously and kept his attention on the two teenage girls hugging.

The two broke apart, Penelopei's smile never wavering. "I've told you a hundred times, Pei, don't go running off without saying anything," the girl continued to chide.

Penelopei huffed. "Our honored guests were here," she countered, pointing at the trio. "*Someone* had to welcome them!"

The other girl exhaled through her nose, before a smile etched across her face. "Hello, my lord," she bowed. "My name is Cornelia Withers."

They must be sisters, he deduced, interested that the two had nicknames; but something bothered him. Penelopei's golden-colored skin glittered in the winter sun while Cornelia was as pale as the flowers in Penelopei's hair. Jarin understood then. *They are orphans, just like Lysane.* He wondered if Lady Vera adopted all the children here.

He focused on the girl. "Hello, Cornelia."

"My lady mother has been waiting for you. Would you like to see her?"

"Yes, please."

"I will lead the way!" Penelopei cheered, skipping deeper into the holdfast.

The thick wet air stuck to Jarin's skin as he walked through the dark and cold hallways. *There are no sigils placed throughout the castle, only flowers.* He observed the two girls ahead of him, unfazed by the nature of the holdfast. "Do you have any other siblings?" Jarin asked quietly.

"Aye, there is Ossian, Nebula, Lucius, Penelopei, and I."

"Sian and Lulu are out hunting right now. They will be back later," Penelopei added, her hands intertwined behind her back.

Jarin held in a groan, his hips aching. "Do you share the same surname?" he asked, and Cornelia nodded. "Why didn't Lysane?"

Cornelia pressed her plump lips together harshly, and Jarin quickly realized that the mention of Lysane was a touchy subject.

"Sansan *did* share our surname, but when she left, she wanted to be no one." Penelopei answered instead, not as affected by the question as Cornelia.

Sansan? Jarin smiled at the nickname. "Why did she leave Widow's Dale?"

Cornelia lifted her head. "My lord, you should ask my lady mother those sorts of topics."

"Oh, come on, Nelia!" Penelopei giggled. "Don't be such a stink!" The jovial girl laughed some more, spinning around as she walked. "Sansan left because,"

"Pei shut up, or else!" Cornelia cautioned, and Penelopei stopped and frowned. "Again, my lord, that is a question you must ask my mother."

Jarin turned to his companions, and they both looked down in response. *They are so strange, yet friendly.*

Penelopei led the pack quietly, with her head down and her hands still behind her back. She no longer spun, nor smiled and laughed; it was like she was not there at all.

Finally, they reached a dimly lit room filled with flowers where a woman sat at a table by herself, reading a book. As they entered, the woman lifted her head and smiled kindly. "Hello," the woman greeted in a wispy voice as her entire face scrunched to smile.

Jarin said nothing in return. *It cannot be.* The woman's face relaxed, and Jarin examined her eyes. *Grey ones filled with life. Sparkling silver hair.* His blood ran cold. *Domeric.* "You're Lady Vera Withers?" Jarin questioned, instead of returning her greeting.

The woman's smile grew larger, reminding Jarin of the day he met her. "Yes, Lord Protector, I am."

"My lord, you know Lady Withers?" Bronston inquired, but Jarin was too deep in thought, trying his best to remember.

He did not know her name, nor where she came from—he knew nothing about the woman. Only that she had silver hair, kind grey eyes, and that his older brother loved her.

King Alen! King Alen! The cheers from that day rang in his head. He stared at the woman as his father's name continued chanting in his mind. He had believed that every person from that day was long gone now. Hamlin, Domeric, Brea, and his father were gone. *Yet she is here. She is alive.*

"I, I, how?"

Lady Vera closed the book and stood gracefully before walking toward him, her body swaying as she moved. She had changed little since the first time they met, all those horrible years ago. By the time Vera approached, Jarin could no longer breathe. She smiled at his tenseness, and looked him up and down, her beautiful grey eyes bouncing around as she observed. "You are still as innocent as I remember," she told him, her voice still delicate and breathy.

"Mother, you know the Lord Protector?" Cornelia asked.

"Aye, I do. Now, Pei and Nelia, why don't you show our guest their rooms while I speak with Lord Jarin," Vera responded.

Penelopei grinned, spinning again as she made her way to the door. "Come, come, and follow me," she sang.

A large and trusting hand touched Jarin's shoulder. "I could stay," Bronston suggested.

"No need," he told his lord knight. "You and Daya need some proper rest."

Bronston nodded and followed Penelopei and Cornelia, with Daya staying right by the knight's side.

Alone, Jarin and Vera stared at each other, silent and tense. "My, my, how you have grown," she began, her smile never fading. "I'm pleased to see that you are alright."

"Why are *you* here?" he questioned, remembering the rest of that awful day. His older brother, presenting the young woman before the King of the Riverlands, flickered before screaming filled Jarin's head. Alen's rants, Domeric's arguments, and Vera's cries bounced around as Jarin continued to stare at the woman. "Why are you here?"

The blunt question startled Lady Withers. "Your brother," she whispered, looking away. "Right before he died, he gifted Widow's Dale to me. I still have the decree somewhere if you need to see it. This place had been abandoned for years, so I thought it was okay. He also gave me several coffers filled with gold to support this place."

A moment of silence filled the air. *Domeric gave her this holdfast right before he died. By then he was betrothed to Lady Ressalia Bayes. Was that why he and my father were arguing on that fateful day?* Horrible memories threatened to replay in Jarin's head as he looked the woman in the eyes. *Domeric really loved her, and it cost him his life.* "Is your name truly Vera Withers?"

She shook her head, her demeanor brightening again. "In the scroll that I received, it said that I was to take on that name."

"What is your real name?"

"Cleophilia," she answered, smiling so hard that she showed teeth. "But, you can call me Cleo."

He nodded, recalling what Hamlin had told him before he left Waterbrook. *Dimia knows who Vera is, but does Vera know Dimia?* His eyes narrowed on the silver woman. "Do you know my wife, Lady Dimia of House Osmont?"

Cleo's grey eyes sparkled, and her smile never faded. "I'm sorry, my lord, but I stay far away in the swamps, not involving myself in politics. I've never met that woman in my life."

HADRIAN

Exhaustion etched into Ser Colvic Rames' face as he swung his sword again, slapping the flat side onto Hadrian's shoulder. The strike swept Hadrian off his feet, and the air escaped his lungs as he hit the ground with a thud. He groaned loudly, his body aching. *I'm going to die. This knight is going to kill me.*

Over a moon had passed, and if the trio weren't traveling, Ser Colvic forced Hadrian to spar with him. The knight placed his hands on his hips as he stared at Hadrian, disappointed. "How often must I explain that Raiders almost always aim for the neck? You would've died many times already! Get it together!"

Tears filled Hadrian's eyes. "I'm trying my best!"

Ser Colvic smacked his teeth and turned away, looking at the afternoon sky. Hadrian watched quietly, observing the man's stocky body underneath the clean clothes. *At least he's not wobbling anymore.* Ser Colvic Rames was a man of many tales as the heroic knight of Valley Pines. Hadrian wished Colvic would tell the stories of his life, but he was a man of action—not talking.

Colvic's got a brother and a sister, too, Lord Peyton Osmont's voice echoed in the breeze. *He's more like Leo than you think.* Hadrian wished he could see that side of Ser Colvic. All he knew was the cold, stoic knight that made him feel small with just a look.

"Alright, get up."

Hadrian moaned at the command, attempting to move. "I need a longer break."

The knight chuckled, but the sound was strange and terrible. "Do you think you get a break during a fight against the Raiders?"

"We aren't in a fight."

"Pick up your sword," Colvic replied, his green eyes beaming down on Hadrian.

The boy's lips quivered. "Please."

"No."

His attention flickered to the young Grasslandi who sat high in a tree, braiding sticks into a crown and decorating it with leaves, ignoring the training below. Hadrian struggled to his feet, wishing he was sitting in the tree with her instead of getting his ass kicked by Colvic. But he didn't get that luxury.

Hadrian closed his eyes, took a deep breath, and heard a single bird caw. He then picked up the sword, which felt heavier this time than usual. His body moved, and he ran towards Colvic on the offensive, where he did best. Without warning, Colvic elbowed Hadrian in his ribs, and the tide of the fight changed instantly. Now, Hadrian was on the defensive, where he was at his worst. He could not read Colvic's next moves. *Left? Right? Up? Down?*

Suddenly, Hadrian was falling to the ground, and everything spun. He sat up and touched his bleeding lips. "You hit me in the face!"

The knight suppressed a grin. "Aye, one of the favorite places a Raider likes to strike."

"That's not fair!"

Ser Colvic shook his head, unimpressed by Hadrian's outburst. "Climb back to your feet, and I'll show you what's unfair."

Raynese stepped between the two, facing the knight. "It's been over a moon. When we aren't traveling, you're training Hadrian until he vomits. I get that you love him and don't want to see him hurt, but if you push any further, *you* could be the one to hurt Hadrian. Long ago, I was told that doing the same thing and hoping for different results means you're insane. You're not insane, are you?"

Ser Colvic sighed. "Fine. What is your suggestion?"

"To me, it seems quite obvious that Hadrian sucks with a big sword," Raynese observed.

Hadrian stood and kicked the dirt. "Thanks, you opinionated re'in."

"Aw, the grumble sounds like you almost hate me," the assassin teased, grinning.

He paused at the statement. *Do I hate Raynese?* Unease shifted in his chest as he realized he loved and despised the woman. *What do I do about that? Nothing? Accept it?* Hadrian didn't know. He was drawn to her strength and independence, but also felt a deep resentment towards her that he didn't quite understand. "I don't, I'm just frustrated."

"Don't be, my sweet," she told Hadrian, embracing the teenage boy and forcing his head to her chest. "I'm going to teach you about the Arts!"

Hadrian's heart beat wildly as he tried to ignore the birds growing louder in his head. It was finally happening; Raynese would teach him about the forbidden Arts. *Maybe then, I will understand life a bit more.*

Ser Colvic buzzed his lips. "You're just wasting your time."

She looked the man up and down. "Seems like you're doing that already. Why won't you let me try?"

The famed knight moaned and groaned before finally relenting. Colvic waved his hand in dismissal and sat on the hard ground, leaning against a stump, relaxing. "The Arts is something I know little about, so I will be listening, too."

"Oh, how wonderful!" Raynese cheered. "I love being an instructor. I can teach you all the things I love!"

"Let's stick to the basics," the knight replied, rolling his eyes.

Hadrian returned to the ground. "No, no, teach me everything you know."

Raynese sat beside him. "Alright, let me start with what the Arts are made up of,"

"The Four Beings, which are elements," Colvic interrupted. "The Nature, the Beast, the Arc, and the Darkness. Teach more important topics."

The re'in pouted. "I am! Hadrian, did you know what the Four Beings were?" Hadrian shook his head, causing the woman to smile. "Exactly as I thought. Since the Austere Ram believes he's so smart, what are the Nature properties?"

"Stop calling me that!" the knight snapped. "Lord Morvan called me that mockingly, and the other highborn laughed along with him. I hate that name, so please, don't use it."

Raynese's hazel eyes narrowed. "You didn't answer my question, *knight*."

Colvic sighed. "I don't know."

"For Nature, it's water, fire, air, and terra. For the Arcs, the properties were their species, higher and lower, but they are all gone now, so you won't ever learn about them."

"What happened?"

"Extinct. The humans killed them all."

Hadrian frowned. *Why?* He hesitated, knowing that Raynese would ignore the question. "What type of Arcs were there?" he asked instead.

"Titans, Valkyries, and their children Valkans were the Highest Arcs, beloved by the gods, and the most powerful. The Lower Arcs were creatures such as giants, elves, nekos, fairies, centaurs, minotaur, mermaids, unicorns, wyverns, sphinxes, griffons, basilisks, chimeras, phoenixes, leviathans, harpies, nymphs, nixes, ogres, and much more."

Hadrian's head spun. *I know some, but not all.* He thought for a moment, repeating the differing Arc species in his head. *Mother told me that the giants, elves, mermaids, and nymphs were not real and that Valkyries and Titans were the children of the gods and never truly lived in this world.* He breathed deeply, accepting that everything taught to him could be a lie. "How do you know the Arcs existed when they died hundreds of years ago?"

She exhaled heavily through her nose. "In Lismure, there are books written by the Arcs that prove how much more advanced they were than how we are today. The Highest Arcs were geniuses, like living gods in our world! Even now, the University is attempting to recreate what the Arcs had invented to advance our societies!"

Lismure is the city that knows all and that none of the Five Great Lands have been able to control. The city that rules itself and floats in the middle of the Lake of Shadows, a lake so large that one might think it is the sea. Hadrian's eyes sparkled with excitement. *I want to go there one day.*

"Sounds heretical," Colvic scoffed.

The Red Cobra's eyes narrowed. "Can't be heretical when you can still see remnants of the Arcs' old world throughout Mystos. Hidden temples deep in jungles. Abandoned arenas constructed in deserts. Intricate stone carvings in caves. I mean, even the Great Sword of Margo in Quiver's Valley is an example."

Hadrian leaned forward. He had once read about the sword that stretched into the sky, but he never thought the weapon would still be there. He believed it was all fake. "Have you seen it?"

"Aye, I could see the hilt of the sword a day's ride from the valley!" Raynese replied, shifting to her knees and bouncing enthusiastically. "Even though the sword has sat there for centuries, the blade isn't weathered down." She showed a faded scar on her palm. "This is from when I touched the sword!"

He frowned at the woman's excitement. *It's like watching her talk about Mikos and the people she never slaughtered.* Doubts filled his mind. "If there is such an enormous, magnificent sword thousands of years old stuck in the ground, why does no one talk about it?"

Raynese frowned. "Long ago, King Mathune Wayward spent all of his kingdom's money on Arcan art and literature. After learning that Margo was a giant princess from the Northwoods, he demanded King Alawi Gardener to sell the sword to him, but the King of the Grasslands refused. Truthfully, no one was able to pull the damn thing out of the ground. Afterward, as King Mathune's life fell apart, he claimed the sword was a fake. Many believed Mathune because of his expertise with the Arcs, but that ugly king was just jealous! As the years went by and the public's opinion on the Arcs and the Arts in general changed, people stopped talking about it. Well, except in the Grasslands, of course."

Colvic crossed his arms. "That sounds like a lot of unnecessary information."

Dust swirled as Raynese kicked the dirt. "Gods, do you always have some shit to say?"

The knight grinned awkwardly. "Aye."

"Fine, since you want to yap so much, what is your Art?"

Colvic frowned and repositioned himself. "The Pack Animal Art. I've said it before."

"But what is it?"

The man groaned and sighed and groaned again, clearly uncomfortable. "An alchemist told me when I was young that I had some kind of Pack Animal Art, so that's just what I say it is. I can tame animals that are used for transportation. The ones I use are the horse, the ox, and the sheep. I'm sure I can do more, but I never practiced."

Hadrian's eyes sparkled. *That's why Colvic can always find a horse!*

"Ser Colvic has the Beast element within him, which usually allows you to work with animals or become similar to the animal," Raynese explained.

His attention snapped to the sparrow that sat in a nearby tree. *I wonder if it's been one sparrow following me this whole time.* The bird reacted by jumping up and down and flapping its wings, causing Hadrian to frown. *Can it hear my thoughts?*

"What's wrong, my sweet?" Raynese questioned, her hand lightly touching his knee.

His frown hardened. "Just wondering if I have the Arts, too."

"Well, I could infuse my allure and see what happens," Raynese suggested. "But it rarely works on highborn, so I'm unsure."

Excitement spread throughout Hadrian. "We don't know who my mother is. She could've been a commoner. Please, try it."

Raynese glanced at Ser Colvic, and the knight shrugged. "Okay, hold out your hands." Hadrian did as he was told, and Raynese hovered her hands over his and closed her eyes. "Try your best to think about nothing," she instructed, her palms glowing green.

Hadrian took a deep breath but couldn't follow the young woman's orders. His mother's sweet songs, his father's random lectures, Leo's short responses, and Maerwynn's adorable giggles filled his head, causing his breathing to intensify. *My family.*

He could hear them all.

A strange gust of wind collected between Hadrian and Raynese's hands before bursting every which way. His eyes snapped open as his palms burned. *What happened?*

"By the gods," Colvic gasped, standing. "Hadrian has the Arts!"

Raynese beamed with pride. "Of course he does! Hadrian has the Nature within him, and the air properties swirl around him. It's beautiful to see."

I have the Arts. Tears filled his eyes. *Raynese says I have the Nature in me.* He studied his hands before turning back to the sparrow, staring directly at him. "Could you have multiple Arts?"

Raynese thought for a moment. "Possibly, but it's rare. Just be happy you have one!"

He forced a smile. "I am happy!"

"Great, now let's practice!" Raynese cheered, jumping to her feet.

Hadrian slowly rose, glancing at the sparrow. *I want to talk to it. I wonder if it will come any closer.* The bird hopped off a branch, landed closer, and Hadrian's eyes widened. *Wait, can it hear me?*

And the sparrow responded by singing a lovely melody.

His body pulsed. *The bird can hear and understand my thoughts.* Hadrian couldn't believe it. *I can't tell Raynese about the bird. I can't trust her fully anymore, so the more I hide from her, the better.*

"Okay, put your hands together and try to push wind from your palms. You don't always have to incant, and it's better to learn without it. It's much faster completing skills when you don't have to say anything."

He looked at the Red Cobra. "What's a skill?"

"It's how you do the ability," Colvic answered, stepping forward. "Much of the Arts is in your head, so you have to practice and turn what you want into reality. Or at least, that's what the alchemist had told me."

Raynese nodded. "It won't always become reality, but if you envision something as simple as a gust of wind and it matches your allure, which is the power you have, then you can create the skill. Now, follow me." The Red Cobra moved her arms, her motions smooth as her hands moved around her head.

Hadrian copied the motions, frowning. "What is this?"

"It will get your mind right."

He continued following along, and even Ser Colvic copied the movements, and for a moment, the three were in sync.

Rustling in the bushes caused them to pause, and Colvic and Raynese readied themselves to fight. The bushes moved again until the sparrow along with a few other birds flew out and into another tree. Hadrian smiled as his two companions relaxed, everyone gathering their breath.

"I'm over this! Thinking every little thing is a Warrior Raider. I feel like I'm going crazy!" Raynese complained, restlessly combing her fingers through her short brown hair.

"What do you suppose we do?" Colvic questioned.

Raynese groaned. "I don't know, something!"

"What if we let them attack us?" Hadrian suggested, causing the knight and re'in to stare at him strangely. "Raynese, you can heal, so you hide while the Warrior Raiders attack Colvic and me. We pretend to die, and when they leave, you can heal us."

The young woman shook her head. "I can only heal myself, sorry. I suck, I know." She thought for a moment. "But if we used the Darkness,"

"No," Colvic interrupted, his face serious. "Using the Darkness brings only death."

JASLYN

The new year had brought nothing but snow, blanketing everything in and around Maryere in a thick white fluff that Kai adored to pounce in. Jaslyn moved the scroll in her hands, trying to calm her breathing. *It's time.*

Over a moon had turned before Jaslyn felt comfortable enough to travel to Queen's Cove. She brought her twin handmaidens and trusted lion to the peasant village to deliver the scroll Lord Asten Dawphrey had given her in the busy streets of Maryere.

Jaslyn hadn't spoken to the young lord since he gave her the scroll, staying deep in the Row of Lords. *Asten even directed me to have Evergreen speak to his grandfather so we could communicate.* She frowned. *I miss talking to him.*

The constant snowfall lightened around Jaslyn, and she inhaled deeply. *I must continue and become the ruler the peasants beg for.* She turned to her handmaidens. "Violet, scout the area with Kai. Learn things."

"Got it," the young woman with bright green eyes saluted before dashing away with the young lion.

Jaslyn held in a sigh, already exhausted. "Alright, Evergreen, talk to the people."

"I don't want to leave your side," Evergreen mumbled, looking away.

She placed her hand on the girl's shoulder. "I will be with Ser Lyon."

"I don't know," Evergreen continued. "Please, let me stay by your side."

Jaslyn silently agreed, and the two walked to Friar's cottage, where Amyn and Sein played outside, creating snow figurines. "My queen, my queen!" the two children cheered as she approached, jumping into her arms for a hug.

"Where have you been?" Amyn questioned with big eyes. "We haven't seen you in almost two moons!"

Jaslyn pressed on a smile. "I've been unwell."

The two children stepped away. "Mama was right," Sein exhaled, looking at his sister. "You might be like that, too," he added and Amyn nodded. "You'll find them inside," he finally answered before grabbing his sister's hand and pulling her away.

When the children left, Evergreen frowned and crossed her arms.

"See, this is why I needed to stay with you. What do those kids mean, 'Mama was right'?"

She rolled her eyes. "Maybe they had asked her why I've been gone, and her answer was similar."

"Or maybe she's a Seer."

"Stop Ev, Seers don't predict the future. They see information and tell it to the Citadel."

Evergreen groaned as a breeze swirled between them. "Fine, let's get this over with before something happens."

Jaslyn nodded and gave a soft knock before Katia opened the door. "My queen, hello," the peasant woman greeted, stepping to the side so Jaslyn could enter. "How are you feeling?"

Jaslyn Wayward took slow steps as she entered the cottage, her attention never leaving the beautiful woman. *Katia's eyes.* Today, the woman's usual brown eyes were a light pink—an eye color Jaslyn had never seen before. Katia's face jumped at Jaslyn's unrelenting stares and she blinked a few times, her eye color returning to normal. Jaslyn outstretched her hand. "What was,"

"I bet you're cold. Would you like some warm brew?" Katia questioned, closing the door and shutting them off from the icy outside.

"No, why,"

"My queen, you're here," Ser Lyon interrupted, walking from another room with Friar at his heels. "I received your letter a few days ago and have been anxious for your arrival."

Jaslyn took a deep breath, no longer wanting to question Katia's eye color. *She obviously doesn't want me to question her about it.* "Well, I'm here."

"What did you want to show, Lyon?" Friar inquired, his voice laced with annoyance like always. "We don't have all day."

As Lyon recounted the contents of her letter, Jaslyn observed the three adult peasants before her, unable to shake off the feeling of uncertainty. *Can I trust any of them? Or are they all just taking advantage of me?*

Katia stepped forward and took Jaslyn's hand. "My queen, I can sense your unease. Your mind is filled with questions, and you seek answers. Am I right?" Jaslyn nodded, her lips pressed together. "I know this because I am an Oracle."

"Katia," Friar snapped, but his wife simply raised her hand to quiet him.

"The queen saw my eyes. There is no longer a need to hide."

"But still,"

"An Oracle can see into the future," Katia continued, ignoring her husband. "I foresaw a lion roaring for a new dawn, just as the Saavant told the peasants. After I saw you riding through the village with that lion clutched in your arms, I knew it was you. I feel it every time I see you. You are the queen the gods have blessed to bring a new age for the people. Do not be afraid of what the gods have given you. Accept it. Embrace it. Cherish it."

Jaslyn closed the distance between them and gave Katia a suspicious look. "Tell me, how will I die?"

Katia exhaled. "My queen, I cannot tell the future that way."

"Why not?"

The woman reared her head back. "I'm from a family of Oracles, and it is forbidden to look into a person's love, birth, and death when seeing the future. There are many tales of ancestors ignoring the rule, and the ending is always the same—they find death for themselves, regardless of what they are looking for. I'm sorry, my queen, but I will not look into your ending. I refuse to look even into my own. Just believe that you will live to be happy and old with a successful life to reflect on. Sometimes, the gods are kind enough to grant us that."

"Katia, that's enough," Friar insisted. "The queen doesn't care about all of that. Right, my queen?"

Jaslyn sighed and held out the scroll for Ser Lyon to take. *I care... a lot.* "Here, read this. We will need to make movements soon. My father plans to send me to the other side of Mystos."

"Is that the Citadel of the Owl?" Friar questioned, pointing to the brown owl imprinted in the wax, and Jaslyn nodded silently.

Ser Lyon Millister grabbed the scroll, broke open the seal, and quickly read through the instructions. "It seems the Citadel planned for the Lord Protector to send you away and want to reroute the destination to Fairpeak."

"Fairpeak, not Shadow's Peak?" Katia asked.

Jaslyn frowned. "Not Snow Creek?"

"Well, technically, you won't stay in one city. You will be going to several places throughout the next few years, but the story the Seers will tell is that you are a ward in Fairpeak. Your father shouldn't pursue further for a while. Jasper Payne is a trusted lord. "

"Where will I be going first?"

"It depends. It says if you leave for another kingdom as the Lord Protector wants, the Seers will declare that a travel party was attacked and you took refuge in Fairpeak, so you will go there first. It says if you decide to run away, ignoring your father's demands, then we will find more information inside a tavern in Eldenhold."

Jaslyn's eyes widened. *The Citadel planned for different possibilities but didn't account for my mother planning to send me to Griffon's Den. I won't be going toward Fairpeak if that is the situation. I'd be going towards;* she held in a gasp. *Eldenhold.* She stood straighter, understanding how far ahead the Citadel was thinking. *And they will claim it's for my sake.* Her eyebrows furrowed. *I need to know more about the Citadel.*

Katia stumbled backward, grabbing at her forehead. Her eyes fluttered open, exposing bright pink irises.

Does eye color indicate an Oracle, like how the Seers have black eyes? Jaslyn frowned. *But only Katia's irises changed. The white parts are black too for*

Seers. She shifted her weight forward. "Katia, are you,"

Friar stepped between the two, holding on tightly to his wife. "She's fine, just tired. Why don't you look through the village? It's grown again since the last time you visited."

Jaslyn nodded and turned to the door. *No point in arguing. There is too much happening right now. I will get my answers eventually.*

"I will make sure things are prepared based on your decision, my queen," Ser Lyon bowed as she stepped out of the cottage.

She studied the old knight, her eyes watering. *It's not my decision. None of this is. Everything is based on everyone else.* Jaslyn inhaled deeply. "Thank you for all your hard work, Ser Lyon." She then walked away, still holding back tears. *I get no real say.*

"What's wrong?" Evergreen asked, catching up to Jaslyn's quick pace.

"My empathy allowed me to fall right into their trap," she grumbled. "Now, the Citadel will decide everything for me until the day I die."

Evergreen smiled. "Not necessarily. Lord Jasper warned me about the Citadel. He said that in order to climb the political tower that the Establishments had constructed; then, you must lean upon one of the pillars. The Citadel is the best to seek assistance as they have some of the most potent influence globally, but are also the most dangerous. I remember my father always telling my older brother, Draigh, that all the Establishments were unsafe and couldn't be trusted. Keep your head down and pretend to be who they want you to be."

"But they are using me."

"Aye, so use them back."

The two approached Violet and Kai, standing beside a young woman cooking outside. *What are they doing?* She saw the two leaning over a large pot and stirring the bubbling liquids inside. *It smells like Maiden Barda's stews,* Jaslyn thought, already drooling. "What are you making?"

Both women straightened at Jaslyn's voice.

"My queen," the woman bowed rigidly, her dark green eyes on the snow beneath her feet. "I am making a chicken soup for my brother. He's very sick."

"I've never seen a chicken soup before," Violet butted in, sniffing the steam rising from the pot. "Syrah is always making foods I've never had."

"Of course, dummy, did you forget," Evergreen questioned, slapping her sister's shoulder. "Syrah is from the Northwoods."

"Most people here in Queen's Cove are refugees from the North-woods," Syrah explained as she stirred, her voice quiet. "There, the winter never ends. It's become too much."

"Like the White Abyss?" Jaslyn inquired, her interest piqued.

The young woman's eyes widened. "I don't know. I wouldn't dare travel there."

"Well, duh, but haven't you read about it?"

Syrah gave Jaslyn Wayward a questioning look. "Apologies, my queen,

I don't know how to read."

Jaslyn opened her mouth before closing it, trying to think of the right words. "No apologies needed, Syrah. That is my fault and my ignorance." She pressed on a smile. "I think I will continue walking while you guys finish up the,"

The sound of hooves beating against the ground caused Jaslyn to pause. She begrudgingly turned to the noises, seeing a knight riding toward her with the golden bear painted on his breastplate. Jaslyn stood straight, ready for any hostile engagements that were about to occur. "Lady Jaslyn," the knight called, and she held her breath, hoping that no one would correct him. "Lady Jaslyn," he repeated, gulping.

Something is wrong, Jaslyn realized, her body tense. *Something is terribly wrong.* She tried to steady her now quickening breaths, but the distressed knight in front of her only made her grow more fearful. A tear fell down the knight's cheek, and Jaslyn closed her eyes, trying her best not to panic. *Knights don't cry.*

"My lady, you must return to Winter's Keep."

"Why?"

"The Lord Protector has fallen ill. The Saavants are uncertain of his fate."

Suddenly, darkness surrounded Jaslyn Wayward. *No.*

Grief made her arms feel heavier than boulders hanging by her side, and her feet sunk into the muddy snow as she tried to process the knight's words. *My father.* Every memory she shared with Lord Borin flashed through her mind. The good, the bad, the ugly. All of it. *My father is sick.* Her eyes snapped to the boiling soup, and her cheeks tingled warmly, reminding Jaslyn of when her father had slapped her. *I said I would never forgive him, but now.* Her heart broke.

What do I do?

Kai answered the question for her by sliding in between her legs and lifting her to ride. He looked back at Jaslyn, and she frowned, understanding her rowdy lion. She then turned to her companions. "Stay here," she instructed as the knight rubbed his eyes harshly. "Syrah, when the soup finishes, could I give some to my father?"

The young peasant woman bowed. "Of course, my queen."

Jaslyn returned her attention to the knight, who stared back with a panicked face. *Syrah called me a queen,* she realized, holding in a sigh. *Now is not the time to act surprised by my title.* She wanted to tell the knight, but instead, she repositioned Kai and moved him forward. She lifted her head, hoping to look like the queen the peasants wanted her to be. *Wait, I'm not a queen. That is only a title the Citadel gave me. I'm a hero. Something is wrong with my father. So, I will be my father's hero, and save him.*

Nothing truly mattered to Jaslyn anymore, only her father.

VICTORIA

Victoria Osmont gripped the report furiously, her hands trembling from the rage building up inside. *Shadows have wrapped Alice Wayward; cursing her. She will not live pass her twenties.* The report stated, not getting into anymore detail.

No, no, no, no, no! Victoria pressed her eyes closed before opening them wide again to reread the findings; but the words did not change. *No, no, no!* She screamed, trying her best not to rip the report into pieces. *Does Falk know? No, he couldn't. If he did, he would've never proposed the betrothal.*

She took a deep breath as anxiety crept up her throat. She read the words again, and again, and again. Each time, she took slow and steady breaths. *Shadows have wrapped Alice Wayward; cursing her. She will not live pass her twenties.* Victoria quit her calming breaths and hyperventilated instead. *If Falk learns the truth about Alice, he would kill her without a second thought.*

She placed the report on her desk, and closed her eyes for a moment. Her fingers pressed deeply into the muscle of her thighs, relaxing her. *How did this happen?* Victoria replayed the memories she had with her niece, and her mind went to a fortnight ago. *It started when Rosert brought Alice to me,* she realized, fingering through her dark brown hair. *That's when I knew something was wrong.*

Rosert's bloodshot eyes matched the pinkness on his wet cheeks. *I don't know what to do, Mother,* her son had cried, holding tightly onto an unconscious Alice Wayward with dried blood smeared all over her face.

Enya can't examine the girl, she had thought. Victoria understood now how vile the woman she once trusted was. Instead, she had her son bring an old, grumpy Saavant named Selkie.

Victoria had the man examine Alice, and when Selkie told her that he had no idea what was wrong with the girl, Victoria forced him to do more research and figure out the issue. *You can even send a report to Lismure to get more information,* she had told the old Saavant.

But then, Alice was better.

The pretty, raven-haired girl continued her days in the Black Castle quietly and contently, as if the episode of excruciating pain never existed. And after a few days, Victoria forgot all about the incident. She forgot about the screaming, the crying, and the look on Alice's unconscious face.

Everyone was happy again.

The girls had their needlework circles in the morning after breaking their fast, and then Alice would spend her time with Doran and Rosert while Victoria and Lady Raya sat in the gardens and listened to the whispers. Everything was well once more, so well, that even Falk left them alone.

The biggest issue in the Black Castle was the disappearance of Alice's handmaiden, but to Victoria, it wasn't an issue at all. *I know who has the girl,* she thought, picturing the missing old Saavant that Lady Raya Vale couldn't find. *But no one needs to know that. I must fight Enya, and that means being patient and making no mistakes.* She frowned. *Although I don't know if Enya will have the patience to keep the handmaiden alive. If she wants the girl's blood, I must act fast.*

Victoria knew she had to prepare.

She grabbed the large, tattered black book that sat on a shelf above her desk, and opened it. *There must be something in here that can help me,* she thought, pressing the pages down. *I must do something.* A majority of the highborn in Mystos weren't Maras, and as Victoria read more about the mysterious Arts, her annoyance at the gods grew for omitting her from the wonderful phenomenon.

She focused on a page and calmed. *The Darkness is the most mysterious of the Four Beings and have four properties; death, fear, curses, and shadows. From there, countless forms can be mastered within the Darkness. Arcan Scholars note that the Darkness came from the dark god, Unmos.*

It is believed that a person can obtain the Darkness by killing an innocent using the Arts and consuming the innocent's blood. This is why the Darkness is banned in a majority of the terrafield. The continent of Eeccess holds the most power for the element, as there are several cases where people have completely mastered the Darkness without consuming any blood. In Eeccess, there are legends that tells of a way to obtain the Darkness by...

A knock pulled her attention away from the passage. Victoria lifted her head, looking strangely at the door. *Who is it?* It was still early in the morning, and her handmaidens never knocked, they just barged in and did their chores. She pressed on a smile, although no one was watching. "Please, come in," she said loudly and cheerfully.

After a moment, no one entered, and there were no other knocks.

Slowly, Lady Victoria moved to her feet and walked to the door. She swung it open, and poked her head from the room to find an empty hallway. *Who knocked?* she wondered, stepping out of her room.

On her first step, she kicked something; and her blood ran cold. *There isn't supposed to be anything at my door.* Her eyes drifted to the floor, and she stared at the object curiously—the darkness making it unrecognizable. She sluggishly bent towards the object to get a better look. *Has someone left me a present? Is it my birthday? What day is it? What moon is it?*

She had absolutely no idea.

Victoria's skin was cold and clammy now, and she felt like she was going to die. Her knees touched the stone floor as she placed her hands around the circular object, feeling hair. *No.* She touched a nose and lips and eyes. *A face; who? Enya? Falk? Rosert? Alice?*

Her hands trembled as she picked up the head and brought it into her room. She understood something now; people might perceive her as insane, but there were others who were much worse.

As she closed the door and locked it, she wondered who was behind this monstrosity. *Enya? Falk? Rosert? Alice?* Any person could be the victim, just as much the perpetrator. Victoria placed the head down and quickly moved to her balcony. She opened the doors and in the early morning sunlight, she recognized the face.

Edmund.

A laugh tumbled out of Victoria as if she was watching a fool dance and sing. Her vision focused on her blood-soaked hands as her cackles continued, and she touched her face. Ser Edmund Archard's blood smeared across her lips, and she licked it away. *This doesn't taste like my tea.*

The cool morning air touched her skin, bringing her back to reality. *No.* She picked up Ser Edmund's decapitated head from the table and stared into the knight's cold dead eyes. *This isn't real. It cannot be!* She lifted her arms before catapulting the head over the balcony. The object flew high into the air, before gradually descending towards the castle walls. "THIS CAN-NOT BE!"

A sickening splat caused screams to fill the air. *Who did this?* She brought her bloodied hands to her mouth again and dragged the blood across her lips. She did this repeatedly, her mind buzzing with questions until she finally realized who had murdered her ally.

Falk.

Victoria turned on her heels and marched out of her bedchamber, still covered in blood. She stomped through the hallways towards the dining hall. *That's where he will be.* It was where Falk spent most of his time. *He loves to cause hell for others anytime he's eating. It's his best tactic in controlling the conversation. And I must stop him.*

As she entered the more populated areas of the Black Castle, the eyes lingered. Most said nothing, while some gasped, and even a handmaiden screamed. But Victoria didn't care.

She approached the dining hall, and the eyes stayed on her. She shook her head, clearing her mind. *I must settle the score with Falk.* Victoria pushed open the doors, and stomped into the dining hall. Her lord husband sat the table, casually eating his meal. *Something feels off.* But she couldn't tell what it was. *Does Falk have something else planned? Is this a trap?*

She calmed her breathing. "I hated my present, thank you."

Lord Falk Osmont put down his utensils and lifted his head. He studied his crazed wife for a moment, before chuckling. "What present?"

"Why did you do it?"

"Do what?"

Victoria paused. *He's going to make me say it.* "You murdered Ser Edmund Archard and left his head at my bedchamber door."

An evil smile spread across Falk's lips, frightening her. "I don't look like someone who just murdered someone. You, however," he moved his hand up and down. "Are you sure *you* were not the one who killed poor Ser Edmund?"

Victoria brought her fingers to her lips again. Her eyes grew wide as she thought about her lord husband's question, and in a moment of panic, she tasted the knight's blood once more.

"You are truly insane," Falk Osmont added, disgusted.

Victoria, however, was no longer there. She no longer stood in the dining hall before her lord husband, covered in blood. She was nowhere, but in the blackness of her mind. *Are you sure* you *were not the one who killed Ser Edmund?* Victoria stood in the darkness, thinking. *I did not kill him, right? I found him like that, right? I did nothing wrong, right?*

The clacking of metal boots brought Victoria back into the dining hall, reminding her of what she was doing, and why she was here. *I didn't kill him,* she decided confidently.

"My lord, a head was found smashed into the ground, apparently thrown. It looks to be Ser Edmund Archard," the knight informed. Victoria gulped as she watched her husband's lips curl into a knowing smile. "My lady," the knight said, his voice shaking a bit, "you are covered in blood, are you alright?"

Slowly, Victoria turned to look at the knight. *Do I dare?* She exhaled heavily, closing her eyes as all the air escaped from her lungs. She then inhaled sharply through her nose, preparing herself.

Preparing to tell the knight the truth.

"Ser," Falk called instead. "Get the other lord knights, immediately."

Victoria whipped around to see Falk smiling wider, seeming more confident. Beads of cold sweat gathered at her hairline and her body felt numb. And yet, a part of her wanted to laugh wildly like she did when she realized the decapitated head was Ser Edmund. *Falk did this. He is the reason I'm in this situation.*

The knight studied Victoria before nodding and exiting the dining hall. When the insignificant knight left, Victoria giggled. *He is going to pin the murder on me. He won.*

"What are you laughing at?"

Victoria straightened and wiped her face, smearing more blood. "How strange," she tried to say with a straight face, but instead, she laughed loudly. "I'm here in a manic mess, yet, the blame is seemingly placed on me. How long have you been planning this?"

"Shut up," Falk growled.

Victoria fell to her knees, still laughing. The laughs were so hard and loud that her ears rang, and her throat became dry.

She wanted to stop.

Her chest, stomach, and cheeks ached, but she couldn't stop. Her laughter continued as she covered her ears with her hands, and laid on the cold, hard floor. Tears streamed from her eyes, and she was not sure if it was from the laughter or pain.

Large hands pulled her hands away from her ears. She fought back in protest, and her laughter morphed into screams. *No! I didn't kill him! I would never kill a friend!* She wanted to yell, but she couldn't. Her words failed her. The only noise she could make now was screams. Her screams turned to wails as she fought back from the large hands. *I didn't kill him!* She knew that was why the hands were grabbing her. They were trying to punish her for a crime she did not commit. *No, no, no!*

"Shut up! Shut up! Please, all the gods, shut this woman up!" Falk's voice echoed around her.

Then, she was silent.

He prayed to the gods, she realized, trembling, as her lord husband pried her hands from her ears. *He never does that.* Her attention then focused on the reflection that shined from the polished floor. *He did this to me.* Blood and salty tears now covered her face, while wild strands of hair went every which way. Even her disheveled dress matched her thoughts. *I cannot let him win.*

And a chuckle thundered in her chest.

In one swift movement, Falk gripped both of her wrists, and pinned her onto her back. He climbed on top and the tip of his nose touched hers as their heavy breathing synchronized. *Why is he holding me down? What does he want from me? Hasn't he gotten enough?*

"This is what you deserve, you bitch!" Falk roared, making gooseprickles appear on her skin. "I know what you did while I was away. You think you're so clever. You think you're Gloriana; don't you? Well, you're not!" Tears filled Falk's dead-looking eyes, startling Victoria. "Those children, those poor children, *my* children."

That was when Victoria knew why all of this was happening. *I sent Falk's bastards into slavery, and Ser Edmund helped me do it. This is our punishment.* She looked deeply into his eyes, and he stared back, both crying silently. "I'm sorry, I was upset."

Falk's face twisted into several different emotions before he smiled wickedly. "Just kidding. I could care less about those children, they aren't mine."

What the hell does that mean?

The door behind them opened, and the clacking of metal against the floor multiplied. *Knights.* Victoria tried to see how many entered, but Falk jerked her back with horrible force. She opened her mouth to scream, but she couldn't.

Falk lifted himself off her, and stood along with the group of knights. "Take her away," he commanded, no longer looking at her. "Lock her in the Tower."

Victoria hyperventilated as cold metal hands grabbed her to drag her away. "Not the Tower!" she howled, startling several knights. *Why would he put me in the Tower? No one has entered the Tower in years. Falk doesn't even like acknowledging it! This doesn't make sense. What is going on?* "Please, put me in the Black Cells instead! Anywhere but the Tower!"

The Lord Protector smiled. "Hm, the Black Cells."

"On what basis should Lady Victoria be arrested?" an older knight questioned.

"She murdered Ser Edmund," Falk alleged.

The older knight, however, did not seem convinced. "Where is the evidence?"

Falk gave a single laugh. "Look at her! She is covered in his blood!"

The knight nodded, accepting that Victoria was in fact covered in *someone's* blood. "By law, we must do an investigation. We should lock her in her bedchamber instead."

Victoria held her breath. *Will this knight save me?*

Falk smacked his teeth, understanding that his plan had flaws. Victoria looked like a woman in distress, not like someone who just committed murder. "Fine, do an investigation."

"Thank you, my lord," the old knight replied, bowing, and turning away.

A twinkle in Falk's eyes told Victoria that he wasn't done yet. "Aye, but there are important guests who live in the Black Castle now. If she is the murderer, we cannot have her going on a killing spree. She must be locked away in the Tower."

Her heart sank as the knight nodded, agreeing with Falk. Without another word, she was sliding across the dining hall floor. "No!" she screamed. "No, no! I didn't kill anyone! I'm not a murderer!" She kicked and thrashed, but the knights continued to pull her away. *It's over. There is nothing I can do now. I'm being taken to the Tower, the place that makes people go insane.* She wanted to laugh. *As if I'm not insane already.*

Victoria Osmont looked over to her lord husband one last time. *To say goodbye.* Yet, when her vision focused, she saw Enya's face plastered on Falk's body. The Saavant stared back, waving, her wrinkling face contrasting considerably with the Lord Protector's younger hand. *What happened to Falk?*

The old woman gave Victoria a nightmarish grin that would haunt her for the rest of her life. "Gotcha."

Then, everything was black.

JASLYN

Jaslyn's heartbeat thumped in her ears with each long stride, and her ragged breaths intensified as she climbed the staircase steps two at a time. Every inch of her body buzzed with nervousness, and tears burned her eyes as she grabbed the door handle. *Father cannot be sick. He must be okay.*

"Father!" she shouted breathlessly. Kai padded past her and made his way to the roaring fire from the hearth. The white lion circled a few times before laying on the floor to nap, unfazed by the situation.

Lord Borin Wayward turned at the commotion, and Jaslyn sighed with relief. *He's alive.* She relaxed a bit, examining his peppery colored hair and beard, and the pinkness of his lips. *He looks fine. How could he be dying?*

"Daughter," he whispered, and then she saw it. The dullness in his usually sparkling copper eyes, the way he struggled to breathe, the purple blackness underneath his skin—all of it. *He's dying.*

"Father, what happened? You were fine a few days ago." She paused, and the muscles and her mouth quivered.

"I'm slowly dying," he informed, "the way *she* wanted."

"She? Who is she?" Jaslyn loved her lord father with every inch of her being because he allowed her to be herself. They had their differences, but she loved him. She would save him regardless the cost; even if it meant her life. *I will be my father's hero.*

"Your mother," the Lord Protector of the Mountain Realm responded coldly.

Jaslyn's eyes widened. "Mother!?"

"She's the reason I'm like this." He coughed violently, and blood spittle stained the inside of his lips.

Jaslyn stayed quiet, her mind racing. *What can I do?* She exhaled heavily through her nose. *Coughing up blood is a sign of death,* she remembered, staring at the floor. *Blood in the lungs means the person is drowning in their own fluids.*

Borin grabbed her hand, the gesture calming her. "There is nothing you can do about this. My death is imminent, and your mother will become the Lord Protector of the Mountain Realm. Just like she wanted."

"No," Jaslyn whispered, gently pulling away. "Jojo will."

"Your mother will claim he is too young and that she should have the title until he comes of age."

"But," Jaslyn began, her eyes shifting to the ceiling. *Josef could die before then.* Her lord father was dying, and soon, it could be Josef. "Are you saying that the exchange in power won't happen?" she asked, looking into her father's sad, dull eyes. "Jojo will never come to age?"

Borin sighed. "I cannot say for sure, but I am frightened about the safety of my children."

Jaslyn shook her head, refusing to believe it. "Mother would never harm us! We're her children; the most important beings in this world to her. She told me that... one time."

"Something has changed. An evil presence surrounds her now. She's not the woman I once loved."

Tears streamed down Jaslyn's face. She couldn't take this anymore. She couldn't grasp at what was happening. *Mother poisoned Father, and wants to take the title of Lord Protector to keep for herself?* "What are we to do?"

Borin patted her hands. "Allow me to tell you three things. Then you can ask me one question. Finally, I have a task you must complete."

She nodded vigorously, wiping away tears. "Yes, Father, of course. Anything."

Anything.

He pressed his lips together. "First, keep Kai close. He is your shield. If he is not at your side, you will fall." Jaslyn nodded, already knowing how important Kai was to her and the people. *Maiden Barda said so many moons ago.* "Second, I need you to continue being the queen that you are."

Jaslyn relaxed at his words and gave him a smile that she did not know she had anymore. She thought she had lost her best and brightest smiles to the awfulness of the world. "Of course, Father. I never planned on stopping."

He smiled back, his just as sweet. "Aye, I know." He chuckled, although his laughed seemed more sad than cheery. "Third, it is okay to make mistakes, but always learn from them and don't make the same mistake twice. I made the same mistakes countless times, but you're a young woman, and many will try to take advantage of you. Don't let them. Take what is yours. But to do that, you must grow from your failures."

She blinked at her father. "What *is* mine?"

"Everything."

Jaslyn's eyebrows furrowed in confusion, but she nodded anyway, not wanting to ask too many questions. "Is it my turn now?"

Borin nodded, and she shifted, having no idea what she wanted to ask. Her father was dying. Soon, he would be gone forever, and all the questions would go unanswered. She tried her best to suppress her nerves, but her heart jumped in her throat. *A question.* She attempted to think of a question, any question, but none came to mind.

Jaslyn only pictured her mother.

Her beautiful mother who owned the sun, whose laughter sounded like songbirds, and her scolding only frightened stray cats. Jaslyn loved her mother even if they didn't have the strongest relationship. She loved her grace, her kindness, and her acceptance—her mother was someone Jaslyn had always wanted to be.

Not anymore.

Jaslyn wanted to forget, but her mother's image kept rushing back, bigger and more vibrant. Her long sleek hair, shining like strange brown diamonds; her dark blue eyes; her rosy, blushing cheeks; her height; her curves; her smile. Jaslyn saw it all.

Finally, she knew her question. "How do you know Mother did this?"

Lord Borin Wayward wheezed as he sat up. "Lady Joan Myster."

Jaslyn frowned. "What about her?"

"That woman believed I wasn't good enough to rule the Mountian Realm and is taking me out using your stupid, vindictive mother who thinks I have a whore."

Her face twisted at the response. "Do you?"

Borin shook his head. "Drowning myself in alcohol was enough. I didn't need to indulge myself further."

"Wait, so you were never violent?"

"I was, although I've recently tried to change," he clarified somberly. "Gloriana was always my target."

"You hit Mother?"

The Lord Protector nodded. "The first time I struck Gloriana my mother, Fallen, encouraged it. As you know, your mother is mouthy, and it infuriated my mother and me. My mother's solution was putting Gloriana in her place with a hit here and there, like a dog. It was the only way I could control her. I couldn't control anything in my life, but I could control your mother with a slap. I was a selfish husband, and I am ashamed of that. My mother told me that Gloriana would be my downfall, but no, this is my fault," he sighed, defeated. "I was a terrible lord, husband, and father."

"No, you weren't," Jaslyn defended, clutching onto Borin. *Lady Fallen controlled Father, even beyond the grave.*

Borin sat up again. "I sent Alice to hell when she could barely walk down the stairs," he replied, sliding back down. "There is nothing I've done that's justifiable."

She released her father and studied him, hyperventilating. *He's blaming himself... and it is his fault.... but he doesn't deserve this.* "I want to give you mercy." *I want to be your hero.*

Borin's face brightened. "You will be a great queen," he complimented. "The task that I ask of you, will bring me mercy."

Jaslyn Wayward held her breath. *His task shouldn't be difficult. Even if he tasked me with killing Mother, I would do it, just in my own time and in my own way. He deserves that.*

"I want you to kill me."

"What!?" she blurted.

"I want you to kill me," her father repeated.

Jaslyn's mouth twitched as she tried to process her father's task. "I cannot," she replied, before breaking into a sob.

"You can and will," Borin commanded. "I'll never get better. Your mother wants me to have an agonizing and long death, but I want a quick one. Don't let her get her way."

I can't. She scanned her father's pale skin, his blood-stained lips, the dimness in his eyes, and how uncomfortable he looked laying in bed. *He will never get up from that bed; and he is never going to get better.*

But Borin Wayward was her father.

He was the man she tried her best to imitate. If he hunted great game, she tried to hunt better. If he got a new horse, she begged for a new one, too. Even when he created a figurine from wood, she tried to replicate it. He was an older brother to her just as much as he was her father. She wanted to be him, she wanted to be better than him, and she did not want him to die. *Is this what it means to obtain power; killing the people, you love? Did my parents ever genuinely love each other?*

She wiped away her tears before nodding. *It doesn't matter. I love my father and this is what he wants.*

Her father smiled widely at her gesture. "Suffocate me."

Jaslyn lowered her head and kept her eyes on her muddy boots. *I don't want to.* She leaned over to grab the pillow her father's head rested on. *I don't want to.* She couldn't remember the last time she prayed to the gods, but in that moment, with the pillow clutched in her hands, she prayed. She prayed for forgiveness, for salvation, and for their wrath to not be severe.

"I love you," Borin said softly, pulling Jaslyn from her prayers. "I love you more than this world, my daughter. I should've listened to your mother long ago. You were the one born to rule. Go and do it. Prove everyone wrong."

His words were so kind, it only made Jaslyn cry harder. She felt the long sobs in her throat, preparing to mourn her beloved father. "I love you too," she whispered, bending over him.

"Promise me, you will save Alice and bring this family together. We are Waywards. We are stronger together," he added, and Jaslyn nodded. "Now, sweet girl, take me to the hell the gods have prepared for old men like me."

Borin kept his smile as she pressed the pillow down over his face. Her sobs grew louder, and his body trembled underneath. She turned her head away from the scene, and Kai stared back with curious red eyes. Her father's body shook violently as Jaslyn pressed the pillow harder onto his face. He did not fight back, he just laid there, accepting death.

When her father's body quit moving, Jaslyn lessened her grip and allowed her sobs to finally grow loud. As she wept, she continued to hold the pillow over her father's face. She refused to see him. She did not want to know what her father's face looked like in death. She only wanted to remember his jolly round face. His body did not move, his chest did not rise and fall. He was motionless.

I killed him.

The bedchamber door opened, and Jaslyn turned to see an old man that she didn't know dressed in a tattered robe. "What're you doing?" the man questioned, his voice rough and strained.

Jaslyn stood straight, releasing her grip on the pillow. She wiped her tears and sniffled, trying her best to calm down. "Nothing," was the only answer that came to her mind.

"You were suffocating the Lord Protector!" the old man claimed, pointing his finger at the dead body lying in the bed.

"No, I wasn't," Jaslyn replied groggily, lifting her hands up to show she meant no harm.

"I saw you!" he shouted. "I saw you murder the Lord Protector!"

Finally, Jaslyn Wayward snapped to her senses. "You saw nothing."

"Guards!" the old man cried out. "Guards!"

Then, everything moved in slow motion. Behind the old man's cries, the clacking of metal boots hitting the stone floor grew louder. She gasped for air as she looked around the room, trying to figure out what to do. *Keep Kai close. Continue being queen. Learn from your mistakes. Take what is yours,* her father's voice reminded her.

"KAI!" Jaslyn screamed before mounting the lion.

At the bedchamber entrance, a sea of knights stood with their swords already out. "That girl!" the old man shouted. "She killed the Lord Protector!"

"Lady Jaslyn did?" A knight asked, confused.

The man groaned. "I saw her! She murdered the Lord Protector!"

"Are you sure?" another questioned.

"Yes! I'm sure! I'm sure!"

Jaslyn's mouth dropped open as she realized what the old man was doing. *He wants me to pay for Father's death.*

She gripped Kai's mane, ready for him to run. She refused to be arrested for mercifully killing Lord Borin. *What I did was a sin, but it was a sin that Father wanted.* And even now, she would do anything for him. *Keep Kai close. Continue being queen. Learn from your mistakes. Take what is yours.*

"Let's take her in for questioning," the first knight concluded, and for a moment, not a single knight moved.

"You heard your leader!" the old man squealed. The knights looked amongst each other, their faces showing uneasiness and despair. "Capture her now!" the man shouted, and the room shook, as the knights' faces morphed to harden ones.

Jaslyn took a deep breath and clicked her teeth. Kai responded by bolting across the room and crashing through the window. The lion landed on a roof with a thud and Jaslyn bit her tongue. Kai stopped moving, and Jaslyn looked back. The old man and the knights stood at the broken window in shock. She clicked her teeth again, and Kai took off towards the gates.

From behind, she heard commands to capture her. "Queen's Cove, Kai," she told the lion, and he picked up the pace. She held on tightly as Kai leaped from a high roof to a lower one, picking up speed with each jump. Jaslyn shut her eyes as the wind burned her cheeks and nose. She felt weightless and realized that she and Kai were airborne.

After several breathless seconds, Kai landed on the ground with another thud, and once again, Jaslyn bit her tongue. All around her, she heard the clanging of metal, boisterous commands, and common folk screaming as Kai ran past. She moved closer into Kai's fur until every part of her body touched him.

"Archers!" someone shouted, and Jaslyn gasped, her eyes snapping open.

Kai had completed his task. They were outside the walls of Maryere and headed towards Queen's Cove. Jaslyn scanned the top of the high walls and noticed tiny metal men standing with their bows. *They mean to shoot us down*, she realized, and turned to lay on Kai's back. *They mean to kill us— to kill me.* Her heart pounded, and her rapid breathing made her chest burn.

"Nock!"

"Kai, run faster! Get out of range!" She screamed desperately, but Kai was at his limit.

"Loose!"

Then she heard it. The agonizing screams of the arrows whizzing through the icy air. She shifted Kai to move in a zigzag position as every arrow missed its mark. One arrow hit the ground on the right of Kai, another shot past. The rest of the arrows hit the ground near Kai's feet, but he continued forward.

"Nock!"

Jaslyn turned to see Maryere becoming smaller and smaller as Kai finally made his way into the lumberyard. She never heard the command; only the arrows screaming once again before striking and splitting on the tree trunks that surrounded her. Jaslyn lowered her head so that no arrow could hit her. *We should be out of range*, she calculated as Kai continued zigzagging through the lumberyard.

Finally, they were in the open air.

With urgency in every step, Kai raced straight to Queen's Cove. As they arrived, Jaslyn slipped off and rushed to the heart of the village. "Help me!" She screamed, waving her arms. "They're after me. Help!"

A small crowd gathered, and Ser Lyon Millister approached hurriedly. "What's happening, my queen? You look pale."

Sweat dotted Jaslyn's forehead. "They're after me! We must leave. Go get your preparations and meet me at the gate!"

The knight nodded and ran in a different direction.

"Who's after you, and where are you going, my queen?" Amyn asked innocently, twirling on her toes, unaware of the looming danger.

Jaslyn knelt and placed a hand on the girl's shoulder. "I'm going to have to disappear for a while," she told the girl. "Go back to your house with your family and hide. The Lord Protector's knights are coming."

Amyn's eyes widened, and she stumbled backward. "Mama said those clad in metal would rain down on us. She meant the knights." Amyn cupped her cheeks and screamed. "THE KNIGHTS ARE COMING!!"

Every peasant in the area stopped what they were doing and started rushing every which way in panic. "They're coming! It's the end! We're going to die!" the peasants cried out, scrambling around Jaslyn.

She looked around, not understanding. *The knights are coming for me, not them.*

"Jaslyn," Violet called, grabbing her hand and pulling her along. "The peasants are going crazy, screaming that the knights are after them. What happened?"

"They're after me," she clarified. "Not them. They need to calm down."

"I don't understand. Why are the knights chasing you?"

She frowned, looking away. "Someone saw me smothering my father."

"Holy shit!" Violet cursed, quickening her pace. "They're going to level this village to the ground in revenge!"

A fire started, quickly spreading throughout the village. *Just as Friar warned.* The girls reached the gate, where a mob gathered at a watchtower.

"Everyone, calm down," Katia told the crowd, her tone motherly. "We might be able to survive this. Go to your houses, gather your valuables, and hide them," she instructed, her face determined. "Gather snow and place them on the fires."

Jaslyn looked at her muddy shoes. *The peasants look to Katia for guidance, not me. I'm the reason for this madness.* Evergreen, Syrah, and a young boy approached, each looking terrified. "Is that your brother?" she asked, and Syrah nodded. "Stay close."

"Giving the knights something to quell their anger will be key," Katia continued. "We will do this by presenting our harvest to them."

The crowd erupted, and Jaslyn looked around. *Where is Ser Lyon? We must leave now.*

"People, please, we must stay calm," Katia begged, but no one listened. Instead, a stampede formed.

A hand touched Jaslyn's shoulder, and she turned to see the old Ser Lyon looking down at her. "I have everything. Let's go."

She shifted her attention to the young peasant girl that stood beside her. "I must go. Go find safety in your home. Things should relax soon."

Tears filled Syrah's eyes as the fire spread to the watchtower. "Please be safe, my queen."

"Of course. Where's your brother? I wish to say goodbye to him, too."

Syrah looked around desperately. "Calas," she called. "Calas, where are you?" Her panicked brown eyes landed on Evergreen. "Did you see where Calas went?"

"There he is," Violet pointed toward the blazing tower.

Syrah turned away as the sound of buckling wood echoed around them. *Something's breaking.* Jaslyn grabbed the young peasant woman's wrist and brought her close. "Stop, let go of me, please!"

Fragile wood crackled, and the tower fell, crushing a piece of the crowd. More screams instantly filled the already chaotic air as another stampede began. *Katia was over there, too.*

"NO!" Syrah wailed agonizingly, falling to her knees. "CALAS!"

"My queen, this is terrible," Ser Lyon informed, shaking his head as he took in the destruction.

She frowned. "Is there anything I can do?"

"Maybe in a few years, but not right now. Right now, we must get out of here before the knights arrive," Lyon answered.

In a few years, Jaslyn repeated. *By then, the peasants won't care and will resent me.*

"Syrah, you come too," the knight added.

"I need to find Calas," she cried.

Ser Lyon's eyes stared at the raging fire. "If your brother survived, someone will care for him. We will be back soon. Leaving is for your protection just as much as the queen's."

Evergreen and Violet helped Syrah to her feet, and the five of them rushed to the horses Ser Lyon Millister had gathered.

Jaslyn got on Kai and returned her attention to the chaos continuing behind her. She could see random body parts in the debris as some of the peasants desperately tried to save the victims. Jaslyn's eyes stayed on the destruction, traumatized. *Did I cause this? Is this all my fault?* She pictured her father's convulsing body in the flames, and tears streamed down her cheeks. *Was I ever the hero?*

"The knights are here! This is the end!" someone screamed, and more people screamed with them.

Evergreen approached, her face sad, yet serious. "Are you okay?"

Jaslyn Wayward burst into tears, and she wanted to do nothing but hug her dead father. "Am I a villain?"

ALICE

Alice Wayward paced back and forth in her bedroom, her eyebrows furrowed. *What can I do?* It was a question she asked herself almost daily, yet she never knew the answer. The best she could do was absolutely nothing at all. She interlaced her fingers, her mind returning to her time with Myra in the wheelhouse. *I wish I could go back.*

"You've been pacing for twenty minutes straight," Doran said, sitting on the other side of the room, grabbing Alice's attention. "Why don't you sit?"

"What if Myra is being forced to stand?"

The boy sighed. "We don't know that."

Her pace quickened, matching the speed of her thoughts. *Who would kidnap a handmaiden?* She could only agree with Rosert's conclusion—someone did it to hurt Alice. *And I will hurt them back.*

"You look cute when you're mad," Doran flirted.

Her face heated at the compliment. Her betrothed had been nothing but pleasant as of late. And she didn't know how to handle it. *I sort of wish he ignored me like when I arrived.* At least then, Doran wouldn't waste his time staring at a girl worried about her best friend.

She stuck her tongue out in response. "Stop it, I'm trying to," a soft knock caused Alice to pause. The pair stared at the door curiously. "Maybe it's Rosert."

After a moment of silence, Doran shook his head. "My brother has no manners. He would have busted in by now."

Alice chuckled, knowing her betrothed was right. She walked to the door and opened it only to find no one there. Darkness filled the hallway, creating a strange shiver to crawl up her spine. Gooseprickles covered her arms in response, and she closed her eyes momentarily. *Why am I afraid?*

"What is it?" Doran questioned from behind.

She exhaled and opened her eyes, yet the hallway's spookiness did not disappear. For a moment, she thought she would just shrug off the fear building inside her and return to her room, but she felt something.

Death was right underneath her.

Frozen in place, Alice Wayward glanced to the floor, and in that one second, when she looked death in the face, she could do nothing but scream. "NO!" She shrieked, falling and scuffing her knees. Her voice echoed through the hall as she slowly picked up her best friend's head. Her face morphed into an uncomfortable frown as she cradled the head in her arms. "NO! NO! NO!" she screamed, the echoes growing louder with each no. "MYRA!"

"Alice, what," Doran paused, taking in the bloody sight.

She turned to the boy with Myra in her hands, sobbing. "Who would do something like this?"

Doran responded by racing to a wastebasket and vomiting his breakfast. Tears streamed down his cheeks when he returned, and he wiped his nose. "I don't know. I'm going to go get Rosert," he replied, rushing out of the room before Alice could respond.

Alice watched as the boy raced down the hallway, feeling helpless. *Someone did this to hurt me.* She held Myra's head tightly against her chest until every part of her body ached. *Someone murdered Myra to bring me pain.* Only one man would do anything to hurt Alice Wayward. *Falk.* The click-clacking of metal shoes approached, but she did not care. *Falk killed Myra.*

"Alice!" Lady Raya yelled out breathlessly, with a group of knights behind her.

She sat up to expose Myra's head in her arms and heard immediate gasps as a few of the knight's faces scrunched in disgust.

"Falk killed her," Alice whispered, crouching over again, hugging tightly onto Myra. "He killed her!"

"Are you certain?" Raya asked, and Alice nodded, sniffling. "I will go and speak with Rosert," she added before pulling away.

"Doran is already going to Rosert," Alice informed, rising to her feet, still cradling Myra's head. Please go tell my aunt Victoria."

The metal-armored knights shifted uncomfortably at the command, but Alice didn't care what they had to say. She only wanted to confront the Lord Protector of the Northern Kingdom of Valley Pines. "I'm going to him," she exhaled, starting her journey. "He must see."

"Alice,"

"HE MUST SEE!"

Another knight stepped in front of her. "It wouldn't be right for the servants to see a highborn lady with a decapitated head in her arms. If the Lord Protector has committed this crime, he's already seen it."

Raya placed her large hand on Alice's shoulder. "Ser Mace is right. Let's take the head, get you a bath running, and then you can speak with Falk."

Alice gave the lady knight a cold look. "I'll give you Myra's head, but I'm going to him now. I don't want to give him more time to convince others he didn't do it."

The knights reluctantly agreed, and Alice stepped forward. *My best friend, my love.* Myra's smiling eyes twinkled in Alice's mind, and her imaginary giggles echoed through the dark hallway. *Falk butchered her like a hog, and for what reason?*

She needed to know the answer—now.

Alice started her march, startling the knights. From behind, Lady Raya gave the men directions, and metal clanking approached after a few moments. Alice couldn't care less who was escorting her. She only wanted one thing.

Lord Falk Osmont sat in the dining hall every morning, sometimes even into the late afternoon, slowly breaking his fast. Alice knew he was there, waiting for her. She knew he wanted her to act hysterical, like the child she once was, sobbing over her dead friend. *I am not a child anymore*, she thought, clenching her fists. *So many things took my childhood away from me.* No one could genuinely bring her innocence back; she was a woman now, and the world didn't allow women to have any innocence.

In the more populated areas of the Black Castle, the servants stopped and stared. It was as if they had seen the strange sight before, causing Alice to shiver, and her eyes grew hot again. *I should cry and make them feel my misery. I want everyone in this castle to feel sorry for the young, highborn girl in a foreign land.* She allowed the tears to flow and kept her head down. Several faces morphed into grief, and Alice internally smiled.

She wanted a revolt. She wanted Falk to pay.

"My lady, are you alright?"

Alice turned to Ser Mace and showed him the miserable face she had perfected. The knight puffed out his cheeks in reply and stayed quiet.

In the dining hall, Falk slowly ate his food. He turned to the opening door and smiled. "Alice!" he cheered, undisturbed by how she looked.

Alice's attention narrowed to her lord uncle, whose clothes were slightly stained with blood. "Falk," she started, ignoring all courtesies. "How dare you,"

"Alice, come eat, come eat!" the Lord Protector interrupted, ignoring her anger.

"W-why did you do it?"

A crazed smile spread across her uncle's lips. "I don't know what you're talking about."

"Myra, you murdered Myra!"

"Myra, Myra," Lord Falk said, stroking his chin, trying to put a face to the name. "I have no idea who you are talking about. Do I look like I've murdered someone?"

"My lord, there was a decapitated head found at Lady Alice's door," Ser Mace informed.

Falk's green eyes flickered to the knight. "I don't believe I was talking to you."

Alice Wayward stepped forward, no longer able to keep calm. *I have played his stupid games for far too long. I don't care if he kills me, too. I must get the truth.* "Stop it! Confess to killing Myra, now!"

"Everyone get out," Falk commanded, but no one moved. "Am I being ignored? Is treason being committed?"

The servants moved around chaotically before flowing out of the dining hall. Ser Mace lightly touched Alice's shoulder, and she felt him move away. *I don't want to be alone with him,* she wanted to tell the knight. *Please, don't leave me.*

When the door clicked shut, another smile appeared on Falk's face, and his body relaxed. "She was supposed to die moons ago, but I was convinced otherwise, so I planned to silence her. I was going to leave the Summeran girl alone, but then she woke up, and I couldn't have that. Yet, again, I was convinced not to kill the girl. That was when your little handmaiden started talking again."

She was supposed to die moons ago. The words struck Alice's heart, and she stepped back. *Does he mean when Myra was attacked? Who convinced him to keep her alive?* "Why?"

The Lord Protector's smile disappeared. "I need you to complete a task for me, and if you refuse, I will kill Rosert."

"You're a piece of shit," she gasped, hugging herself.

He laughed at that. "Aye, I am, but for a good reason."

Why must I be a part of this? Why can't he leave me alone? "What do you need me to do?"

Falk laughed again. "Imagine? Using my wild son as a tool to get what I want." A glint in the hilt of a blade made Alice step farther away from Falk. "Come here," he commanded, but Alice continued to back away. "I said to come here," he repeated, his voice harsh.

Alice's entire body shook as she stepped toward the man she hated. "Please," she cried, "don't make me do this."

"You must," he told her, his voice soft as if he cared about her well-being. "For Rosert's sake."

She brought her hands to her mouth. "Please, I am not a killer."

"No, but soon, you will be."

Alice broke into a sob, grabbing the dagger. *What did I do to deserve this?* She believed she had been good and kind, just like Myra. Alice studied her reflection on the metal blade. "Who?"

Falk smiled, showing his straight white teeth. "I need you to stab Victoria in the heart."

"That makes no sense," she replied frantically.

"It doesn't matter if it makes sense. You just need to do it. For Rosert's sake."

Alice gulped. *How could a Father be so cruel?* "Alright, I will do it."

Falk beamed at her response. "Good girl," he said as if she was a dog. "Alright, now, let's set some conditions. One, Victoria is suspected of killing one of my lord knights," he informed, scoffing. "So she's already being held in the Tower, and I don't feel like doing an investigation. Second, you have a fortnight to kill her. Lastly, if you try to stop me, I will make you wish you were never born." The fight in Alice's body escaped her, and she fell to her knees. "Get up, get up! Don't be so dramatic. You can do all that later." Falk shifted to his feet, and Alice scooted back, causing the Lord Protector to smack his teeth. "Remember, all you have to do is kill your aunt, and I will leave you alone."

He then left the dining hall as Alice continued to process the conversation. She studied the dagger before slipping it into a pocket in her gown's folds. *I must kill Victoria in the next fourteen days. If I don't, then Rosert is dead.* Alice had already lost Myra and Ser Damien. She wasn't going to lose another person close to her.

She gathered the strength to leave the room as a thousand scenarios played out in her head. *Is there any way I can stop him? He said if I try to, he will kill me, but at this point, I don't care. No one else will get hurt because of me.*

She approached her bedchamber and entered to see Rosert sitting on her bed, looking paler than she had ever seen him. "Alice!" he sighed, running up to her. He hugged her, but Alice felt strange touching him. She felt empty. "What happened? Doran was speaking nonsense, but I understood something had happened to you."

"Where is Doran?" she questioned, her voice pained.

Rosert pulled away, and Alice saw the jealousy in the teenage boy's face. "I had some maids take him to his room so he could rest," he grumbled before truly taking in Alice's appearance. After a moment, his face downturned. "Why is there blood on your clothing?"

She looked down to examine the mess, but tears immediately blurred her vision. "Myra was beheaded," she answered in a sob, falling to the floor, and Rosert embraced her again. "He murdered her and threatened to murder you if I don't kill aunt Victoria."

"Wait, kill my mother!? Who?"

"Falk," she cried loudly, finally releasing the pain she felt losing her best friend. Memories she shared with Myra flooded her mind, and she bent over, unable to take it. "Falk took her away from me!" Alice could still feel Myra's warmth, hear her soothing voice, and smell the lavender the girl enjoyed to bathe in. *She can't be gone.* Alice refused to believe it.

"My father has gone mad. We must do as he says, but we can't be here anymore," Rosert told her, his voice melancholy. "We must leave."

She lifted her head, her emotions stirring. "When?"

"The night you take my mother's life."

Alice Wayward shivered at the darkness in Rosert's voice. *I must take a life, so others can live.* The realization sickened Alice, but she knew there was nothing she could do. *Falk won.*

GLORIANA

Spiced tea warmed Gloriana's insides, causing her to hold back a moan. The brew had been crafted in Honeygrove, and just the smell alone reminded Gloriana of home. She was so pleased when Ser Bradberry had brought her the tea bags that she invited Lady Joan Myster to enjoy some. Now, the old woman sat at the table across from Gloriana, and a skinchanged Esme stood behind her silently.

When the Lady of Bear's Creek mentioned pseudoskins, Gloriana believed the woman was mad. *What do you mean you can change skins? If that were the case, I would have changed how I looked long ago!* Yet, Gloriana trusted the old woman's words, and now, she couldn't decide if she was annoyed or excited.

Esme's orange hair had become brown, just like her eyes, which were once sparkling green. *She is a whole new woman.* Gloriana's attention flickered to Lady Joan, and she sipped more tea. *Is skinchanging the Arts? Is what Joan did illegal?*

"The Old Copper Bear continues to hibernate?" Joan questioned cryptically, and Gloriana nodded. "Have the Saavants decided what has ailed him?" Gloriana responded by shaking her head and gulping more of the cooling tea. "How are you feeling?"

"Fine," she exhaled, refusing to show too much emotion. "A new moon has turned, and with it comes a new year filled with new opportunities."

Joan rolled her eyes. "What's that? Some kind of Summeran saying? Your people are known to talk nonstop. How many Summeran sayings do you know?"

The mocking tone burned Gloriana's insides. Joan had stood with Lady Fallen Wayward for years, criticizing a young Gloriana for being different. *Joan always made my life a living hell. I can't fully trust her.* She exhaled heavily. "It's not a Summeran saying, and no, I don't know any."

"A shame, the Summerans used to be the only thing you'd talk about."

"Lady Fallen told me it wasn't polite to speak about a group of people who never visited the Mountain Realm. So, I stopped, and after a while, I'd forgotten what I enjoyed about them. I guess that was what Lady Fallen wanted."

Joan Myster eyed Gloriana before taking another gulp. "Lady Fallen always got what she wanted."

"A little like you, I guess," she grinned, covering her mouth with the teacup. "Anyway, since the bear could continue sleeping for a few years, we should start training Josef immediately."

Joan snapped her fingers, and Esme stepped forward, placing papers on the table. "These are the differing strategies we will be using with Josef."

Gloriana read one of the pages listing potential marriage candidates: *Emeline Osmont. Rose Glisten. Vivah Thoren.* The list continued, and Gloriana's stomach churned at the idea. *How much say do I have in all of this?* Her attention moved to the next page, which laid out potential education based on who the Mountain Realm aligns with. "You think the Establishments will create an alliance with us?"

"We will try using Josef's name or yours. Whichever works," Joan replied, uninterested in Gloriana's questions. She then looked Ser Bradberry up and down. "Who is this lord knight?"

"Don't worry, he's trustworthy," she answered, and the young man smiled.

"Trustworthy, hmm, tell me more."

Gloriana turned to the knight and smiled. "Please, Ser Bradberry, enlighten Lady Myster."

The knight bowed. "Aye, what would you like to know, my lady?"

"Bradberry is such an interesting first name," Lady Joan replied. "Are you from the Hearts Grove?"

"Aye, right outside Grove Fort."

"Are you familiar with House Bradberry?"

The knight nodded. "My mother loved Lord Colton Bradberry."

Chuckles erupted from the old woman. "Ah, Lord Colton, I haven't heard that name in years. So why didn't your mother just name you Colton?"

The young knight blushed. "My older brother's name is Colton."

Lady Joan Myster burst into laughter, clapping. "Your mother sounds like a joy!"

"Aye," Ser Bradberry smiled. "She was."

Gloriana took in the interaction, trying her best to calm her nerves. *Joan can befriend people so quickly. If I'm not careful, she will wrap both Esme and Ser Bradberry around her wrinkly fingers. Can I even trust those two anymore? Could I ever trust them?*

"Do you have any other fun stories about your mother?" Joan questioned, and Gloriana burned with jealousy. *The wretched hag never wanted to know more about my mother. Joan was quick to insult her, too.* When Ser Bradberry confirmed, Joan grinned, showing a few missing teeth. "Take a seat and tell us, please. You too, Esme."

The two sat, and Ser Bradberry took a deep breath. "My mother used to tell me stories when I was a child and my favorite is about Ihphy's deity."

"Ihphy, the goddess of the Sea?" Esme quizzed, and the knight smiled.

"Everyone knows about her banished deity, Zilaidat. It's an island now."

"Do you know why he was banished?"

The three women at the table shook their heads. "Ihphy didn't have one deity; she had two, and openly adored her second deity, Caenum, while ignoring her first, Zilaidat. Enraged by his mother-goddess' favoritism, Zilaidat slew,"

The door swung open, interrupting Ser Bradberry's story. An old man waddled into the room, his breathing ragged. The strange man wore a holey brown robe, and his grey, matted beard made him look dirty and unkempt. He wiped the sweat from his round, yellow face as he licked his chapped lips repeatedly. "Lady Gloriana."

She looked at the old man with disgust. *Who is this man, and why does he speak to me so casually?*

"Who are you?" Ser Bradberry inquired, standing. The chair crashed to the floor, making Gloriana jump with nervousness. She glanced towards the knight whose hands were readying to fight.

Something is wrong. Gloriana Wayward knew it. *Something is terribly wrong.* She pressed her sweating palms against her dress and steadied her attention on the man.

"The Lord Protector is dead!" he shouted, flinging his arms in the air.

"WHAT?!" Everyone screamed, and the old man nodded, looking contemptuous for being the first to break the news.

Esme grabbed her skinchanged face. "No, this wasn't supposed to,"

"How do you know?" Joan interrupted, shutting Esme up.

"I saw Jaslyn Wayward suffocate him!"

"What!?" Gloriana shrieked, falling to the floor and scuffing her knees. The pain intensified as she grabbed clumps of hair. *How could this happen? The plan seemed so perfect.*

"Aye, she suffocated him with the pillow he laid on!" the man continued, his voice growing louder. "It was a disgusting act to witness."

Kill him! Gloriana demanded internally, but she couldn't find her voice. She just stared at the floor and listened to the conversation.

"Lady Jaslyn would never lay a hand on the Lord Protector!" Lady Joan Myster shouted at the man. "It sounds like you came in here speaking treasonous lies."

No, Jaslyn would do it. Gloriana let go of her hair and brought herself to her feet. *If Borin told her to. Damn it!* Her lord husband had beaten Gloriana at the game she created. *I failed.* "Where is my daughter?"

"Gloriana," Joan gasped.

"I told the knights to arrest her, but she escaped the city. Knights are currently chasing her," the old man explained.

"You WHAT?" Gloriana fell into her seat, completely exasperated. *Jaslyn is gone.*

Ser Bradberry stepped forward. "What gave you the right to command that?"

"What do you mean? I saw her murder the Lord Protector!" the old man countered desperately.

Kill him! She wanted to order. *Kill him! Kill him!*

The Matriarch of the Mountain Realm rose to her feet. "Take us to the Lord Protector," she demanded as Esme assisted her toward the door.

"Of course, my lady," the man bowed and led the group to Lord Borin's chambers, huffing and puffing.

Anger, despair, and heartbreak swirled within Gloriana as she walked a few steps behind the group. *My life is like the stories of the gods Ser Bradberry told earlier. There is no happiness, only grief.*

Gloriana stepped into the room and saw Borin Wayward peacefully lying in his bed—lifeless.

She rushed over to her lord husband's bedside and fell to the floor. *I didn't even get to say goodbye.* Slowly, she grabbed his limped hand. *I loved you for so long that I ignored the evil within you. I even tried to save your life. Then I hated you so much and so quickly I wanted to see you dead.* She squeezed his hand as tears streamed from her eyes. *And even then, I still have love for you. I thought, maybe if you got sick, and I knew that you would never get better, it would be easier to get over you.* She kissed the knuckles of his cold, dead hand, her own still aching. *Honestly, this is what you deserve.*

Gloriana turned to the group behind her, knowing that was all the goodbye she needed to say. *Borin can rest in peace now.* "You," she began, pointing at the old man, her face frowning harder than ever. "Gather more knights."

"Yes, my lady," the old man replied and scrambled out of the room.

When he was gone, the room grew silent.

"This shouldn't have happened," Esme screeched, gripping her hair. "He was supposed to have been bedridden for several more years. That is what the alchemist told me. I promise! I promise! This isn't my fault!" Esme sobbed, yet her sobs made Gloriana feel nothing.

"Quiet now, girl," Lady Joan Myster hushed. "We don't know what happened."

"That man seems to be telling the truth," Ser Bradberry informed, his hands on his hips.

Gloriana nodded. "He is, but he doesn't know the full story."

"And you do?" Lady Joan inquired, unconvinced.

Her eyes burned from the sunshine that beamed through the broken window on the other side of Borin's room. *Is that how Jaslyn escaped?* Her attention then narrowed on Lady Myster. "Aye. Jaslyn wouldn't hurt her father, not unless he commanded it."

"You think he told her to do it?"

"I know he did," she confirmed before pointing at his corpse. "Look, he's smiling."

Joan Myster groaned. "Well, it's time we pivot. Josef is too young, so we will make you the leader until he comes of age."

Gloriana's eyes widened. "What, me? A woman can't rule the Mountain Realm."

"We can have you be Regent, like Queen Taylia Wayward," Esme concocted. "The other highborn should accept that claim. Taylia the Good is beloved in Mountain Realm history and ruled well until King Fane came to age."

Joan nodded. "And King Fane's first child was Queen Rayleen Wayward. The greatest there ever was."

Gloriana's attention returned to her dead husband, and her heart broke. *If I'm going to rule, I must have Jaslyn in Maryere. Jaslyn is my Rayleen.* She then turned to Ser Bradberry. "Send knights to find my daughter, but they cannot harm her. I will see that every knight's head is on a spike if she is hurt."

"What if rumors spread that Jaslyn killed the Lord Protector?" Esme questioned.

"I'll put down all rumors about anyone murdering Borin," Joan confirmed confidently. "He died peacefully in his sleep and that's that."

Gloriana's vision narrowed on the old woman. *Joan does everything for the benefit of House Myster, so what is she doing this for? I thought it was to put Josef on the throne, but now I'm unsure. I don't believe who sits on the throne matters as long as Joan whispers in their ear.* Gloriana clenched her stiff fingers, and the pain reminded her that she was alive. *I must keep this old hag nearby. I can't have her scheming against me.*

She then reached out and grabbed Joan's frail hand. "My lady, will you guide me?"

"Of course," Lady Joan reassured. "You need friends around you, especially now." Joan wrapped her arms around Gloriana in a tight embrace. "Worry not. Everything will be fine." The women separated, and Joan's soft, saggy finger wiped the tears from Gloriana's cheek. "But you must trust me."

I'd rather trust anyone else. "Of course, my lady," Gloriana replied, giving the old woman a false smile. She then turned to Ser Bradberry. "The old man hasn't returned with knights. Go find him."

Ser Bradberry bowed and exited the room.

"We should leave too," Lady Joan said, grabbing Esme's hand. "Please, call if you need us."

She nodded and waved goodbye, now alone with her dead lord husband. She sluggishly moved to the other side of the room and stuck her head out of the broken window, feeling the freezing wind burn her skin. *Run Jaslyn,* she could almost hear her husband say, *don't let them catch you.*

Gloriana grabbed the window sill, cutting her palms on the broken glass. "Please don't listen to your father, Jaslyn. I need you here, please," she whispered to the frigid air, knowing her youngest daughter would never listen even if she heard the plea.

HADRIAN

After several days of attempting to converse with the sparrow, Hadrian decided that its name was Myp, the only name the bird ever responded to. He didn't know how they got to that name, but he was pleased to have a secret he could keep to himself. The sparrow was small, chirped a lot, and had endless sass. It slightly annoyed Hadrian, but the bird still wanted to stay by his side, and that was all he wanted.

Myp wants to be my ally.

"I'm going to try again," he informed the sparrow, and Myp replied by quieting his song. Hadrian closed his eyes and steadied his breathing. *If I want the skill to work, I must imagine it.* He had a hypothesis—if a wild animal wanted to have a relationship with him, maybe it was the Arts too. *Which would mean I have two Arts.* He grinned, hoping it was true.

So far, however, Hadrian Osmont had yet to find success.

Still, he wanted to try. *Let's try with a skill I've gotten good at.* Hadrian outstretched his arms and pictured the wind. "*Wind Skill: Swirl!*" A gust gathered in his hands, and he pushed the air forward, causing a horizontal tornado to crash into the tree before him.

Myp flew out of the tree Hadrian had hit, squawking wildly.

"Whoops," he chuckled, and the bird pecked at his head. "Ow, stop! I didn't know you had changed trees." Myp hovered before Hadrian, and he could feel the attitude radiating from the bird. "I'm sorry. I'm sorry. Let me try the next one, please."

The sparrow tweeted out a sigh and moved out of the way.

"Thank you!" He then narrowed his vision and thought about exactly what he wanted. *I want to hear from afar, and a bird can do that.* His eyebrows furrowed, and concentration filled him. He cleared his head, just as Raynese had taught him. "*Bird Skill: Aural!*" he shouted, yet nothing happened. *My mind isn't clear enough. I must get this right.* He repositioned himself and closed his eyes, once again trying his best to think of nothing but the skill he wanted to manifest. "*Bird Skill: Aural!*" he incanted again, and when he no longer heard the echo of his voice, everything else became loud.

His eyes snapped open, and his ears throbbed. *It worked! I have a second Art!* He jumped around excitedly, and Myp tweeted cheerfully. The differing sounds were loud, and after a moment, it turned maddening. *Wait, I've felt this before.* Tears filled his eyes as realization kicked in. *I've had it this whole time, probably before the Wind Art. But why wasn't it working before?* He touched his ear lobes as Raynese's humming intensified. *I didn't know she was near.*

Hadrian turned in a different direction when he heard another voice. "The lil lord is near and alone. We should kill him now."

"No," another voice said. "Let's go speak to Sakala for now."

Fear ripped through Hadrian Osmont. *The Warrior Raiders are here!*

A branch slapped him in the face, alerting him that he was already running. *I must get to Raynese, and we need to plan. The best option is having them attack us to near death, and Raynese will heal us even if she has to do it using the Darkness.* His hands squeezed into fists. *What if things go wrong? I don't want to die.* Hadrian pressed his lips together, his entire body pulsing. *There is nothing I can do. I must put my trust in Raynese.* He continued forward, and the Red Cobra's humming grew louder. *She's near.*

"My sweet, what's wrong?" Raynese questioned, suddenly blocking his way.

He dug his heels into the dirt and forced himself to a stop before he ran into the woman. *Where did she come from?* He sighed, knowing Raynese wouldn't answer the question. "The Warrior Raiders," he told her breathlessly. "They're here!"

"How do you know that?"

Hadrian stepped back. "I-I saw one!"

"And they didn't attack?"

He puffed his cheeks. "Why are you questioning me? We need to plan! The plan I had mentioned before will work, but I would love it if we have a less violent way to escape them."

"Worry not, my sweet, I've devised the perfect plan. A plan that will shake off the Warrior Raiders once and for all," she replied, waving off his concerns.

"What is it?"

The Red Cobra gave a frightening grin. "I'm going to let the Warrior Raiders kill you."

Everything became silent as Hadrian stared at Raynese. "Huh?"

"I'm going to let them kill you, then I'll resurrect you," she repeated, barely making sense. "Hopefully, everything goes great! You trust me, right?" Hadrian stayed silent, and the woman moved closer. "You trust me, right?"

He looked into her hazel-colored eyes and could only see darkness within. His lips twitched as all the moments he spent with Raynese weighed him down. *I can't do this anymore. I don't even want her to resurrect me. Just leave and let me die.* Hadrian opened and closed his mouth, and his heart shattered into a million pieces. "Fuck you."

Anger blanketed Raynese's face before she relaxed. "Please, have some faith in me. You'll never have to worry about the Raiders again in a few hours. Okay? I'll be back. See ya!" The young woman jumped high, disappearing into the trees, and leaving him alone.

And your faith shall kill you.

Hadrian fell to his knees as he processed what happened. Myp landed on the ground before Hadrian and stared, staying quiet. "She," he started, tears filling his eyes. "She betrayed me." Myp chirped twice before leaning against Hadrian, showing some compassion. His cry grew louder as the situation sank in. *My mother betrayed me. The girl I was enamored with betrayed me.* He gripped his chest. *Will I ever be able to trust anyone again?*

"Hadrian," Colvic's voice boomed from behind, but Hadrian didn't react. Shrubs rustled, and a presence approached. "There you are. What's wrong? Where is Raynese?"

Slowly, Hadrian Osmont turned to the knight who had been by his father's side since childhood. His twisted, distraught face caused Colvic's eyes to widen. "The Warrior Raiders are near."

"Where is Raynese?" he questioned again, his voice laced with rage.

The tears continued. "She left."

Ser Colvic stomped on the dirt, releasing some frustrations. "Damn it! Damn it! Was this her plan the whole time?"

"She said she would resurrect us, but I've never heard of someone doing that before."

"No, she's got some ulterior motive and is trying to separate us," the knight replied, turning to the trees. "I felt it when we met her, but I had to deal with other things. I'm sorry, Hadrian. I failed us."

He shook his head. "No, I'm sorry. I forced you to trust her."

Colvic relaxed and sat on the ground. "So, the Raiders are coming?" He nodded, and the knight patted the parched dirt for Hadrian to sit. "How much time do we have?"

"Not long," Hadrian sighed, leaning against the tree. "That stupid Raynese! I will never forgive her!"

Ser Colvic Rames roared with laughter. "If we survive this, you will learn there are a lot of Red Cobras out there. You must be cautious."

"Aye, but it's hard."

"It is," Colvic agreed. "Strangely, sitting here like this, waiting for death, reminds me of a time I spent with Peyton."

Hadrian turned to the knight, smiling through his tears. "Please, tell me the story."

The knight shifted uncomfortably. "When the Single King's War started, Kiandy wavered on its support because the ignorant Lord Protector banished Lord Othenel Kiandy's wife, Maleka Waters, and their children although no crime had been committed. To resolve the situation, Morvan sent his heir, your father, to Kiandy for negotiations. But you see, Lady Maleka and their children never made it safely to Wilderton. Lord Othenel was sure Morvan did something to them, so when Peyton and I arrived in Kiandy, he imprisoned us."

"He wanted payback," Hadrian notated, understanding the Lord of

Kiandy's anger.

"Aye, but Othenel was kind, which was his biggest mistake. He placed us in a guest room instead of in chains in a dungeon. For fifteen days, Peyton attempted to negotiate with Lord Kiandy, and when he finally made a breakthrough, Morvan arrived with his army and sacked the city, even destroying the castle. Peyton and I were locked inside our room, listening to the agonizing wails outside. We knew we were going to die. But then, we didn't. Valley Pines knights found and freed us. Morvan executed Othenel and installed Othenel's estranged half-brother, whom Morvan legitimized. The end."

Hadrian frowned. "That wasn't a very good conclusion."

"Aye, but we survived, and that was enough for me."

A cold chill ran over his body. *We survived.* That's what Hadrian wanted. "What should we do now?"

Colvic sighed and got back on his feet. "I really didn't want to do this, but I have a good friend in House Branch that may be able to help us, and I don't think the Raiders are willing to attack an enormous city like Oysterhelm, so let's head there."

The slightest bit of hope tingled inside of Hadrian as he stood. *Maybe we can survive.* He followed the knight north, and a little more life filled him with every step. *I can't give up because of Raynese or my mother. I will live and succeed despite what they've done to me.*

He looked at the back of Ser Colvic's head as they walked. "Who is your friend in Oysterhelm?"

"They aren't actually in Oysterhelm," Colvic clarified, "but we can seek shelter and contact them when we arrive. We just have to get there."

The pair quickened their pace, barely stopping to take a piss.

We can do this. Hadrian chanted during their quiet journey. *We will survive. Everything is going to be okay.*

"We're less than an hour now," Colvic informed, almost running. "I feel them around us. We need to get there soon."

"I feel them too," Hadrian confessed, his eyes on a frantic Myp, circling above the trees. "That bird is freaking out up there."

The knight lifted his head. "There is no bird."

"Aye, there is, and he squawking quite loudly."

Ser Colvic Rames stopped, causing Hadrian to run into his back. "There is no noise." Hadrian looked up as the knight turned around. "Where is the,"

An arrow flew between the two, stopping the conversation. Colvic pushed Hadrian in the chest and jumped back.

"They're here!" A voice called, and movements shifted around them.

Oh gods. It's the Warrior Raiders.

Berserk roars filled the air as figures appeared from the shadows, coming closer. There were at least twenty, and Hadrian's entire body trembled. *The time is now. I need to do something, or else I will die. What do I do?*

Colvic threw a second sword near Hadrian's feet. "FIGHT!" the knight commanded.

Hadrian scrambled to pick up the sword, causing the Raiders to begin their assault. Another arrow flew as Hadrian dove, and he busted his chin on the ground. He didn't have time to react to the injury and grabbed the sword. *I must survive.*

Lady Arla Osmont's smiling brown eyes appeared as the trees around him began to burn. *My sweet Hadrian,* his mother cooed in the air, and he closed his eyes, unable to take the sound of the voice. In the darkness, he still saw those eyes, and now, they were frowning. *Why don't you just die already?*

Gusts of wind pushed from Hadrian's body in a wave, creating an enormous boom and taking out all the flames. Everything stopped.

After a moment, there was a gasp. "That's the Arts."

"He took down four of our men, Sakala," the squeaking voice of a child informed, causing Hadrian's eyes to snap open.

There are children here.

He scanned his surroundings, noticing a few attackers backing away. *Can I fight to the death against a child?* A violent cough erupted from him, and he fell to one knee, using the sword to stay upward.

"Hadrian!" Colvic called, giving a finishing blow to a Raider before rushing toward him. "Hadrian, are you okay?"

The woman named Sakala, dressed in animal pelts decorated with bones, stepped forward, clutching a bow. "I know about the Arts," she said, readying her weapon and pointing it at Hadrian. "His body is broken. He won't be able to do that skill again for a while. Let's kill him while we can."

A skill. Hadrian scooted backward, his body burning from the inside. *I used a new skill, but my body can't take it, and now I'm going to die.*

The woman let loose the arrow, and Ser Colvic Rames jumped in front of Hadrian, allowing the arrow to strike him through the shoulder.

"COLVIC!" Hadrian screamed.

The knight groaned and broke the arrow piece sticking out of him, not yet pulling it out. "This is nothing," he exhaled, struggling to stand. Colvic inhaled deeply and swung, and a thin young man jumped in front of the woman, mirroring Colvic's sacrifice. Ser Colvic struck down the strange-looking Raider.

"Dinan!" the woman in bones cried, falling to her knees and grabbing the slain Raider. "He's dead."

The others reacted by rushing the famed knight and starting a fight, eleven versus one. No one paid attention to Hadrian; they only wanted vengeance. Hadrian moved away, unsure of what to do. *I want to help Colvic, but I must stay alive.*

"Why Dinan?" the woman continued to cry as another child raced over and attempted to bring the woman to her feet. "Our Oracle, Selese, our Oracle!"

"The lil lord is right there!" the young girl replied. "Cry for Dinan later, Ma, please!"

Ma. The word echoed endlessly as Myp cawed along with it. *That's a mother and daughter.* His attention then turned to the dead man. *Who was he to them? What's an Oracle?*

The little girl grabbed the bow from her mother. "We don't have time for this," she groaned, pulling the string back with force before releasing the arrow.

Hadrian steadied his footing and lifted his hand. "*Wind Skill: Swirl,*" he incanted, and his Art collected in his palms before pushing out toward the girl, forcing the arrow to blow away. He released another gust of wind without saying anything, pushing the girl on her bottom, and her eyes grew wide. Hadrian's attention snapped to a ragged Ser Colvic, who had already taken down six Raiders. *We must end this soon and get to Oysterhelm. This might not be all of the Raiders chasing us.*

His eyes snapped back to the mother and daughter, frightening the pair. *I hate this. This is all Raynese's fault. I don't want to be a murderer.* "Leave," he told them mercifully. "I don't want to hurt anyone."

The women didn't move, and Myp's squawking became unbearable. *Myp, why are you doing this?* He then refocused on the fight, where Colvic was now losing against the remaining Raiders. *I must help him.* His hand lifted without thinking, "*Wind Skill,*"

An arrow hitting Hadrian Osmont's chest stopped the incantation.

Panicked, he looked down, staring at the wood sticking out of his body. His eyes lifted to Selese, still holding the bow, crying. "I'm sorry, but we must take you down, here and now. We need the gold." The little girl released another arrow, piercing his arm.

Hadrian cried out in pain and fell to the cold, hard ground as the young girl approached, readying another arrow. "Please," he sobbed, sitting up. "My mother did a wicked thing and paid you to kill me. Could we not work together instead? I will give you the coins, just like she did."

"Ya got two hundred gold?"

His eyes widened. *That's how much Mother's paying them?!* More tears streamed down his face. "No."

Again, Selese struck Hadrian, this time in the thigh, furthering his torment. He pulled the arrows out of his body, breathing heavily. He attempted a skill, but nothing happened. He was too weak. *I'm going to die.*

The fight quieted, grabbing Hadrian's attention, and he saw a dying Colvic lying in a puddle of blood. The knight looked at Hadrian, the light in his green eyes dulling. "Peyton," he exhaled, lifting his hand. "Peyton, don't leave me, please. I can't be without you."

"COLVIC!" Hadrian screamed as a Raider took Ser Colvic's sword and plunged it into his chest. The knight quit moving, but his eyes still stared at Hadrian. *Colvic is gone. They killed him.*

Rage ripped through Hadrian Osmont. *And it's Raynese's fault!*

Selese was now in front of him, with the bow lowered. "You seem like a kind boy. As the daughter of the tribe leader, I was taught to enslave kind boys like you and make them my husband." The girl sighed as if the situation hurt her. "Maybe in another life," and in one swift movement, she leaned over and slashed his neck.

Hadrian grabbed at his throat, unable to stop the gushing blood. He stared into the young Warrior Raider's cold eyes, unable to understand. *She's so young, yet she killed me without a second thought.* He laid on his side, still holding his neck, as his consciousness faded away. *It's so cold.*

"I really would've preferred to take the highborn boy as a slave," the girl complained, turning on her heels. She returned to her mother, still frowning. "When we create our settlement with the gold, I want a highborn husband."

She's continuing with her life like she didn't just take mine. Hadrian observed a blood pool gathering near his head. *This girl, Selese, she's like Raynese. Colvic was right. There are many Red Cobras out there.*

"The Lady wants his head," Sakala whispered, still looking at the dead man in her hands. "Finish the job."

The girl groaned and stomped around before coming back to Hadrian and straddling him. "Fine, but I'm holding the head until we get to King's Berth. It's my prize."

A loud howl caused Selese to pause, and she looked into the trees, her eyes now terrified. "Ma, that wolf is here!" She clenched her teeth and grabbed Hadrian's hair, pulling at the wound across his neck. Hadrian moaned in pain, barely conscious. "This sucks," she whispered, lifting the knife and rubbing her body against his. "Dumb beast is going to make this a hack job."

An enormous black wolf sprung from the forest, immediately attacking several Raiders.

"It's here!" Selese plunged the knife into Hadrian's neck creating another wound, yet Hadrian felt no pain.

Mother. I want you to get the justice you deserve.

The animal's growls and howls grew closer before it sprang forward, forcing the girl off Hadrian.

"Selese, let's go," the woman in bones instructed, moving to her feet and keeping the dead man on the ground. "We can return when the wolf is gone. The boy is dead anyway."

The ground rumbled around Hadrian, and each of his breaths grew shallow. The wolf, now calm, booped Hadrian's nose and licked the blood puddle before howling. *It acts like it knows me.* He attempted to lift his hand, but death was heavy, and his arm plummeted into the dirt.

He blinked slowly and watched the beast walk to Ser Colvic as Myp sat in Hadrian's open hand. He gasped for air as the wolf prodded at Colvic's dead body. *Please don't eat Colvic. He is a famed knight. He doesn't deserve to be a meal.*

The wolf's pained howl started again, and Hadrian's heart slowed. "I got here too late," the wolf cried in a frantic feminine voice. Hadrian wanted to be surprised by the sight of a talking animal, but it was too cold for him to care. "Aye, they are both barely breathing, but I don't know what to do," the wolf continued. "Those Raiders are still near, and so is that woman who was traveling with them."

Raynese.

The wolf transformed into a beautiful, naked woman with fluffy blonde hair. She pulled the massive sword from Colvic's chest before pouring liquid into the wound. The woman then hurried over to Hadrian and poured something into his throat, but still, everything was cold. "Oh no, Hadrian has lost too much blood. The medicine won't help."

She knows my name. He opened his eyes. "Who,"

"Sh," the young woman interrupted, not covering herself as she pulled the knife from Hadrian's neck and rolled him onto his back. "I'm so sorry, but I can't help you. I promise I will get revenge for you and take down those Warrior Raiders."

Life continued to slip out of Hadrian Osmont, and breathing became impossible. *This wolf-woman can't save me, so how could Raynese? This is the end.* The woman moved away, and he closed his eyes again, feeling death take him.

You finally got what you wanted, Mother. Your beloved son, the boy you cherished more than anything in this world, is dead. He took one last breath. *And I'm going to haunt you until the end of your days.*

JARIN

Widow's Dale was a haven. The pleasant holdfast gave Jarin Ayers the peace he needed, and in a short time, he realized that he didn't want to go back to Waterbrook. He loved everything about the old holdfast —the peaceful silence in the early mornings, the floral aroma that filled every room, and the taste of the game Ossian, Lucius, and Ser Bronston hunted.

He loved it all.

Jarin also loved spending time with Vera. *Or should I call her Cleo?* He spent any moment he could with the Lady of Widow's Dale. They often spoke about the past, of better times when the people they loved were still alive. They also talked about their time apart. How she found her children, and how he dealt with the darkness in his mind.

Cleo brought him solace, but Jarin was conflicted. There were too many lingering looks, touches that lasted too long, moments where they were in each other's air, breathing in. Jarin wanted more. He wanted to stare at Vera longer, to interlace his fingers with hers, to embrace her with a kiss, but he couldn't. *She was my brother's, and he loved her,* Jarin constantly reminded himself.

"Good morning, my lord," Cleo greeted in a sultry tone. She walked into the dining hall, taking long strides, and her hips swayed seductively underneath her form fitting dress. Her face was bright, and her smile invited more than just a simple greeting.

"Good morning, Cleo," he replied.

She changed direction and moved toward Jarin. She leaned to his ear. *Too close. She is always too close. Do I want that?* "Aye, I'm Cleo, but don't forget my highborn name," she exhaled, making his skin tingle. Their eyes met, and again, they were too close. Jarin could do nothing but nod, and she pulled away. "How was your sleep?" she inquired, sitting at the opposite side of the table.

"Fine."

"And the pain?"

"Subsided. I feel young again."

"Well, you aren't," She joked, clapping her hands. "But see, I told you! Chewing on wetwood can cure all!"

Jarin grinned. "Aye, much better than the crazed pills I took before."

"Aye," she agreed as the door opened.

The servants filled the room with wonderfully smelling food, yet Jarin felt empty. *What is this feeling?*

Cornelia entered first with her hands held together and her eyes low. "Good morning, Mother. Good morning, Lord Jarin."

"Good morning," Jarin replied in a cheery tone.

"Morning, Nelia." Cleo greeted. The girl waddled a bit as she walked to the chair next to her mother and sat down, ready to eat. "How was your night?" Cleo asked, touching the girl's hair softly.

Cornelia kept her attention on the table. "Fine."

"Want to talk about it later?"

Cornelia shifted her gaze upwards to Cleo's grey eyes and nodded, staying silent.

Next, Penelopei came in twirling and singing. Cornelia immediately sighed, already tired of her sister's antics. "Good morning to you! Good morning to you! Good morning to you!" the teenage girl sang as she pointed to each of them.

"Morning, Pei." Cleo and Cornelia greeted simultaneously in vastly different tones.

"Good morning, Penelopei," Jarin grinned.

Penelopei turned and clapped her hands. "Oh, oh, I have a new song!" She informed Jarin happily. "I want you to hear it later today!"

Jarin gave a small smile. "Of course."

Ossian, Lucius, and Bronston walked in together, already dressed for a hunt. "Lord Jarin, Ser Bronston said we are going to try and find a moose today!" Ossian informed excitedly, as they all sat at the table.

Jarin rose his eyebrows. "A moose? Are there any this far south?" All three shrugged causing Jarin's smile to widen. *Of course, it doesn't matter to them. They are going to try regardless.*

The room buzzed from conversations, and Jarin felt at peace. *This was what I have always wanted.* In Widow's Dale everyone was part of a family that loved and trusted each other. They spent their days doing nothing, barely having any responsibilities. *I could never have that in Waterbrook.*

The last to arrive were Daya and Nebula, walking hand and hand. The two girls were always together laughing and whispering and making flower crowns. *Finally, Daya can have a childhood, far away from deception and death.*

Today, the pair wore pretty matching sundresses that complimented each other. Daya wore a yellow dress with white lacing, while Nebula twirled in a light green dress with blue lacing.

A squeak and a giggle came from the other side of the table, and Jarin sighed at the same time as Cornelia, who was already rolling her eyes. "Nebbie!" Penelopei laughed aloud so that she could be the center of attention. "It's winter now, you can't wear summer dresses!"

"Spring will come soon enough, Pei." Nebula replied, not looking at her sister.

"Spring isn't summer!" Penelopei countered, crossing her arms.

"Enough girls," Cleo commanded, her voice light and airy. "We need to break our fast and carry on about our day, not argue."

Penelopei humphed loudly in response, while Nebula sat silently beside Daya.

When everyone settled, Cleo smiled. "Let us pray."

"Thank you, Korta, for blessing us with this food. Thank you, Slait, for blessing us with protection in our home. Thank you, Axone, for blessing us with life. We are forever grateful." All the children said in unison.

Jarin, Ser Bronston, and Daya stayed silent with their eyes lowered as House Withers recited their prayer. *That custom,* he thought as the room grew loud once again, *it is not from the Riverlands. River people really only pray to Axone, Obum, and Krella. Maybe even to Unmos if they wish for death.* He glanced back at Bronston and Daya, who now ate happily along with everyone else.

"Is something wrong?"

Jarin focused on the silver woman. "What do you mean?"

"You aren't breaking your fast."

Jarin pressed on a hard smile. He grabbed some bacon and blackened bread, and broke his fast. *There is no use worrying about the strange customs House Withers takes part in. They are kind and friendly, that's all that matters.*

Ossian and Lucius shamelessly scarfed down their meal. "Done!" the boys shouted, slamming their plates on the table as they stood. The pair eyed each other before chuckling and running out of the room. Ser Bronston took one more bite of his breakfast, stood from the table, and followed the boys out.

Penelopei laughed just as loudly as her brothers did. "You guys are having so much fun!" She cheered, now standing and hopping from one foot to the other. "Fun! Fun! Fun!" As Penelopei took up the attention, Daya and Nebula made their silent escape. "I'm going to go swing in the garden now!" Penelopei announced, not really to anyone, and made her exit too, twirling and singing until she disappeared.

Cleo snickered at each of her children as they finished their meal and left the dining hall. The only time Lady Withers kept a straight face was when Cornelia finally stood.

Cornelia said nothing, and as she took a step to leave, Cleo grabbed her wrist. "Will you be in the library later?" Cornelia frowned harshly, but nodded. When she did, Cleo let go, and the girl walked out of the room without another word.

"She hasn't been eating," Cleo informed passively when they were alone. Jarin examined the empty plate where Cornelia had sat, before looking back at Cleo confused. Lady Withers sighed at his confusion. "She didn't grab any food to eat. She just sat there, being invisible, like always."

Jarin matched her frown, upset that he had not noticed. "Why?"

"I have no idea," the silver woman sighed. "I want her to talk to me, but she refuses to open up. Last time I pushed too much, Lysane left me."

The Lord Protector thought about the situation for a moment. Her children were difficult just like Jarin's. He could never tell how Terryn and Dain truly felt. He would just study their faces and shrug off any suspicions until they finally came to him with their problems; which they rarely did. "Perhaps you should wait until she wants to talk," he suggested.

"I don't know," she groaned, placing her forehead on her hand and slumping over to relax. "I'm all about conflict resolution. You can't sit around and wait forever."

"My lord," a servant said, approaching. "For you."

A letter. Jarin inhaled sharply, took the letter, and broke open the seal. *Who wrote this? It isn't Dain's handwriting.* It wasn't Dain's nor Terryn's nor Dimia's. Jarin had no idea who wrote the letter. *What is this?*

"What does it say?" Cleo asked pryingly.

After a few moments, Jarin pulled his attention away from the letter and looked at Cleo, and her eyes sparkled with curiosity. He stared back silently, before returning to the letter. He scanned through it repeatedly, still not understanding. *Lady Dimia Ayers is dead.*

"What is it? What's wrong?"

Instead of answering, Jarin Ayers raced out of the dining hall.

He wandered around the holdfast for hours, with the letter gripped in his hand, mumbling to himself. After a while, Jarin went outside, hid in the small grove near the exit, and cried.

Ser Bronston Hedge was the first to find him. "Why are you hiding? Lady Vera is worried about you." Jarin quietly handed the knight the letter. "So, she's dead?" He huffed, his voice raspy and cold.

"I have no idea who wrote this," Jarin confessed, chewing on wetwood for comfort.

"A priest did," Bronston replied, examining it. "If it was a Saavant they would have mentioned what killed her." The knight thought for a moment, his eyes scanning the letter repeatedly. "We need to return to Waterbrook." He handed back the letter and Jarin reread it. "We need to return to Waterbrook," the knight said again after a few moments of silence.

Jarin placed the letter on his lap. "Can't we stay a little while longer?"

Bronston sighed. "The Lord Protector of the Riverlands should be in the capital city. We've vacationed here long enough, we should probably leave tomorrow." Jarin could only sigh in response. "I will make preparations and let Daya know, there is no reason for her to stay here now." Jarin continued to stay quiet, which made Ser Bronston groan. "Are you going to tell Lady Vera?" Still nothing. "You can't leave without saying anything."

"Why not?" Jarin countered. "It's not like they are a major house or anything. I owe them nothing."

"The children would be disappointed if you left without saying goodbye, and so would Lady Vera."

Jarin knew his trusted knight was right. *I'm not a cruel person.* He took a deep breath. "What do I say? 'My wife died so I gotta go, bye!'"

The knight shrugged, "That is why you are the Lord Protector and I am a knight." He smiled a kind and reassuring smile, before leaving Jarin to his thoughts.

After spending more time mulling, Jarin decided how he would say goodbye to each member of House Withers. He returned to his bedchamber and laid there silently to think, skipping his lunch and dinner. He hated this, he hated all of this, but there was nothing he could do. *It's time for me to go home.*

The door to his bedchamber swung open suddenly. "You're leaving tomorrow!?" Cleophilia started, her voice raised; and all Jarin could do was sit up in his bed and stare. "And you weren't going to tell me? You were just going to leave?"

How did she find out? Jarin's mind spun. "I was going to tell you,"

"When?" she interrupted.

"Tomorrow."

As soon as the words escaped his mouth, Cleo fell to her knees crying. Her reaction surprised Jarin, so he got up from his bed, and hugged her as she cried on his shoulder. She looked at him, her grey eyes dull against her now pinkish sclera. "You're leaving, just like Domeric did," she responded in between sobs. "Never to return."

"I must go back home. The Lord Protector must rule and protect."

"You can do that here."

Jarin shook his head. "I must rule in Waterbrook as my family has done for generations."

His answer made her cry harder. "You're just like your stupid brother!" They sat in silence for a moment, as Cleo calmed down. "Let me come with you."

Jarin choked on the air he breathed. "What?"

She grinned, her face still flushed from crying. "Let me come with you," she repeated simply, but Jarin stayed quiet, not knowing how to respond. "Please," she begged. "You bring me so much warmth and joy, I refuse to lose that again."

She means my brother. His face grew hard and intense. *My brother was her warmth and joy—not me.*

"I fell out of love with your brother long ago," she confessed, as if she had read his mind. "Domeric abandoned me during the war to follow your father's orders and marry that ugly Bayes girl. I couldn't forgive him. He gave me Widow's Dale as an apology, so I dedicated my life to rescuing and caring for wayward children." She softly cupped his face. "As I raised my children I promised I would never give my heart to another person. That was until I met you. Please, don't abandon me, too." When Jarin didn't answer, she looked away, pouting. "You don't feel the same way?"

The question made his stomach drop and he looked away, too. "I do."

Cleo reacted by jumping onto Jarin and kissing him passionately. "Then take me with you!"

"No. It wouldn't be right," he replied, dazed from the kiss. "My lady wife just died."

"From what you've told me, Dimia dying should bring you joy."

Before he could respond, Cleo leaned in and kiss him again. Jarin couldn't get enough of her soft, warm lips. Kissing Cleo felt safe. When Jarin kissed Dimia, it always felt forced, like something he should never do again. As he kissed Cleo, however, he knew he could kiss her forever.

They moved to the bed and Cleophilia straddled him, kissing him deeper. *She wants me,* he thought as her tongue slipped inside his mouth. *She wants me. She isn't forced to want me. It's willing and lovely and special and beautiful.* Cleo pulled away to untie her dress and Jarin grabbed her hand, stopping her.

"This isn't a dream, right?" he strained to say, still surprised by it all.

Cleo smiled seductively and leaned in to kiss him again. "No, it's not," she whispered, making him shudder. "It's something that I want, and it's something that you want, too." She pulled her hand away from his and began to untie her dress again. When she exposed her breasts, Jarin couldn't help but to grab for them and massage them in his hands. She moaned at his touch, making his manhood stiffen. "Take me with you," she exhaled.

"Anything for you."

Gooseprickles covered Cleo's skin as she giggled happily. "Thank you, my love."

Jarin Ayers smiled, knowing that this was what he desired and had longed for. He never wanted the Osmont girl who had comforted him as a child. He never wanted the Valley woman with the cinnamon colored hair and eyes the color of diamonds. He never wanted the Whore of Waterbrook.

I want Cleophilia.

And yet, when he closed his eyes in ecstasy, he only picture the venomous grin of Dimia Osmont.

ALICE

The air around Alice Wayward was still and cold. She ignored the gnawing frigidness as she folded two sheets of paper, hiding what she had written. She folded methodically, thinking about everything that could go wrong tonight. *I could die, but then, I'll be with Myra.* Slowly, she poured hot golden wax on the seams of the paper and pressed on her House's seal. She lifted the paper to examine the imprinted bear. *Our sigil is pretty.*

Every Wayward had the blood of the bear within them. Lord Borin was the Copper Bear, once because of his eyes and energy, but now the lords and ladies whisper that Borin was now the Old Copper Bear—weak, corroded, and tired. Jaslyn was the Golden Bear, a name given to those with the most promise, and Josef was the Lush Bear, as the child always demanded the finest things.

Alice, however, had always been the Silent Bear. Amounting to nothing and keeping mum all the while.

The journey from home forced Alice to destroy the Silent Bear. Even though everyone begged her to stay calm and collected, she couldn't. The Silent Bear had become the Raging Bear. *I can't let Falk get his way anymore,* Alice thought, watching the wax dry. *He believes I will complete his task and return to my room like nothing happened. But it's not going to happen like that.*

It took four days before she finally understood reality. *I must kill Lady Victoria to get what I want.* She knew it was selfish, but she had no other choice. *I can't stay here anymore.*

Rosert Osmont planned everything for his and Alice's escape. He decided the day and included Lady Raya Vale in the party, whom he believed would be good at smuggling them from Hard Pine Bay. Rosert also refused to bring Doran, no matter how much Alice begged. He insisted Doran was too weak and forced Alice to keep the plan of running away from her betrothed. *I don't want to leave Doran behind.*

A sudden knock came to the door.

Finally. She stood from her desk and fixed her dress and hair before slapping her cheeks lightly to brighten her face. "Come in," she tried to say politely, but it only sounded like a croak.

The door opened, and Ser Mace slipped into her bedchamber. "My lady," he bowed.

Alice put on a pretty smile. "Thank you for coming."

"Of course," he replied. "How have you been these last few days?"

She drew in a deep breath. *Horrible,* she wanted to say. "Fine. I've been staying in my bedchamber."

It was the truth, although most of the time she had visitors.

Emeline visited to pray, and Alice appreciated the calming silence her cousin brought. Catrain visited too, although the girl never wanted to pray. *I'm going to be strong like a bear,* the young girl would tell Alice during her visits. *Rosert told me your sister is a queen! You know we have the same eyes? When I get older, I'm running away to find her and be a queen, too!* Alice had told her little cousin over and over how lovely that would be.

Doran visited, too. He apologized and sang and read to her. Alice craved Doran's attention and he was willing to give it. *Soon I will never see him again.* He was her innocence, and she loved him so much for it.

When Rosert visited, they usually sat in silence, waiting for the moment when they would leave Kingment forever. She begged Rosert not to come, that he didn't deserve to live a life on the run. *I'm not leaving you,* he had told her, his face harsh. *I will never leave you.*

"My lady, I promise, whatever you called me for, will be in confidence," Ser Mace said, bringing Alice back to reality. "I promised to serve the kingdom. I cannot do that with who is in power now."

Alice grabbed the letters she had written. "What I'm asking you to do is a lot, but you are the only one I trust. My friend, who was murdered, her name was Lady Myra Nores."

"She was a highborn?"

"Aye, she was, and *he* murdered her knowing this." Alice sniffled, trying her best to contain her emotions. "I need you to take these letters and her corpse, then travel to Lakefort."

"In the Summerlands?"

She nodded and folded an edge of one of the letters, "This one is for Lord Nores, and this one is for Lord Wayward. When you arrive in Lakefort tell them you are there as my ambassador. From there you can send whoever to give the letter to Lord Wayward."

"Yes, my lady. Of course."

Alice smiled. "You must leave today and tell no one. I will not forget this, and when all is done, I will make sure you are rewarded."

"Protecting the innocent is my reward." He bowed, turned on his heels, and left.

Alone, Alice broke down in tears, falling to her knees. *I never want to see you cry again,* Ser Damien whispered, but hearing his voice only made her cry harder. "Please!" She begged. "All the gods have mercy on me! Allow me to escape this evil life!"

Instead, another knock came.

She didn't answer, continuing to cry on the floor, but the door opened regardless and Rosert Osmont walked in. "Get up," he commanded. Alice studied him for a moment, before looking back down at the floor, ignoring him. "Get up, we need to go." His voice was so cold and angry, causing a pain to twist in Alice's chest.

"I want to see Doran, one last time."

Rosert scoffed. "We don't have time for that, now, get up."

She snapped her head towards the boy. "Why are you being so mean?"

"Tonight, you are murdering my mother and then we are escaping Kingment, my home, to never return. Do you expect me to be happy?"

More tears fell from Alice's eyes. *Do I ever stop crying?* "I told you already, you don't have to come. Go back to your bedchamber, I can do this by myself."

"And I already told *you* that I'm not leaving your side." His words made Alice cry harder. *Why do I have to do this?* "Come on," he sighed, embracing her. "You must stop crying. The world doesn't care about that."

"I know," she whispered, "but I can't seem to stop."

Rosert helped Alice to her feet and hugged her tighter. She inhaled everything about him; his smell, his warmth, his touch, everything that reminded Alice of home. When he pulled away, she felt cold. "It's late, we must get this madness over with before the sun begins to rise."

Alice nodded and Rosert grabbed her hand to lead her from the bedchamber. As she walked out, she turned and looked back one last time. Everything from Maryere was in there—and she would never see it again. Another sob came to her throat, but she pushed it down. *I must be strong.*

When they arrived at the Tower, Rosert let go of Alice's hand and handed her the dagger. "Go inside, I'll hide in the bushes until you return."

She looked at Rosert, then to the Tower, and back over to Rosert. She nodded slowly and took a step forward. As soon as she moved, Rosert rushed over to some bushes and hid.

Alice Wayward walked to the entrance of the Tower, and quickly slipped in.

Inside, everything was dark, damp, and silent, reminding Alice of the Bloody Tower. *Must all towers be so awful?* She shook out her nerves and found the courage to climb the stairs at a fast pace. *I can't be here long. Rosert said this place is haunted.* She stared at the door that held the single room at the top of the tower. *Do it!* Each time she gripped the handle, she let go as if it burned her. *Do it! Do it! Do it!*

Finally, she swung the door open. Her skin crawled as she stepped into the room. *What is this feeling?* In the bedchamber, Alice saw nothing but the darkness.

"Aunt Victoria?" she called out quietly.

Rattling answered her call, and she shifted toward the moonlight. There, in the corner, was a restrained Lord Falk Osmont. *What?* She dropped the dagger and stumbled backward. *This can't be.* A shifting from behind caused Alice to grab the dagger, turn on her heels, and swing.

The person caught Alice's arm and knocked the small weapon out of her hand. "My, my, who would've thought you would try to fight me," an old woman said, stepping into the light. "Did Falk's abuse bring the true Wayward bear out of you?"

Alice yanked her arm, but the woman gripped tighter. "Who are you?"

"No need to be hostile, child. I am going to grant your wish." The old woman let go of Alice and moved to Falk, who furiously rocked back and forth in the chair. She smiled and removed the cloth from Falk's mouth.

"Enya, you fucking bitch, this wasn't the deal!" the Lord Protector raged. "Where is Victoria, and why the fuck is Alice here? What,"

The old woman stuffed Falk's mouth again, shaking her head. "His voice can just grate your ears."

Enya. Doran's kind eyes appeared in her mind. *The Darkness that radiates from her is worse than my father.* She glanced at the old woman, pretending to be oblivious. *She did something to Falk. Things have changed. I must get away from here.* "Aye, it does," she agreed, and Falk's eyes widened. "But he's right. Why am I here? What is happening?"

"That dagger," Enya pointed before motioning her head toward the Lord Protector of the Northern Kingdom of Valley Pines. She then pretended to stab the man repeatedly and grinned at Alice. "Your wish."

Murder Falk. It was something Alice Wayward wanted not even a few days ago, but now, she just wanted to be in her family's warm embrace. *I refuse to make that only a dream.* "My wish is to go home."

Enya stood straight and placed her hands on her hips. "The only way to go home is if you kill him."

Tears filled Alice's eyes. "Why?"

The old woman's eyes narrowed. "Don't you want to get revenge for your friend's death?"

Her chest throbbed from her heart pounding, and the room spun. "I hate the man, but I'm not a murderer," she croaked, already sweating. "Can't I do anything else?"

Enya's frown turned ugly. "Great, you're health is already declining." She walked up to Alice and stared into her eyes momentarily before flicking her on the forehead.

Alice's head slung back in reaction, and memories filled her mind. When Falk's eyes wouldn't leave her's at the feast. Or when he spoke to her in the garden. *Is Enya... forcing me to rage?* Her mother's screams rang as images of Falk repeatedly slapping and punching Alice played in her head.

Then, she saw the sad blank face of Lady Myra Nores.

If the only way to gome home is to murder the man that caused me so much pain, I shouldn't complain. In an instant, Alice grabbed the dagger, raced to a wide-eyed Falk Osmont, and pulled the cloth from his mouth. "This is for Myra!"

The Lord Protector inhaled sharply. "What are you talking about? I,"

But it was too late.

Alice Wayward had already unleashed the Raging Bear that lurked inside her. Over and over, she stabbed her lord uncle, and blood splattered everywhere.

It was like she was in a dream. *Was this what I always wanted?*

After several strikes, Falk was dead, but Alice didn't stop. She couldn't. "This is all your fault, you bastard!" She screamed, plunging the dagger into his chest.

The door opened, and two men walked in. "What the?"

Alice kept the dagger in the air and scanned the room. *Did Enya trick me and call for the knights? I didn't want to kill him!* Her continuous tears grew more intense. *Was I just a puppet?*

"Is that Lady Wayward?" one knight asked.

She stepped away from Falk's corpse and dropped the dagger. *I must escape. I cannot get captured. I will be sentenced to death and can never go home.* She moved to the other side of the room, her entire body numb. *I can't leave. My only escape is the window. It seems I'm going to die regardless.*

"It doesn't matter!" Enya shouted. "Lady Alice Wayward murdered the Lord Protector! Seize her!"

The knights rushed forward, and Alice turned to run. *This is it. Either I get arrested and die or jump from the window and die.*

Alice Wayward knew what she had to do.

She took several steps back and then, she ran, crashing through the window. Glass shards flew every which way as Alice plummeted. *I'm sorry Mother. I'm sorry Father. I'm sorry Jaslyn. I'm sorry Josef.* Her tears flew upwards and she took in the starry sky. *Life isn't fair,* she wanted to explain to her family, *so I've decided to let go. I wish we could've had a better relationship, but maybe in another life.*

She stretched out her limbs, ready to crash into the ground.

Instead, strong arms wrapped around her and the pair tumbled onto the grass. Her attention narrowed to the Tower and saw Enya dangling out of the window. "Alice! You get back here!"

"Why the hell did you jump from the window?" Rosert roared. "And why are you all bloody? What happened?"

Alice freed herself from Rosert's grasp and pointed at the delusional woman, hanging from the window. "Aunt Victoria wasn't in there, it was Saavant Enya who held Falk as a prisoner."

"So, where is my mother? Where is my father?"

"I don't know where Victoria is," she exhaled. "And I murdered Falk."

Rosert grabbed her hand and raced away from the Tower as the Saavant screamed for more guards. "Murdering the Lord Protector is worse than killing his lady wife," Rosert explained, leading her to a passageway. "You must leave, quickly."

You. The word echoed in her mind. *Not we.*

Outside the passageway, the sun shone lightly on her cheeks, and she breathed in the salty air. *We're on the beach already, how?*

"Over here!" Raya greeted, waiting on the shore with a small rowboat.

Alice raced to hug Raya, but Rosert pushed them both into the boat and kicked it into the waves. "What are you doing?" Alice cried, grabbing onto his pants to stop them from drifting farther.

"I'm staying here," Rosert informed with a frown. "I must find my mother."

"Please!" Alice wailed, gripping his pants tighter. "I thought you said you would never leave me. I can't continue on without you by my side," she gulped. *It might be selfish, but I must. I can't lose another loved one.* "Please, come with me."

The Osmont boy's face turned cold. "Of course this is happening," he scoffed as the bells above them began to toll. Rosert turned his eyes to the cliff where the Black Castle reached the skies, taking in the view for a moment, his eyes watery. Rosert then suddenly snapped his head and stared at Alice before the tension on his face melted. "Fine, let's go."

"Rosert, what happened?" Raya questioned. "Why are the bells ringing? What do you mean you must find Victoria? What's going on?"

"Shut up and row!" he demanded bitterly, jumping into the boat, and Raya stared back in shock as Rosert rowed as fast as possible.

Alice sat in the middle of the rowboat, keeping her eyes on the rough surface of the wood. "I murdered Lord Falk," she mumbled, causing Raya to gasp. "Saavant Enya made me do it."

Lady Raya Vale jumped to her feet, causing the small boat to rock. "Enya?! We must return to the castle. Victoria was wary of the old woman."

"We can't," Rosert replied, his voice hoarse, "The Saavant captured Falk. She could've done the same with my mother. We don't know what she is capable of, so let's continue our journey as we planned and see what news trickles out of the kingdom. Now, sit down before you tip us over!"

Raya sat in response and matched Rosert's quick pace.

In the distance, the bells continued, signaling that something had happened. As Raya and Rosert rowed farther away from Kingment, Alice stared at the sunrise. Against the Sapphire Sea, the sunlit sky looked like glittering jade jewels. *Like Doran's eyes.* "What about Doran?" Alice questioned in a soft tone.

"What *about* Doran?" Rosert repeated, annoyed.

"Will Enya do something to him, too?"

The young man groaned. "Who the fuck knows? We can't go back, so stop asking about the people still in Kingment!"

Again, everything was quiet, except for the bells.

"There is a ship waiting for us in about two leagues," Raya informed.

"We need to get there quickly," Rosert replied, his voice still demanding and harsh. "We don't want anyone stopping us."

"We have a head start, and I doubt they will turn toward the sea to search for us for another few hours."

"How can you be so sure?"

Raya smiled knowingly, although her brown eyes showed the sadness that was underneath. "Because, everyone knows that Alice just wants to go home."

APPENDIX

of major characters in A Death at Dawn

As of the New Moon 506 SM

Maryere, the Mountain Realm

BORIN WAYWARD, Lord Protector of the Mountain Realm.
Wife: GLORIANA, of House Thoren, from Goldspire, the Summerlands.
Their Children:
ALICE, their eldest child, a girl fifteen years of age.
JASLYN, their youngest daughter, eleven years old.
   - KAI, a white colossal-lion, companion.
JOSEF, heir to the title of the Lord Protector of the Mountain Realm, ten.
Their Household:
ASTERIN, from the Black Ice Tribe, the Deadlands.
BARDA, from a village in the Northwoods, the Mountain Realm.
MYRA, of House Nores, from Lakefort, the Summerlands.
EVERGREEN, from the settlement of Kiloweed, the Mountain Realm.
VIOLET, from the settlement of Kiloweed, the Mountain Realm.
BRADBERRY, Lord Knight to the Lord Protector, a Customary Knight of the Heart's Grove.
Others in Maryere:
JOAN MYSTER, Lady of Bear's Creek.
      - ESME, from Valley Pines. Lady Joan's attendant.
JASPER PAYNE, Lord of Fairpeak.
ASTEN DAWPHREY, Lord of Snow Creek, fourteen.
HEARTHRA SEAMANN, Lady of Accrid.
WYRRA TUDOR, Lady of Shadow's Peak.
ALLARIC CANTREE, Lady of Cantree Castle.
CYRUS CASTER, Lord of Windshire Fortress.
HAYLISE HAYWARD, Lady of Winterhaven.
MILTON WARD, Lord of Goldharbor.
Wife: TAMRA, of House Green from Greenharbor, the Northern Kingdom of Valley Pines.

RALLOR FLETCHER, Lord of Riverhold.
Wife: TAYLIA, of House Blackmour from Eldenhold, the Mountain Realm.

Others in Queen's Cove:
LYON, a Knight of House Millister.
SYRAH, a peasant woman in Queen's Cove.
CALAS, Syrah's little brother.
FRIAR, Leader of Queen's Cove.
Wife: KATIA, an Oracle.
Their Children:
SIEN, a young boy.
AMYN, a young girl.

Kingment, the Northern Kingdom of Valley Pines

FALK OSMONT, Lord Protector of the Northern Kingdom of Valley Pines.
Wife: VICTORIA, of House Wayward, from Maryere, the Mountain Realm.
Their Children:
DORAN, heir to the title of the Lord Protector of the Northern Kingdom of Valley Pines, seventeen years of age.
ROSERT, their youngest son, fifteen.
EMELINE, their eldest daughter, twelve years old.
CATRAIN, their youngest child, a girl of eight.
Their Household:
ENYA, a Saavant.
DAMIEN, Head Lord Knight to the Lord Protector, a Knight of House Clay, from Saltspike, Valley Pines.
EDMUND, Lord Knight to the Lord Protector, a Knight of House Archard, from Pinerun, Valley Pines; eighteen years old.
RAYA, Lady Knight to the Lord Protector, a Knight of House Vale, from Steephorn, Valley Pines.
Lord Falk's bastard children:
CLERIC, also a member of the Osmont household as Catrain's handmaiden.
IVAR, blacksmith, a man of twenty-three.

The Southern Kingdom of Valley Pines

PEYTON OSMONT, the Lord Protector of the Southern Kingdom of Valley Pines.
Wife: ARLA, of House Ashe, from Ashington Keep, Valley Pines.
Their Children:
HADRIAN, the once heir to the title of the Lord Protector of the Southern Kingdom of Valley Pines, fifteen. Has the *Wind Art* and *Bird Art*.
  - COLVIC, a Knight of House Rames, from Craven Hill. Once the Head Lord Knight to Lord Peyton Osmont. Known as the Greatest Knight in Val-

ley Pines. Has the *Pack Animal Art.*

    - RAYNESE, a Zaiku assassin and member of Quiver's Pit, known as the RED COBRA. Art Unknown.

    - PATTY, a handmaiden.

    - MYP, a manifestation of Hadrian's Art; shaped into a sparrow.
LEONIDAS, heir to the title of the Lord Protector of the Southern Kingdom of Valley Pines, twelve.
MAERWYNN, their youngest child, a girl of ten.

WARRIOR RAIDERS, a group of various tribes from the Kingdom of Valley Pines known for their violence.

Waterbrook, the Riverlands

JARIN AYERS, the Lord Protector of the Riverlands.
Wife: DIMIA, of House Osmont, from Kingment, Valley Pines.
Their Children:
TERRYN, heir to the title of the Lord Protector of the Riverlands, seventeen.
DAIN, their youngest child, seventeen. Also a member of the Council of the Riverlands.
Their Household:
HAMLIN, member of the Council of the Riverlands, a monk.
BRONSTON, Head Lord Knight to the Lord Protector, a Knight of House Hedge, from Salonia, the Riverlands.
KAYLIEN THOREN, of House Thoren, from the Black Hills, the Summerlands.
DAYA, a Dykon assassin, from the Derich Family.
JOSSA, Dimia's handmaiden.
HARRWYN, Head of the Defenders of the Oar, a Knight of House Brooks, from Rivergrove, the Riverlands.

House Withers:
VERA WITHERS, Lady of Widow's Dale, the Riverlands.
Her Children:
LYSANE, member of the Council of the Riverlands, nineteen.
CORNELIA, a girl of seventeen.
LUCIUS, a boy of sixteen.
PENELOPEI, a fifteen-year-old girl.
OSSIAN, a boy, fourteen years old.
NEBULA, a girl of twelve.

*This story occurs from the Harvest Moon of 505 SM to the New Moon of 506 SM.

**SM: Secession of Man (the current era)

ABOUT THE AUTHOR

Gabrielle Grey is the author of the *When the Fires Broke Through* series. She graduated from the University of North Carolina at Charlotte with her MA in History. When she isn't writing and researching, she loves playing the Elder Scrolls Online, watching anime, and scrolling endlessly through Twitter.

Growing up in a creative and expressive household allowed Gabrielle to become interested in several different hobbies, one of which is writing. She has been writing since she was a young girl, and in 2014, at 18 years old, she began a new story – *A Death at Dawn*.

BOOKS IN THIS SERIES

When the Fires Broke Through

A Skinchanger's Journey: A Novella

Lord Peyton Osmont, the Lord Protector of the Southern Kingdom of Valley Pines, requested the famed Ser Colvic Rames of one final duty: protect his bastard son, Hadrian. However, when the Warrior Raiders attack in the middle of the night, he finds himself captured with Hadrian nowhere in sight. In A SKINCHANGER'S JOURNEY, Colvic learns the secrets of the world as he searches for the boy he was tasked to protect. As he stares into the eyes of his captors, he wonders how he will ever be able to complete his last duty.

The events in this novella happen simultaneously as Hadrian runs through the Great Forest in A DEATH AT DAWN in the series WHEN THE FIRES BROKE THROUGH.